ALSO BY ADAM SYDNEY

My Heart is a Drummer

Yolanda Polanski and the Bus to Sheboygan

Welcome Home

Adam Sydney

Newcraft Press ‡ Tucson, Arizona

WELCOME HOME

Published by Newcraft Press, Tucson, Arizona.

Copyright © 2015 Adam Sydney

The moral right of the author has been asserted.

ISBN: 978-0-9851636-4-8

newcraftpress.com
facebook.com/NewcraftPress
adamsydney.wordpress.com
twitter.com/adamsydney1

Acknowledgements

This novel can at times be quite a challenge to the reader. Consequently, those friends who have been kind enough to offer their thoughts about it have performed a service above and beyond their pay grade. I wish to express my most heartfelt thanks to:

Michael Baun, Tre Cox, Ginia Desmond, Joséphine Dubois, Ben Gell, Bode O'Toole, Cassandra Rohland, Germaine Shames, Matthew Sydney, and Simon Woodham.

Before

My god, I wish I were you. You've probably had some bad times in your life, some challenges, but they've always fit into the realm of reality, of expectation. And even if you've experienced something that can't yet be explained through rational science, there's always been that question in your mind, that wonder if there isn't some other, sensible explanation. Even if you don't admit it to yourself because you want so badly to believe in the mysteries of the cosmos, that question's still there. And it's that tiny question that keeps you sane. Just that tiny, niggling question. Believe me.

Now, the closest I can ever come to believing in the mercy of rationality is when I think about being physically close to people. If you're wondering if that's a euphemism, it is. Only then can I bury my face and occupy my hands and feel the innocence so close to me, just on the other side of that skin. It's the only consolation for me: knowing that unawareness can still exist and imagining the feeling of its beating heart. Judge me if you'd like because shame is something that's been burned out of me.

In fact, I'd like to be intimate with you. You know all the places on your body that are electrified when another person touches them, all the ways your vulnerability can be unfolded and explored by another. I want to give that to you, to share that privacy of exposure. And I know your heart is generous enough to give someone like me a moment away from this unbearable knowledge. Surely there can't be a better reason for you to open yourself up in this too often colorless life.

I suppose I should say here that one of the consequences of all of this has been that I've grown very gentle, very appreciative of the needs of others. Although this is an ultimately self-serving skill, it has very definite collateral benefits.

And what I've got isn't catching. No matter what I say or do, no matter how often our bodies might commingle, that tiny question of yours will always be there for you, keeping you from where I've been sent and am now lost. So no matter what I share with you, you will always wonder about my account, always question its truthfulness even if you tell yourself you believe me completely. My fervent belief in this is why I feel secure in offering all of this up to you—it can do no real harm. I hope you'll see it as a kind of intimacy, one that might convince you I can be as open and raw as you might ever ask of our physical union.

19182 Penobscot Road is a modified four-square house built in 1906 and considerably altered in 1952, 1965 and 1980. It had originally been erected as a farmhouse on land east of Pacific Bay, Oregon, on 210 acres of land. Today, whatever farm had once existed has been taken back by the deep forest that's closing in around the house, and the property only extends about an acre around the structure in every direction. If you count the basement, there are four floors, plus a small attic. After the last addition, even the property appraiser lost count of the square footage, but the house is enormous, with nine bedrooms and at least that number of other rooms that cannot be called bedrooms merely because they lack a closet. From the front of the house, in view on the first floor are a full-length porch, bay window, and small casement window next to the door. The second floor has two, smaller windows, and the third floor has a small, fixed window in a dormer. Wide, dull, white aluminum siding encloses the entire building, and the hipped roof is covered in dark green, failing shingles. The house is deep, so the initial impression is very deceptive, but once inside, you find that hidden behind the facade are additions that continue haphazardly on and on toward the rear.

I hope you can't tell how hard it was for me to write that paragraph. Reading over it myself, I can imagine it through your eyes: mildly descriptive, informative, a report. I wish I were still able to remember things as simply, but I know what that casement window really means, what that dormer really holds within. Still, to share that knowledge with you now would be to force you immediately to end this relationship we've just begun to build together. I must be as gentle with you as I promised. I ask only that you understand I don't share these things with you to harm you but because my story is the only thing of value I have left to give you beside my physical attention.

In fact, I ask you to consider this: offering our knowledge can be much the same as offering our bodies. After all, we may be born ignorant, but we spend so much of the rest of our lives scrabbling for information from others. So I hope you experience what I'm about to offer up as a kind of gift.

I suppose I should begin with the first thing that happened. Well, it's the first thing that I'm aware of; I can no longer ask the others. It might not even have been the first thing that happened to me, but it's always been the first thing I remember when I think of Penobscot Road.

See how gently my gift begins:

I was standing next to Nicole, who was at the sink. She was washing her grandmother's old Corelle plates, and I was drying them. I was about a foot away from her and about six inches away from the counter. Remember that, because it will be important in the future. It was our first day in the house, October fifth, and it was seven in the evening. She was telling Alphonse and me that we should start in on cleaning the dining room, while she was going to work on the living room.

"The parlor." Alphonse was sitting at the table behind us.

Nicole shook her head. "I'm not calling it 'the parlor.'"

"There is at least one other 'living room' in this place. We have to establish a nomenclature."

"You can establish whatever the fuck you want, but I'm not using words from the 1800s."

"Well, I'm going to call it 'the parlor' because it is a parlor. And you're going to have to stipulate which 'living room' you're referring to whenever you use the term, which will be a waste of time both for you and the person to whom you're speaking."

"Fine. I'll stipulate. You guys get to work on the dining room, and I'll clean 'the *fucking* living room.'"

"That's funny."

But that was it. The subject was closed, which was a relief to me. We'd all been on edge since we'd agreed to rent the house, and I just wanted some peace and quiet.

Some things to note: Alphonse didn't bridle at being told what to do; Nicole didn't agree to a reasonably innocuous request; and I didn't weigh in on the situation at all. It's important to keep all these facts in mind, as they illustrate how things were when we first moved to Oregon, how they'd been our entire lives together up until this point.

But then I said, "The parlor is where nuns go to spread rumors about each other."

And that's it. That was the first thing that happened to me in Penobscot Road. You see? That wasn't so bad, was it? I promised you I'd be mild, and I have been. I'll never break any of my promises to you. I hope you recognize it as a sign of my utmost respect.

Of course, such a large part of respect is honesty, and I also owe you this. So I will explain just why I feel as if this simple statement was the first thing that happened. There are several brands of honesty; I will try to make mine as painless as possible.

My comment annoyed Nicole because she interpreted it as if I were dragging out the subject. It annoyed Alphonse because he interpreted it as a presumption on my part that this information was something that he didn't know. And it annoyed me because I had no idea why I'd said it.

Well, it annoyed me at first, but very quickly, it frightened me. Something told me to keep this fear to myself, however, so I just kept my head down, drying those old plates.

Alphonse's annoyance always expressed itself as soon as it bloomed in him. "Where on earth did you get that little tidbit from?"

"I don't know," which was true. "The internet," which was a lie.

"What do you mean, 'where nuns went to spread rumors about each other?' That doesn't even make sense."

"It doesn't matter."

"Then why did you say it in the first place?" Nicole finally weighed in. "I don't want to ever hear that word again."

"Okay. I'm sorry I brought it up."

And I was, in more ways than one.

Have you ever known that you knew something, but you just didn't know what it was? I realize that may sound ridiculous, but that was what it was like for me from the first moment I laid eyes on that house, and I honestly think Nicole and Alphonse had the same experience. They knew me well enough to know that I would never say something like that, and even though I did my best to hide it, maybe they could tell that I was more surprised than they were by what had just come out of my mouth. That must've been just as disturbing for them as it had been for me.

But none of us acknowledged any of this at the time, and soon enough, we were back to cleaning.

Do you ever wish that you could go back in time and comfort yourself? I wish I could've been there that night to stroke my hair and tell myself that I had to toughen up for all the things that were about to happen. I wish I could hold my old self in my arms and smell the ignorance erupting out of every pore, feel the limp muscles under my clothes not yet perpetually contracted against what I now know about Penobscot Road. You're probably thinking that if all of this is true, then what I really should be wishing for is the chance to go back and scream at myself that the nun comment was the first sign and that I should drop that dish and get the heck out of there. But I see the world too fatalistically for that now. I think the most I have the right to ask for is to make the whole thing a little easier on my old self. I just can't believe that anything else could've happened to me. It was too immense, as if it had its own gravity.

Anyway, this is a perfect example of what I'm saying: I'm kind to my old self; I'm kind to my present self. I'll be just as kind to you. And even though I'm about to tell you everything that happened in Penobscot Road, please remember that I wish I could be there with you, holding you as I would my old self, stroking your hair and telling you to prepare for what's about to happen.

*   *   *

As far as I know, the second thing happened to Alphonse, and it was only a few minutes later. But I've painted no picture! You must be wishing that I would describe the house a bit more, maybe talk about who the three of us were at the time. You know how much I need to satisfy you. So I should exhibit some of that kindness I've been talking so much about and fill in the picture a bit more. Talking about Nicole and Alphonse is painful, but I think it will be good for me. Talking about the house won't help anything, but as you can see, I'm driven by some urge to use it, to offer it up.

And as I've sworn I'll always be honest with you, you're about to see many things I'm not proud of, many shameful admissions. One of the first has to be that my recounting of Penobscot Road is a self-destructive act that I'm unable to control. The second is that I risk being just as destructive to you.

But I'm still avoiding my descriptions! Alphonse, Nicole and I met in our freshman year at college, became roommates in our sophomore year, and have never lived apart since. All three of us had spent our entire lives in Sacramento until Nicole decided that we should move to Pacific Bay. Nicole was the ringleader; she was always the active one—physically, emotionally, mentally. She was the agent of change in our little team. Alphonse was a customer tech rep for a software company. Socially, he was maladjusted, but like most nerds, he was perfectly comfortable with this. You could trust almost everything that came out of his mouth; you just usually didn't like it. And I'd earned a degree that focused on eighteenth-century English literature, so I'd been a server in mid-grade restaurants since graduation.

We were three parts of a whole, a single organism that couldn't function if dissected. And just as this codependency was a kind of strength for us all—possibly the only real strength any of us had—it was also a fault that atrophied us, making us vulnerable to so many forces both within and without.

Should I describe us further? Nicole was short, thin, and wiry. She was built like a gymnast. Her great-great-great grandparents were part of the Chinese immigration to America's Second City in the coolie days, which was what the Chinese called Sacramento. Her taste ran to athletic wear for most occasions, and she wore her uncle's signet ring of garnet and silver on her left thumb. I'd always imagined him as a kind of Asian Dean Martin, a strangely appropriate focus of ancestor worship for Nicole. Of the three of us, Nicole was the least damaged, although this wasn't saying much. She was the runt of her family, the last born, the least born, and so she'd learned from the best of them how to run a relationship. Nonetheless, you need something more fundamental than this knowledge to succeed, and she had nothing else to offer others; it just wasn't there. The best she could do was Alphonse and me.

Alphonse was very tall, extremely skinny, and physically placid with brief periods of spasmodic gestures. His parents had come to Sacramento from Trinidad, although any sort of island breeze stagnated around him. Instead, he'd spent his youth with computers, and they'd been his friends, his family, and his punishment. I often wondered if he'd been initially attracted to Nicole and me because we were like computer characters in some way: oddly flattened out, one-note, the process of dealing with us so straightforward and simple and always the same. Likewise, he was ultimately very pliable, although fussy every step of the way. In fact, there was something about his parents, something tactical, masterful, that left me with the impression that they'd conquered him by using his whining to drown out their blows. He was simply smart in all the wrong ways.

I was the fat one; I was the white one.

But what difference does any of this make? We changed so much during those days in Penobscot Road that this all feels pointless, almost masochistic on my part. What happened before things started happening doesn't seem material to me, either: the trip in the U-haul, the first night in Pacific Bay, the panic at noticing that most of the town's inhabitants appeared to be retirees, Caucasian, uninspiring.

Yes, this seems unimportant to me, but more than anything, it's terribly painful to think that when we first arrived, we were so close to what was about to happen and yet had no idea.

Nicole was terrified by the fact that she'd moved us all to a place none of us had ever been to before, while at the same time she was exhilarated in a way I'd never seen before. To her, coming to Oregon was proof that she was alive, that she was still young and in charge of her own destiny. Of course, that rubbed off on Alphonse and me, so we were energized and nervous in our own ways. I grew quieter; Alphonse grew more combative.

For your consideration: our second day in Oregon. The three of us were being driven around town by Flo, the property manager with whom we were working. Just like everyone else we met, she was desperate to know how our group worked but was too mortified by her own, base curiosity to ask. I suppose I should say here that none of us had ever been sexually interested in each other; our bonds were much more perverse than that.

Flo was one of those white, older, conservative-looking people that were the majority of the population in Pacific Bay.

"And how many bedrooms were we going to look for?"

Alphonse spoke before Nicole could. "Well, we had two bedrooms in our apartment in Sacramento, so I guess that's a minimum."

"Two." She said this as a declarative statement to cover over the furious math going on inside her head.

"But three or even four would be fantastic."

"Oh, fine." Flo seemed a bit relieved by this, but Alphonse was merely setting her up.

"That would give us a room or two for a study, or workspace."

Nicole moved in to stop the game before it got any worse. "A big reason why we moved here is that we need more space. Things are so much more affordable in Oregon." I think she sensed that Flo was a brittle person and that she wasn't dumb enough to miss what Alphonse was doing. Nicole could be abrasive, but she would never intentionally embarrass someone else if she didn't feel they deserved it—although Flo's dirty mind might have been reason enough for the teasing.

Of course, if Nicole believed that someone deserved a piece of her mind, they'd be lucky to get off with just a little embarrassment.

"Oh, we're a lot more affordable than California. That's why most of us have moved here. I'm from San Jose, originally, but I just love it here. You can really breathe. And then there's the beach."

We were parked in front of Flo's business, and as with so much of the real estate in Pacific Bay, we had an astounding view of the ocean. It was a good thing for Nicole, too, because when Alphonse and I looked over the gray water extending out to meet the horizon, it was very hard to regret our decision to follow her. The vistas were amazing, and they were going to belong to us.

"Okay, so three and four bedrooms go for about $900 to $1500, based on views and number of bathrooms. You saw many of our available homes online, but we have quite a few that haven't made their way to the website. And speaking of views, that's usually one of the first things that I ask: how important is a view to you?"

I would've said 'very important' if I ever chimed in on discussions of this nature. But I never did. I knew that if the others agreed with me, then they'd say what was on my mind, anyway. And if they didn't agree with me, then I'd go along with their decision rather than advocate for myself because I avoided conflict at any cost. Part of this was that I was awfully weak; part of it was that our lives had been so monotonous up until this point that we'd yet to have anything really important about which to disagree.

That being said, I was disappointed with Nicole's response: "I think what is most important to us is the house, rather than the view."

Alphonse was disappointed, too. "But a view would be cool."

Still, Flo responded to Nicole, a sign that she might've been on to Alphonse's mockery. "Great, because if a view isn't an absolute requirement, you're going to get a lot more house for the money."

"Awesome! I printed out a few of the houses that I wanted to take a look at right here..." And Nicole handed Flo a handful of dog-eared pieces of paper.

"I love it when my clients are proactive!" And we were on our way.

Now that I consider it, I realize that this meeting with Flo was a lot more consequential than I'd originally thought. Maybe this is part of the reason I have to write all this down: it forces me to really look at everything for the first time since it all happened. And maybe if I really look at it, it will finally make some kind of sense to me. Or at least, it will make some sort of sense to you. I don't really believe that, but it's still something I could hope for, right? Because besides imagining that I'll be with you, the future doesn't hold much value for me. I guess that at one time, I would've said that without hope, there is no disappointment, but I know better now. So why not try to let myself hope for something? It would at least occupy my time.

Anyway, the reason I say that this meeting with Flo was so consequential was what happened when we were in the second house. Alphonse was in rare form—never a good thing—because of what I suspect were his simultaneous impulses to run back to the safety of Sacramento, and to jump for joy at the thought of eating breakfast in a wainscoted nook while looking out over fog-wrapped outcroppings and the Pacific Ocean's majesty below. Alphonse had difficulty managing even one emotion at a time; this was simply pushing him too far.

Of course, his entire wrath was aimed at Flo because he knew this would have the maximum effect on Nicole. "So this shower stall is kind of small."

Flo looked inside, as if she previously hadn't noticed the size of it. "Do you think so? It's a standard size, I think."

"Do you mean for one person?"

And then later: "How big is this room, Flo?"

She looked down at her fact sheet. "It is 12 feet by 14. Not a bad size for a master bedroom."

"Yeah, but our California king would really be a tight fit."

Of course, I would never say anything to disavow Flo of the conclusions she must have reached because I was too shy, and Nicole couldn't directly address her conclusions without getting more explicit than she liked. So she did what she usually did when Alphonse acted up: she changed the subject. "Would we have to buy our own washer and dryer for this one?" And so things calmed down, and so Alphonse knew that he'd scored.

This is honestly the first time I've ever realized that Alphonse was ultimately responsible for everything that happened to us. Of course, I could blame Nicole for bringing us there in the first place—as well as for inspiring Alphonse's nastiness. But Nicole was genuinely trying to improve her life—and by association, ours. Alphonse was just being mean.

His skin tone was very dark, which he sometimes used as a weapon. "So what would you say is the general make-up of the neighborhood, Flo?"

"Well, mostly three and four bedrooms. I think they all have similar floor plans."

"Oh, I don't mean the houses. It's just that, you know, we come from the big city."

"You mean the shopping?"

"Did you know that Sacramento is one of the most ethnically diverse cities in the world?"

"Is it?"

But I saw it in Flo's eyes. I see it now, the rapid succession of reactions. At first, she struggled to connect what sounded like a non-sequitur to what they'd been discussing a second before. Then she realized exactly what he meant. Then she realized that it hadn't been her imagination: he really had been trying to make a fool out of her. It was terrible to see someone who had been struggling to be pleasant, who'd grown so unused to thinking the worst of others that she'd intentionally misinterpreted Alphonse's comments up to this point. Nicole was right; Flo wasn't an idiot. It's to our eternal bad luck that she wasn't.

But now, I can see that perhaps I should be blaming myself for everything that happened. I shouldn't be too quick to judge Alphonse and Nicole. Because I saw what Alphonse was doing, and yet I also recognized Flo's awareness of it. I don't think either of my roommates was paying close enough attention to see that glimmer of goodwill extinguish itself in Flo's eyes. But I saw all of it and yet never acted on my knowledge, never mentioned it to Nicole or Alphonse afterward, never put the pieces together until today.

I didn't think that I could feel any worse about all of this, but now I do. So my effort to recount everything that happened in Penobscot Road may turn out to be infinitely more self-destructive than I'd ever imagined.

Because at that moment, the last trace of a smile slipped from Flo's mouth, and she said, very quietly, "Actually, there's another house I think you might like to see."

* * *

Something else I'm realizing: my desire to be with you physically increases in direct proportion to my desire to stop all of this. Remember this as I continue, because I wouldn't be continuing at all if it weren't for you. My need to please you alone is what's counteracting my horror. So in a very real way, this final act of Penobscot Road is due entirely to you.

* * *

We all knew the second that we laid eyes on the house. And looking back, it's clear that Flo must have known, too. On some level, everyone knew. The closest I can come to the experience is staring at a series of black and white dots and circles. Right away, there's something warning you about them, and as your eyes adjust and you back up, you slowly realize just what you're looking at: an old crime scene photo or archival images of a lynching. It was all there, in front of us when we pulled up; on some level we knew it, but at the time it was still just dots and circles. I can't say how we recognized that something wasn't right, though. Perhaps the human eye just sees too many things to handle at once, almost like kinds of infrared light that only register on an unconscious level. Whatever it was, I found myself squinting at every detail, every surface of the building in an attempt to see what I somehow sensed was there.

But if this is a human ability, we've certainly developed the capacity to counteract it. I wonder if in our desperation to deny these other actualities, we don't respond in the most inappropriate way possible. We certainly like to laugh at the idea of a sixth sense. And truth be told, I can't help but wonder if all of this isn't just a revisionist take on the first few moments we were exposed to Penobscot Road. Maybe I've just added this extrasensory perception to make the telling more engaging now.

But we knew something wasn't right. We did.

The great irony of it all was that the house couldn't have looked less extraordinary if it had tried. The dull aluminum siding, the replacement screens, the almost austere design—there simply was no place where my eyes could catch, where I could recognize just where that sense of dread was emanating. So I chose to recognize nothing, just as Nicole and Alphonse did.

"It doesn't look that big." But there was so much wonder in Nicole's voice, more than was appropriate for her comment.

And there was just as much in Flo's. Even then, this disconcerted me. "I know. But it goes on forever behind."

"Does it?"

I finally realized that we'd been sitting in Flo's car for a couple of minutes, staring up at the house, although no one else seemed to find this odd. I think that in an effort to deny what we were experiencing, I acted. "Well, let's take a look." And I opened the car door.

Nicole opened her door next, about five seconds later. Then Alphonse a few seconds after that. But Flo just kept on gazing up through her windshield, almost mesmerized. It didn't seem so dramatic at the time— after all, it was only about a ten-second period. But a lot of significant things only take ten seconds, so why do I still try to excuse our stupidity this way? There were just so many signs.

Here's another one: "You know what? I have to make a quick call. Why don't you guys go ahead on in, and I'll join you in a few minutes." Flo merely rolled down her window to tell us this.

"Okay. We'll just need the key, then." Nicole approached her open window.

And yet another sign: "Oh, it's probably unlocked. The last tenants should be... I think you can just head on in." At our confusion, Flo strained a smile out. "It's so far out in the woods. Who would try and break in?"

I looked around and wondered if there could be any better place on the planet to burgle: no neighbors to see what was going on at the house and thick stands of trees completely surrounding the small clearing in which we stood. Even that low, gray Oregon sky seemed to invite illicit activity, cloaking it, almost condoning it.

But it was just a house and some trees and the sky! How can I blame myself at this point? I've always had a hyperactive imagination. And how can I blame you for the fact that I'm visiting all of this again? You're just a person, and I'm just a person. Why do I feel this need to blame anyone at all? It's simply something I have to tell, just as Penobscot Road is simply something that happened. There may be whys, there may not be. All I can do is recount what I went through.

I'm sure you can see at this point that I'm trying to psych myself up to continue, and the fact that you can see it makes me feel so much better because you're getting to know me. If all of this had never happened to me, I wouldn't be the person I am today and consequently could never have been able to do anything like this for you. I certainly never used to understand how much I could need another person. So in short, we would never have built this relationship, such as it is. I know that I'm still psyching myself up, but it's all true, and I need to get a running start at this.

Because I really don't want to remember that first time.

Alphonse went in first, then Nicole, and finally me. The front door was really wide, and it must have been original because it was made of silver, weathered wood. In fact, this would prove to be one of the areas, but I didn't know that yet. I just remembered as we stood in the front hall how much I loved my mother's baked ziti, and then the sounds and smells and colors of Sacramento came back to me in a terrible wave shooting up through my veins all at once. I know that at the time, I was staring at a large chip in the paint of the fourth step of the staircase that stood in front and to the right of me. That chip was in the shape of regret, and whenever I looked at it again, I'd always feel exactly the same way I did that first time.

But it wasn't long before the other sensory stimuli of the house distracted me from my dismay. It was ice cold and damp inside, the kind of freezing humidity that had been around for a while, that had seeped deeply into everything. It was the house's normal state; I could feel that looking around, and it was profoundly disturbing to me. A house is supposed to be warm and dry, and when it isn't, this should feel like an anomaly, a momentary lapse or accident. This was no accident.

"Fuck me, it's cold in here." Nicole immediately approached the old thermostat on the wall of the central hall.

"It'll take hours to warm up." Alphonse was staring into what he would later call the parlor as if he'd just heard or seen something. Of course, if he had actually seen something, he would've told us, so I returned my attention to Nicole.

"Yeah. Too bad."

But Alphonse had already wandered into the room on our left and was stroking the mantelpiece.

"This place is enormous." He almost seemed to say this to the fireplace. "We don't need anything this big."

"But we haven't even seen it yet." Nicole still kept her back to us.

"Look at this room! It's the size of a garage. We don't need that."

"Why not? Look, Flo said the upper end of rents around here is $1500. We can do that with no sweat! So why not live in a big house? It would be fun."

"Yeah, and a ton of work, cleaning and taking care of things. And who's going to mow that huge lawn?" But the tone of Alphonse's voice seemed to be in agreement with Nicole, rather than defending his position. It was a very strange phenomenon—especially coming from Alphonse.

It was the opposite with Nicole. "It's so private. Think how awesome it would be to have all of this room for a change." She was saying positive things, but her tone was so hollow, almost as if she were play-acting. This was even stranger than how Alphonse was behaving.

I saw all of this, but my reactions to the house were so strong that it's only now I can really wonder what my roommates thought of each other's behavior. Ever since I'd known them, they'd raced to name anything unsaid among us all. They'd both come from families in which undercurrents were ignored—for Nicole's family, it might have been some cultural form of respect, for Alphonse, an attempt to avoid the pains of unhappiness. On the other hand, I'd been raised by people who delighted in laying everything out on the table—the term "warts and all" comes to mind—so it really is no wonder I was so quiet. Of course, I'd joined a new family that was just like my old one in this respect. Perhaps I gained some feeling of superiority by being the one who sees all but says nothing. In our group, there were precious few other ways for me to feel superior.

So why didn't they call each other out?

"And you're going to get a second job to heat the place, I guess." But Alphonse was rubbing the edge of the mantel, watching his finger move up and down with the kind of expression on his face that he'd get when he was petting a cat.

And Nicole was now staring into the shadows of the other rooms, which got murkier and heavier as the number of windows diminished toward the back of the place. From our vantage point, I really did get the impression that they just kept going, farther and farther back.

"We'll just heat the rooms we use. Then when it gets warmer, we'll have a bunch of bonus rooms. I don't know what you're so afraid of." But she sounded as if she did.

"I'm not afraid of anything." And for once, Alphonse sounded as if he really wasn't.

The parlor was big—and I suppose it still is—with a wide baseboard that had been painted a dozen times, and one of those big, spherical, rice-paper light fixtures hanging in the middle of it all. It was an expansive room made larger by a wide bay window facing the front yard that had tall, slightly crooked panes.

It was my opportunity to say something, ineffectual and inconsequential as it was: "I think the house might not be level, anymore."

Surprisingly, it was Alphonse who put me in my place. "We'd be renting it, not buying it. That doesn't matter. We're not putting in a bowling alley." I got the impression that he said all of this for the benefit of someone other than Nicole or me, as if we were being bugged. But he quickly corrected: "But come on. This place is ridiculous in so many other ways."

Nicole still hadn't even bothered to turn around for any of this. Her face was still aimed away from us and toward the darkness of the house's interior. "I vote that we take it. I love it."

"Nicole! We've seen one room! That's crazy." In fact, it was so crazy that I actually spoke my mind for once. "Come on. Let's at least see the rest of it first."

"No. Don't you see? We can, like, discover it all when we move in. Like an adventure or a dream." She still hadn't turned around. "Imagine opening up a door and deciding right there and then that this is the room you want. What a fucking awesome story that would make."

Only a minute before, she'd been arguing with Alphonse that we needed to look around before we made a decision.

"Nicole. That is crazy."

"Exactly." Now she did turn around. "When have we ever been crazy before? The whole point of this move is that we get a little crazy. I want this all to be a surprise. I'm serious; I don't want us to walk through the place. I just want it. What do you think?"

I had no answer for her. Nicole's words were in such contrast to the tone of her voice, the look in her eye, that I honestly was waiting for her to tell me that she was kidding and that this would be the last place on earth she'd ever consider calling home. Of course, this kind of joke was definitely something that Alphonse would've played on me, and it could've explained his present behavior. But it just wasn't Nicole's sense of humor.

She continued to stare at me, asking more than her original question. I wanted it to stop. "Are you sure?"

"I vote no." And Alphonse's long, bony finger made little, affectionate circles on the top of the mantel. Then he said, "You're the tie-breaker, Chris," which may have been the strangest thing yet. What about looking at other houses? Why wouldn't he want to wait until all three of us agreed on one? *A tie-breaker?* I'd never heard him use that phrase in my life. Alphonse had always been just as all-or-nothing as he was logical.

"So what are you thinking?" And this was even odder from Nicole, who was normally so circumspect. We'd been there for five minutes, and she was already joining Alphonse in trying to squeeze an answer out of me. I won't say that I panicked, but I distinctly remember feeling artificially on the spot.

I can only liken all of this to a kind of sensory overload for me, but there was the overload being generated by everything else, too. Perhaps I failed to react to their inexplicable behavior because it was the least of what I was dealing with. After all, I'd left the only city I'd ever lived in— and rather hastily, too; I was in a strange new part of the country that was very different from anything I'd known before; and I'd ended up in a huge, old house in the absolute middle of nowhere that might soon be my home. But more than any of this, the house was pulling me in two directions at once, just as I suspect it was for them. Truth be told, the closest experience I can offer is the act of using politically incorrect pornography: I felt a need to reject something fundamentally wrong with it, which was, at the same time, what generated my very desire to consume it.

But my biggest problem of all was that I was about to agree to move into the house.

Here, at least, I was self-aware enough to rein myself in. "I'm thinking that we should sleep on it, maybe look at a few other places. You know, to get a better perspective on things."

Nicole shivered violently as she studied the space around my head. "I'm freezing. Let's go."

So we never did look at the rest of Penobscot Road. When we came up to Flo's rolled-down window, she informed us that the rent was $750 a month, and Nicole told her we'd sign the lease that afternoon. Alphonse said nothing. I said nothing.

In my own defense, I was too busy staring up into a small window set in that third-story dormer, its paint curling up at the corners. The darkness behind it was like velvet, and as I moved to open the car door, I realized that my underwear had dampened with sexual fluids.

The First Day

I feel so close to you right now! It's extraordinary—we've never met, and I predict that we're far apart in distance and time. Yet I have the ability to make you feel, and these feelings are just as much mine as they are yours. So even if I cannot yet lose myself for a few moments in your arms and know that I'm giving you the sensations your body craves, we have produced something just as precious together. Thank you.

For the next two days, the three of us waited, and it was the wait in an airplane before a sky dive, the wait at cool dusk with your slacks rolled up, ready to walk across a bed of hot coals. We'd promised ourselves exhilaration in our future, transformation, but behind the smiles were the whispered rumors of those instances when risks bear terrible fruit.

Nicole, Alphonse and I had grown up in California, a place in which satisfaction is just on the other side of the thinnest plastic film. This satisfaction is most dramatically illuminated by our bright sun and so is clearly within our reach if we can only determine a way to push through this thin membrane that separates us from what we've learned we want. And what we want is always on display: the march of expensive cars; the orange-tree-shaded, backyard tennis courts; the couture faces and relentless manicures. We're informed that while this existence is ugly, it's still the best kind of ugly, and there are only worse and worse kinds of ugly, all of which inhabit our dry, hazy streets, too. These worse kinds of ugly gave birth to most of us and hold us down only until we can find a way to pass through to the other side.

So it's no wonder that Nicole, Alphonse and I assumed that moving to the mysterious Oregon coast and living in a huge, old house would elevate us, somehow, move us a step closer to an existence that was a little less ugly. After all, changing place is an external action, and for Californians, changing the external is the first step in changing the internal. For Californians, changing the internal is just as easy as that.

But there was still some sort of risk in the move to Penobscot Road; we just couldn't state it explicitly. There wasn't much of a monetary risk— the rent was nearly what we paid just for parking in downtown Sacramento each month—and it wasn't as if we'd left anyone or anything of value behind. While we didn't have jobs yet, each one of us had skills that were pretty much in demand anywhere. In terms of a big move, this couldn't have been much less risky. Yet we were strangely on edge, those two days before the first day.

"Let's just stay another hour." Nicole was staring out over the ocean almost hungrily, as if the time and effort put into looking would allow her to carry more of the experience away with her.

We'd agreed to do fun things in the morning and work on moving in the afternoon. It was 12 p.m., and we were walking along the beach. It was foggy and rocky and sublime, and I was doing more staring around than usual.

"Nicole." Alphonse was the least fascinated with the wetness of the area, including the beach and the moody grayness of the water particles that seemed to float everywhere and coat everything nearby. Sacramento got some of the worst fog in the country, and it certainly rained, but those were events. They started and stopped. They were contained. I could sense that the Oregon coast's moisture was perpetual, invasive, and it inspired a great deal of awe in me.

"All right! We wouldn't want to enjoy ourselves too long."

"Apparently you think that enjoyment is some kind of constant, but I stopped enjoying myself about two hours ago."

"I think *we* decide whether or not we're going to enjoy ourselves."

"Why didn't they think of that in Auschwitz."

"Sorry you feel like you're in a concentration camp."

"Oh, please. Let's just go."

Just to annoy Alphonse, Nicole stayed put for a moment, still gazing out toward that indistinct horizon. She knew that he wouldn't go until she did; that was just our way. Finally, she turned back toward town without looking at either one of us.

"Yeah, you're right. Enjoyment sure as fuck isn't constant."

Alphonse was especially worked up because he'd just realized that we had no tools of any kind, and we'd probably need a slew of them in a big, old house. There had been the promise of a handyman in our contract, but living in Penobscot Road was going to be different from living in an apartment. It was supposed to be owned, not rented, by its inhabitants, and Alphonse felt a certain level of possession that he never had with our places in Sacramento. He wanted to play at being a homeowner, and with this, at least, Nicole had no argument. So we went to a local hardware store.

"What about this?" Alphonse held a yellow and black reciprocal saw that he was turning around in his hands, as if he knew what he was looking at.

"What about it? We're moving into a house, not building it." Nicole had two different kinds of hammers in her hands and was weighing them both, as if she knew what she was looking at.

"But this thing will cut and saw and all sorts of things."

"It's $50. If we need to do any of that, we can always rent one. Or borrow one or something."

"The nearest neighbor is like a mile away."

"But they're still neighbors. Probably even more so."

"What's that supposed to mean?"

"We're not on top of anybody now. People will be more likely to want to see us, maybe. I don't know. We're going to meet the neighbors eventually, right?"

"We're in rural Oregon, not heaven."

"Maybe we're in both."

"That has got to be one of the most disturbing things I've ever heard you say."

"I said maybe, you know? I'm open to anything. You might want to try it."

"And what kind of anything are you expecting?"

"It sounds like you know what to expect."

"Maybe I do."

"So what is it?"

But Alphonse didn't answer. He just put the saw down, shaking his head. At the time, I was glad that he remained silent, but now, I wish that he'd responded, so that whatever it was he was expecting after we moved in would be out in the open, a broached topic of conversation.

Still, Nicole came the closest: "We can buy as many power tools as we want, but there's no way to be totally prepared for something like this."

* * *

As I've already said, the first day was pretty quiet, or maybe I should say that we were so noisy and distracted that we didn't notice too much. But as we drove our U-Haul up the long, dirt driveway to the house, we were unbelievably quiet, at least as compared to our normal behavior.

I've already mentioned that Alphonse and Nicole hated silence, and when they were in good moods, they loved to talk about politics, philosophy and art. It was such a warm feeling, knowing that when I returned home each night to our apartment, something uniquely ours would be waiting for me there, these edifying, important conversations. So I guess I haven't really made it clear for you: we weren't bound together entirely for codependent reasons. There were other levels of need that yielded positive results for us. For instance, we were very well-suited to each other intellectually, and although we often didn't agree on these sorts of subjects, we had such a healthy level of respect for each other in this regard that it didn't matter. We'd known one other too long to let debate represent more than an opportunity to work out our own thoughts, to gain broader perspectives. I'm proud of us for that.

Of course, I usually only listened to these discussions, and that was okay, too. Alphonse and Nicole knew that if they asked me to weigh in, I'd at least have an intelligible answer, and that made me part of it all, somehow. But since we'd seen the house, something about our group had been turned on its end, and so it was I who began to talk when the first glimpse of the house shot through the trees. It felt like panic: I couldn't stand the thought that a moment such as this, which should have been a happy one, could instead state some murky truth as eloquently as our silence. So I did what many of us do: I blathered. Just not about the house.

"Oh, god, I just thought of something. Did either of you remember to let Jesse know that we moved? What if he goes to the apartment? That would be horrible for him. You know how he hates surprises. It's just that we haven't heard from him in so long that I guess he kind of slipped my mind when we were calling everybody. God, I can just imagine him standing there at the door, waiting for us to answer. What a terrible—" At which point I became aware that my eyes were fixed on the front door of Penobscot Road.

I regrouped. "But anyway, I'll call him soon. We didn't think about what we're going to do for dinner tonight, though, did we?" The driveway was endless. "With all this hauling and unpacking, I don't think any of us will want to cook tonight. So maybe there's a restaurant that delivers around here?" Once again, though, my words caught in my throat as I looked up at the house. Every corner, every wall and shadow seemed to confirm the idea that any local person delivering food to this place was unimaginable.

I have to say again that the house looked perfectly mundane! There was nothing concretely threatening about its appearance at all. In fact, as we pulled up to the front door, I was even able to imagine it being almost pretty in the sunlight. Or maybe not pretty, but honest, straightforward, with its weathered planes and simple craftsmanship. It was just a big farmhouse, and I envisioned the man who built it: quiet, calm, and practical about his possessions and life.

No. That isn't right. That was what I was telling myself to imagine, rather than what I really saw. I've promised to be honest with you, and a large part of that is being honest with myself. So no, I wanted to imagine a sunburned, docile farmer, but instead, I saw a figure whose face was eradicated, somehow, as if someone spiteful had scratched it off in an old photo. Even in these early moments, even with something as innocuous as wondering about the house's past, things weren't right. Long dead people remained veiled even in my imagination, as if an unknown entity could reach out and seize things in my own mind. This sounds appalling now, and it was then, too, but please remember that I was experiencing all of this for the first time. I'd hardly been outside of Sacramento before, so I told myself that all of these strange experiences were just part of the process of dropping one life and building another, that anyone's imagination would create a kind of gothic horror story out of these unknown elements. Moving is scary.

As it turned out, the experience of failing to imagine Penobscot Road's first owner was something I shared with my roommates. We only discovered this much later on and found that for each of us, it was quite a different phenomenon. But it seems terrible to me now: during those first few minutes, as Nicole backed the truck as close to the front door as possible, we were each struggling to grasp who could've built such a home for himself. I've said that I wish I could go back in time to give myself a hug. Well, this is the moment I'd give almost anything to return to so that I could just hold Alphonse and Nicole's hands. At this point, we still shared something that wasn't a secret or a suspicion.

Moving our few things into the house would have been unremarkable if we'd actually walked through the house before agreeing to rent it. As it was, the cold, damp, dark rooms just extended out in front of and above us, not so much representing exciting mysteries as much as indistinct threats, nasty proof of our stupidity in renting a house mostly sight unseen.

We were standing just inside the front door, and again, I was overcome with a wish to return to Sacramento and make up for the inexcusable error I'd committed when I'd agreed to come to Oregon. From whom I was seeking this pardon wasn't clear. And that chip in the stair's paint a few feet in front of me was proof somehow of my blunder; I don't know how better to describe it. I was staring at it so intently that Nicole had to repeat herself to me.

"Chris? Do you want to weigh in on this?"

"Sorry. Weigh in on what?"

"Should we walk through first, or should we just get everything inside?"

Were they actually discussing whether we should continue to avoid the rest of the house? I looked up the stairs into the reaching bleakness of the second floor.

"Why don't we just get everything out of the truck first."

There wasn't any beer to lubricate our work; there wasn't any celebratory pizza to make the whole thing lighthearted and fun. As I said, Nicole and Alphonse deplored any kind of dishonest communication, and beer and pizza would have been a denial of this oddly solemn event, a claim that we were doing something normal. Plus, by this time, we'd shelled out nearly $2000 and had signed all the papers. We'd sensed then what was only being reinforced now, so we couldn't even plead innocence of what we were doing.

 Instead, as we hauled everything into the parlor and dining room, we either remained silent or grunted requests specific to our tasks. We didn't wonder about the best arrangements for our furniture. We didn't debate the perfect spot for Nicole's large bronze statue of a football player. We didn't marvel at the house's huge rooms or amazing view. It was grim.

I'm tempted to liken the three of us to mesmerized prey, but I knew something was wrong and have to take responsibility for my inaction. I know you'd never retain any respect for me, otherwise, and your respect is one of my primary concerns. At this point, you've come to realize that it's one of the most precious gifts you can give to me. Of course, there are other things I'll be craving from you as my story continues— understanding, indulgence, pity—but above all, I need to know that you believe I've done the right things for the right reasons. If not, everything we share will just become the latest chapter of my nightmare, and I know you don't want to be responsible for that.

*   *   *

As the whole point of this exercise is to share everything with you just as it happened to me at the time, I suppose I must be completely truthful with my descriptions, regardless of how insane I might sound:

The window closest to the front door, a small, casement window to light the front hallway, has a brass latch on it with a handle that curves to the right, as if to fit perfectly into the palm of a right-handed person. It wants a right-handed person to touch it, to utilize it, yet when you do, there is a sharp edge out of sight that bites into your flesh, scraping, and occasionally cutting, the area just under your fingers. In fact because of this, I discovered that this area of your palm is the body's gateway for regretful emotions. So when that handle scratches you there, it's easier for those feelings to seep into you because this spot by the front door is a place for regret. The effect is most concentrated at the window as you look through it but billows out for a few feet in every direction.

The phenomenon is immediate. You start off feeling sorry about the immediate situation: you shouldn't have squeezed the handle so hard, you should have remembered about the sharpness there. At the beginning, this feels normal, logical. That's how things often start in Penobscot Road; on the surface, they make some sort of conventional sense. But then you glance out the window at the gray sky and the stand of forlorn trees across the clearing—naked trees that seem almost ashamed, nervous that they're the ones forced to be bared to the house in such a way. They're victims, and they see you through the window, and they wonder why you only stare back, and they wait for you to do something, but instead of a future waiting, it's a backward waiting that only results in your remorse getting worse and worse with the passage of time. At first, you tell yourself that it's insane to somehow be sorry about failing to help a line of pine trees, but then the specifics of the situation disintegrate, and you're just left with the feelings, which are as real as any you've ever had and can't be diluted with common sense because common sense only works in the regular world.

You see? Insane. The problem is that humans just don't have the right words or concepts to accurately describe the experience. I'm so sorry to distance you like this, but I just don't see any way around it. Nevertheless, I believe that the more you hear about the oddities of the house, the more they will become familiar to you—and with that familiarity, the more believable. Then we'll grow closer again, and this will have all been worth the discomfort it's causing both of us.

By the time we'd spent our first evening in Penobscot Road, this spot by the front door had already caused me to be twice overcome with the desire to return to Sacramento and make amends for having left it in the first place. It wasn't the chip in the stair's paint that had made me feel that way; it was my proximity to that little window. Only from that spot could the chip be seen clearly, and so my first impulse was to blame it. In fact, during my time living in the house, I often had to shift blame from one implausible cause to something even less plausible for what was happening. As you can imagine, plausibility no longer holds any value for me.

That night, after we'd cleaned the dishes and I'd made that strange comment about the nuns, something even stranger happened with Alphonse. We didn't know it at the time; I only discovered it the next day.

We were all sitting in the kitchen, and next to us was a long, pitch-black hallway that led into the increasingly incomprehensible additions built onto the back of the house. Because of them, the kitchen had been robbed of any windows or door to the back yard, and it felt wrong, as if the room had been frustrated, trapped in the core of the house. But how could a room feel trapped? And even if it could, there would be no way for it to writhe and scream as if it were an animal clenched in iron jaws.

Alphonse and I avoided looking down the hall, but Nicole was facing it, squinting into the void. It was ten o'clock at night, and we hadn't unpacked anything. We didn't even have anywhere to sleep, as the mattresses were piled up in a corner of the parlor. We were exhausted and sore and unable to move onto the next part of the process. We still hadn't been anywhere but the parlor, dining room and kitchen.

Alphonse suddenly sprung up. "There's got to be a restroom back here, right?" None of us had even bothered to find a bathroom in the house. We'd just relieved ourselves in the woods. It was bizarre.

"Yes." Nicole was still staring down the hall. Maybe she could see a bathroom somewhere in there?

"All right, well…" And so Alphonse clomped down the hall, feeling the walls for a light switch. He was completely swallowed up by the murkiness for a moment, but then a blinding light threw everything into a different form. On the surface, it was an absolutely unremarkable, filthy hallway, except for the fact that it was longer than most and seemed to jog to the left and out of sight at the end. I couldn't help but ask myself why someone would deny the kitchen its light, its proper place within the home to build something as squalid and sloppy. And then I knew the answer: it was out of spite, although at the time, I couldn't say why.

"Found it." Alphonse had disappeared around the corner of the hallway, and his voice sounded remarkably far away. I'd never lived anywhere where someone needed to shout to be heard. In the little rambler I'd grown up in, I had only to barely raise my voice to be heard across the entire house. Needless to say, the apartments I'd shared with Alphonse and Nicole were even worse. So the idea sent a little shiver of excitement through me: the house was larger than I'd imagined, and the luxury of space would make living there a remarkable experience. Each of us could be in a different room, and we'd have no idea whatsoever what the others were doing—or even necessarily where anyone else was! I'd never dared imagine that I was worthy of such privacy before.

I was to have very many normal feelings like this over the next few days; I hope that you might take this as proof of how ordinary I was at the start of everything and that this might make up for some of the other things later on. Ironically, though, it was precisely these reasonable responses to the house that kept me there—and the others, too—so our normal reactions actually turned out to be worse for us than the irrational emotions we were being subjected to. If we'd experienced only these strange feelings, we might have been shocked into leaving within the first 24 hours, rather than having our real selves imperceptibly robbed a little more each day, never quite being able to pinpoint the urgency while one set of our perceptions was replaced with another.

Eventually, Alphonse returned and sat down, his back to the hallway. He'd switched the light back off, the draping of a shroud.

"There are a lot of rooms back there."

"Really?" Nicole was still staring into the darkness over his shoulder. I tried to keep my eyes on his face.

"I don't know what we're going to do." He jerked his shoulders up in an awkward shrug. "We don't have enough stuff for all of it."

"There's nothing wrong with a few empty rooms." But it sounded like a lie the second it passed Nicole's lips. How could we call a place home if the cold and damp and silence still owned so much of it? It couldn't really be ours.

"Whatever. I'm dead, guys. I'm just going to pull a mattress out and sleep on it in there. We can deal with the rest of this tomorrow."

Nicole and I didn't ask what "this" referred to. We all knew that "this" was about to dominate our lives.

The Second Day

As I mentioned, the second thing had already happened to Alphonse, but I didn't discover this until the following morning. Only then had I convinced myself that the healthy behavior was to explore the house, and so I worked my way through all of those rooms behind the kitchen. There were so many of them that I almost immediately forgot which one was which. So I wandered around, my mouth open, as I stared at blank walls and scratched-up door handles.

Forgetting about rooms in your own house might sound like the height of luxury, but I know now that the details of home are not things that should slip your mind. You have to know the place where you live as well as you know yourself. Otherwise, you don't really live there at all; it's just a structure that holds you.

Of course, you can tell that I'm procrastinating again. All right: I don't know where he got them from, but the previous night, Alphonse had apparently found five, old, pink washcloths with pretty little flowers on them, which he'd folded neatly and placed directly at the foot of the sink in that back bathroom. I know this because when I finally made my way back there, I found that he'd urinated on the washcloths, rather than in the toilet. There was so much of it that some had run to the center of the room, where it had dried to a sticky residue. The smell was nauseating.

Then I looked up. The state of the entire room indicated that over the years, quite a good deal of urine hadn't made it into the toilet, which helped explain some of the odor. I let out an involuntary gasp when I realized that I was standing in some of it and suddenly felt overwhelmed, frozen in place. I couldn't walk out of the room in my shoes because I'd track Alphonse's piss all over the house, and I couldn't take off my shoes where I was standing because then I'd have to make contact with the floor in my socks. Of course, now I see many alternative courses of action, but at the time, I was unable to move, and I could feel the foul residue of the room rising into the air and coating my body.

I wasn't yet able to acknowledge that something strange was happening to me, but I couldn't move, either, so I did the next best thing: "Alphonse!"

I knew enough to yell loudly in the new house, but after waiting a few moments, no one responded, so I yelled even louder. How could no one have heard me? But of course, the house was that big, and again, I realized that what had struck me as an extravagance was increasingly looking like a liability. Home is not a place where your screams can't be heard.

To make things even more disorienting, I was beginning to think about the preposterousness of the situation. Why would Alphonse pee on several washcloths and then leave? Even more unnerving to me for some reason: how could he have come into a room like this and not mentioned its disgusting state to us right away? After all, this was Alphonse, a man who commented on everything and then commented on the comments. But he'd never said a word to us about the bathroom the previous night. He'd behaved as if everything were normal.

My need to get these thoughts out of my mind somehow gave me the strength to walk right out of the bathroom, and I promised myself that I'd clean the floor in the hall as soon as I could.

I found Alphonse and Nicole in the parlor, sitting around a pile of old photographs.

"Didn't you guys hear me?"

Alphonse looked up, glassy-eyed. He was leaning against the mantel. "No."

"I was in that back bathroom."

Absolutely no reaction from Alphonse. No flinch, no grimace, no brazen grin. Only: "What did you need?"

And suddenly, I didn't need anything. I didn't need to know why he'd pissed on the washcloths in the bathroom; I didn't need to know why he couldn't even remember doing it now. I didn't need to say anything at all because the only thing I needed was for that look in his eye to remain there forever, that aura of mild incomprehension, that old Alphonse expression. Already, I knew that it was old, of the past, and this was doubtlessly another reason why the three of us continued to avoid any mention of what was happening for so long. We wanted to see the old versions of ourselves reflected in each other's eyes for as long as we could manage it.

"Nothing. I just think I'm going to clean it."

In Alphonse's left hand was a faded Polaroid of the three of us at a freshman Halloween party, lined up against a wall and posing awkwardly. At the time, Alphonse had handed his old camera to another student to take the picture, who'd pitied us good-naturedly as he told us to say "penis." I still remembered. We had a history.

Alphonse returned his attention to the old photos. "God. We're going to need our cell phones to get ahold of each other in this place."

I knew then that Alphonse must have heard my yelling and had ignored me. He must have realized what I'd discovered in the bathroom and didn't want to deal with it. Perhaps he'd even ignored me because he knew I'd clean it up. In my perpetual quest to smooth things over, he knew I'd get on my hands and knees and wipe up his sticky, foul, dried-up urine, his waste getting under my nails and seeping into my skin, and I wanted to take the sharp corners of that photograph and slash at his face, make those droopy eyelids bleed.

Then I forgot about it and cleaned the washcloths and the floor.

But you should know that things weren't always strange between the three of us in Penobscot Road. Not at first, anyway. We had lunch that afternoon—Nicole made hamburgers—and it was as if nothing wrong around us mattered. Although the weather was as depressing as it could have been, we were in our own house and no one could hear us talking, and the kitchen was warm from the stove and the old furnace, and for the first time ever, we were in the middle of a big-league adventure. In the past, our riskiest behavior had been staying to watch a second movie at the multiplex or taking a day trip to Napa.

"I think I met my first Oregon friend." Nicole smiled at us over her burger just before she stretched her mouth over one corner of it.

Alphonse was delighted. "Already? Who is it? What happened? You're such a friend slut."

Nicole snorted over her full, working mouth. "Fuck you!"

"You know I'm jealous." And he was, although "friend slut" could have been one of the most damning accusations among us in other circumstances. We had such an intricate relationship, which was more important to each of us than anything else, so any other kind of interaction with other human beings often seemed redundant, and therefore, not worthy of respect. This was because we felt that the rest of the world, which didn't have what we had, was to be pitied when we were feeling generous and loathed when we'd been injured by it. But before you dislike us too much, please remember that we never purposefully harmed anyone else, and for the most part, just minded our own business. We were busy giving one another a family.

Finally, Nicole swallowed. "It was at that convenience store just where our road goes into town, the one at the corner? She was standing behind me and she saw that I was buying bagels, so she told me that there was a bakery in town that made awesome bagels."

"That's your new 'friend?' Some lady who told you to buy bagels somewhere?"

"Why not?"

"You liar."

"All right. So there's more. I told her about us moving here and everything, and she was really impressed! She's an organic florist! Did you even know they existed? I think she's going to make us an organic arrangement and deliver it in her electric minivan. So you're totally making fresh cookies so that when she comes over, we can invite her in and act like grownups who have casual, like, Martha Stewart moments all the time. She needs to believe that we *entertain*."

Now it was Alphonse's turn to have his mouth full, so I felt as if I could contribute. "She sounds great. What was she like?"

But Alphonse was a fast eater. "Who cares what she was like! Nicole's right: we're country folk now, so we need to be always ready with a howdy and some nice brown betty or whatever."

Nicole giggled. "Brown betty! I don't even know what that is. Or what about apple dumplings."

"Or Jell-O with fruit in it."

"No, we need to make pandowdy."

Alphonse snorted. "Pandowdy. It's probably made with panda. Grandma cooked with panda."

We all laughed at that, and it was a laugh no one else in the world knew about but us. Then Alphonse said, "So what's she like?"

"I don't know. She's older than we are, and she had some really cool, pink glasses on. She just seemed cool. I think she'd like us."

Alphonse nodded for a few seconds, stopped, then nodded some more. Then he got up and started rummaging through the cabinets, which were only half full at this point.

"Am I getting any help with these cookies?"

And so we started trying to gather the ingredients for chocolate-chip cookies, only so many of our kitchen supplies were still boxed or not yet restocked that we ended up making one too many substitutions, and the cookies came out like little, dry cakes. Of course, we should have been continuing to unpack, but I think we sensed that these kinds of moments would be finite, so I'm glad that we didn't return to the stacks of boxes right away. After the cookies came out of the oven, we had one each, and then two, and then we realized that we couldn't serve them to company, so we ate the rest of them, carving out a little, warm space of domesticity in Penobscot Road. We'd still managed to avoid going upstairs or downstairs, and those places sandwiched us, dead weight. But we ate cookies to spite it all, to hold it back, the stars of our Oregon adventure.

The woman with the pink glasses turned out to be named Ruth, and when Nicole and I visited her shop the next day to tell her where we lived, she was politely mortified that she'd given Nicole any impression that she'd be stopping by. But it was more than that: her eyes slipped off of us one too many times, so I dragged Nicole out before any more could be said.

"What the fuck was her problem?" At that point, we already kind of knew, but we hadn't actually spoken it out loud yet, so Nicole's question just sunk in the heavy, humid air. We were used to being rejected socially, just not accepted and then rejected. That seemed entirely too cruel.

"Hey, let's get some ice cream." I'd learned a long time before that the best way to handle a grenade was to gently toss it away and hope that it never rolled across our path again. But there were so many at this point of our time in Oregon that I was losing track of where I'd thrown them.

When I do things like torturing metaphors, what I'm really trying to do is distract both you and myself from the fact that I'm not playing fair. And I'm not: I shouldn't bounce around our timeline like this. It's only going to disorient you and push you further from me and my story. And I need you here, with me.

But I realize that at this point, it's going to take more than my weak begging to keep your interest. I respect that. So let me promise you here that I was only a day away from finally taking significant action, rather than simply reacting to what the house was doing to me.

You're going to be impressed, and that kind of response in you has a very aphrodisiacal effect on me, so please understand all that you're giving me, as well. I admire powerful people, too, and you wield just as much power over me as I ever could over you.

After we ate the cookies meant for our hospitable welcoming of Ruth that day, the three of us toured the rest of the first floor together, a little knot of hesitations and frowns. At first impression, the back of the house was terrible. But this was one of the main reasons why I decided to do something about our situation—my momentous, impressive decision the next day—so I don't look back on it with as much pain as I could.

I want you to experience the first floor exactly as we did that afternoon, so I'll imagine you as one of our team while we wandered around, saying little to each other, occasionally touching a broken light switch or grimacing at a smell. You'll be the fourth, a ghost that slips between us. It's somehow easier to relive, imagining you there, silently supporting me through it all. And the beauty of this is that you weren't really there at all, so you haven't been ruined like the rest of us. You can still look at the world and see something familiar.

The three of us began by reviewing what we already knew: the parlor, dining room and kitchen. As they were in the original part of the house, they had thick, plaster walls, high ceilings and a little self-respect. The parlor was a large room, with a sturdy, well-finished opening into the dining room and a bay window facing the front yard. But I want you there with me. So if we were standing together in the window, we'd see the wall of pine trees that stood about a hundred feet in front of the house, and an insistent, light draft would pass back and forth across our faces, slipping always through the gaps in the old panes. There would be the smell of wet bark, and below that, of leaves rotting in the dirt, and below that, of the sea. You'd sense something unusual about this view, but that's all.

The walls in the parlor were a relatively innocuous sea-foam green, so everything there had a green cast, which is the color of mild sadness. Standing with me at the center of the room, you would find yourself constantly searching out my face to see what's wrong, why I seemed so down. Would it be because I was lightly tinted green that you'd feel I was unhappy, or would it be because the room colored your entire vision green, in effect making you sad no matter what you saw?

We moved on to the dining room. Unfortunately, it turned out that any proximity to the newer portions of the house had a toxic effect. In the case of this room, its rear windows had been replaced with a narrow opening that led to an addition, robbing the room of almost all of its light and basically turning it into a hallway rather than a place to gather. Although there was a high, odd window facing the side of the property, it bathed the room only in a strange overhead murkiness, which caused its occupants to feel as if they were underwater. In fact, it was always the dankest room in the house (except the basement, of course), so you would draw instinctively closer to me after we'd entered it, knowing that a dining room should be more air than water. Perhaps this would lead your mind to wonder what it would be like to float over a multifarious coral reef with me, but this momentary, happy thought would be quickly extinguished. That's what the dining room did. As a consequence, we never paused long in this room, and so you would join us as we escaped into the kitchen.

It was even darker here, buried as deep as it was from any natural light source, but it did have merciless fluorescent lights that helped counteract the impression of being swallowed whole by the house. I imagine your specter sitting up on the counter, the worn and cut-up Formica cooling your backside, as you tried to decipher the particular odors there. Years of frying had packed hard grease into the corners of the room, so the first thing you'd think you were smelling would be rancid fat. And you'd be right. But then, things would become more complicated for you. The scent of strange, pungent herbs would rise up next, at first medicinal rather than palatable, and then not even that. Suddenly, you'd sense that their purpose had grown obscure, not necessarily for the health of their recipients. This would remind you then of pitiless nature, of the ugly, hidden things that grow in abundance where nothing else will take root, and your whole concept of "kitchen" would mutate. Now, you'd see it as a place where dead things were brought to be cut up and boiled, a stripping of their identities in the grinding, endless cycle of earthly digestion.

It would be an odd thing to think of, so you'd grab ahold of the counter, feeling the right angles biting into your palms and wondering if the rest of us had been corralled to the same odd conclusions. This would be my turn to draw close to you because once I'd recognized what you'd just experienced, I'd regret the loss of your old, domestic understanding of the kitchen: a place to nourish, to gather, to live. That would be gone for you now, and it would sadden me.

At this point, Alphonse said that he was going to buy a waffle iron because the room begged to be filled with waffle steam, and the three of us laughed. It had also been redone in the 1970s, country kitchen chic, and his comment was definitely appropriate. You'd hover near the exit, hoping to move on, but the corporeal in our party lingered. There was a kind of safety in being swaddled in the room, as it is difficult for a predator to maul prey already inside of its gut.

We also hesitated because the back hallway stood so close to us. Alphonse and I had rushed through it, but that made it even harder for us to move. Finally, Nicole tried to casually wander toward the nearest door in the corridor, and we helplessly followed. But you'd be ahead of her; without the vulnerability of flesh and blood, your curiosity would outweigh any vestigial instincts of self-preservation. And if you were there with me, just out of sight, I'd know that at least one of us had nothing to worry about, and this would calm me, help move me into what we were about to refer to as the family room.

It was large, as large as the parlor, but the ceiling was much lower, and with only one small, aluminum window, the room compacted the space within it, rather than elongating it. However, this wasn't necessarily a bad thing, and the initial experience for us was one of coziness on a somehow more human scale than the parts of the house we were already familiar with. The walls were covered with ash brown, fake wood paneling, and a wood stove sat in a far corner, promising a kind of heat that the fireplace in the parlor couldn't. In fact, we all felt a little relieved, as I think we knew that we'd be spending a lot of time in the family room, and so for the first time, we actually discussed things like furniture placement and whose posters were going where. To our credit and our detriment, we did this completely ignoring the fact that the floor vibrated the whole time we were in the room. I told myself it was just something mechanical in the basement, but even then, I could tell it was organic. Even then I could feel the pulses reaching up into my legs and viscera.

Of course, you'd be floating above it all, so you wouldn't even notice the vibration, necessarily. Perhaps you'd only see traces of it in our upturned mouths, a little stiffer at the corners than natural. But we did like the room, and even its stained beige carpeting didn't worry us because it was so dry it was almost crunchy. Even though the entrance to the dining room stood only a few feet away, the family room seemed as if every last ounce of moisture had been squeezed from it. It smelled like sandy dust, like baking rocks. You'd circle the space over and over and over, glad at least that we took one room on our tour to be welcoming. I know you'd be generous enough to celebrate that.

Passing back into the corridor, we found two more doors on the far side before the hallway made a ninety-degree angle to the left. Both were closed, and faint light glowed under each, illuminating the uneven surface of the hallway. The quality of construction in this part of the house was very inferior, almost amateur, and no lines seemed to run parallel or perpendicular to any other. This was deliberate, somehow, which made it worse than amateur, but already we'd developed the ability to overlook these sorts of realities, and instead, we quickly approached the second door across from us, joking about funhouses or something.

You'd pause at the first, suspended there and wondering, only this time, I'd ignore you. I'd have no choice, and so you'd continue on and join us, understanding me enough by now to know that I'd answer your questions just as soon as I was able.

We entered an old lady's room. The odor of lavender and moth balls was the most insistent sign, but there were others. The walls were painted a particular shade of light tan that was the color of women's face powder in the 1950s. Of course, I didn't see this at the time, but you'd know it immediately, because ghosts understand much more than the mortals dragging their feet around them. You'd recognize that colors are born and die, too, and that this color had been dead for 60 years.

The floor was covered in stiff, sensible vinyl the pattern of parquet, and I could picture a rag rug, veiled with long, silver strands of hair, under the old brass four-poster that must have stood there. There was a set of ecru gossamer curtains, mossed over with years of dust, that framed a small, aluminum window.

I saw, just as my friends did, that this was going to be Nicole's room, so there couldn't possibly be anything to make us uncomfortable here. After all, the woman who'd inhabited it had been dead for years. None-theless, you'd remain at the door, watching me, pained and silent.

Although the three of us had wondered about who'd built the place, this was the first time we'd come across tangible traces of a former inhabitant. I see now how odd that was. In fact, the rest of Penobscot Road seemed as if it had always owned itself, as if the previous genera-tions of people who'd lived inside of it had been like a race of tattoo artists, insignificant themselves, leaving only anonymous flourishes of significance behind. These flourishes were then subsumed by the house and used to shift and sharpen its identity for its own sake. I know that it sounds as if I could only ever describe this in hindsight, something I've promised you I wouldn't do. But I did sense it even then, standing in that room, which struck me as if it represented some kind of gall that had taken root in one of the house's vital systems. As I was already well aware of the house's negative nature, this kind of mutiny seemed a good thing then. But being a spirit half in this world and half in another, you would have had a much better perspective on the situation. You'd have known that cancerous abnormalities are never things to welcome or trust.

A little further down the corridor, it turned, dead-ending into the bathroom I've already shared with you. As we hesitated there for a moment, I keenly watched Alphonse to see his reaction to the room, which was so much cleaner than the day before and no longer stained with his urine. He merely turned the shower on and off, watching as the rusty water pooled up around the black drain. I knew Alphonse so well then that I knew he was wondering how he'd deal with all this decrepitude. What was on the other side of that drain wasn't all that different from what we now called home.

Next, we found a large storage room that up until then had been hidden behind the corner of the hallway. Its old, gray asbestos tiles were stained by the slow excrescence of countless containers; in one corner was a rusty circle and in another a rectangle of yellow discoloration. The room couldn't have been more than a degree or two warmer than the land that stood beyond it, and it smelled of rotting vegetables, even though it had been empty for a long time. As Nicole hated the cold, she immediately scanned the walls to find that there were no registers in the room—yet another odd construction decision.

Besides a door to the back yard and laundry hookups, the only feature worth noting was that a section of the room had been walled off, and a hollow, pressboard door opened into it. At first glance, it appeared to be a closet.

You would hover before it, wishing you had material feet to plant onto the ground and wondering how you could make yourself known to Alphonse and Nicole before they approached the door. I, of course, would sense your presence but would have only your reassuring aura to read; your sudden alarm would remain mercifully undetectable to me.

Then the door would pass through your specter and then so would Alphonse, Nicole and I as we clustered on the other side of it to find that the intrusion into the store room actually housed a set of narrow, steep stairs, headed up on our right side and down before us. Doors must have stood at the end of each staircase because the one on our right was completely swallowed up by blackness not even six feet above us, and only the first two steps descending before us were visible. It was even colder here than the store room, a dank draft rising up from the basement. Alphonse wanted to investigate the cellar at this point, but Nicole and I convinced him to wait with a little more animation than we could have explained at the time. You would have explained it easily, if I could have only heard your wails.

Nicole quickly dragged us out of this room because it was so cold, and we returned to the kitchen, whose familiar squalor I actually found comforting. Without being specific, let me just say that this comfort borne of familiarity was going to prove to be my undoing, and although it's a trait that's far from exclusive to me, there can be no excuse. You would've known this, pausing next to me here and hearing my breathing slow, my heart rate return to normal, surrounded by the warped cabinets. You would've caused a warm breath to drop down from the ceiling and lightly pass over my forehead, as if to brush the hair gently off of my eyes. Don't I remember that?

There was still a door in the kitchen that we hadn't opened. As she opened it, I remember Nicole warning whoever was listening that the room behind it had better be the last one on the first floor.

Having just come from the rear section of the house, the first thing I noticed was the room's genteel proportions: high doors, high ceiling, large, drafty windows. It was painted lilac and had apparently been built as a bedroom, although its exits—into the kitchen and into the front hall— made it feel so exposed to the busy areas of the house that it seemed far too unsettled to provide much rest or privacy.

Slowly, I became aware of a scent like sourdough bread—only in no way appetizing—and underneath that, clinical disinfectant. So this was Penobscot Road's annex for sickness. I could practically see the hospital bed in the corner, a wheelchair backed up next to the door, stacks of starchy white linens in the closet. But even though it was a place of infirmity, I could get no sense whatsoever of the presence of any previous invalids. Here, too, the house had drained the space of any personality, leaving only anonymous, obscure clues that humans once existed there.

Alphonse loved the room at first sight, and as neither of the others speculated how the room had served earlier inhabitants, I never shared my understanding of what it had been, either. I didn't want to take anything away from Alphonse at this point.

Your spirit, swirling madly around and around the space, would immediately sense what I was sensing, but you'd recognize other things, too, so you'd draw near, silently urging me to tell Nicole and Alphonse what I knew about the room. But I would feel only the friction of your movements, something so pleasant and intimate that any worry I had about the room would disperse, and soon I'd come to believe that the space was harmless.

And so, after two days of living in that house, we'd finally managed to explore the first floor. Alphonse and Nicole were looking around the front hallway blankly, talking about window coverings. I stared at the front yard through the small casement window and felt the stairs rising up behind me. I could also perceive the presence of another basement door under the staircase, its damp draft wrapping around my ankles as it passed up and out of the house's many fissures. Upset that we'd waited so long to look around, I wished that we'd done it before agreeing to rent the place. It really wasn't nearly as nice as I think any of us had been expecting, based on the condition of the parlor. But it was too late, now, so I'd have to pretend along with Alphonse and Nicole that making the best of it was the right thing to do. The thought made my stomach drop. And we were doing it already, discussing cheap mini-blinds as if a few homey touches would somehow erase everything that was alien in the place.

As I joined the babble, you'd shake your head, fading, and you'd rise, slowly, slowly up and away from me and my predicament. Sensing that my steady companionship had gone, I'd lose whatever strength I'd once had to suggest checking out the rest of the house and would instead find myself drawing up plans in my mind as to how the staircase might best be walled off. It wouldn't have to be permanent, just something makeshift until we were able to leave Penobscot Road in a year. I'd simply sleep in the parlor every night, next to the fireplace, the last graying embers collapsing in on themselves as I drifted off to sleep.

These were my thoughts after you'd leave me.

The Third Day

I didn't think it was possible, but I feel even closer to you. Your generous acceptance of everything I've given you has made revisiting Penobscot Road actually bearable for me this far, one of the greatest gifts you could have ever given me. If I were with you, I hope you know that I'd do everything in my power to show my gratitude, to give back one-tenth of what you've allowed me to have. Life on earth is endurable solely for the hope that I might one day make your body sing.

Do I want to continue with this? Absolutely not. Events up to this point in my story are at best only mildly disturbing. You and I are still able to relate in what is for the most part a natural, comfortable, almost mundane way. I haven't really shocked you yet, made you question yourself or me or the world. But I can't stop. So please try to establish a kind of distance, a way to view everything else without letting it fundamentally change who you are. Because I know you have that kind of power.

The comment about the nuns had been my first inexplicable experience in the house; urinating all over the downstairs bathroom had been Alphonse's. I suppose you could say that our failure even to glance around the other floors after living in Penobscot Road for almost 48 hours could be categorized as strange. But Nicole's first incident in the house was much more distressing than anything that had happened previously. In fact, it was what convinced me to act on the suspicions I'd developed the day before.

We spent most of the third day moving around our few bits of furniture and unpacking. Alphonse made a flavorless turkey tetrazzini from shrink-wrapped meat, and we continued to discuss everything that didn't matter over lunch, such as our spring plans for the yard, and the best places to start to look for jobs, and our need of a good coffee place. Alphonse and I had slept in the parlor the previous night; Nicole had moved her mattress into the old woman's room. She looked as if she hadn't gotten much sleep. This was one of the facts we would use, for a few days, anyway, to explain the behavior she was about to exhibit in the kitchen that evening.

I was washing the dishes, and Nicole stood next to me, her eyes a little unfocused and bruised, and dried what I handed her.

We were still speaking of all the things that I think we knew were never going to happen. I was unusually talkative: "We can grow so many flowers from bulbs here, I bet. I've never planted bulbs. If we do it right, the entire yard could be a carpet of color from spring to fall. They can't cost that much. We should see if we can find a nursery today."

Nicole was rubbing a pan absentmindedly. "You got some sauce on your leave."

"What do you mean?"

"The stain's going to set in."

"What are you talking about?"

"Right there!"

"Right where?"

"What do you mean, 'where?'"

"I don't know what you're talking about."

She finally put the pan down and pointed at my left sleeve. "Alphonse put too much fucking oil or butter or something in it. It's going to stain if you don't wash it off."

"Oh, my *sleeve*."

"Yeah. Your *leave*."

I looked over at Alphonse, who was sitting at the table behind us. His mouth was open.

"What the fuck's wrong with you two?" But she asked this casually.

Both of us had stopped our work; the water was the only thing moving in the room.

I didn't want to answer her. I could see her utterly blank face. But Alphonse was farther away. He chuckled a little. "Nicole, you're crazy."

"What do you mean?"

It certainly wasn't her sense of humor. It didn't even make sense. But Alphonse wanted it to be a joke. I think this was easier for him because he didn't have much of a sense of humor, himself. "'Clean your leave!'"

"What are you talking about?"

"It's weird, but funny, I guess."

Nicole was getting pissed, which was never what anyone wanted. "All right. I need one of you to tell me what in fuck's name is going on here. Right now."

Suddenly, I realized that the worst thing we could do would be to tell her what was going on. "Don't worry. He's just being an ass. I'll take care of it. So can we look for nurseries tomorrow?"

But she could tell I was lying. She always had, the few times I ever tried. It always enraged her. "Bull fucking shit."

And she waited.

After I threw him an especially significant glance, Alphonse finally realized the danger if Nicole found out. Luckily, he was better at lying than I was.

"Chill, Nicole. We just misheard you. That's all."

"You thought I was saying 'leave' instead of 'leave?'"

"Umm. Yeah."

"That's not funny."

"No."

And then she returned her attention to me. It didn't take her long to run her eyes over my face, almost abrasively, reading me like an extremely detailed newspaper article covering some senseless accident. Just as I wasn't a good liar, I couldn't much control my expressions, either, and she instantly recognized that something was still wrong.

"I said 'leave,' Chris. I did not say 'leave.'" But there was a question in this, a buzzing level of fear.

"Yeah."

"I said 'leave.' Leave!"

"We just misheard you."

"Yeah, and I'm saying 'leave' right now. I can hear myself."

"Why don't we just drop it?"

"Because every time I say 'leave,' I can tell that you think I'm still saying 'leave.' But I know what I'm saying. I can hear myself." Now she looked scared.

"Leave!" And her voice rung through the house, a prosecution.

Obviously, this would've never happened in Sacramento, but if it had, I think Alphonse and I would've rushed Nicole to the emergency room. It seemed like one of the signs of a stroke.

Now, however, we did nothing. On one level, we didn't know where a hospital was, and even so, it was just one word; she wasn't slurring all of her speech. On another level, we'd already been lying so much to ourselves and each other about the house and everything we sensed there that this was just another thing to deny. We knew it wasn't a stroke, but instead of addressing this with her and then discarding it, we pretended. It was terrible, and all the more so because it seemed to be her subconscious, warning, begging us.

I had to get away, so I cleaned off the table—something I wouldn't have done until I was finished with the dishes, ordinarily. We all knew that, too, and Alphonse or Nicole would've normally commented on it right away. In Sacramento.

I made sure my back was to her. "You're saying 'sleeve,' and we're hearing 'sleeve.' So what do you think about my idea for a yard full of flowers?"

She didn't respond, and I couldn't read what was happening with her by Alphonse's face because he was intently examining his cuticles. No one was looking at anyone else.

Finally, there was a clank behind me. "I think that if you'd like to spend $500 of your money on bulbs then you might want to get a job sometime soon."

And when I returned to the sink, she abandoned the job of drying, and we argued lightly about plants, pushing the strange phenomenon as far away from us as we could.

Nicole had been standing one foot away from me and six inches from the counter. She never used the word 'sleeve' again.

*   *   *

Still, we'd only been in the house three days, so Alphonse and I were sort of able to discuss things. We were following Nicole on the empty road into town as we returned the rental truck, and I remember that everything seemed as if it were made firmer by that cold night, as if slippery things exposed to it would freeze and could be dissected without danger.

As I was less in denial than Alphonse, I broached the subject. "Don't people who are having strokes do things like that?"

But he only shook his head. "She was doing it on purpose."

"Why?"

"You know she likes to screw with us. With you, especially, because you're so gullible."

"No. *You* like to screw with me. *She* likes to boss me around."

"Yeah, well, we both like to do that."

"Alphonse. She was right next to me. She wasn't doing it on purpose."

"Eehhh." This was how Alphonse dismissed pretty much anything he disagreed with, which was most of what came out of my mouth.

"She had no idea she was saying… anything different." I couldn't say the actual word out loud; it would've just echoed around and around the car.

He hunched back down into his seat and watched the silhouettes of the trees we passed catch an occasional light ray from the headlights. I remember how black it was, that night. Rural Oregon was darker than anything I'd ever experienced before, and it was scary. If you stood in the middle of the blackness, the air pushed in on your eyes, forcibly crushing out your most vital sense.

Alphonse's response was unsatisfactory, but I found myself glad that we'd stopped talking about Nicole's behavior. That's why I was disappointed when he added: "She was kidding." He knew that wasn't true. I knew that wasn't true. And physically, before my eyes, the night suddenly dropped into a deeper blackness. I remember that, too.

But the first Nicole episode was ultimately a good thing! In a way. Because if it hadn't have been for the shock, I don't know how long it would've taken me to act on those early suspicions of mine. And if I'd waited even a day longer, I don't believe you'd be reading this right now.

So here's where you're going to be impressed with me, see me as the protagonist of my story. Here is where I finally get to elicit that raw, undeniable response in you that's so close to the raw, undeniable response I'd elicit from you if we were in the same room together: *I decided to find out what was going on.* Even then, I recognized that things were getting worse and worse, and that something essential in me and my friends would be lost forever if I didn't fight against this unnamable process. It was up to me to be our savior.

I remember promising myself this, driving our car down that twisting road, following that white box of a truck in front of me. In fact, my decision was a white box; it was definite and substantive and before me, as clear as everything around it was obscured. I think I might've even smiled a little to myself, an action-adventure star, my hands gripping the wheel a little more tightly.

Looking back, I think I came to this decision as easily as I did because I was out of the house, where everything could sometimes seem a little clearer. That incredible resolve I felt—while Alphonse and I watched Nicole deal with the rental agent as we sat inside the car, and then when we stopped off at a drug store, the relentless fluorescent lights there reminding me of just how real everything on earth actually is—that resolve was the best thing to happen to me for days. Even though not that much had happened yet, I knew that there was something fundamentally not right with Penobscot Road. So I was elated to realize that I had power, that I could still do something to make the world better. It would be the last time I'd ever feel that way—at least, rationally—so you'll forgive me if I seem a little more romantic about it than what may seem appropriate to you right now. But I think you'll look back on my "decision" with a little nostalgia soon, yourself. I love the thought of us sharing fond, little memories.

So that night, as I stared up at the blackness beneath a ceiling that held back the things we still weren't able to face in Penobscot Road, I reviewed the situation. There were the three instances of odd behavior—for me, Nicole's was the worst because she was so unaware of what was happening to her. There was the strange shifting in our interactions: the lies, the denials, the sudden silences. And then there were the inexplicable emotions that seemed to wash over me when I was in the house, a majority of which were negative. What sense could be made of any of this?

I had to start with the rational explanations. We'd never lived outside of Sacramento, we'd never lived in a big, old house, and we'd never lived in the country. All of this could've just been symptomatic of our struggle to deal with the new. But I quickly rejected this argument because I'd never heard of anyone coping with change by pissing on washcloths. There was stress, and then there was insanity.

Which brought me to my next hypothesis: could it be that we were all going insane? I wasn't assuming that this was a coincidence, though; I merely wondered if there were a cause, like a radon leak or lead in the water. This was my favorite explanation because it was logical, measurable and rectifiable. It would still be my favorite if subsequent events hadn't completely obliterated it.

But that was it for my sane explanations. After this, I had to delve into the occult. First on my list: haunted house. Something evil in Penobscot Road was tormenting us. This fit the bill, although it didn't wholly explain why we were doing strange things; for that, I had to consider demonic possession. But was this what it felt like to be taken over by the devil? Momentary and confusing and kind of banal? When I'd made my odd comment about the nuns, I'd had no idea where it had come from, but I never felt as if something had taken control of my mouth or my mind. It had just sort of popped out, like thoughts occasionally do. I certainly hadn't felt like Satan at the time.

So what about a poltergeist? I knew that strange things were supposed to happen in this situation because an inhabitant's energy was seriously out of whack. It certainly wasn't immediately clear which one of us could have the disturbed psyche. So maybe all three of us were generating super-poltergeist activity?

Then I became aware of someone in the dining room. I could see nothing and I could hear nothing, but I knew, just as surely as I know you're there, that a presence was right on the other side of the wall. Right behind my head. And I can describe it, too: it was male, and it wasn't young but it wasn't old. It was looking for something; more than anything, there was an overwhelming sense of fevered searching, although I couldn't say for what. What's more, it had been searching for quite some time. This wasn't a new phenomenon. I knew that it sensed us—sensed me right now—and it knew that I was aware of it, there in the dining room. Our dining room. But I also somehow knew that this wasn't supposed to be happening, that exposing itself like this was wrong. It was a perverse presence, which was the most frightening thing about it. It was a loose cannon of some kind, an anomaly.

I describe all of this with a kind of detachment now, but it pitched me into a terror that pressed me down on that mattress, almost like a spasm. I could feel every square inch of my body exposed to it in that blackness that blinded me yet somehow also provided a medium for the searcher to exist. In fact, it and the utter darkness were very well acquainted; the closest word I can use is that they were *associates*, somehow. I know this makes no sense whatsoever, but I can't take the chance of keeping it from you and regretting it later, so I have to tell you.

And then I sensed the presence moving off into the darker parts at the rear of the house, and then it was gone. This kind of fright takes a while to be processed by your body, and I remember breaking out in a sweat, stars flashing at the corners of my vision as the blood poured back into my skull. It was good to feel like a stunned animal for a moment because this meant I wasn't thinking about what had just happened. Actually, my first coherent thought was an attempt to dismiss the jealousy I suddenly felt for dumb animals and their happy ignorance.

It didn't take long, however, before the physical shock relented, and I began to question myself. How had I known so much about the man so quickly? Why was he in our house? What did he want from us? What had been certain knowledge only a moment before seemed now like the tailings of a dream, and it was true: as I looked up at the ceiling, it was different. It was closer, and its surface was differently flawed. How could the house have changed? A disembodied spirit was one thing, but ceilings growing suddenly lower? It had to have been a nightmare, but I couldn't remember waking up, opening my eyes. The event had been seamless, and I couldn't accept that it had just been a product of my imagination.

But you've probably already recognized the answer. And even I, after a few minutes, realized that when I'd sensed the being in the dining room, I hadn't been able to see the ceiling at all. Now I could, albeit darkly. The level of light in the room couldn't have changed to that degree, so it really had been a dream, and I'd just woken up.

Nonetheless, it had felt as if it weren't *my* dream, somehow, and this only strengthened my determination to figure out what was happening to us as soon as possible.

You'll have to excuse me if I don't go into any further detail with this episode. I give it exactly as much weight as I should at this point in my story because this is about as much weight as I gave it at the time. I have to respect the evolution I was undergoing and attempt to communicate it as faithfully to you as I can. If something in the back of your mind is troubling you about the presence in the dining room, I hope to answer all your questions as soon as possible.

I'm not teasing you with all of this, but if I were, would it be such a bad thing?

The Fourth Day

The fourth day in Penobscot Road was the best day we had there.

It all began with me waiting in the car—historically my refuge for privacy—until exactly nine o'clock and the start of everyone else's working day:

"Southwestern Properties?"

"Hello. May I speak with Flo, please?"

"This is her."

"Hi, It's Chris. We're renting the big house on Penobscot Road?"

Her voice brightened, like crystal. *"Hello, Chris! How are you?"*

"Fine. The place is huge, isn't it?"

"I knew you'd love it."

"I was wondering if you might have some spare time to meet with me. Only a few minutes—"

"Did the previous tenants not move all their things out? You know how uncomfortable I was, moving you in there without someone from the office going down our checklist first. I really broke the rules for you guys. Let's see; I could have someone out there tomorrow?"

This was the first I'd heard of any rules being broken, but Alphonse never bothered me with technical details, and Nicole never bothered me with procedural ones. I thought nothing of it at the time. "I don't think they left anything behind."

She was oddly silent.

"I just had a few, quick questions about the house and thought you'd be the right one to speak with. If you have any spare time."

"Well, you know, I don't know too much about all that. I'm just glad that you're settling in so well!"

"Have you talked with Alphonse or Nicole?"

She sighed, of all things. *"Oh, well. Not since your move."*

I'd only expected Flo to try and answer my questions over the phone, so I hadn't developed tactics to force her into a face-to-face meeting. I needed to see her, to have access to all her reactions. Otherwise, clues could be overlooked.

Instead, she'd dismissed conversation of any sort. Her evasiveness actually caught me off guard.

I had to be smart in the way an investigator has to be. Unfortunately, I'd had so little practice that this was all I could muster: "But I really need to talk to you."

"About what." There wasn't even a hint of a question in her voice.

I couldn't just be Chris, now. I had to be more. "Don't you know?"

But that wasn't right: *"Is there some sort of problem with the plumbing or electricity or something? Would you like me to send out our handyman?"*

Violently I realized that for my entire life, I'd hardly ever asked questions. Most people learn how to manipulate the answers they want through the questions they ask. I'd certainly never experienced a day in which I hadn't felt manipulated in this way. So how did people do it?

"So you'd rather not meet with me?"

Wrong: *"It's nothing like that. I'm just very busy right now."*

"Why didn't you suggest this place right away when you were showing us properties?"

Wrong: *"I have more than 50 properties to manage. Sometimes one or two can slip my mind."*

But this was a lie. I just knew it. So Flo was taking the time to lie to me, yet she was also answering my questions—and in the same hard, sparkling voice. Why wasn't she trying to get off the phone?

"Why aren't you trying to get off the phone?"

"Well, because I don't want to be rude!" And this as if she were talking to a very pleasant, very slow person.

Next came a loud shuffling of papers on her end, so clearly a cry of frustration that I knew to remain silent. After all, remaining silent was my specialty.

Finally, something worked. Her voice shifted, suddenly harassed and defeated.

"All right."

*   *   *

Nothing strange occurred that day, at least as far as I knew, and we spent the morning cleaning the first floor. This was another way to feel in charge, altering the state of the house to our liking. I recall that Nicole had a framed photograph of Marilyn Monroe that we spent an hour moving around her room searching for the perfect lighting, a spot where it would make just the right impact on someone who entered the space but would also be best appreciated by the person living there. It was a waste of time when we had so many more pressing responsibilities, but we'd come to Oregon to learn to waste more time.

I think the cleaning helped Nicole feel more in charge, which led to her broaching the subject she did as we scrubbed away at the family room.

"There's only one Pilates studio in town."

Alphonse was scraping at the walls. "Are you going to apply there?"

"I was thinking of starting my own."

"Wow." But Alphonse sounded discouraging.

"Oh, please. Rent is dirt cheap here, and I'd be able to keep all the money, rather than hand 70 percent of it over to some pretentious shithead."

"But maybe there's only one studio in town for a reason."

"I could fix a room up here, and then we wouldn't even need to pay rent for a studio."

"Might want to check our contract on that one. And how long before you start to turn a profit after all the marketing you'd have to do? Can we afford that?"

Nicole was strong, but sometimes she was easily swayed. "Forget it. When are you two going to start looking?"

"God! We just moved here a few of days ago."

"Exactly. You've got to get started on that."

I wasn't as annoyed by the subject as Alphonse. "There are a lot of restaurants in town. It shouldn't be too hard for me to find something. I'll check them out tomorrow."

"And it's going to take me about ten seconds to find a new position." Alphonse worked remotely in technical customer service, so as long as he had a phone nearby, he could do his job anywhere. "I've already contacted a couple of people."

"Hey, Nicole, were you wandering around last night?" I thought this was as good a time as any to continue my investigation.

"You mean around the house?"

"Yeah. I'm pretty sure I was dreaming, but I thought I heard you in the dining room." I was careful not to say that I heard "someone" in the dining room, which would've sounded even more awful. Just asking this question was horrible enough.

She was cleaning the sill of the window, but she stopped. "Yeah. I was looking for something."

I wasn't expecting this answer and so wasn't the best detective for a few seconds. I only said, "Oh."

Finally, though, I realized that there was something not quite right about the way Nicole had just sounded. "Did you find what you were looking for?"

"In this mess! No." Then there was silence for a good while, and then she said, "I was looking for the masking tape. I wanted to tape up one of the boxes full of my crap."

I'd learned enough from old TV cop dramas to know that people who answered more than the question, who built up elaborate and detailed responses, were lying. But why?

"Nicole. That's bull." Any pride in my brilliant deductive ability was immediately dashed because it was Alphonse who said this, casually and without recrimination.

She was equally as casual. "Maybe."

Alphonse considered this a moment. "So now that we're in a new place, we're going to invent these, like, exotic lives that we'll tell each other about?"

Nicole grew animated at the thought of this. "Totally! We'll only ever say interesting things to each other, and it will all be bullshit, but we won't really ever know for sure. And so our lives will suddenly seem all sexy and mysterious. And the people in town will start to pick up on it, and we'll get this reputation for being the most interesting people in the area. We'll be Pacific Bay's celebrities."

"Awesome."

Now how was I supposed to figure out what had really happened the night before? I couldn't just ask again. The rules of our relationship prohibited getting serious in the middle of joking around.

I said only, "So the next time, you might want to come up with some-thing a little more glamorous than 'you were looking for some tape.'"

"I'll have to work on that. Are you guys getting hungry?" And the discussion was closed.

But even though I didn't get an immediate answer as to why Nicole had been evasive about being in the dining room, I was still satisfied. I still had a lead of some kind, anyway.

So what did I have to work on? First there was Nicole. I wasn't sure if she'd been in the dining room or not, and if she had been, what she'd really been doing there. I also needed to find out why she would make up something like that to begin with. And while it was distressing to find out that one of my closest friends was lying to me, at least I had some thread to follow. I couldn't directly address the incomprehensible behavior Alphonse and Nicole had exhibited earlier in the week because neither of them seemed wholly conscious of it. But Nicole's lie was deliberate, so she had some sort of additional knowledge. I was actually glad she was hiding something from me, if you can believe it.

Then there was my meeting with Flo the next day. I was going to be more prepared this time, so I'd not only jotted down questions, but also different ways to ask the same questions. Then, I'd ordered and memorized them. I'd won the last battle with her, but I wasn't exactly sure why. Next time, I would have a deliberate victory.

For someone with a history of passive behavior, those first few days of investigation were thrilling to me. Historically, Alphonse had always acted as the smart one in our group; we all depended on him to do the heavy lifting in that department. But I wasn't less intelligent than he was, I just didn't want to be criticized if it turned out I was wrong. So I generally played dumb. After all, Alphonse had always been much better equipped to deal with judgment, with disappointment than I'd been. He didn't care so much about what we thought of him—at least when it came to intelligence. There were other areas, though, that he was very touchy about.

Still, the supposedly bright one wasn't the first person to look into what was wrong in Penobscot Road. If he had been, he would've definitely said something already. So who was the smart one now? That's right: yours truly. Would you like to know what I did next? Do you want to hear how I gathered my body of evidence and then constructed a hypothesis from it? How I set my traps? You know, I think sometimes it's a good thing to tease. I never did it much with Alphonse and Nicole, but the relationship you and I are building is different. I'm an adult in this one.

I think I'm going to like it.

* * *

Afterwards, we had our only adventure. It had started lightly enough:

"We're going to work to live, not live to work." This particularly familiar platitude came from Nicole as we stared at the kitchen table and empty lunch dishes scattered there.

"Wow, you should really copyright that." Alphonse's sarcasm was in direct proportion to his annoyance. This wasn't the first time that year we'd heard the cliché.

"Fuck you. I'm serious. When did we ever do things that we wanted to do in Sacramento? I mean, really. Everything was always about fucking work. Nothing ever frivolous or spontaneous. We planned our fun."

"Umm, real world?"

"No. No! This is the real world, too. Look what we've done! Where we are! How hard will it be to come up with $250 apiece for rent, you know? We're not fucking capitalist slaves anymore!"

"You might change your mind when you see what kinds of wages we'll be making here. Same shit, different state."

"But even the minimum wage—"

"Let's climb that mountain behind us. Right now." I'd wanted to say it since I'd arrived, but we'd always had other things to do. It was frivolous and it was spontaneous, and more than anything, it was a test. I was still gathering evidence, after all. I would no longer be passive.

Alphonse and Nicole looked at me, then at each other.

Another surprise: Alphonse was the first to speak. "I just have to find my shoes."

Nicole always rose to a challenge, just as she rose to bait. "Let's do this, bitches." And even though it was Alphonse's bait she'd risen to much more than mine, I knew that my friends were still on my side.

There were no roads, no paths that we could find, no signs telling us to keep out. Nature in Oregon hadn't been circumscribed as it had everywhere else we'd ever been, and it was a little scary just as it made me feel more important, somehow. I was an individual here; I could make my own decisions.

Mercifully, it was a gradual slope—more of a hill than a mountain. But I was unused to the exertion, and Nicole and Alphonse had to pause once every thousand feet for me to catch my breath.

They never pointed out my physical inadequacy. They never questioned why we were climbing to the top of the hill. And once we'd pulled free of that strange, dolorous, magnetic field of the house, we were almost our old selves again—another reason to believe that our unease in the house could be managed.

"Even the pine needles turn to mud." Alphonse couldn't repress his scientific interest in our surroundings, which indicated that he was happy. "You're doing the laundry tonight, Chris."

"I wonder what we'll be like, now that we can do shit like this whenever we want." Again, Nicole's Californian belief that what you tell yourself you are is what you are. Maybe it's true.

"Guys, I think this is a great place to pause and enjoy the view." There was no view, and I could barely get the words out. Alphonse and Nicole stopped without complaint.

"Our future is, like, a mystery. We don't have to be the same for the rest of our lives. We're young. How could we forget that?" Even Nicole was becoming philosophical, despite the freezing condensation from the trees towering above us that seemed to find its way into every crevice leading to raw skin. Despite the overcast bleakness. Despite the fact that no matter when and where we turned around, our new home was somehow always in view.

"Human beings are the most adaptable animals on the planet. We forget everything pretty quickly. It's supposed to mean that we can change more easily, but sometimes, it has the opposite effect." This was Alphonse's way of saying that he agreed with Nicole.

"So we get used to bad situations, which is good, but we get used to good situations, which is bad." Nicole and Alphonse were even having a Sacramento conversation!

I couldn't help myself: "I don't think that getting used to bad situations is a good thing."

Nicole had been looking at Penobscot Road as I said this, and she started walking forward before pulling her gaze away. "Come on. We've got to get you to the top of this mountain."

And my friends did get me to the top. I would never have done it on my own. It was cold and drizzling, and the sky was so low there that we couldn't even see more than ten trees ahead of us. It should have been disappointing, but I really did feel as if I controlled my own destiny for a moment. Nicole and Alphonse had given me that.

"When we tell our grandchildren about this, let's spice it up a little. Maybe throw a mountain-lion fight in, maybe some inbred hillbillies that tried to rape us." Even Alphonse was glad that we'd climbed all the way up.

"They don't have hillbillies in Oregon. And you want to tell your grandkids about being raped? Nice." But Nicole's voice was dreamy, thick. "You're right, though: we'll have stories to tell the grandkids now. We're going to have a whole butt-load of stories."

We could all feel it there, at the top of the mountain, almost as if the thinning of the air had thinned out the normal chaos of life: it was the beginning of something we didn't know and the end of everything we did.

I want to tell you something else. You don't mind me jumping forward a little in my story here, do you, offering a little information before I'd actually gained it myself? Because in reality, I'm jumping back hundreds of years, too. So I guess it's one of those instances in which truth is so primordial that, either forward or backward, time ceases to matter.

I discovered later that what we stood on had a name: Klalakis Hill. And much later, I found out what this had meant to the natives who'd long since disappeared from that particular region of Southern Oregon.

We were living beneath the "Silent Widow."

The Fifth Day

I woke up on that fifth day and knew it was going to be different. First of all, there wasn't a cloud in the sky, and the watery, fall sunshine made the interior of Penobscot Road simultaneously more cheerful and much, much dingier. It revealed so much—the old-fashioned, saturated colors; the subtler stains; the waviness of the walls—and as I pushed my body off of that mattress and onto the floor of the parlor, I could sense that it would be a day of revelation. Of course, we hadn't even been there a week yet, so discovering more about our new home was still an interesting proposition. And I planned on discovering a great deal on my own, too.

So why didn't I join forces with my roommates so that we could solve the case together? I wouldn't have hesitated for a moment in sharing my suspicions with Alphonse and Nicole in Sacramento. But they were a slightly different Alphonse and Nicole now, and I was a different Chris. I had to gestate on my own. Still, I did plan on sharing my findings with them as soon as I'd developed a theory. My furtiveness was temporary, and that made it okay.

I think we all knew that this day of revelation meant that we'd have to explore the rest of the house. It's still baffling to me to think that we'd been inside of Penobscot Road for more than four days and had never walked up the staircase. The three of us had even piled up boxes on the first few steps in an attempt to make it seem as if we *couldn't* go up yet. But that was no longer going to fly; the sunshine, which was clearly a rare event in southwestern Oregon, somehow demanded exploration. The question was: who would bring it up, and how would we go about doing it?

"The satellite guy is supposed to be coming today between one and five." Nicole was usually in charge of making appointments with tradespeople, and Alphonse and I were usually responsible for dealing with them.

"I'm going to tell him that we moved here from Las Vegas. I lost everything on red 23; Nicole, you were running a strip club north of town that went bankrupt; and Chris… What's your story going to be? Maybe you're connected with the mafia? Running numbers, maybe?" Alphonse was still joking around about reinventing our past.

"Don't say that. I don't even know what it means."

"Yeah, me, neither. Hey, maybe we can tell him that we don't even know what your past is. You just showed up in town one day. That way, if he asks you, you can always be mysterious about it or make up your own thing."

"Sounds good." It actually sounded horrible, but I wasn't allowed to say that. Our jokes were still too sacred at that point. So I had to change the subject and just hope that he would forget to say anything to the satellite guy. "Hey, how was your room?" Alphonse had moved into the invalid room the night before.

"It was awesome." Was this another story? He didn't say anything for a while, so I began to hope that maybe he was just being uncharacteristically positive for once in his life. But then: "There was something in there with me. I could hear it breathing. I think it was in the closet."

We all tensed up. Then Nicole giggled. "So the boogeyman is your roomie. Fun."

"He's not my *roomie*. He's my *life-partner*."

"Even better."

"We're going to make it official."

"So where are you guys registered?"

"Macy's."

"You're getting a toaster from me."

I had to join in. It wouldn't totally work unless I participated. "And I'm going to get you a blender." This wasn't even remotely funny, but I hardly ever was.

"So what's he like?" I think there was tension under Nicole's levity.

"Oh. He's dreamy. He's tall and dark. So dark that I can't tell if he's handsome. And he's got a deep voice. I can tell by his breathing." Alphonse winced; he'd missed the mark. "He sends his regards to you guys." Which really missed the mark.

But Nicole had to laugh, so she did. "Can't wait to meet him."

"Me, neither." My inability to joke made it even worse, but I continued. "What's his name?"

Alphonse was cleaning one of the door handles in the family room with some kind of solvent. He was bent over the work, hesitating—but it didn't seem as if he were cooking up a funny response. He was hesitating for some other reason.

Then he spoke. "You know, it's strange, but his name is Alphonse, too. Crazy world, huh."

I really wanted this to stop, but I also knew that I was supposed to be figuring out what was happening to us. So I plowed on. "His last name must be different, though."

"Oh, he's going to take my last name. It's in the pre-nup."

"A pre-nup? You two are never going to split up."

"This isn't working at all. This doorknob looks just like it did twenty minutes ago."

And Nicole pulled us farther away still. "And today's the day, you know: we're finally going to deal with the upstairs."

Sure, I'd managed to gather a little information before the others changed the subject, but what sense did it make? Still, I had to remind myself that this was the fact-finding period of my investigation; interpretation came later.

"And the downstairs. We've got to deal with that, too." Alphonse had been especially fascinated by the idea of a basement. None of us had ever been in one before, let alone lived above one. To him, this was the most decadent aspect of our new home: a whole floor that was virtually ignored by inhabitants.

"God. What are we going to do with all this fucking space?" I was on the other side of the family room re-hanging some drapes I'd cleaned in the sink the night before when Nicole said this. She was standing with her hands on her hips, looking around the room, and she seemed so far away from me. Were human beings meant to live close together or far apart from each other? I wondered this for the first time in my life as I stared through all that air at her. She was an outside distance from me, only we were inside.

*   *   *

Anyone who's cleaned a large, dirty area will guess what I'm about to say: we ran out of all our cleaning supplies by 10 a.m. What that same person may not expect: the previous night, I'd poured just enough of each down the drain so that no one would notice the difference. I'm sure you're glad to see that I was growing craftier by the minute.

Consequently, Alphonse and Nicole were in town on a restocking mission when Flo knocked on our door. I was so sad when I saw her face through that little window, thrown into deep shadow by the blinding light illuminating her hair. In spite of my childish efforts, I would never get any answers out of her because Flo, a real, grownup lady, would know just what to do to frustrate me at every turn. Suddenly, I realized what my silly, memorized questions had been reminding me of all along: third-grade multiplication tables.

I opened the door, and her hard, shiny eyes remained entirely on me. Never once did she peer over my shoulder into the gloom of the house. Then there was her smile, an independent force. It was enormous and sharp and matched nothing else on her person.

Also thrown into shadow by the relentless sun was a bottle of wine in her hand. It was thrust at me. "Look at you! You look fantastic! It must be the country air."

I took the bottle and moved aside to allow her to enter. "Oh! Thank you. Well, you've just never seen the real me. Remember, I'm from California. I'm only real when it's sunny."

She didn't laugh at my frail humor, nor did her smile change. "I'm just so glad we found you the perfect place!"

I didn't know how to respond to this, so I didn't. Flo remained on the porch, waiting.

"Please, come in—"

"Oh, I didn't want to interrupt anything. I just wanted to drop off my little gift real quick and welcome you to your new home!"

I'd worked so hard to see her in person that I knew I shouldn't let her take the victory—or credit—away from me. Yet now that Flo was in front of me, all my questions seemed so awkward, far too blunt and obvious. And just like everyone else, now that she was here, her strange behavior aligned itself with Penobscot Road's strangeness—adding to it and fueled by it. Everything just seemed so systematic, so inevitable that I could no longer see any reason to struggle against it. I was fixed to that spot at the front door just as I was fixed by the house in a position of groping ignorance.

Of course, you know the truth about that spot by the small casement window, but I hadn't realized its effects yet. I bring this up only to help you understand what I was up against when I made my next move. I'm still impressed to this day:

"What's wrong with it?"

The question had pushed itself up through my guts, the sharp point of all my planned interrogation, a separate force to eradicate her smile. In fact, my first reaction had been to not even assume responsibility for it, but I knew it had been me, some part of me that still had the power to cry out. Perhaps I wasn't the world's weakest detective.

"What's wrong with what." Flo's smile pushed up at the rest of her face, the frown at her nose, the fear in her eyes.

Perhaps it had been that sad area of the house, perhaps my instinct for passivity, but I couldn't find the strength to continue, and silence proved to be the right move again. Eventually, she spoke: "Look, I've only been in Pacific Bay for a year. What do I know?"

I was a fast learner; I remained quiet.

"I just think the rent is so inexpensive because no one really wants to live out of town. But it's not even fifteen minutes away! I mean, we both know what a real commute looks like, right?"

Flo should have been asking why I thought there was something wrong with Penobscot Road. Even through my dismay, I realized that.

It gave me my course of action: "What about previous tenants?"

"I told you! I don't know about all that. Apparently, it's just always been one of those properties that's been difficult to collect rent on. That's all. People just up and break their leases, and then it's impossible to track them down after that. Kind of a common story with cheaper rentals." Her eyes remained on me as if she were coming toward me on a tightrope, a chasm gaping beneath her.

"So there's nothing else?"

She looked down at the phone in her hand as if there were something of importance on its dark screen. If she had been on a tightrope a moment before, she was swaying fatally.

Flo's smile fell away. "Look, maybe somebody else can tell you more. Some people just know more or can sense things or whatnot. I mean, I'm not the only person in Pacific Bay, right?" But she only flinched after this and continued, "I can get you out of your lease, if you want. Just let me get you out of your lease."

Why did this admission of guilt feel like a challenge to me, too—some sort of test that encompassed a great deal more than just the two of us on that porch, momentarily seeing everything but a way of acknowledging what was happening?

And why in god's name did I answer as I did?

"Oh, that's all right. I was just wondering."

* * *

So far, I've told you only what I thought was significant at the time, so life in that house must seem like an unremitting series of inexplicable events right from the start. Yes, our behavior was odd, but maybe not so odd if you factor in all the "normal" time we spent there in the beginning, the details I've left out. We had normal conversations; we did normal stuff. In fact, I'm pretty sure that if things had ramped up any more quickly than they had, we would've reacted differently, maybe gotten out of the house right away.

Also affecting our escape was the fact that our behavior was becoming more and more altered by the house, bent into stranger and stranger angles, so our responses and the time they took grew increasingly inappropriate. I need you to understand this before I tell you about the upstairs.

* * *

Alphonse, Nicole and I procrastinated until after lunch, but the sun outside was too unrelenting; it seemed to say that this was our last and best chance to confront the rest of the house. Finally, we gave in and pulled enough of the boxes off of the front staircase to get through.

Nicole went up first, of course, then Alphonse and then I. The bright afternoon was strangely altered by each, unknown window above us, and as I stared at the tag on the back pocket of Alphonse's jeans, I told myself that if the sun could exist up there, so could we. It was just another floor of another house. Downstairs had been a little creepy and a few strange things had happened, but this didn't mean that the rest of the house had to be like that.

I reached the top step knowing that I was about to enter the level on which I'd have to pick a bedroom for myself. I could no longer sleep in the parlor; I had to move away from my friends at night.

So it came as a profound shock when I stepped into the upstairs hall. It was nothing like the first floor; at the same time, it was much better and much worse. The second floor was better because the atmosphere wasn't nearly as filthy and negative. Right away, it smelled fresher and more like a house should smell, and the surfaces weren't covered in nearly as much greasy dust. But the second floor was worse because it felt as if I were sneaking around in someone else's home. It was as if the people who lived there had just stepped out for a moment and would be returning at any second. Or maybe they were up there, just out of sight. This feeling of being an intruder was immediate and overpowering, and I had to fight an urge to creep back downstairs and show some respect for the family's privacy.

But *what people?* I glanced at the others. This time, neither seemed to be sharing my experience; they were joking about a third-floor staircase to our left and how important it was that we should have at least four floors of living space. At first I was astonished that Nicole and Alphonse couldn't feel the presence of the family right there with us. All along, I'd been under the impression that—although we never discussed it—the two of them were sensing the same things I was. I could see it in their eyes, hear it in their jokes. Now, I was alone.

The sensation of breaking and entering was bad enough, but being isolated in the experience upset me much more. I was cut off now from the others, burdened with something that we could never tackle together, and this terrified me more than might seem reasonable to you. But as we advanced down the hall to the door directly in front of us, I also realized that if Alphonse and Nicole continued not to notice what I was noticing, I'd face a much tougher time figuring out what was happening. Because my impressions just didn't seem as if they were enough.

When we stopped at the first door, to our left was the third-floor staircase, and to our right a very long hall leading toward the back of the house. The join was visible between the old building and the new; the ceiling dropped a foot, and the corridor narrowed about six inches on either side. At the far end, the light seemed to be swallowed up by its stingy construction.

Where we stood, transoms stood over each door with a circle of colored glass at the center of each. The door in front of us had a ruby-colored insert, and I could imagine the face of an early twentieth-century boy on a step ladder, peering through the glass, a scarlet oval of light covering half of his face like a birthmark. I could go no further, though; I didn't guess at what he was witnessing.

"And behind door number one…" Nicole pushed the door open to reveal a large, high room with scratched up wooden flooring and two sets of water-stained, mint-green curtains. A large window faced the front yard and another provided a view of a dark stand of conifers on the side of the house. A corner had been partitioned off by sloppy drywall, and the hollow-core door in it revealed the rounded shine of a toilet emerging from the shadows.

So that's what the room looked like. Now I should describe what I felt there. But first, let's pause so that you can take a deep breath and settle your mind. You wouldn't know to do that, otherwise, and as I've promised you again and again, I want to make this as painless as possible for you.

Really, though, I'm pausing for myself, too. I need to recount the room dispassionately, from the distance I must constantly remind myself now exists between it and me. I'm not inside it, anymore. It no longer has me.

Because this was my room.

But none of this matters to you! Not really. You don't want to pause; you just want to find out what's making me so melodramatic, to see if my fear of the room lives up to what I'm about to describe. Right now, you're not concerned about the trauma I experienced there; you just want whatever thrills you can extract from me. I can't help but wonder if I'm really nothing more than a story to you.

So I should be more of a storyteller, then. And as a storyteller, a premeditating, scheming narrator, I should only reveal information at the right time. Of course, up to this point, I've shared with you what I lived through exactly when and how I lived through it, so I've been playing by the rules. We've shared the same experience, you and I.

But I understand more about you than you think I do. On the surface, you long to know immediately what it was about that room that still makes me bolt awake at night, my sheets wadded into a ball at my feet. Yet on a deeper level, you want me to keep some things back. You want to wonder about my bedroom, look for clues, anticipate all the things that happened to me there. In short, you want to work for it, to earn it—the difference between a lover and a whore. And you know I have to give you everything you want eventually, anyway, so I guess I should yield to your deepest desires here, too. I'll hold back like the lover I am and keep from you all the things I understood the moment I entered. As I said, a little harmless tease can go a long way in spicing up a relationship. I'm pretty sure that's true.

So all I'll say at this point is that I knew that this would be my bedroom, just as the others knew it. It felt like me, only different, and in fact,

Alphonse said this not two minutes after we'd entered. Perhaps it was the room's misplaced formality, so similar to the one Alphonse and Nicole constantly criticized while dissecting my personality. But there was something else, too: an angry, refusing sadness. We all recognized this, although just as in the hall, I sensed much more.

Maybe this is why I've come to believe that just like people, rooms develop a character from the many things they've endured, from all of the furious drama whirled up inside of them over the years. New rooms are just smooth, soft infants, but an old room is a veteran. In fact, we tell ourselves that we recognize the life scars of others through our five senses—the lines on faces, the scent of panic sweat or overpowering cologne, the smiles that shouldn't be smiled and the glares that can't be helped. But I think we receive most of this information through other sense receptors, just as with old rooms. The residue's there whether we acknowledge it or not, and just as my own, terrible residue is in that room right now, its residue has been deposited inside of me.

But that's all I'm going to reveal at the present. And if I'm honest, it's a relief not to have to face all of that yet. Not yet.

Still, this isn't about my comfort. It's about yours.

Coming out of my bedroom, we noticed for the first time that we'd missed a couple of narrow doors near the main staircase. Although this was in the original part of the house, someone had added these doors and the wall in which they stood. The spaces behind them were too small to be bedrooms but too big to be closets, and although they were definitely built with some kind of purpose in mind, we never could figure out what it was. The one on the left had a window facing the front yard, but the one on the right could only be lit artificially. The one on the right had a baseboard covered in one spot with deep gouges and scratches. The one on the right drew me in.

Maybe it was because it had been built later that the room didn't feel as saturated by the presence of previous owners, and I didn't want to leave when Nicole and Alphonse pulled me back into our new upstairs hallway. There was still a door on our left and a door on our right in the original part of Penobscot Road. One had a sapphire orb in its transom, and the other an emerald. The sapphire room on the left was painted gold, and the emerald room on the right, gray. The sapphire had old, beige carpeting with a series of reddish-brown stains clustered in the left-hand corner under its large window. None of us walked into the room that first time, so we didn't stand on those stains, the soles of our shoes never coming into contact with those crusted, marked fibers. The room on the right, the emerald one, had been completely and recently renovated, with sharp, brilliant pink paint on the woodwork and a brand-new laminate floor, the only room in the entire house in anything near presentable condition. The three of us walked right in, smiling, and then walked right back out again, the smiles still there, but now like old photos of our smiles, distant and fixed. We didn't speak about it then, but I know now that leaving the room had been a physical reflex for each of us, rather than a response to something we recognized.

"Oh my god. It keeps going." Nicole was staring down the hallway, which had appeared to end about fifteen feet from where we'd been standing, but which now clearly jogged to the left and out of sight. We'd just stepped down and into the addition. "How big is this house?"

"Maybe all of the people who worked on the farm lived here." Alphonse was still looking for a logical explanation for something that felt fundamentally incomprehensible. "Maybe they were Mormons? Lots of wives and kids?"

"Maybe." She had paused next to a newer door with no transom above it, only dusty cobwebs at the corner of its frame. "So I wonder which wife lived in here."

"Cinnamon."

"Angelique."

"Chastity."

"Champagne."

"Dakota."

"Cheyenne."

"Tiara."

"Uhh… La Toya." Nicole always lost the stripper name game, and Alphonse made the "loser buzzer" noise.

"If you want to do Jacksons, I would have accepted Paris. But only Paris."

"Fuck you. If I was a stripper or a Mormon wife, I'd totally pick La Toya."

"That's why you're not a stripper or a Mormon wife."

"Fuck you."

And Nicole opened the door, and the most horrible smell of death came out of the room. She slammed the door shut and choked while she laughed. "Jesus! What the hell died in there!"

"God. Some rat or something, probably. We have to get rid of it." Alphonse was backing away from the door, the most squeamish of the three of us.

"Why didn't anybody fucking clean before we moved in? That's totally nasty." Flo had commented that she'd bent the rules for us by not having the place cleaned, but she must have known that would never have really been possible.

Standing there in that fetid hallway, it actually enraged me to think that one of the rooms in our new home could stink like that. I was overcome with the desire to claim the house as ours, because this stench seemed as though it were a dare, a challenge to us to take complete possession of Penobscot Road and of ourselves. If I took up the challenge, maybe the second floor would no longer feel as if I were trespassing. Maybe it would feel as if it were ours.

Alphonse had his shirt over his mouth. "Guys, this is going to have to be your thing, unless you want to clean up my vomit in there, too."

"All right. Let's keep going and deal with it later." And Nicole turned toward the darkening space leading away from us.

"No." And I opened the door, quickly closing it again behind myself. Whatever had died I planned on throwing out the window, which I would then leave open.

But the smell was a physical assault. Even when I breathed through my mouth, I could taste the rotting flesh and entrails, the maggots burrowing into the never-to-be-evacuated feces. A yellowed blind was pulled down against the sun at the only window in the room, and the murky light it produced was actually the *color* of that smell, somehow. My eyes watered just looking around.

I could feel the gravity of my friends and the hallway pulling at my back, but I'd made a pledge to be proactive about the situation we found ourselves in. I was going to be proactive.

The small window was actually quite a distance away, and I realized that this room had the same dimensions as the family room directly below. Finally reaching the far wall, I found that the window was painted shut, and I looked out at the stand of trees a few feet away, desperate to breathe in their fresh air. In the bright sun, the swaying branches were cheerful, inconsequential, and I considered breaking the window just to be adjacent for a moment to anything that could still be inconsequential. But this would be akin to admitting some kind of defeat, so I turned back to the shadowed space, focused on finding whatever was left of the dead thing.

The carpeting, very old and very orange, was covered in a thick coat of dust. Even in the midst of that horrific smell, I remember wondering why some of Penobscot Road's rooms were so dusty, while others were totally free of the stuff. As my eyes adjusted, I saw that there were dozens of dead flies scattered in the corners, but no dead animal. I couldn't hold out much longer, so I raced to the closet and found it empty, too.

But then I looked again: on the top shelf, almost entirely hidden in that yellow gloom, was a box. Had someone deliberately put a dead animal in it? Or even worse, a live animal? I grabbed the box and ran out of the room, slamming the door behind me like a communication of victory—even if the flimsy thing hardly made a sound.

"Oh, god, is it in there?"

I was gasping. "The room's empty, otherwise."

Alphonse had retreated back up the hallway to the corner, his hand squeezing the wall. "Does it smell?"

Nicole and I looked at each other. "No," she said.

So I opened up the box. It was packed full of Christmas lights, all in their original packaging. They appeared to be about twenty years old, and their festive package design was like a slap across the face. More than anything yet, they made me realize how deep we were, how far we were from real life.

But then I reminded myself that Nicole had been right: this *was* real life, too. "I guess we have our decorations for the holidays."

Nicole looked down into the box as forlorn as I'd felt a moment before, and then angrier. The lights had never been used. I expected her to throw the box against the wall, but she giggled instead. "Twinkle."

"Twinkle?"

Nicole directed her gaze at Alphonse, who was approaching. "Twinkle. That's an awesome stripper name."

"That's the worst stripper name I've ever heard in my life. That's, like, the name for a doll that pees. You need to actually go to a strip club to see what they're really like." Alphonse rummaged through the box.

"Oh, like you've been to one?"

"I don't need to go to one because I already know what makes a good stripper name."

The three of us were absolutely clueless. Maybe this was the way things actually were for the rest of the population—the people who went to strip clubs and threw Christmas parties and had sex and lived in houses. Maybe weird things happened to everyone else all the time.

I think Alphonse and Nicole were considering the same thing because they joined me in just staring down into that box for a while.

Christmas. In Penobscot Road.

Finally, Nicole put the lid on it. "What's making that smell then?"

Alphonse, as was his style, already had an answer. "Something died in the wall."

"Oh. Yeah." Satisfied, Nicole put the box on the floor. "We'll have to call Flo, so we'd better make a list." And she pushed us farther into the house, the dense shadows now eating up many details.

But why weren't we turning on lights? Sure, it was sunny out, but it was actually getting hard to see back there.

Then it all made sense: turning on a light would be admitting that the hallway was robbing us of our sight, that we couldn't handle the situation without flinching.

But I was flinching. "Where's a light around here?" Reaching out, I flicked up a nearby switch. Nothing.

And then a cloud passed before the sun, and I could only make out an occasional flash of my roommates' eyes. Suddenly, a chill went through me as I noticed a door handle in my hand. It was classic.

But I'd shivered because it was freezing in there! And the sun would come out again in a minute. I spoke to cancel the spell. "Put that on your list: replace bulb."

I couldn't blame everything I felt on unknown forces. I lived in the real world, too. Although my real world might not have been everyone else's, there were light beams and clouds and old furnaces in my world, as well. There was my fertile imagination.

I reminded myself that the doorknob in my hand was just a dented piece of metal. Someone had bought it in a hardware store and stuck it on because he needed to open the door and because all doors have door handles. I twisted it and pushed the door open. It didn't squeak so much as it screamed, but a little oil would take care of that. It needed lubrication; it wasn't begging us to stay out.

And sure enough, the room behind the door was just a room. I didn't sense its previous inhabitants; I didn't smell or hear or see anything out of the ordinary. Sure, the walls needed to be cleaned of yellowing kids' stickers, but that was perfectly normal. The window had no curtains, and as we looked around, the sun came out, hitting us all right in the face. It was wonderfully warm and exactly the same sun we'd always known.

Yet we were quiet because commenting on how normal the room was would be admitting that the rest of the house was not normal. So we just wandered around the room, lingering much longer than we had in the other rooms and talking about nothing in particular. In fact, we more than lingered, we pressed our behinds against corners, explored the closet and caressed the smooth walls enclosing us. Alphonse and Nicole even stopped joking.

"How far out belongs to us?" Alphonse was looking at the trees that were waving at us a hundred feet on the other side of the dirty window. His crotch was resting on the window sill. "I could be completely nude right now, and no one would ever see me."

"Uhh, hello? *We'd* see you." But Nicole said this desultorily; she'd come up to Alphonse's side and was inspecting the forest, too.

"You know what I mean. People who count. Neighbors. We don't ever need to close our curtains here. We never have to worry about anybody else."

"And nobody else is ever going to worry about us." But she said this as if it were the most attractive prospect in the world.

In point of fact, not too many people had ever worried about us in the first place. Still, there was a definite freedom in the idea of extricating ourselves completely from the complex web of society that we'd never really mastered. So I could see why Nicole said it the way she did, wistfully, as if remembering a pleasant dream.

As I idly flicked a Scooby-Doo sticker on the window frame, I wondered if people pulled away from us because as they got to know us, all they could do was worry. That couldn't have been enjoyable.

Finally, we didn't have to worry about that kind of worry, either. We were free to do whatever it was we wanted to do.

I came up between Alphonse and Nicole and put my arms around their shoulders. I felt both their arms grasp me around the small of my back. We began to sway like the trees before us, lightly, indolently. Being free and being together: it was what we each needed more than anything else in the world, and now we'd found it.

"Ready to keep going?" Nicole said this excitedly, and I realized that we were only halfway through our adventure.

"Absolutely," I said, nodding my head just like the branch I'd been staring at, which was pendulous with pine cones. "Let's see what's next."

The light had shifted quite a bit in the room, and one of the walls that had been in shadow was now bright with sunshine. I noted this in passing as we moved back out into the hallway. Then I peered into the creaky darkness and winced in bewilderment. Why were we continuing deeper into the house? Why on earth had I agreed to live here? Had the three of us just been *touching* each other?!

I kept my eyes down, embarrassed and frustrated and confused. As this was often my state of mind, I could at least take comfort in the fact that Nicole and Alphonse might not read too much into my behavior. They, however, were easier to decode: I could see that they were struggling with the same emotions I was. Alphonse escaped back into the sunny room, and Nicole plowed down the hallway to the next door, which she flung open and entered.

I wanted to join Alphonse, but that would have been admitting too much. In many ways, I was stronger than he was; I hadn't reached my tolerance yet and so didn't have to retreat. But there was a palpable level of danger on the second floor now. The real occupants must have just returned home and were mounting the stairs to investigate the odd noises. I knew they had a gun.

I rushed into the next room and closed the door as nonchalantly as I could. Had Flo leased Penobscot Road to another group of renters? Maybe the people who really owned the place had decided to move back in? I was learning that the mind has to run through all explanations before facing the possibility of never knowing.

"Christ. Why would somebody do this?" Nicole's back was to me, the familiar annoyance back in her voice.

This room had been painted black, and even the carpeting was such a dark gray that it might as well have been black. The meager light from the smallish window didn't even make it far into the room. It smelled like adolescent deodorant and Windex and rat droppings. And there was someone's body odor under all of this, musky and insistent.

"Some teenager must have thought it was cool." And as if to prove her point, Nicole opened the closet door. On the back of it was an ancient, ripped poster for Slayer.

I'd never been happier to discover something than when we found that poster because I could so easily imagine the 15-year-old who'd put it up, nothing like the others there whose traces refused to let me pin them down, to shrink them into my imagination. Boring, predictable, pathetic people had been inside that house before us. I couldn't help but laugh, and then I felt my eyes well up.

Of course, I kept all of this to myself. If Nicole was thinking the same thing, she hid it pretty well. She was genuinely surprised to find me wiping tears from my eyes.

Nicole could take a lot, but instead of asking me why I was so over-come, she redirected her attention to a hole in the drywall behind me. "I don't think I've ever slammed a door open in my life."

I wished she could've seen what a wonderful thing that poster was, but she was right: telling her would only make it worse right now. So I only said, "You're not dramatic enough."

"You're one to fucking talk."

A shoe scraped the floor behind me, and I jumped into the closet door so hard that I bruised my temple. At first, it seemed as if the house had hit me rather than the other way around, and in one sense it had, because if I hadn't been worried that the people who lived there were about to hunt me down, I would've immediately recognized Alphonse's shuffling gait.

The joy that the poster had just given me slid into fear for my physical safety: what other harmful reactions could the house elicit from me?

But we were finished in the room. Alphonse and Nicole fussed over my bruise a little, and we kept moving.

"You know, we can have more than one room of our own in this place. Like an office for me where I could work, and an exercise room for Nicole." Alphonse skipped me because I didn't really do anything very specific with my free time.

"I could have a library." But I didn't even want one room to myself up there, let alone two.

"I want the sunny room." It was as if Nicole had been waiting for the opportunity.

"But I want that one." And Alphonse sounded scared. "Why don't we rock/paper/scissors for it?"

Which they immediately did, Nicole's paper covering Alphonse's rock.

"Shit!" But he wasn't going to be the first person to admit that the sunny room had some sort of perverse hold on him. "Shit. Oh, well. No big deal."

"Don't worry, Alphonse. You can have the room that smells like death."

Her joke wasn't funny, hanging in the dark air, and as he opened the door in front of us, he replied only that, "There's a whole floor we haven't looked at upstairs. I get first dibs."

The thought of going through other strange halls and more and more empty, laden rooms made me realize how tired and hungry I was. It was almost time for dinner.

But we'd started up the stairs not long after lunch. How could it almost be nighttime?

Nicole and I followed Alphonse into another bathroom. This one had cracked, gray tiles rising up the walls and a leak in the faucet that sent a rusty trail to the drain in the middle of the floor. It flickered as if alive in the last of the electric dusk that comes after a particularly sunny day. And through the window, the woods did look shocked, the light forcing an exposure unnatural for them. Even the bathroom seemed naked, violated.

But maybe it was just sundown and just a bathroom. I was worn out by our tour, no longer willing to make sense of what I was finding out about my new home. I hoped no one would say anything because I knew I was too fatigued to properly audit how I'd respond.

At this exact moment, Alphonse spoke up. "Why are all the bathrooms in this place so gross?"

"Chris's bathroom isn't gross. The *master* bathroom." But Nicole and Alphonse both sounded as flat as I felt.

I was right about my tact, which was one of my only strengths. It had finally been wrung out of me. "You guys picked your rooms before even checking out the second floor."

"I thought you two wanted to stay camped out downstairs. You know, so that you'd be really close." Yet Nicole's comment sounded even more laconic than the last one.

On some, distant level, I knew things were going out of control, but I didn't feel it, and so I responded, "I'm upstairs now. That way, I'll have my privacy, and *you two* will have *yours.*"

I remember my eyebrows rising on this very meaning-laden *"yours,"* which was an overwrought and consequently uncharacteristic behavior for me. You see, my face, which is something people have to get used to, isn't a particularly animated organ. So almost immediately, I was thankful for the darkness that hid this anomaly. Then I realized that we hadn't turned on any lights because the enclosing night was insulating us from certain aberrations, such as my sudden facial expressions. I could only imagine what the others were grappling with in those shadows.

Later on, and to my regret, we'd discover just how little we'd seen of the second floor in that darkness.

Of course, our groping around in the dark seems now to me as bizarre as our initial reluctance to explore that floor. So yes, I can see my story as you do and am overcome with a desire to apologize for my stupidity then. But haven't you looked back on things you've done and wondered what you were thinking? I just pray that the looking back for you isn't continual and toxic, as it is for me.

At this point, my energy had drained out along with the light in that room, and I couldn't find the strength to stop arching my eyebrows melodramatically and speaking my mind in the blackness. In an almost trancelike way, I continued: "I guess you guys will just have to learn to amuse yourselves while I'm up here. *Somehow.*"

Nicole's response was just as automatic. "And you'll just have to amuse yourself, *as usual.*"

Alphonse had been standing closest to the door, and he grunted out of a kind of frustration and pushed back into the hallway. After a moment of staring at the empty door, Nicole moved to follow him, and because I was in the way, I had to shuffle toward the door, too. But it was as if I'd just woken up and couldn't quite remember why I had muscles or how to coordinate them.

"Move it, Chris." And Nicole actually shoved me out of the room. As soon as I was back in the hallway, I became aware of the dropping temperature and the end of dusk and the sharp sounds and smells around me. I was ashamed of what I'd insinuated in the bathroom and angry at what Nicole had said. We never said things like this to each other. But I also never admitted to having regrets and so immediately fell back into old ways as we felt our way toward the last door at the end of the hall. And even though Nicole always admitted to being pissed off, curiously, she said nothing, either.

Alphonse heaved against the door and jiggled the handle. "Locked. We're going to have to leave this one for another time."

"It must be where the back stairs lead." Nicole did her best to make this sound casual, but there was a strange echo that made every word sound as if it were just behind you.

And so we ended our tour of the second floor. As we retraced our steps down the hall, I became aware of how long the walk was and how much I'd experienced over the past few hours. My other life almost seemed fake now.

Other life? I felt a metallic constriction in my throat while the three of us passed the third-floor staircase, completely ignoring it. Even that morning, my "other life" could have meant Sacramento and everything I'd known before coming to Oregon and Penobscot Road. But what I'd meant was my life previous to mounting the steps I now stood above. What could have possibly changed so profoundly that afternoon?

I knew the answer to this and I didn't know it. The wooden steps were creaky and sturdy and cold as I descended them and passed back into the front hallway of my new home.

*   *   *

I can't be the first person to equate telling a story with making love, can I? The careful, expansive start. The quickening pace and urgency. The climax. Then there are character and dialogue, and both even share conflict—in each case, a kind of friction of wish-fulfillment. Should I suggest that good storytellers make good lovers? I long to make this apparent to you in more immediate ways.

But they have something else in common: a dynamic of revelation. When to lay oneself bare and when to hold something back. If Penobscot Road were a map of your body, then I've bared you everywhere but my bedroom, so far. Here, I've only grazed. And then there are other parts that I haven't even touched yet: the basement, the third floor. I suppose you could say that we're at third base. And the idea of skimming over some areas of the house, while concentrating all of our attention on others allows me to feel as if I have some sort of control over the process.

But just as with making love, when overanalyzed, a story breaks down into a scattering of unappealing *objects* that push the *subject* farther away, rather than making it more tangible.

Any fetishist will tell you that.

The Sixth Day

The next morning, I had a chance to continue my investigation. As we drove down the little road away from our house, I peeled layer after layer of confusion and doubt and passivity off the skin of my mind. Eventually, I had to admit to myself that the cliché, "the farther away I get, the better I feel," was the only way to describe my experience. And even though the weather had returned to its perpetual gray, I remember looking down at a storm drain at a corner in town and marveling at how simple, clean, and pure it was. It was nothing more and nothing less than a storm drain, with one function and one lifespan. If I stared at it or sat on it or grabbed it or smelled it, it would never do anything but perpetuate its relationship with me as a storm drain. A series of humans had designed it, built it, and placed it next to the road, and just like those humans, it only ever obeyed the wonderful laws of nature. And it was connected to a sidewalk, and then a building, and then a reality that was completely familiar to me. That's how it felt, going back into town after a couple of days. What just a short while earlier had seemed profoundly alien was now like coming home. I honestly wanted to hug every unexceptional senior we passed and breathe in their smell of cauliflower and denture paste. They would be dead soon enough, but in the right way.

You know, it's the same urge I have to breathe you in physically. Perhaps I make a little more sense to you now? If I don't, I will soon enough.

The three of us were mostly quiet while we accomplished our errands, but I'm sure we could all feel the same kind of relief radiating off of each other. Our lives had shifted out of bounds in the house, but *only* in the house; the rest of the world was exactly how we remembered it, how we'd always demanded it to be. Because it's true: I think things stay sane in our world because we demand reality. Human beings have quite a powerful collective will. It's just that the house's will was stronger than ours.

Finally, I stood at the end of an aisle in Pacific Bay's party store. Seventy-five percent of the place had been given over to Halloween, and Nicole was inspecting a string of jack-o'-lantern lights because she'd decided that we were going to get into the holiday spirit and decorate the hell out of Penobscot Road. She wanted the families that came to our door with their little Luke Skywalkers and fairy princesses to recognize that we were serious house dwellers, that we meant domestic business. I saw a couple of flaws in this line of attack but managed to hold my tongue, which was easy for me again in the cold light of normality. No one was going to bother driving all the way out to our house just to collect a few pieces of candy, but this wasn't her real motivation. Now that Nicole felt stronger out with the rest of the world, just as we all did, she'd come to the conclusion that she could somehow strike a responding blow to the house by forcing it to display humiliating Halloween decorations. She wanted to *own* it. The only problem with this line of reasoning was that she was looking at Penobscot Road as her opponent, that there was a battle to win or to lose. This was very characteristic of Nicole. I, on the other hand, felt that the house existed outside of any conventional structure of competition; my whole experience with the place had already been too fundamentally alien for anything as easy as that. Instead, I suspected that the three of us were as impotent as ants crawling up its drainpipe, although if you'd asked me then, I wouldn't have been able to say why. I'm still not sure I could.

"This is the fucking tackiest thing I've ever seen in my life." She was holding up a cardboard elephant wearing a witch's costume that was perched on a flying broomstick, its chunky feet not even physically able to grasp the handle. "I'm getting, like, ten of these."

On some level, Alphonse was aware of Nicole's motives and tacitly agreed. "And we need a few of these." He threw a group of ugly rubber scarecrows into our cart.

None of us had jobs. None of us had really even started looking. We didn't "need" any rubber scarecrows.

"You guys are so much better at this kind of thing than I am. I'm just going to head down the street for a second. There are a couple of things I need to pick up." I rolled the cart in front of Alphonse and stepped away. "I'll be back in a couple of minutes."

Nicole looked back at me, astounded. I'd never abandoned her army before. "We have to decorate for Halloween, Chris."

"So get to it! I'll see you guys later." And I beat a retreat before she realized that although the outside world was the same, I wasn't.

On the way into town, we'd passed an older house that had a sign in its window: Fortune Teller. It had reminded me of Flo's suggestion to consult with someone who "sensed things or whatnot," and despite my terminal passivity, I found myself watching each of my feet actually hitting the sidewalk, one after the other, as if they could walk wherever they wanted.

In fact, I'd never really considered the possibility of the occult before the move, so I'd never bothered to form an opinion about it. I know that must sound a little ridiculous, but nothing even remotely supernatural had ever happened to me, and I tended to consider weighty issues only as they were lobbed at me. I was the kind of person who took only little bites and then chewed a very, very long time. So as your average, maladjusted nerd, I'd managed to keep myself eternally distracted from the important questions of life. At one time or another, I'd been obsessed with the writings of Willa Cather, Dixieland jazz, and unicycling, although when we'd moved to Oregon, I'd been in fixation-remission. This may help to explain how I so easily embraced the possibility of the paranormal in Penobscot Road: I had nothing better with which to occupy myself. But more than that, it was a goal that, rather than just taking my mind off of my life, would also allow me to solve a problem the three of us faced. I'd never felt such determination.

Soon, a young, blonde woman in sweat pants opened the door holding a toddler chewing on the head of an Elmo doll. I'd been expecting someone more stereotypical, and my first impulse was to ask to speak to her grandmother.

"Hey." She didn't sound like a fortune teller; she sounded like a college student. But why couldn't you be both?

"Hello. Is this a good time for the whole fortune-telling thing?"

"Yeah. Come on in."

Sure enough, the house was kind of like her: prosaic Ikea furniture, lots of photos of her son in plastic frames, a gallon of milk sitting on a white-tiled breakfast bar. It even smelled like sweet, tropical air freshener. Still holding the baby, she moved to put away the milk.

"Sorry. People don't usually show up at this time of day. I don't know why not. We're going to go into that room over there. I just need to give Colton to my boyfriend." And she disappeared into another part of the house, leaving me to peer into the fortune-telling room. But it was just like the rest of the house: pedestrian and white, with an older computer perched on a flimsy cantilevered desk and a poster of a strip of hotels on a sugar beach that read: "Cancun."

"Go on in and have a seat." And she followed me into the room, shutting the door behind herself. "Okay! So 'the whole fortune-telling thing.' My name's Melissa, and I've been doing this for just about ten years now. So what we're going to do is figure out your situation first, and then I'll choose the tools that I think can help you the best. Does that sound okay?"

As she sat before me, I saw how light blue her eyes were, almost gray.

"Sure."

"So what's your name?"

"Chris."

"And what's your situation? What brings you here?"

"Something weird is happening in my house. Or my house is weird. Or something weird is happening to me in my house. Or none of the above. I'm not sure. I guess that's why I'm here."

"Wow. So what's, like, specifically happening?"

"Well, each room makes me feel different things or remember things. Or something. And my roommates and I have been doing things, too. Things that don't make any sense. But only since we moved in. I just don't feel like myself when I'm in the house. I don't know what to do, or if there's even anything I can do. Should I even be here?"

"What do your roommates think is going on?"

"We haven't really discussed it yet."

"Really?"

"Well. We're a little weird about some things."

"Hmmm." She looked up, over my head and to the left a little, her eyes moving back and forth in little sweeps. I was sure she was calculating.

"How much does this cost? I just want to be sure before we start."

It was as if she hadn't heard me. Her eyes continued their little movements, scanning the wall behind me, just below the ceiling.

I could feel the muscles in my legs getting ready to contract, to hoist me into the air. "I'm not even sure—"

"So do you think it's haunted? Or possessed or something?"

"I don't know. Nothing like this has ever happened to me before."

"Because I'm a fortune teller, you know? I'm not a medium or anything like that." But Melissa said this as if she wasn't sure, somehow.

"What's the difference?"

"A fortune teller tells you what might happen in the future, and a medium can communicate with other… but you know, I'm kind of wondering if there really is that much of a difference, you know? Maybe there isn't? Like, where do I get my information from?"

"So you're real, then?"

She smiled a little at this, but it wasn't a nice smile. "What, you mean because I'm young and everything?"

"I just don't know anything about all this stuff. I've never had any reason to do something like this before."

"Yeah." And her eyes unfocused again. This time, she'd pointed them on the smooth surface of the table. "It actually sounds kind of cool, in a way."

I didn't like that she'd said this and rose to go. "So I guess I should speak with someone else. Maybe you know somebody? A medium or something? Because I'm not really sure what to do next."

Her eyes flashed on me, and it felt as if they cut through the air, sliced through all the nonsense. If she were a fake, it was the eyes that worked for her, the way they grasped onto you, like a wolf's. I could imagine feeling duped five minutes after leaving her house, but not then, not when she was looking at me.

"I kind of know a guy up in Seville. He's pretty well-known around here. But maybe I can help you. I'm getting a vibe. I don't know. Would that be okay? I wouldn't charge you anything."

If I was going to explore the possibility of something supernatural happening, I wanted an expert. I'd never feel as if I had a real answer, otherwise. Of course, would I *ever* feel as if I had a real answer that way? Or maybe I should have been comparing answers between mediums? "What would you do?"

Melissa pulled a set of large cards out of a dark-blue velvet pouch and shuffled them, her white-hot gaze back on me. "Let's just see what I'd do." And she handed the deck to me. "Go ahead and pull three cards out of there. Whichever ones feel right to you."

I picked one from the front, one from the middle, and one from near the back. I can still feel their sharp edges, their rounded corners pressing onto my fingers. They felt so definite, and this comforted me, somehow.

"Okay. Now just lay them down in front of you in a row. In whatever order seems like the best one."

And I did: the second one, then the first, then the third. They had animals on them, strange symbols and some writing on the bottom, but before I could really get a look, she'd whisked them off of the table.

"All right. So let's do this."

"What did they say?"

Now her searing gaze was on the cards as she returned them to the pouch. "They were about something else."

*   *   *

Returning to the house was horrible. Looking back, I don't know if I could have even done it if I hadn't committed myself to determining what was happening with Melissa. Honestly, I have no idea how my friends were able to return to that place.

Pulling up to the front porch was a much different experience than the last time, now that I was becoming familiar with what was behind those walls, those windows. Honestly, it was the thought of putting myself back into something abject, like freeing myself from a fall into a toilet bowl only to return to it, pushing my private area farther and farther into the foul, chilling liquid. Going back into that house made just as much sense.

What were the three of us talking about at the time? Nicole was still solidifying her plans for Halloween, Alphonse occasionally making brief suggestions. I remained even quieter than usual. We all managed to keep our eyes on the paraphernalia we were unloading; to look up was to give away whatever power we might have had.

"What about covering the porch with those spider webs? Let them hang down so that they kind of create a new room out here."

Nicole stopped for a moment to consider Alphonse's idea. "That way, we could hide behind them and jump out at the kids when they come up the steps. Nice. Hey, and what if we set up some of this stuff inside and kind of make a haunted house? Like the parlor and front hall or something. Make those brats work for their candy."

Regardless of its innocent origin, Nicole had uttered the phrase "haunted house." If our behavior was stiff before, it grew doubly so now. Alphonse could only muster a "Yeah," in response. He and I were fiddling around more than was necessary with the bags and boxes we had, and it took Nicole to open up the door and pass back into the house before we made our way inside.

It smelled like mildew and burned toast; the walls radiated cold; there was a kind of negation in everything, a rejection. Why had I agreed to let Melissa in here? She could never do anything to help; she only wanted to snoop because it was "cool." And anyway, I knew everything I needed to know about Penobscot Road already. I knew the emotions I felt, the things I sensed. What did it matter where they came from or why they existed? Their origin wasn't the problem.

I noticed then through the small window by the door that Nicole had turned our car's headlights on accidentally. Our car was ancient, so the color of their light was pinkish yellow, their incandescence much closer to fire than the newer, cooler headlights on cars. Imagining that they probably used much more electricity too, I thought of that battery draining so quickly, only to be charged and drained, charged and drained, charged and drained until at last it failed to charge. I thought of how dependent we were on something so weak and fickle. I thought of how much damage cars could do to people, but in order to do damage, they needed a battery that hadn't drained completely. I thought of all the lives that would have been saved if only their batteries had drained completely. But they hadn't.

"Hello?" Nicole was dragging a box into the parlor. "Chris? What are you doing?"

"Oh, nothing." And I wondered if letting her battery drain would save us as I joined her in pushing that box into the other room. I never did tell Nicole about her headlights, but Alphonse turned them off when he returned to the car to retrieve his scarf a minute later. I saw him come back into the house, and he paused at the front door, inspecting me as if he wished I were someone else.

My plan was this: first, I'd draw up a map indicating the locus of each phenomenon I'd experienced so far. This I'd date and send to myself in the mail to prove to Melissa (and my roommates) that she and I couldn't have matched up our stories—consciously or unconsciously—before we'd heard each other's. Then, I'd get Melissa in while I'd surreptitiously gotten Alphonse and Nicole out. I'd already done it once when Flo came; I was certain that I'd come up with another brilliant ruse. And following her through the house, I'd videotape everything that happened.

Any concurrence on Melissa's part might help convince me that I wasn't going insane, but I didn't see how it would solve the problem. I wasn't even sure what the solution could be: should I try to stop the strange phenomena? Gather evidence hard enough to convince the others to move? Develop some sort of skillset necessary to deal with the house's peculiarities? I think I assumed that these questions, along with how I would sneak Melissa in and what she'd actually do, would be answered soon enough.

I can see now that I was afraid of broaching the subject with my friends without some corroborating evidence. How would things have turned out if I'd just had the guts to share my suspicions with Nicole and Alphonse the moment I'd had them? I'm haunted by the possibility.

The time came before I was ready. That day, we were planning on cleaning the second floor. It wouldn't take the days that the first floor had; the leavings of time and previous inhabitants were subtler here. Still, as I mounted the stairs with Nicole and Alphonse, I guessed that it would be harder to scrub away the sensations and responses that the second-floor rooms engendered in us.

I was right. As soon as I hit the landing, I knew there was a family up there, behind the closed doors, performing acts that were both private and peculiar to them. But there wasn't. I studied my friends out of the corner of my eye. Alphonse was frowning at the floor as if he were listening to far off music; Nicole was clanking together the many cleaning products she was toting around much more loudly than was necessary. She also spoke right away: "Shit. Pledge."

My first thought was that she was chickening out, and I couldn't blame her. But that was a grand example of projection.

Alphonse's eyes darted down the dark hallway. "Pledge?"

"Pledge." Now Nicole dropped everything in front of my bedroom door. "I just want to get this done. I don't want to be cleaning this place for fucking years."

The third-floor staircase was right there, right next to us. We never looked at it directly.

"And we need something to get all those hard water stains out of the bathroom. Shit. We were just in town! Why didn't we think of any of this then?"

Alphonse and I remained mute. I knew the reason why but would've never uttered it.

"I need to get a DSL splitter. And a filter. I mean, I don't need them right this second, but if we're going back into town." Of course, Alphonse sounded more relieved than he should have been.

"What about you, Chris? What have you forgotten? Fuck, this is a pain in the ass! Everything we're ever going to need is going to be, like, this long-ass drive into town."

"Nothing."

"Nothing?! Really?"

"No, nothing."

"Well, then." And she handed me the bucket she'd been carrying. "I guess you can get started on your own room."

The two of them watched me, curious and nervous at once.

Nicole was even less absolute than usual. "I mean, is that okay?"

In rapid succession, my brain performed a series of calculations. I'd never been up the stairs that were six inches from my ankle. If Melissa were to come over that afternoon, I'd need to have already recorded my responses to whatever was up there. And to the basement. But this meant that I'd have to go up to the third floor and down into the basement before Melissa got there. By myself. Now.

I didn't have enough time. I wasn't prepared. The third floor was bound to be worse; I could feel its discharge weeping down onto me. Yet what came out of my mouth was: "I want to get started here."

"Okay. See ya wouldn't want to be ya." And with that, Nicole and Alphonse disappeared, clearly glad of the reprieve of an hour or two.

Then I was alone with Penobscot Road. I could feel all of the imprisoned space there, stretching out into the smaller, darker, nastier surfaces that pushed backward into the rear yard. It all generated the kind of silence that city dwellers can't understand, a vice around my head that centered on my ears. The house was so patient; I could feel it then, the waiting almost a kind of observation.

The day was dark with swollen rain clouds that hadn't yet decided to present what they were carrying. So it was pitch black at the top of the third-floor stairs. I'd refused even to look up there over the previous 24 hours.

I called Melissa.

"Hello?"

"Hello, Melissa?"

"Yeah?"

"This is Chris. I was in earlier. About the house."

"Sure, Chris. What's going on?"

"What do you mean?"

"You sound—I don't know—upset."

The blackness that overtook the light at the middle of the staircase seemed almost solid, the exact color and mass of the silence waiting above me.

"I think it's a good time for you to come over. If you can. My room-mates just left for a while."

"Is anything happening?"

"No." But this sounded like a lie to me. I'm sure it must have sounded the same to her.

"Okay. Yeah, sure. I can come out now."

Even if she left at that minute, it would still take Melissa twenty minutes to reach the house. I had to experience every inch of the place before then. And record it. And be ready for her. There was no way of knowing if she'd ever come back, so we couldn't skip any corner of the house. I'd always wonder about it, otherwise.

I didn't see how I could get it all done.

"Thank you." I'd never been less thankful in my life.

Racing downstairs, I hunted for a pad and pencil. Here, I focused on the feel of the different flooring under my socks. I noted the slight movement of air over my ears and hair as I rushed around corners. I observed the changes in temperature from room to room: cold, frigid, cold. I kept my head down, as if to keep from tripping, a coolie cowed by my oppressor yet aware, always aware. I recognized that every scent and every stench in the house was always in some proportion to an undercur-rent of mildew or something rotting, a constant element in Penobscot Road that I hadn't yet named.

What I didn't do was think about what I was doing or where I was or what was about to happen. It must have been the same reason that hospital workers race soon-to-be-dead people around on gurneys, shouting things and earning their pay in a way that none of them can ever acknowledge.

The pencil and then the pad were retrieved. My path took me through the dining room and then the parlor before I mounted the first set of stairs and then the second.

I was on the third floor.

There was a door at the top of the stairs; it had once been padlocked on the outside although the lock had since been removed. It was var-nished; probably the same, dark stain that had once covered all the wood of the house, rough now against my hand because of a hundred years of humidity. I felt nothing strange and did nothing strange. This was noted on my pad, and then I opened the door.

A dark hallway, narrower than any on the first two floors. That smell of mildew was offensive here; clearly this was the source from which it spilled down the cracks in the house, infiltrating the walls. I flicked on the light, and the first thing I saw filled me with such dismay that I nearly turned around and walked out of the house forever: there was a large hatch on the hallway ceiling, evidence of an attic. The house had another floor; more fouled space lingered above me. Space that I would have to expose myself to.

But the attic was too much to face at that moment, and so I squinted around the third floor, experiencing a kind of vertigo at the thought that I was so far from any means of escape. At least on the other floors, there were windows that helped reassure me of the mournful woods outside, that could be broken and jumped out of when it became necessary. But this level seemed to have none; no light even leaked underneath the two doors nearest me, and the silence was so much more overwhelming here, like being sealed up, suspended in the thick air.

I started to whistle "You Are My Sunshine." I don't whistle very well, and I don't whistle very often, but it just started. The whole thing was appalling, the noise somehow being eaten up by the surfaces, by the atmosphere, rather than reflected back at me. But I needed to put something of myself up there, a cross between a defense and an offering. I just knew I did. Still, the sound was terrible and small, and I wished that it would stop.

I pushed on. As on the other floors, the hallway had been extended toward the back, and there were a couple of steps down into a passage so tight that my arms brushed both walls and I could feel a stray hair on the top of my head snagging on the rough ceiling. I wanted to start at the far end and work my way back to the stairs; this seemed like a slightly less terrifying plan than moving farther and farther away from the exit—even though it wasn't really an escape and only brought me back to the chaos of the second floor. There was no longer real safety for me anywhere.

When I finally made it to the end of the corridor, it opened into a small T crowded by four flimsy doors that were stained a color mocking the original woodwork. Two faced me, and there was a door on my left side and a door on my right. I opened the door that faced me on the left and walked in.

It was a storage room with chipped, darkened asbestos tiles on the floor and feces of various sizes and shapes scattered from the corners and into the center. A small window overlooked the back yard through which someone had tried to get out or flung something so forcefully that its screen had ripped out down the middle. My whistling became more and more tuneless as my lips dried and I felt my pulse at my neck and ears.

The ceiling was low to begin with, and it sloped off to my left practically to the floor. I noted in my pad that I was relieved to find that no one had been forced to live in such a room, that it was just a standard attic space. But then I noticed darker spots on the floor that seemed to indicate where small-scale furniture had stood for years and years.

"They just stored it up here." Now I was talking to the third floor, refusing to take its bait. The weakness I could hear in my voice made everything so much worse. But I couldn't stop myself. "Kids would love a room like this." In response, the room increased its silence. I strained to hear the wind whistling through the grizzled screen, but there was absolutely no sound. "Kids can have fun anywhere."

I turned my back on the room. *"You are my sunshine, my only sunshine."* Now I was fighting with the silence, pushing back at it, denying it. *"You make me happy, when skies are gray.* And they're always gray around here. But that's just Oregon for you." I opened up the closest door. It revealed a room that was the mirror opposite of the first and that threw a stench of mold into my face along with silence. The smell was so strong that it was almost a sound. I should have been able to hear it.

"You'll never know, dear, how much I love you, please don't take my sunshine away." I was shouting at this point, enraged. This room had been amateurishly painted with toy blocks and teddy bears and rocking horses. A nursery. "It's so cozy up here, perfect for a baby. What a great idea." The ceiling was actively leaking, a slow brown drip on a darkened spot on the carpet, ground zero. The screen had been forced open here, too. I could hear my pulse vibrating in my ear drums. *"The other night, dear, as I lay sleeping, I dreamt I held you in my arms.* I know all the words to this song. All of them."

I slammed the door, and opened the next one: a bathroom. The roof angled down so sharply at the bathtub that I couldn't see how a person could keep their head above the water. *"When I awoke, dear, I was mistaken, and I hung my head and cried."* The toilet was missing, and someone had shoved a nice, white towel with pink and blue roses down into the hole it left. There was no window. "This is so convenient!"

I flung open the door facing me across the hall. Another bedroom with ash-colored, fake wood paneling that had been wet so often that it undulated across the walls and ceiling. The silence was becoming physical, tightening around me. I stomped a dance onto the gold, loop-pile carpeting that threw up the smell of rancid foam rubber. *"I'll always love you and make you happy, if you will only say the same. But if you leave me to love another, you'll regret it all one day."* The inside of a small dormer here had been covered—floors, walls, ceiling—with stringy, orange shag carpeting. A gnarled branch from one of the trees next to the house was so close that it reached out, scraping against the roof under the window, pointing at me. "What a great decorating idea!"

I ran into the hallway, breathless and screaming at the top of my lungs: *"You are my sunshine*—what else do we have here? Come on. Show me." A door farther down the hall revealed a huge, long room in the original part of the house. *No window at all.* It was decorated all in pink for a little girl, now not much more than a filthy gray. *"My only sunshine!* How sweet! I'm sure she grew up to be a healthy young lady!" Across the hall, another long room with no windows. This one had a bunk bed shoved at the end farthest from the door. On closer inspection, it had been bolted onto the walls and ceiling so tightly that it must have been too much work to haul out. The old mattresses were circled in myriad piss stains. *"You make me happy when skies are gray."* When I turned the light off, the room couldn't have been more like a mausoleum. Fresh, open air was just on the other side of its ceiling, unbreathable, impossible.

"You'll never know, dear," the attic hatch was directly above me. How could there be another floor? *"How much I love you,"* I had to go up there; I had to see everything. I couldn't allow any part of the house to be unknown to me. That would give it too much power.

But then I froze. The silence ate all of my sounds and movements, leaving me the loser in our fight, the victim. I froze because I'd just pictured the front of Penobscot Road: there was a large dormer on the third floor with an octagonal window in its center. But there were no other rooms up here.

I let the silence follow me into the bunk-bed room: only one door, which led to a closet. I ran across the hall to the little girl's room: a closet door just like its twin, but another, short door on the wall facing the front of the house. It had a latch on it that was locked. I kicked at it and kicked at it, glad to feel the wood injured by me, feeling it crack and bend and eventually give way to my force.

Inside, there was a sort of crawlspace, only about three feet high and two feet wide, but it had been completely covered with faux Victorian flowered wallpaper. Someone had actually taken the time to shove themselves into this claustrophobic nightmare and wallpaper it. It turned sharply to the left and out of sight.

I scrambled through it and found myself inside the dormer. It was at most five feet high, wide and deep, littered with cheap, plastic toys: a headless doll, a ray-gun, a tiny tea set still set up for a party in the corner. The ceiling was at a terrible level—it encouraged adults to stand but then frustrated them every time, their necks bent forward at the exact same angle as a hanging.

An astounding view of the driveway and the clearing at the front of the property was revealed by the octagonal window. It somehow informed me that everything I saw out of it was under the influence of Penobscot Road, that everything exposed to the house's presence by sight or sound was part of it and not the safety I'd imagined it to be. And coming down the driveway was a silver car—Melissa. It was too late for her, too.

But I was immobilized by the little tea room, suddenly enervated by the distance and awful trial I'd have to endure just to get to the front door of my home. I couldn't stand up or lie down in the little cell, but I could crouch, which I knew would become quite a comfortable position over a period of time, and I felt that period of time suddenly stretching before me, inexact but necessary. The stained, sloping wood floor already looked familiar, the floor on which I now realized I'd always been fated to remain. I'd never straighten my body up as I once had, but that was part of my previous behavior, no longer required or accessible to me. The silence swaddled me here, immobilizing me in such a way that I imagined at some point would be reassuring. This was my new way of being.

You see, the third floor had so easily won because it wasn't like the other floors. It wasn't a group of varying experiences and effects but rather a single, concentrated force. Each room was an organ of the larger fury of the space, banded together in an attack on me. So in a matter of days, the house had beaten me, and now it was going to do the same thing to Melissa. Was I responsible for what was about to happen to her? That responsibility belonged to the old me; here and now, I was required only to crouch and gaze out at the dominion of Penobscot Road. I accepted that becoming part of the horror was easier than fearing it.

Melissa's faraway knock swam its way through the dense quiet, each impact thinning it more and more. First the need to move, then to save myself rose up in me as I felt my stupor loosen its grip. I had to get to Melissa, although I couldn't say why, and already several minutes had passed. Pushing against the incredible inertia that I already felt solidifying on my skin again, I stretched my muscles and bones into rescuing themselves, crawling back through that awful tunnel, picking up speed as I raced down one flight of stairs and then the other.

I was screaming something at Melissa, too, although I only became aware of this when I reached the front door and the screaming stopped.

She was starting up her car, and so I ran at her, my stockinged feet immediately shocked by the ice-cold mud.

I must have looked awful because when she saw me, she just stared at me through the windshield, the car idling and idling, the most indecisive sound I'd ever heard.

After a minute or so, it became clear that she was rethinking her decision to come. It's true, I hadn't told her much about the seriousness of the situation, and in fact, I hadn't even been up to the third floor before she'd arrived, so I couldn't have warned her about that even if I'd wanted to. But she could see how much worse it was than she'd imagined, and she hesitated. I would've driven off immediately.

Then, the engine stopped, although the keys remained in the dash. She got out of the car, a frowning smile twisting her face up. "Hey."

"Hey."

Melissa remained behind her car door. "Are you, like, okay? You know what? Hold on a sec." She pulled a cell phone out of her jacket. "Hey… I just wanted to let you know that I'm checking out a house on Penobscot Road, 19182 Penobscot Road. It's a little ways out of town on 47… For paranormal activity… Could we talk about this later?… Well, I'm not." She put her hand over the phone. "Chris, what's your last name again?"

"Szabo."

"Hun? Listen, I've got to go, but we can talk about this later. I'm with Chris Szabo, okay? I'll be back in an hour, tops, so, don't worry… Yeah, do that… Okay, bye."

She put her phone away but made no move toward me. "So I just realized that I don't really know anything about the house or you or anything. I just got in my car and drove out here, which was really... That's why I just called my boyfriend. Because—"

"Because I look pretty crazy right now."

"Yeah. Because of that."

"Something just happened."

"What happened?"

What could I say? "I just have to process it for a while."

"Okay." She remained firmly behind her door. "You know, I don't even know if I can help you."

"I know."

"Something really weird happened?"

"Yeah."

"Huh."

She stared up at the house, searching but coming up with a blank expression. "Huh."

"But after—but anyway, I think it might not be a good idea now. I'm so sorry about getting you all the way out here."

"God, what happened?"

"It was just, kind of, intense."

"Really. Like paranormal intense?"

"To be honest, I'm a little worried for you. That's why I don't think it's such a great idea."

"Because you know I can take care of myself. Those kinds of things can only hurt you if you let them." But she looked up at the house again, unsure. "It's just a house."

"No, it isn't."

She slammed her door and walked toward me. "Yes, it is. I had a feeling about you back at my place, but I'm not getting any vibes here. So I'm not scared of the house; I'm worried about you. Come on. Let's just see what happens, okay?"

"No, I think you should go."

She walked past me and up the steps to the porch. "Come on. It'll be fun."

"Please!"

"I'm here already! Just five minutes, okay? I want to see—"

"What?"

"I want to see if it's real or not. I want to see if I can tell. So it's not just about you. Does that make you feel any better?"

She stood next to the front door, looking down at me. She was so small against that house, rising up, rising back past her sight and awareness.

"I don't care what I feel. I don't want it to happen to you."

"Well, I do." And she entered Penobscot Road, the door closing over the image of her, momentarily shadow-swept and fragile.

But I hesitate here! I've never been more aware of your presence, of its importance to me than at this very moment. And the reason why is that flooding through my mind are many, many things I could share with you about what happened next.

The first thing that comes to mind is to lie. I think of this first because I think first of you and how I've promised to be as gentle as possible, to do only what I must to give you this. But in actuality, that promise was to be gentle *with the truth*, so I know it would be wrong. Still, I can picture you receiving a cushioned lie and exhaling, all the stress and frustration I've caused you leaving your body for a blessed moment.

In fact, the right lie might convince you to end our relationship forever, a grievous thought to me but one that at least would leave me somewhat merciful in all of this. If I were stronger, I'd end it now, myself. Of course, if I were truly strong, I would've never begun to do this to you in the first place, but what kind of strength is that? Aren't we given our strength so that we can join up with others to create something new, something greater? I know, too, that I can only grow rougher with you from this point forward if I accurately recall how things slid out of control at Penobscot Road. So I may lie.

Or I could restrict the telling only to what I experienced at the time, as I have since I began. This would be factual and respectful, and honestly, much less wrenching than anything else I could do to you. And I do want to share with you what happened when Melissa entered the house. I cherish the thought of widening your knowledge of the world, of my world, if only slightly. So I may continue to restrict the telling to my own experience.

I could also tell you what others have said about that afternoon, though up to this point, I've told you nothing that I couldn't personally swear was the god's honest truth. Besides, repeating other people's recollections and claims and suppositions and opinions and half-truths and mistakes would be allowing strangers into our relationship. There would always be that testimony between us, potentially keeping us further from the absolute truth and, therefore, each other. I've promised to be as respectful and gentle with you as possible; the others haven't. Plus, you might prefer their version and choose their more logical, sensible interpretation over mine. I don't think I could stand that.

There is another course of action. I could be perverse, and in this way, the closest to the truth. Because at the heart of what constitutes our relationship—this shared recalling—is a perversity so fundamental that it makes even the consideration of other approaches deceitful. I see now that this is the only course I could ever take. Forgive me:

The foreign element enters, at first similar to the other, recent flutterings. Immediately, though, it is identified as a threat different from the others. It gropes, it pries in a way that irritates. It is stronger, although the strength is chaotic, unfocused. Because of this erratic power, it is more dangerous. Because of this heightened state of danger, it must be dealt with immediately, rather than buffering, cocooning the threat until it is fully immobilized and readied for consumption, as with the others.

The first action is to observe, to monitor for the weaknesses that underpin strength. Several soon make themselves clear, any of which may be exploited to expel the irritant. The number and depth of these weaknesses reduce the severity of the danger, and consumption becomes an option.

The threat's primary weakness is targeted first. Reaction time and type to stimuli will determine whether its excretion or utilization is preferable. Soon, it is concluded that utilization is viable, and strategies are employed to set this sequence into action.

The door was flung back so violently that it hit something inside. Melissa was in the process of vomiting across her sweater, her face red and swollen, her eyes teary slits, as she stepped across the threshold, craning her head before her.

I was at the bottom of the porch steps, feeling what anyone who sees another person throwing up feels—sympathy layered over disgust layered over fascination. She'd been inside for no more than a couple of minutes.

The sound of the vomit hitting the wooden floor of the porch was the worst somehow, and I felt my own throat constrict. But she was off the porch and away from the house before a few seconds had passed, dry heaving next to her car, her hand on the hood, now as red as her face.

What could I do? I came to stand next to her, making worried noises until she finally stopped. Her head remained down for the next few minutes, and she spit and coughed intermittently, ignoring my questions.

Eventually, she found her voice. "I have to go."

And with that, she got into her car and flew off, never a look back in my direction. Or the house's.

The freezing grains of dirt were working their way up through my socks and in between my toes. It was uncomfortable and wrong and I knew that the longer I stood there, the worse it would get.

I had to find someone who knew what to do about Penobscot Road immediately.

The Seventh Day

Have you tried imagining me? It's getting more difficult to picture what I must look like, how I sound, the ways in which I move. Isn't it?

I wasn't used to keeping things from Nicole and Alphonse. But what had I ever possessed to keep from them before? Secrets imply importance; secrets imply *self*-importance. I'd never had anything worth keeping from the two of them, and even if I had, my privacy just wasn't valuable enough to justify the bother. Now, I was acting without their knowledge, and I'd done okay. I'd identified the problem and taken steps to solve it. I'd not needed to consult with them or give way as they took over. I'd been, on some burgeoning level, an effective individual. At the time, I was actually proud of myself.

So this made it easier to deceive my friends. I'd been sure to eradicate any signs of Melissa's visit—including scratching over her tire tracks—so on that seventh morning in Penobscot Road, the two of them sat before me, unaware and yammering. But it was more than that; they almost seemed like fools to me, their comments pitiably ignorant, their suggestions idiotic. I finally understood the real power of knowledge.

"So should we even bother with the third floor right now? Because I really have to get started on my job search. It's not like we need the space." Alphonse was slouched down in his chair, playing with his spoon and cereal bowl. He didn't look at either of us.

"We'll deal with it once the other floors are cleaned up." And so Nicole provided her determination to the rest of us. You'll note that my opinion was never requested; if it had been, I might have told them what had happened the day before, how going up to the third floor was like being eaten alive, how only a couple of minutes spent in our home had made a sensitive person violently ill. I would have told them everything, if they'd just asked, but they were concerned only with themselves.

Neither one of them had even been up to the third floor yet. At the time, I wasn't sure if I was thankful or disappointed by this. But I can say that their responses to the house were growing less important to me. After all, I knew what I was experiencing; I no longer needed some kind of slavish confirmation from my roommates, some final decision as to whether I was right or wrong. I was sure that Melissa's response had proven that this wasn't just my imagination; the next step would be to convince her to track down the medium she'd mentioned. I'd get the real answer from him.

Plus, I'd been the one who'd had the guts to go up to the third floor—by myself! Unassuming Chris, follow-the-leader Chris. The two of them were busy making excuses to avoid it entirely; they couldn't even take five minutes out of their hectic lives to check it out. Sure, I'd been scared, too. But meek Chris had had the guts to push past that.

Because of this and other things, I found Alphonse and Nicole growing less important to me.

"What are you going to do, Chris?" Alphonse was referring to that day, which I think the two of them had been discussing for a while.

"I might apply to a few restaurants in town."

Nicole was powerfully silent for a moment, then got up to put the breakfast dishes into the sink. I think she believed that having her back to me softened her comments. "Oh. I thought you were thinking about looking for work that, you know, would let you use your degree a bit more."

Nicole was all about self-improvement, regardless of the consequences.

"But it might take me a while to find something like that. I mean, it's Pacific Bay, not San Francisco. Don't we need money now?"

"I know. But you could, like, *try*. That's all I'm saying. At least *look*."

"I think I'll be *looking* at every job in Pacific Bay. The list can't be that long."

"Yeah." But she wasn't done. "Because, like, the purpose of this whole move was to improve things, right? I don't know if any of us are living up to our full potential."

I thought that was exactly what we were doing, but I said: "I'll check it out." And I rose to help her dry the dishes, which Alphonse would never have dreamt of doing.

"Awesome. Because we're putting some seriously positive vibes out into the universe with this whole thing. Moving to Oregon, getting a house in the country. Doing what we've always wanted to do. When you put out good vibes, I think they come back to you. That's why I think you might just get lucky."

We lived in a house that hated us! How was that lucky? If the universe was telling us anything, it was to drop dead.

But I was an intriguer now. I was a soap-opera star. "I'm sure you're right. Thanks."

"Because someday, you know, we might not all be together, and we need to be able to get by on our own."

Even during our worst fights, even when we'd annoyed each other to the extent that we would cry in frustration, we'd never discussed splitting up. The future had always been the three of us. I glanced at Alphonse, and he actually looked down the hall and past me, guilty. Already quite familiar with the concept.

Was this the real reason we'd moved to Oregon?

I could feel my throat constrict, but I had to respond. I had to keep them from knowing how this betrayal devastated me. I'd been an actor just a moment before; I had to continue.

But instead, I said, "The condemned were often forced to wear a mask of black velvet."

A spoon clanged into the sink. "What?!"

It was the same question I was asking myself. That statement had come out of my mouth like someone else's steady exhalation. And before I could even recover: "It is a material best at absorbing light and curiosity."

Nicole actually chuckled! "What. The. Fuck, Chris!"

She looked at Alphonse, who wasn't smiling. "Why would you say that?"

I needed to leave and so headed toward the parlor, which I knew would be cooler, calmer. Where people wouldn't be staring at me. "You brought it up."

I thought of that area, just to the left of the kitchen sink, and then suddenly, I could delineate it perfectly. On some level, I'd been aware of it all along; I just hadn't had the vocabulary to define it until now. It was a column of space about a foot and a half wide and about five and three-quarters feet tall, centered on the handle of the cabinet door next to the sink and about four inches away from it. The best way to recognize it was a slight bump in the vinyl floor, an almost invisible raised section that had managed to trip up everyone in the house at least four or five times already. It was a place to be mischievous, for the want of a better term. To confuse or embarrass or humble or annoy. The hump actually felt like mischief, if you ran your bare foot over it. It had the shape and density of mischief, and it was like the button that dying people pushed to have morphine flood into their bodies. When you pressed down, the warm urgings flowed up through your legs, up through your mouth.

I was usually the only person who bothered to dry the dishes; otherwise, they just dripped onto a rubber mat. That must have been why I'd said such odd things there twice already.

But Nicole had had her episode with the word "leave" while standing there, too! The location had had a different effect on her, but wasn't this some sort of objective proof? I'd blurted out someone else's arcane comments, and she'd screamed her subconscious urge for us to get out.

She didn't remember doing it, though, so I could only use it as proof with Alphonse—and I really needed to share what I knew with both of them at the same time.

As I gathered myself at the mantel, I could hear Alphonse and Nicole whispering in the kitchen. I couldn't blame them, but it was still uncomfortable. We'd always talked about each other in secret—concerns and praises and rantings to let off steam—but this was different. Still, I had faith that the need we had for each other would always overcome life's need to tear us apart.

Still, I became less and less assured as I approached the kitchen to find them smiling a little guiltily.

"So you coming into town with us today?" Nicole's grin remained, but it was presented as merely cheerful.

I was careful to avoid the space next to her as I approached the counter where I'd left Melissa's number. "I think I'm going to do a bit more cleaning. My bedroom."

"Okay." And then Nicole moved over to straighten some of the dishes in the drainer—her foot just in front of the bump!

"Do you know whose number this is?" I held the slip of paper just far enough away from Nicole that she would have to step onto the bump to read it.

But she just squinted at it and turned away again. "It's your handwriting, dipshit. Why don't you call it and find out?"

"Yeah."

If I hadn't known better, I would've said that she was avoiding the bump. But why would she do that?

*   *   *

So I was finally doing some serious scheming. That's got to be attractive to you. And even if I'm just the protagonist of a melodrama, isn't melodrama at the heart of all stories? Admittedly, its divide between good and evil is as sharp as a blade, but that's what makes melodrama so reassuring. Real life's divides are so sloppy, just endless gradients perpetually pulling you to one side and then the other. There is no absolute right, no undeniable wrong. Only levels of regret.

In fact, I think a little melodrama was exactly what I needed. Before the third floor, I'd been immobilized by all the grays, all the tugging and shoving of life's divides. The first two floors were inconsistent, somehow. Indeterminate. I'd found it just as difficult to make decisions there as I had in the real world. But after going up to the third floor on my own, I knew exactly what I had to do, and I never once wavered.

That's the definition of a hero, isn't it?

So you must be drawing closer to me. I can feel it. What we're creating together finally has some thrust to it. I can imagine the thrill this must hold for you, and it reassures me. In fact, you're giving me the power I need to continue on because things only get worse from here. So we'll have to share whatever strength we can muster. Still, I'm confident that we can do it together, so doesn't that make us both heroes?

After Alphonse and Nicole left, I put my plan in motion. The first step was to make arrangements with Melissa for the medium to come by.

"Oh, hey." It sounded as if there were someone else in the room with her.

"Hey. Are you okay?"

"Yeah." But that was all she said.

"You can't talk right now?"

"Uhhh, yeah."

"Okay. When's a good time to call?"

"I don't think so."

"What? I was hoping you could help me get that medium friend of yours to cleanse our house or something."

"I don't think so."

"Is it because of what happened to you yesterday? What happened?"

"Okay. Bye." And she hung up on me.

The experience had been much more damaging to her than I'd imagined. And she'd only been in the house for a couple of minutes! I was relieved to think that I sensed so little of what was going on in Penobscot Road that I wasn't continually wracked with nausea.

But then I felt a cold draft pour down my collar, and it brought to mind everything lurking behind me in the room, down the dark halls, hidden in the endless closets and damp nooks of the house. I was alone with it, and it was apparently much worse, much more powerful than I'd even imagined. What in god's name was I living with? Why did I continue to remain inside of it?

At the time, I was in the parlor, and I went to stand before the fireplace, running my hand over the mantel's smooth surface. Without a fire, the area still seemed to radiate phantom heat, reassuring in spite of its alien quality for the house. It was always so cold everywhere else.

But I was the hero now! And heroes won; they didn't lose. Only a moment earlier, I'd felt the awareness of the house spreading toward me, overwhelming me with some faceless threat. But now, the army retreated, its power sinking, dissipating at my feet. It was just a house. True, there were areas that seemed to take me over, my mind jerked one way or another, but I was coming to recognize these areas now, and with this understanding came the ammunition I needed to win the fight. It was that simple, although my strategy was still a little fuzzy. But all would soon make itself clear, once I got confirmation and direction from the medium. I just knew it would.

My laptop was in my room. Strong now, I casually strolled into the hallway and up the stairs, although my courage bled away as I passed through one empty, gray space after another. I was alone. Anything could happen to me, and then the wound of my absence would quickly scab over, the police having no recourse against a building. How many other unexplained deaths came about this way? How many *explainable* ones? As the upstairs hallway gaped into darkness before me, I knew that despite all that I'd discovered about the house, there was so much more waiting for me, there in the shadows.

But I was the protagonist! I am the protagonist, even now. And to ensure that role, I've kept from you what I knew about my bedroom from the first moment I entered it, in part to pique your desire for future revelations. But I've also glossed over the reality of my bedroom because it is so painful to relive and because if revealed too early, it would distance you. Again, I exhibit the behavior of a lover.

I have the strength to face my bedroom now, to share it with you, and I believe you've earned that strength, too. You've lived through enough to know that I'm no longer just a passive victim, that I have the capacity to be admirable. So we'll go there together.

You know already what it looks like: the faux Victorian wallpaper, the slapdash addition of a private bathroom, the tall windows that afford it a civilized amount of light. In fact, it's one of the nicest areas in the house, at least to anyone who doesn't know better. So whenever I entered it, my first reaction was always a momentary stab of pleasure perpetrated by the room's agreeable contrast to the other filthy, uneven spaces around it. More than at any other point during my stay in Penobscot Road, those first few seconds helped me remember what the concept "home" meant and that I'd been searching for that feeling my whole life. Of course, I never actually felt *at home* in my room; it would never allow that. But those first few seconds gave me faith that there were places in the world that were welcoming and safe and familiar and absolutely nothing more. Maybe this faith is the only reason I'm able to share all this with you today.

In any event, my warm feelings didn't remain for long. All too quickly, I'd be confronted each time by the fact that there was something else happening there, and my heart would be hollowed out again, each time a little more. It's true that there were other areas in the house that inspired the thought of past inhabitants, but these were impressions, as if literally pressed into the air—or at least that's all they seemed at the time.

But in in my room, there was a single, active, conscious presence.

I don't even need to guess what you're thinking: why on earth would I stay in a room in which there was "something else?" That's if you're not still asking yourself why I remained in the house to begin with. Well, persisting in Penobscot Road was the same as persisting in my room. Just as the proverbial frog in hot water, my relationship with all these phenomena changed so gradually that I couldn't get perspective on them in time to react appropriately. At first, I was aware that there was something heavy in the room, something shifting, but I told myself it was my imagination. Then, as I came to accept the truth, it was only a presence and not a bona fide danger. Over the course of days, I realized that it was, in fact, a threat, but one I could handle. And finally, it was something I was destined to live with, regardless of what it did to me and my room-mates.

My first day in the room, the thing was a pet under the bed, making only a mild, forgettable impression. The second, it was a mother checking to see if I was still breathing in the night, stronger as I was dropping into sleep, weaker as I became more conscious of my surroundings. On the third day, it was a father, angry about something, disappointed and fussing in a corner. Finally, it became a sibling, following me around, encouraging behavior that it considered too risky for itself, and then jealous and prone to hideous outbursts. I say "finally" because that was what it had become for me on that seventh morning I retrieved the laptop. It was other things later.

I didn't see it or hear it the first day. But just because you don't see or hear a tree outside your window doesn't mean it isn't there. You don't *think* it's there; you don't *believe* it's there. *It's there.* Although I had ways of denying it at the time, on the deepest level, I knew all along what was happening in my room, just as you know that what I'm telling you is the truth. Any denial you're feeling is just as paper thin. Senses lie just as often as they are accurate, but the knowledge the two of us share rises above nerve impulses, just as your understanding of the entity needs only this disclosure to bring it to life for you. And I think on some level, I felt as if I were its audience, a receiver, like you, waiting to see what would happen next from the safety of my own corner. Terror isn't as linear, as progressive as we're told. I know that, now.

So when I say that the stranger in my room took on different person-alities, I think that it's more about the relationship it developed with me. That first night, I remember staring at my old bed, knowing that it belonged in my apartment and not here, not in this chaos. The California sun had bleached its cover a bit on one side, and the thought of it made me very sad. I could feel the second floor expanding out into the dark-ness, another kind of activity buzzing just beyond my door where other, more urgent lives were being lived in a privacy that I was invading. But their sensation was weaker in my bedroom, seemingly mitigated by the light and the sounds I made. And by the presence, although I would only realize this later. The family on the second floor almost seemed afraid of it.

Still, sensing them just outside my door was a frustrating experience, and I'd just felt the worst of it that first night when my attention was drawn to the bathroom. Not in any violent way, just as a kind of reminder, as if I'd remembered that the dog was waiting for dinner. It was an unquestioning waiting, so mild that it barely registered in my mind. Try it, yourself. Imagine a pet nearby right now, simply waiting quietly for dinner under a table. It's not scary, is it? It's too minor to be anything other than a flight of fancy, forgotten as soon as it occurs. So that's exactly what I did. And when the experience occurred again and again that night, the presence shifting its location around my room, it just seemed like a silly day dream my mind kept revisiting and revising, some sort of mysterious coping mechanism inspired by the stress of the previous days.

Why on earth didn't I recognize that it was a part of the house that first night, just like all the other strange things that were happening? I know this seems so obvious from our perspective. But you've got your dog right now, in the next room or under your bed or just around the corner, watching you silently and waiting. Are you panicking? Are you barely escaping with your life? It's just the same thing.

The second day I cleaned the room on my hands and knees, scraping brown crust from the baseboards and rubbing the woodwork with toxic solvents to get the strange scuffs and stains out of them. The presence knew enough not to make itself known during the day when the few, competing sensory inputs, merely chemical fumes and the watery light, might have made it too plain to me, too clear in contrast. No, it held off until that night, when I was sinking into sleep. It exploited the landscape of dreams then, and stole up to me, studying me, only a few inches from my face.

It was at its full strength then, fully present, and I awoke gasping and cringing into my pillow. Just as if I'd had a bad dream.

So while it had made itself known to me at this point, the state I'd been in provided explanation enough for me. Strange things had been happening; why wouldn't I have strange dreams? And so I was periodically reawakened that night, the entity directly over me, frozen in the space above my head, or in the bed, its intense scrutiny coming from the pillow right next to mine.

In semi-consciousness, the mind accepts things it otherwise wouldn't. Importance is somehow dialed down and everything becomes evened out, equally plausible. That's my excuse for the second night. Only a part of me was aware of the presence, and so the next morning, I remembered my experience but didn't act.

It wasn't until the third night that I came to appreciate what I was dealing with. This was the day that I'd visited Melissa, that I'd gone up to the third floor and found the secret room with the tea set. At this point, I knew too much to feel anything without questioning it. The house knew this. Penobscot Road was moving with me, shadowing me, through its revelations.

The cold dusk of that evening was endless; the wind felt as if it pushed right through me, as if my body wasn't even worth slowing down for. I remember because I'd gone out to the car to retrieve something from the trunk, and when I turned back to the house, my attention was drawn to the large windows of my room. It was up there, looking down at me. Its reflection wasn't reaching my retinas, yet I could see its presence nonetheless, as if its molecules were vibrating at a different frequency. I could see the absence of normal space, if that makes any sense, and I know it doesn't. More than that, I could see that the presence was angry. The area it occupied, a section in front of the rubber backing of the curtains, buzzed with a fury that only flared up when it entered my peripheral vision. Strangely, I could even tell what kind of angry it was: contained, easily rectified—a father waiting up for me past my curfew. It knew enough to reveal only part of its emotion, allowing me to become very gradually used to its reality. So at this point, it was full of rage, but the manageable, finite kind. Later, I was forced to see much more.

Standing outside of Penobscot Road on that bottomless night, I finally and completely understood it was there. I understood that it had been the same presence since the first night, slowly blooming into itself. And I understood that the process wasn't over yet. But I also knew that Melissa had understood everything I did—and in a much shorter time. She was going to help me, so I couldn't give up. I suspect that even if she hadn't come, I still would've stayed because I felt that the entity was ultimately powerless, that a creepy, angry presence could do no more to me than be creepy and angry.

It beggars belief that I could return to that room all by myself on the second floor, close my eyes against the dark, and sleep. Even trying to bring myself back to that frame of mind is impossible. I can only report.

But I must be completely honest with you, too. Choosing to return to a room I finally knew I was sharing with something malevolent is the act of someone looking to explore a private darkness. Because just as the entity initially presented itself as if it were a series of family members, it felt as familiar as family. The attachments that bind us to relatives are there for a reason and cannot be severed merely by distance or time. Resolution often only comes in the form of confrontation or cooperation for the sake of peace. Often, not even after that. So we tolerate our family and pray that this leads to a deeper understanding of ourselves and humanity.

Well, it felt the same with the presence. I was obligated to explore its relationship with me in order to grow wiser, to understand the truth of existence. And a large element of that existence is the blackness, the cruelty of life. If I didn't confront this evil, inside of me somewhere, buried under a denial that was shored up by weakness and inaction, how could I ever become a whole person, a *real* adult? Chris was a forgettable, harmless nothing—but that wasn't all. I accepted this, too, that night.

So I walked up those stairs and I entered that floor possessed by the past of others and I closed my door behind me and I was alone with it. It hadn't gone away. And while it didn't have a location at that moment, its presence was draped over the room, diffused and placid. It accepted my acceptance and waited.

What else could I do but prepare for bed? I had to function in the real world, too. My corporeal body still demanded normal behavior, as did my roommates and the three-dimensional objects around me. I wasn't exactly scared, either—the entity felt too familiar for that—but I was definitely anxious. After brushing my teeth, I'd looked down at my toothbrush to find that I'd put more toothpaste on it. I could feel the presence delighting in my unease.

Yet sitting on my bed gave me some sort of strength, its years of service reminding me that ordinary still existed, too, and could reach back up from the past. I just had to learn how to live where normal and abnormal intersected—and I couldn't be the only one. In fact, the thought that there were doubtlessly others out there struggling with the same chaos gave me comfort, and so I waited for it, prepared, almost optimistic.

But nothing happened. Apparently, if it remained amorphous, it was unable to act. And so it just filled the corners and the shadows and the heedless drafts with itself, whether curling up to rest or to strike, I couldn't tell. Of course, it wouldn't be truthful to say that I was disappointed, but I wanted to find out what I'd been living with to gauge its bare power once and for all.

But I fell asleep. Right in the center of it. Inside of it. If that's not embracing my dark side, I don't know what is. You have to agree that it's brave, though. You have to admit that it's arousing. And when I awoke, it was gone.

So this brings us back to the next day, and my race upstairs to search for a psychic to help me. There, the residue of past inhabitants was stronger than it had ever been, and I remember nearly tripping at the top of the stairs after just missing some sort of movement in the dark end of the hall. It was a Tuesday, but on the second floor, it was a Sunday, and the family was finally rousing itself after sleeping in. There were a lot of them, too; I sensed what could only be called a crowd all around me in those rooms, and they were just about to catch me on the other side of their doors. Slamming my own behind me, I remember looking at the space between it and its frame, wondering if the phenomenon of the family could seep into my room like some poisonous gas and make it Sunday everywhere.

The presence was right behind me. I immediately knew it was there and that it had mutated again. It was no longer angry; it was something else.

My eyes grew blind to what was in front of them, and instead, I focused whatever was left of my acuity on the space a few feet from my back. I could hear nothing, smell nothing, yet I *knew* it was there. I just knew.

I was too exposed to remain that way for more than a second, and so I whirled around, my face distorting in what must have been a ghastly flinch. In fact, I'd pressed myself so close to the door that I hit my shoulder against it and left a bruise. But the presence was gone! Or so I thought at first; it only took an instant to realize that it was right behind me on the other side of the door, so I whirled around again. And once again, it had instantaneously concentrated itself within the space at my back, only a little closer, this time.

I backed myself right up against the wall to the right of the door, actually glad to feel the clammy, ugly wallpaper touching my neck. But the presence remained behind me, occupying the area just on the other side of the wall! It was so agile, so alert, that I could almost imagine it bouncing on the balls of its feet, smirking at me.

Strangely, this thought slowed my heart rate, and I gasped for air. Apparently, I'd forgotten to breathe. True, there was an alien force directly behind me, and I had no idea what it was about to do to me, but I'd already sensed that the presence was no longer angry. What did I actually have to fear? At this point, I could also tell that there was nowhere I could go that it wouldn't be there anyway, peering down my neck, a millimeter from some terrible embrace. It was no longer confined to my bedroom; my new awareness of it meant that it was now confined to me, at least while I was in the house.

Knowing just how the entity would respond, I nonetheless rushed to my bed and got under the covers. Not the most heroic act ever, but that's what I did. I didn't even take off my shoes. You know I can spare you nothing.

Of course, the entity was right there, right under the bed—or rather, *inside* the bed; I could feel it just on the other side of the sheet, a hair's breadth away from actually coming into contact with me. Touching my skin. If you've ever slept in a water bed, it was just like that: something that isn't supposed to be near you when you sleep is right there, right next to your body. There's nothing more uncomfortable than the thought of lying in dampness. And people *drown* in water. Yet just like a water bed, it somehow made itself insidiously benign, and so I remained still, willing myself first not to bolt out the door, then to accept its proximity.

After a moment, I came to realize that the *bed* wasn't supporting me—*the entity* was. Almost undetectably, I'd been lifted up a microscopic distance from the mattress and was being held by it, almost cradled. And all at once, I understood so much. The way in which the presence occupied and manipulated space around me was the way in which it communicated. It was like dancing, wrestling, or making love.

Now, the force was playful, curious, and so I lay with it for a while, trying to get used to what I could only call true paranormal activity. You see, up until this point, everything that had happened to me could have just been in my head—although I'd always known better. But now, as I was levitated by some unseen force, there was no longer any room for doubt.

I studied the grimy roses in the wallpaper on the ceiling above me, which repeated and repeated every few feet, their stems curling to the right, right, left, right. Right, right, left, right. The people who had pasted that wallpaper all over the room must have really had to concentrate to get those patterns to line up so perfectly. But they must have also sensed the presence in the room. So how could they have strained, hour after hour on top of their ladders, smoothing the paper, fixing the places where it had folded over itself, all while this thing was expanding and contracting in the air around them, hemorrhaging emotions and concealing schemes? Or was I more sensitive than I thought?

As I pulled myself out of the wad of blankets and stood, I was even more determined to get a third opinion. But the presence was no longer behind me; it was gone. So had it gotten what it wanted from me? There was clearly more to what had just taken place than I could make out, but at that moment, I was too focused on finding someone who could tell me what was happening to stop and analyze the situation.

There were pages and pages of psychics in Oregon, but I could only find one in the Banana Belt, which is what locals call the southwestern corner of the state. Evan Maggiore. His website looked as if it had been designed in 1997, with awkward, animated GIFs cluttering it up, and my heart sank. Who knew if he was still even alive? But he was in Seville, so he must have been the medium Melissa knew.

"Hello." This was a statement, rather than an interrogative. But at least someone was answering.

"Hi. I'm trying to reach Evan Maggiore?" This should have been a statement, but it came out as an interrogative.

"What about?"

"I found a website and—"

"Oh, for pity's sake! Is that thing still up? My nephew was supposed to… Yeah, I'm not uhhh… That's not happening, anymore."

His voice was old and ragged, as if he'd drunk and smoked his way through life.

"Really? What happened?" I must have sounded pretty disappointed because he sighed on the other end, with healthy pauses on either side.

"What happened. Man, well, you know. Stuff. Life. What do you want me to say."

I didn't know. "I called because something's going on in my house, and I need to know what it is."

"It's probably swamp gas or radon or some such stuff like that. There's no…"

"No such thing as ghosts?"

"What do you want me to say?"

"I don't know what else to do."

"You've got to understand something." But he stopped here. I waited, but all I could hear was his breathing.

Finally: "What?"

Still, he only breathed, hoarsely, somehow. I began to wonder if he wasn't sick.

"You can't do it, anymore?"

"Look, just get somebody else, all right?"

Now it was my turn to be silent.

"All right? All right. Goodbye."

I decided to look a little more closely at Evan's website. There wasn't much to it, only that he was some sort of earth father, a Wiccan sensitive who ultimately believed in the goodness of all things. To him, the spirits from beyond were helpful, caring and wise, and the only emotion that superseded his respect for them was his love. *"Angels are real. Let me help you grow closer to those who love you still."*

There was nothing angelic about Penobscot Road, and I was tempted not to destroy his illusions. But he sounded so grizzled—and as far from a hippy-dippy New Ager as he could've—that I guessed he'd had a change of heart since the website had been built. And something about our exchange resonated with me. I didn't believe that another telephone conversation would be fruitful, but there was an address on his contact page, and he was only two towns up the coast. Now, I just had to dream up an excuse to use the car.

I was becoming a different person. I know how obvious that is now, but at the time, this was the precise moment I realized it. I was looking out my window thinking that it seemed as if our dirt driveway were scrambling to escape from the house, racing toward the road and safety. It wasn't moving, but I knew about the other kinds of movement now. I could see more.

Those dirty, stinking rooms spread out around me, out and down and up and back, their walls defiant gestures that they existed, their floors hard and undeniable. They seemed to be saying that I was here, now. That I was a part of them. I'd entered Penobscot Road for a reason, and that reason was gradually making itself known. The house was horrific, unspeakable, but there was nonetheless a place in it for me. A place in which I fit perfectly. And that place was my dark side, although it was too nebulous to name it more than that. At the same time, I knew I would fight it, that I might even overcome it. But there was no way I could stop. And no way that I was going to change back to what I'd been. So this was the moment in which I gave myself permission to acknowledge my new life both through thought and behavior. I didn't seem to have a choice.

How did this manifest itself? Well, I must have been there for a while, absorbing my altered reality, because I was only reminded of the regular world when I saw Nicole and Alphonse coming up the driveway. I needed to get out of the house and to Evan before they noticed anything too different about me. The only hope I had was to mitigate my new self by being the one to present the solution for our predicament to my room-mates—hopefully backed up by a legitimate psychic.

So I ran downstairs (not ignoring the fact that the second-story feeling of invasion now struck me as almost ordinary) and met them at the door.

"Oh, hey." Nicole had her arms full of bags. "A little help?"

I could see the car out the little window, and all at once I realized that the whole thing was going to end badly. Evan would no longer be at that address, and if he were, he would never agree to help me. Even if he did, there was no such thing as tidy as "help." "Help" was something from my old world.

"What? Did I leave my lights on again?" Nicole craned her neck toward the window. "What?"

"Can you grab this, Chris? Chris?!" Alphonse was holding a huge bag of potatoes out to me. I hated potatoes, and both of them knew it, yet they insisted on spending our money on huge bags of them, and they would shrivel up and get black abscesses on them before finally being thrown out. Potatoes don't have feelings, but I felt sorry for them. Then I felt angry at them for existing with the sole purpose of making me feel sorry for them. I saw their weight pushing down the skin on Alphonse's hand, denying it blood and causing it pain, and I thrilled at the thought of it.

I was definitely a different person now.

"What the fuck, Chris?"

I stepped away from Alphonse and toward the parlor. "Can I have the keys? I just need to… I need them."

"What? Why?" Nicole dropped the bags next to her feet. "What's wrong?"

"Nothing. I just need the keys."

"Where are you going?"

"I need the keys."

"But where do you need to go?"

"I need the keys."

"Chris, you look like—"

"Can I have the keys, please?"

"I just don't—"

"You don't what? You don't understand that all three of us bought that car together and that I have as much right to the keys as either of you?"

They both froze. Apparently, it was harder to hide my new self than I'd hoped.

I saw the keys in her hand and tried to pull them out, but she tightened her grip. "Hey!"

"I need the keys!"

"Well, you're not getting them until you tell me what the fuck is going on!"

My voice dropped. "I think I've got an infection. I want to get it checked out." I slathered these statements with cryptic meaning.

Nicole would never ask anything more about my little problem. "Oh, okay."

"What kind of infection?" However, Alphonse would.

I didn't have to think about what part of my body would be the most embarrassing for long because Nicole came to my aid. "Jesus, Alphonse." And she handed me the keys. "I hope everything goes okay."

It says a lot about me that I'd never really, purposefully lied to Alphonse and Nicole before coming to Penobscot Road, yet it was already second nature. As I walked out of the house, I thought back to all the times when a simple lie would have made my life with them so much easier. Lying was putting my needs first while exhibiting enormous disrespect for my friends.

I liked it.

*   *   *

We hadn't yet explored beyond Pacific Bay, so it was a surprise to find out how far apart the towns along the coast were. On a map, Seville looked kind of close, but an hour later, I still hadn't reached it.

There was something else I should have been surprised about but wasn't. The other times I'd left the house, I could see things clearly. The real world reminded me of itself again, and the house became an anomaly for which I produced a wealth of explanations and excuses. But this time, Penobscot Road stayed with me. Now, it was real life, and the road up the coast was something merely to be discounted, distrusted. Even today, I couldn't really tell you what that road was like; I remember only fog, both literally and figuratively. In a week, the house had taken reality away from me.

So I guess this is the point when we need to address something that's bothering you. I know you don't really believe it, but I understand you so much more than you think I do. And I just can't stand the thought that anything poisonous could seep between us.

You're wondering if I might have been going insane, and I'm sure if I saw things from your point of view, I'd entertain the same possibility. I admit that my growing disconnect with reality did have many similarities to mental illness. And I'm not sure that anything could categorically convince you that I was and continue to be just as sane as you are. A crazy person swearing that they're perfectly normal is possibly the most unsettling symptom of insanity there is. But remember that if this is the case, I'm not misleading you; I've honestly reported my experiences as I perceived them at the time. And how can anyone completely trust perception, anyway? You have just as much responsibility for creating all of this as I do, so at what point should you question your own sanity?

But maybe you like the thought that I was—that I am—insane. It's so much easier to feel superior to others than it is to struggle to truly understand them. That's so much more work, a continual battle against baser instincts. So if this is the case, I've got a struggle on my hands, too. Should I simply be glad that I'm providing you with the pleasure of believing that you're better than I am? You know, even if you're calling it pity, it's much the same thing. Or should I continue to wrack my brain to somehow convince you of my sincerity? Maybe the answer is to change some of the facts around to cast my sanity in a better light. Fiction is popular for a reason.

But no, my primary goal right now is to involve you as fully as possible in what we're sharing, and I honestly believe that telling you what happened—and just as it happened—will give you more excitement than anything else we could do at this point. Because even if you do believe that I'm crazy, you can't be completely sure. You need more information; you need to keep going with me to find out. So I shouldn't bother trying to convince you—maybe it's the last thing I should be considering. Let me just say this: you'll have, by the end of all this, what I consider undeniable, unquestionable proof. I'll just have to hope that this is what you need to believe. And anyway, I can't expect you to overlook my many faults without excusing a few of yours. This is the fertile seed at the heart of every loving relationship.

The address on the website led me to a small, wooden cabin high in the mountains that rose over Seville. There was a little clearing in front of it filled with what struck me as significant garbage. Piles of rocks were placed in strategic locations, and old, colorful glass bottles were stacked up and cemented together, their worn surfaces barely reflecting the murk of coastal Oregon. Dozens of wind chimes and mobiles and other faded wind machines moved repetitiously in the hard breeze coming off the ocean. But no matter where I looked, everything was caked in dust, stuck into the soil years and years earlier to tear itself slowly apart. The place looked deserted.

Still, there was a track of mud leading to the front door, so the weeds hadn't been able to grow completely around the cabin. I took this as a good sign and followed it, surprising myself at how softly I knocked.

"Who is that." Evan's voice.

"It's Chris. We talked on the phone a little while ago—"

"Oh, for pity's sake. I told you to leave me alone."

But then I heard him talking to a woman, and a moment later, she opened the door.

Her huge, almost obscene smile was so incongruous to the scene that I think my mouth might have been hanging open for a second. She was grossly overweight and had light-blonde hair that had been permed into frizz that rose off her shoulders. The huge, bright sundress that hung all around her was an affront to the moody, harsh beauty of our surroundings. She was hypnotic.

"He knew you'd come. I'm Suzy." Even her voice was the opposite of what it should have been: singsong, high-pitched and frivolous. In the dark recess behind her, the scent of cinnamon and pot rolled out to meet me.

I shook Suzy's hand, and she used this to pull me into the house after her. "Your hand's freezing! Don't you have a heater in that car? We need to warm you up a little. Do you drink? Or smoke? What can we do to get you back up to your normal, operating temperature? At least sit over there by the stove, and then you can move once it gets too hot for you. It won't take long because Evan likes it really warm in here and overloads it with wood all the time. You know, I sweat more in the winter than I do in the summer, if you can believe it. I mean, look at me now! Or don't because it's gross."

Evan was in a dark corner, his old La-Z-Boy cranked back and his TV tuned to MSNBC. He didn't get up, so I couldn't really see him except to say that he was small and thin.

"Thank you."

Suzy paused at a doorway that led into a cramped kitchen that was all wooden surfaces. "For what?"

"Oh. I don't know. For inviting me in?"

"Certainly! Did you drive far? Are you from Seville?"

"Pacific Bay."

"I'm from Pacific Bay! Where in Pacific Bay?"

"Really kind of outside of it. Off of Highway 47. On Penobscot Road."

She quickly moved from my field of vision, and there was a moment of silence. "Is that right?" But her voice rose even higher, straining at nonchalance.

"Do you know it?"

She returned to the living room with a fresh smile plastered to her face. "I'm just making some blackberry tea. How does that sound? So Evan told his nephew to take that website down a long time ago, but Sean kind of lives by his own rules, I swear. Evan thought that maybe Sean had the gift, but I don't see why designing a website about it would tell us whether he did or not. And then Evan... well, he just kind of didn't want to do it, anymore. So that's why he wanted the website down, but you're only the second person to contact us off of it, anyway, so we haven't really bugged Sean, anymore."

I didn't know what to say. "Oh."

My eyes were beginning to adjust to the light, so I could see Evan more clearly. He was in his fifties, desiccated and pinched. All of his facial features seemed to be pushed to the center of his face, which made his large forehead and chin look even more expansive. I could see evidence of a pony tail behind his head, and he was dressed in an old flannel shirt, stained painter's pants and Birkenstocks. There was something so flat about him that I couldn't imagine him being "gifted" at anything.

"So Evan tells me that you're having some issues with your house."

"Suzy."

"Hon, when someone drives for an hour just to talk to you, you listen. I didn't say you had to do anything."

"No, you didn't." But this was especially sarcastic. Evan still hadn't taken his eyes off of the television.

Suzy returned her attention to me, and I realized that it was my turn. "I think there's something living with me in my room. And the house just seems—bad."

"Something living with you?"

"I can sort of see it. Not directly, but kind of out of the corner of my eyes."

"I'm going to kill Sean."

Suzy rolled her eyes at Evan's comment. "You've never killed anything in your life, Evan Maggiore."

"Then I'm going to kill you." Once again, this was said with more significance than made sense to me at the time.

"Just hush." At which point, the kettle started to whistle, so she jumped up and out of the room. "Can you tell that we don't have many people over, Chris? I feel like I have to train Evan to deal with guests. Sugar or lemon?"

"No, thank you."

"'Thank you!'" She returned with a couple of old mugs. "I forgot what that sounds like. So how is the house 'bad?'"

"I don't know. It seems like certain areas inside make people feel things. Or do things."

"So others are experiencing it?"

"I think so. But I don't want to talk about it with my roommates until I'm sure that it's real."

"You don't want to seem too crazy." At least Evan looked at me when he said this. He was trying to be rude, but there was something else underneath it, a kind of searching. His eyes were jet black, so they seemed all pupil, as if they were devouring me. Then he returned to the TV.

I had to be honest: "Yeah."

"Oh, come on, now. Nobody thinks anybody's crazy here. You just want to get to the bottom of it all. It must be so scary, in your own house and everything. How long has this been going on?"

"About a week. That's when we moved in."

The couple exchanged a really odd glance at my comment, and then Suzy tried to cover it, a little feebly, I thought. "You're not originally from Pacific Bay?"

"Sacramento."

"Oh, wow! That's quite a change. What brought you to southwestern Oregon?"

"I guess we needed a change. And my roommate, Nicole, always wanted to live here."

"What about you?"

"It's really beautiful."

"So you always wanted to live here, too, then."

"Well, not really. I didn't want to live anywhere, I guess."

Another very significant look passed between Suzy and Evan, and she timed a huge smile to distract me from what was going on. But I could tell that Evan was growing a lot more interested in what I was admitting than he let on.

Suzy said only: "Moving is a very stressful period. New people, new town. New house."

"Yeah. And this is the first time I've ever lived outside of Sacramento before."

Now Evan frowned flatly, and he didn't even try to hide it from me. There was a lot going on in the room that I didn't understand, and his next comment didn't help. "Well, finish up your tea because you've got a long ride home."

Remember: I was a different person at this point. I'd changed, and I'm still not sure if it was for the better or worse. "Why can't you help me? What's wrong? Why do you keep looking at each other like that? I don't know what else to do, and I'm afraid of… I'm afraid."

"I know! I can see that. Of course, you're afraid." And Suzy shot Evan with her most meaningful stare yet. "Maybe you're not the only one."

"That's real easy for you to say." And Evan crossed his arms even more.

"But what is it? What's wrong?"

I could see that Suzy was about to tell me, but then Evan got up, and she did, too.

Her huge smile returned. "Let me just talk to Evan for a second, okay, Chris? You just hang out. There's some Utne Readers under there, and a loaded bong right behind the couch, so make yourself at home, okay?"

I rose. Why would I want a guy like Evan to help me, anyway? The ludicrousness of the situation finally dawned on me. "You know what? Evan doesn't want to do this, and I don't want to waste any more of your time. Thank you for at least taking me seriously for a second." The door was only a few feet away from me, and I remember feeling an enormous, heavy dread as I approached it, the ride back to the house more than I thought I could manage without any hope of resolution. I didn't even know how I could face Nicole and Alphonse, but part of my change was that I didn't care as much as I used to about that. In fact, the absence of that concern distressed me more than anything else, and for the first time, I considered just driving away from it all. But I still couldn't just abandon my friends, and the weight of understanding Penobscot Road only enough to be haunted by it forever was too awful. I had absolutely no idea what I was going to do.

"No, no, no! Chris! Okay. Okay. You have a right to know what's going on."

"Suzy! What the heck is wrong with you, man?"

"What difference does it make if you want to pull the site, anyway? It's not like this would generate more business or anything. It would be just one, last time."

Evan was at least six inches shorter than Suzy, and he looked up at her with such a sudden flash of affection, his bloodshot, intense eyes moistening up, that I felt much better. I'd seen it so infrequently that I'd completely forgotten what love looked like, but it told me that there was still a regular world out there. Everything wasn't Penobscot Road.

"Exactly, Suzy. *One last time.*"

"Evan."

They both stood there for a moment; Evan was the first to look away. He swung around and returned to the television, wiping his eyes and then re-crossing his arms. He had removed himself from the discussion in as theatrical a fashion as possible.

"Chris, why don't you sit back down, and I'll explain all of this goofy stuff. Then you can make up your own mind about it. You know, you're not the only one here who might be crazy."

I'd actually cracked through their resistance. It was so surprising to find out what a little assertiveness, a little brutal honesty could achieve that when I returned to the couch, I held myself more erect than the moment before. I was worth looking at, paying attention to. I was effective. It was such a rare experience for me that I suspect I was a little theatrical, and if I hadn't been so worried, I might have viewed this scene featuring the three of us almost sentimentally.

Suzy sat right in front of me and leaned as far forward as her stomach would allow. "Okay. Okay. So what's going on is that we're worried about you. We've been doing this a long time, and what you just described is kind of the worst-case scenario."

"What do you mean?"

"Well, a new town where you don't know anyone. And not really caring about being here, maybe not a lot of support, except for your roommates. And even there, it sounds like you're not really communicating with them completely."

She looked at me for confirmation, and I had to shrug.

"Okay, so there's that. You're kind of a good candidate, in a way. Kind of cut off, emotionally and physically and spiritually."

She glanced over at Evan, but his entire body radiated such absolute denial that she could only return her attention to me. "And the reason why Evan is so grumpy is because it's not just him. I mean, he isn't the only member of our psychic roadshow. I'm kind of a part of the whole process, too, only I don't really remember anything. What I mean is that when we go to places where stuff is going on, I go into a trance, kind of, only people don't know it. And I whisper weird things to Evan, who's the only person who can understand what I mean. And then he translates. So we're more of a team. He just kind of doesn't want people knowing that I'm so involved."

Evan watched television even harder.

"And the last time we did it, I was sort of physically affected—"

"She had a heart attack and nearly died."

"Which is why Evan doesn't want to do it, anymore. But he knows that the real reason for that was because of my weight, and going up and down all those stairs all night. And he also knows how many people we've helped—"

Evan swung around and focused squarely at me. "Do you want to be responsible for her death? Is your house that bad? Criminy, this is ridiculous, Suze! There's no way I'm going to let you do it. Get real."

Now, it was Suzy's turn to aim all of her energy at me. "Do you know what you're probably dealing with? It's not ghosts or a poltergeist or anything like that. You haven't really told us everything yet, but everything you have told us makes us think you're being victimized. By a demon. That land east of Pacific Bay—"

"Suzy! Why on earth would you say that! You're making things worse! Just get out of here, Chris. Find somebody else to help. We just can't do it! I'm sorry."

During this exchange, I'd gradually adopted my customary slouch. Even though I didn't believe that I was dealing with a demon, it was still unnerving to be in the same room with people who did. And Evan was right: I might have been distressed by everything, but things weren't bad enough yet to risk someone else's life. "That's okay. We'll just move—"

"Suze—!"

"That's just it, Chris—"

"Suze!"

"When demons find the right victim, they don't leave you alone. No matter where you go. That's why I have to do this—"

"We don't know any of that for sure! Not really. But I do know that you're going to die the next time we try any of that stuff! That's a real, live fact!"

I got up, and I could feel the dark hall right behind me. Their certainty was infectious. "Is it here, now?"

They both froze, and the absence of sound only made the space around me seem stranger. For the first time, I could hear the breakers down below us on the shoreline, muffled by the pines.

Finally, Suzy replied. "We don't know. I can only tell you things like that when I'm in my trance."

"Geez, Suzy!"

"But I usually only go into a trance when there's something around! So probably not."

I couldn't believe in demons, but at that moment, it didn't make me feel any better. "So am I possessed? Is that what you think?"

She chuckled. "Believe me, you'd know it if you were possessed. We all would."

"Suze. You can go if you want, but I'm not translating. So what would be the point?"

She frowned flatly at him. "What would be the point? Come on, Evan. What's the point if we don't help?"

He turned to me. "You could just do some of those tests for paranormal activity yourself. They're real easy, and they're all over the internet. Your roommates would believe you with proof like that."

Suzy's frown deepened.

Evan was beginning to sound hopeful. "Or we can find someone else for you. Maybe those guys up in Vancouver. We'll just send them down. They've got all that equipment and stuff, man! They do it all the time."

She smiled sadly at me. "Maybe they can detect things, but they can't get rid of them. Look, let me talk to Evan. Because he knows that I can't let somebody in trouble just walk out of here. He can't, either."

"Yes, I can."

"And we'll talk about how to reduce any risk to me, if there is any."

But I wasn't comfortable with any of it. They both seemed too earnest, too dramatic to be right. They just took themselves too seriously. In a way, this was the moment when I began to hope that I *was* just going crazy, rather than becoming like them. Demons! "Listen, don't worry about it. I don't think it's a demon, anyway. To be totally honest, I don't think I believe in demons." I began to sidle toward the door. "I'm sorry about all of this. I didn't mean to, uhh—"

"Chris, you don't need to believe in demons." And again, Suzy exchanged a weird glance with Evan. "In fact, it's kind of worse for you if you don't. And anyways, if you don't believe in them, then what would be the harm of having us stop by?"

Evan pulled himself out of his shadowed corner and approached the door, readying to close it behind me. "You've got to understand that this is how Suzy can feel like she's making a contribution to society. It makes her feel important. She likes the attention because it makes her look like an expert—"

"—which is exactly why Evan took all the credit—"

"Yes! But I don't want that kind of attention, anymore! Because it isn't worth it."

I had the door open now. "Okay, well, thank you!"

Suzy came right up to the doorway and pushed past Evan. I could actually feel the heat that her body was radiating. "We'll call you. We'll just stop by. That's all. Just take a quick look. That way, you can just cross 'demon' off your list."

Evan craned to see around her. "No, we won't!"

I needed to leave. "Thanks. Bye!"

Seeing that familiar car made me think of Nicole and Alphonse, and then swiftly of the house, and I again contemplated just walking down the steep driveway and off into the wilds of the Pacific Northwest. I wasn't at all sure I wanted Suzy and Evan coming to my house, but what else could I do? *Something* was happening; maybe they could fix problems other than demons. *They* certainly believed so. And if I was really just crazy, then maybe I could believe it, too.

"Don't worry about anything, Chris. We'll call!"

I smiled dismissively, waved, and drove down the side of the mountain as fast as I could. It was getting late, and Alphonse would be angry if I missed his dinner.

* * *

What was happening wasn't a demon. So what was it? As I drove home that evening, the absence of cars on the road again reminded me of how nature stood between everyone in Oregon, how it insulated each of us from the others. But was that natural or wrong? Weren't we supposed to be closer together, like in Sacramento? Did these huge, moss-covered spaces in between the people around me mean that other things had more of an opportunity to wriggle up between us? Even in the house, Nicole, Alphonse and I were physically far apart, and for the first time, I began to wonder if that was somehow a deliberate thing, if the house had been specifically designed to separate us from each other. For the briefest of an instant, the words "herd" and "cull" came to mind. Ever since moving to Penobscot Road, I certainly felt farther from the two of them, even though they both seemed as cozy together as ever.

But hadn't I been distanced by my family and the people I came into contact with in Sacramento? Even in that crush of humanity—where you stared at people's shoes five feet ahead of you as you walked through the mall, and the people five feet behind you stared at yours; where there were lines of consumers everywhere you were forced to join; where even the parks were filled with evidence of visitors who'd been in your exact same spot only two minutes before and two minutes before that—even there, buffers could be erected to isolate me. So wasn't that why I'd always clung so closely to Alphonse and Nicole, and presumably why they did to me? I still couldn't say for sure whether we'd been banished by our hometown or had simply chosen to live in a place that was a little more geographically honest about how we felt about others.

But that implies a lot more conscious thought than I think the three of us could have scraped together at the time. Things are so different now. In fact, my time in southwest Oregon has helped me appreciate the advantages of distance, I think. I'm not the same, needy Chris I once was. Even this expanse between you and me of time, of space, puts me at ease and allows me to appreciate our relationship in a way that just wouldn't have been possible if I were right there, with you.

Then the house was upon me, and I strained to see if the presence was up there, in my window, but then I knew that it was right behind me, in the empty space of the back seat, now making itself known to me, and the first thought that crossed my mind as I opened the front door and saw all the black spaces inside yawning at me was "demon." The entity was no longer confined to the house.

The two of them were in the family room watching television, the almost vanished smell of meat indicating that I'd missed the dinner I was supposed to make by about an hour. They sat in cheap, white plastic lawn chairs, adrift in expansive shadows, yet this did nothing to weaken the coziness of the scene.

Alphonse had had time to craft his reaction. "How are you doing?" He really did seem concerned about me, and I felt this, along with the dry warmth of the room, as something approaching my concept of home. Nicole looked up, serious in her waiting. She even muted for me.

"The doctor said it's no big deal, and if I follow his instructions, it will clear up in a week or so."

"Oh, awesome." But she couldn't let other things go as easily. "You were gone for a while."

"Yeah. I had to drive a couple of towns north of here. Seville."

"What was it like?"

"Nice, I guess. Smaller than Pacific Bay. I didn't really look around too much."

"I got a job at the Pilates studio in town."

Of course, we were already off of me, which I had no problem with this time. "That's great! When do you start?"

"In a couple of days. They don't pay nearly as much here as they do back home." It was the first time I'd ever heard her call Sacramento "back home." Penobscot Road was changing Nicole, too.

"Well, things are so much cheaper here."

Alphonse shifted in his seat, a symptom of his eagerness to speak. "And I'll have a job tomorrow. Tommy at Bright Solutions is supposed to hook me up. So, yeah. That just leaves you." He always had to release into the world what everyone else was thinking but knew enough not to say.

I wanted to throw him off-balance for once, put him on his back leg. "How's the boogeyman treating you? You said something about him living with you in your room?"

Alphonse stretched a smile across his face as he returned his gaze to the silent television. "Oh, you mean Alphonse? He's awesome. Always asking after you. I never know what to tell him."

"Oh, tell him I'm fine and that thing we discussed is going to happen really soon."

"I'll do that." But this response was perfunctory, as Alphonse was no longer even listening to me. "I'll do that."

"How dried out is dinner, I wonder." I drifted toward the kitchen.

"At least clean up," was the only response I got from Alphonse.

In the kitchen, I carefully avoided the spot in front of the sink, but the greasy, peeling atmosphere of the room immediately turned my mind to grayer things. The presence was still with me, and I suspected that it was perfectly visible behind me except for the few moments when I could catch a reflection of it. Then, it would pass into that strange trans-visible state for an instant. The entity was smarter and faster than I could ever hope to be, and it was in its element here, so there was really no reason for it to conceal itself. This was its house. It had nothing to hide, and in fact, it seemed to be hiding less and less from me every day. Plus, I sensed that keeping itself entirely from me was tiring, an inconvenience.

Of course, what should have most distressed me—and what you're doubtlessly screaming at me right now—was that I was becoming too used to it too quickly. I was reminded of what Alphonse had said about humans being earth's dominant species because of our uncanny ability to adapt to our environments so quickly. It was growing increasingly clear to me that this ability was having a negative outcome for the three of us. Everything was wrong, and yet we were sitting on plastic chairs in the middle of it all, cheerfully watching reality TV. And now I was frequently forgetting that some force was right behind me, observing everything I did with a mild curiosity that was nothing more than an ominous prelude to god knows what. I did want it to stop, to go away, but that night, as I started in on my flat, crusty meal in that flat, crusty kitchen, I knew that the only and best thing was to be patient and see how Evan and Suzy could help. And not to make any sudden moves.

The Eighth Day

At 2:23 the next morning, I was awakened by sounds outside my door. Or more accurately, I was awakened by the memory of sounds that skewered my sleep until I awoke. Because once I'd opened my eyes, Penobscot Road's second floor was completely silent. The presence was gone, though; I could tell that immediately. It had better things to do in the blackness. At first, I wondered if it hadn't been responsible for the noises, but I found that I knew better. Instinctively, I understood that sound wasn't one of its tools; rather, the presence was a torture movie with the speakers disabled. It was a mouth gaping in an endless, silent scream. The entity's muteness only made it more intense, more violent. As I lay in my bed, the cold, damp air pressing down on my face, I distinctly remember being unhappy about making this realization, that the thing manifested itself through darker, nameless senses and that one of my primary ways of knowing that it was near me was disabled, useless.

Determining the source of the noise was even more distressing. I didn't want to wander around that hallway and its traces of previous inhabitants, but I needed to identify what was happening. I knew that whatever it was would be bad, yet I also knew it wasn't about me, somehow. I wasn't that valuable to the house. Plus, I had to provide as much information to Evan and Suzy as I could, and whatever was happening was new.

If you're wondering why on earth I would actually go in search of the source of strange noises in the deepest part of that darkness, please remember that ignorance is the basis for bravery. I would never dare step out into the house's night world today, so don't let this behavior distance you from the me you know now. I was still in my "interested" period; I was still able to see myself as intrepid, resolute.

Sure enough, when I passed into the hall, the sensation of others sleeping behind all those doors around me was stronger than ever. I could even hear their breathing, heaving lightly in and out, until I realized that it was my own. Even then, I marveled at how calm I was, my breath so regular, so shallow. Why wasn't I on guard?

In the dark, I felt my way to the back of the house, my hand often pulling away from the sharper, cheaper surfaces of the walls in the newer sections. We hadn't replaced the hallway light bulb because I'd honestly believed I'd never want to walk all the way down there at night. But even if we had, I doubt I would've turned it on. My fear of alerting the sleeping family of my intrusion was actually stronger than my fear of what the blackness hid. Maybe that's because I knew there were things hidden there just as much as I knew that I didn't want to see them. And since the house wasn't concerned with me this time, why put myself through that?

I finally reached the door to the room that we believed housed the back staircase at the dead end of the hall. It was still locked, but when I put my hand against the door, I could feel its particular energy. Behind it was a slaughterhouse, a place furiously ignored because of what was performed there. In fact, my sense of being an invader had evaporated here because I could tell that even the family was afraid of this part of the house. It was unclean, even for them, with much more to be lost than gained, so the end of the hall was forgotten, effaced by the suspicions and fears echoed by the former owners. Back here, they clearly were leaving me to my own devices.

The bathroom was next, but after that, how would I manage to enter the rooms in which the family felt safe? What would that make me?

Closing the bathroom door to keep any light from alerting the others, I flipped the switch and was immediately overwhelmed by the ridiculousness of my behavior. The room's ordinariness seemed to reproach me: the ugly, stained fixtures and dumb necessity. What was wrong with me? There was no sleeping family, just their unintentional mark on the air. Nothing was even threatening me this time; I was implicitly able to understand this just as I was beginning to understand so many other things about the house, albeit slowly. So why skulk around?

And then I heard the noises again. They were far away, at the other end of the floor, and as I quickly re-entered the hall, I felt the others becoming conscious, waking up around me. But it wasn't because of me or the ruckus; the family was on its own, spectral clock. As I approached the two, small rooms near the head of the front stairs, I quickly sensed that this indentation of another time was a Tuesday morning and the start of another busy day around the farm. For the others, it wasn't even October; it was spring and the end of another comatose winter. I could even sense their delighted anticipation of swiftly moving, billowed clouds against an Easter blue sky, of muddy puddles that would soon be shrinking up rather than joining up across the land.

But what surprised me the most was my dismay at the thought that for me, it was the depths of an autumn night and those very same puddles were pooling up outside, growing toward the house, preparing to crust up and provide yet another Oregon danger to me and my friends. Because of course it was raining outside. You can just assume that it was raining unless I point out otherwise.

I remember wishing that I was greeting that ancient March sunrise, too, rather than the awful moment I found myself tied to now, although the people—the family or whatever it was—had always been a part of what made the house so awful. Even back then, on their brisk spring morning, something wasn't right.

The noise was coming from the small room closest to the third-story staircase, and I was very relieved to recognize that it was just an animal, a rat or mouse or something. It was scrabbling at the walls, intent on performing something completely natural and therefore nothing to do with the strange alterations and intentions that constantly swept through Penobscot Road.

But when I opened the door, I found that it was Nicole. She was balled up on the floor, face down, scratching at a baseboard with her right hand. There was a good deal of paint chips and dust covering her sweat pants, so she'd been doing it for a while.

"Nicole?"

"I just have to get rid of this." Her voice was absolutely ordinary; she wasn't even whispering, as I had just done.

"Get rid of what?"

"And because they're coming and they."

"They what?"

"It's just a task or a *task* or."

She wasn't awake. She'd walked in her sleep up to this room and was now speaking to me from somewhere other than consciousness. I'd never known her to do this before.

"Why are you in this room?"

"Why are you in this room?"

"Nicole—"

"Why are you why are why."

I knew that I shouldn't wake her, but I couldn't let her spend the rest of the night with her face on the floor, scraping at the baseboard until her fingers bled.

"I'm just going to take you downstairs and back to bed—" But the moment I touched her, she slid to the left, got up, and casually walked past me and out the door. Her eyes were open, but they were seeing other things.

Consequently, I was very worried that she'd hurt herself on the stairs or wherever it was that she was headed. Because she was very intent on going somewhere farther down the hallway. Every move of hers was utterly confident, as if she'd walked this passage a thousand times before. Even in the dark, her body knew where to go, while I trailed behind, carefully feeling my way farther and farther into the blackness.

Then she was gone, and I frantically tried to determine which door she'd just passed through. I could feel my face squeezed into a terrible grimace, the natural response to rushing into a potentially hazard-filled area while robbed of sight. Then it was suddenly bright, and I could feel the light reflecting up from my pinched cheeks, off my dry front teeth.

She was up ahead in the room with the Scooby-doo sticker, the room in which I'd put my arms around my roommates. Once my eyes adjusted to the light, I approached the door slowly, worried about what I was about to find there.

Nicole was naked and turned toward the door, smiling, her sweatpants around her feet and the large t-shirt she'd been wearing flung into a corner. I'd never seen her naked before, and absurdly, the first thing I found myself doing was checking my years of suspicions about her body against the real thing. Her areolae were smaller and darker, her hips narrower than I'd imagined. I'd gotten her pubic area right.

I would've turned away except that rather than looking at me, she was staring at something over my shoulder, and I couldn't tear my eyes from hers. Her gaze was illuminated somehow, lascivious, unashamed and very private. I wasn't supposed to be seeing it.

I backed into the hall, away from her gaze. "Nicole. It's Chris. Why don't you put your clothes back on." I could hear her start to moan; at that point, and didn't care if it was appropriate to wake up a sleepwalker. "Nicole! Nicole!" I stuck my arm through the doorway and began to knock furiously on the door. "Nicole, wake up!"

At the precise moment her moaning stopped, I felt her hand smash mine against the door, painfully.

"Chris! Stop." She sounded annoyed.

"Are you awake?"

"Yes." I could hear her pants sliding up, her t-shirt being pulled down.

She came to the door, one half of her face bright from the naked bulb in the ceiling, the other cratered by the shadows of the hallway. "I was just sleepwalking."

"I know, I—"

"Just go back to bed." And with that, she walked right past me and downstairs.

But I was still frozen there, at that door, a new but equally silly grimace on my face. How could she have woken up so soon and instantly comprehended what was happening to her like that? I found myself momentarily contemplating the impossible: that she'd been awake the whole time and had tricked me with her expert facsimile of someone asleep. Perhaps she was so annoyed because I'd backed away, backed out of the room. Perhaps she'd sensed my body responding, surprisingly and intensely, a sexual agitation impossible to hide completely.

It was easy to let these thoughts fade away, though, because the artifacts of activity in the room and the hallway were increasing, moving nearer the surface. As I hurried back to my bedroom, I couldn't help but wonder if the family continuing on underneath might not be able to break through soon. Because with every day that passed in that house, the membrane between their lives and mine grew weaker and weaker. I could sense this, too, on that horrendous October night.

* * *

Something had changed since the night before. Something downstairs. I could feel it even up in my room, even through the aching cold radiating off of my huge windows, even through the weird smell of bacon that had worked its way up to my nostrils. Bacon was a change, too. Breakfast in our house was normally a pretty paltry affair.

But something else was going on down there, and as I descended the staircase, I grew aware of how fatigued I'd become coping with Penobscot Road, this endless shading of darker and darker changes. Even with a good night's sleep—thanks in part to the absence of the entity in my room—I felt my thoughts roll over hysterically in my head, just as they would when I'd been awake two days straight. My senses were heightening in some ways, scabbing over in others. My limbs were weak and sore just as much as they were taut and twitchy. All of this scared me more than might seem likely to you, but that's because I knew I was growing less and less able to properly consider things, to make the safest choices. My reactions would be growing increasingly ragged and unpredictable— and in direct proportion to my need of correct responses—as events continued to spiral downward in the house. It wasn't good.

Alphonse and Nicole were sitting at the kitchen table, chatting in low voices and gnawing on the last, two strips of bacon. When I entered, they kept their heads in exactly the same positions, allowing their voices to trail into silence. Neither one looked at me.

A sign that I was no longer functioning at full capacity: only when I saw the bruised smudges under Nicole's eyes did I realize that I hadn't given the first thought to how I would handle the previous night's scene. What did she remember of what she'd done? What did she remember of me? And I hadn't even considered the ways in which the house might have provoked her sleepwalking. Or why.

Finally, Alphonse looked in my direction, although not directly at me. He actually chuckled. "Look who's up."

"Hey."

The two of them exchanged a strange glance, as if they were trying to smooth down frustration with a thin layer of amusement. It was an attitude we three had often shown for strangers; I'd just never known any of us to apply it to each other.

"Hey." Alphonse moved toward the sink.

Nicole still hadn't looked at me.

I knew the answer, but I wanted to see how it would be delivered: "Is there any bacon left?"

"No."

"Oh."

"You get a job yet?"

"You paid for that bacon with our money from Sacramento. My money."

"So make some more for yourself. We didn't know when you were planning on getting up."

I glanced at the clock on the stove. "It's seven o'clock."

"Make some for yourself, then."

What had changed downstairs had been Nicole and Alphonse. They both were really angry with me, the kind of angry they usually reserved for everyone but me. I'd always been annoying, but my meek nature had precluded ever drawing wrath from them before. I'd just never been enough of a force for that.

Strangely, their anger had an odd effect on me. "Great. I'm just going to eat the rest of it."

Now Nicole did look at me. I was fat, but I never usually ate much at one time. In fact, I'd always been a little too conscious of appearing like a pig, a little too decorous at the table. In short, I'd been kind of a prissy eater—which was doubly galling, as I continued to pack on weight.

"It's been so long since I've had bacon."

The pack was three-quarters full, and I dumped it all into the frying pan that was still sitting on the stove, surrounded by a horizontal halo of splattered fat. The wedge of meat banged around obscenely in the pan.

"What the fuck are you doing?" Now Nicole sprung up. Now I'd gotten a response.

"You guys had yours. Now, I'm having mine."

She pushed me out of the way and yanked the pan off of the burner. "What the fuck is wrong with you!?" The resonance in her voice made it clear that she was talking about more than the bacon. "I'm serious. Something is wrong with you."

Nicole looked at Alphonse flatly, her mouth a pursed line of conflict, and he flicked the edge of the table with his fingernail.

"What do you mean?"

"We shouldn't be mad at you. It's not your fault."

"What's not my fault?"

"Last night."

How could either of them blame me for what had happened then? But I found myself actually refusing blame, rather than welcoming it this time, a rage rising up in me that I'd never known before: the kind that is expressed.

"Well, I'm glad that you two got together to decide how we should all feel about what happened last night. So I guess that I'm somehow responsible for it, and yet at the same time, I can't actually be *responsible* for my own actions because I'm too clueless to know what to do in that kind of situation. So thanks. Next time I won't wake you up. Is that what you want me to say?"

"I don't want you to say anything! But I guess this is good, that you're finally saying what's actually on your mind. I guess that's a good thing." She hesitated here, looked at Alphonse. "But that's not like you, either."

"So what was I supposed to do? Not wake you up? Because I can't figure out what else I did wrong! Did you want me to wake Alphonse up, instead? Would he have known the right thing to do?"

Alphonse's frown reminded me of the way he looked when he read an article about technology that didn't make complete sense to him. How could an expert on the subject get it wrong? "You *did* wake me up."

"How? I didn't make any noise. Nicole woke you up, if anyone did."

He paused, looking at Nicole for guidance.

She'd never looked so uncertain before. "Maybe we shouldn't talk about this now—"

"No, I want to talk about it. How did I wake Alphonse up?"

Nicole had been furiously holding the handle of the pan for the entire conversation. Now, she released it, the insides of her hands lined in red, and sat back down at the table and her empty plate. "You don't remember?"

"Remember what?"

"You were sleepwalking last night."

I grabbed the edges of the counter, digging my fingers in. "What?"

"And you came down here and woke us both up. You were—" another significant look toward Alphonse, "—shouting. Saying stuff that was pretty bad. About us. And doing things."

"*You* were sleepwalking last night!"

"Some of the stuff that you said was really hurtful. We can't blame you, exactly, for what you said, but—"

Alphonse shifted abruptly and awkwardly in his seat. "But we can't help wondering if it isn't what you really think of us but never had the guts to say before."

"But *you* woke *me* up!"

"You mean you weren't sleeping when you said all that?"

"I don't know what you're talking about! I didn't say anything about you guys, and I didn't come down here. You woke me up because you were sleepwalking upstairs. You were in that room with the stickers, and you were—let me see your right hand." Her fingernails were ragged. "See? You were scratching on the wall."

Nicole held up her left hand, which was just as torn up as her right. "I was ripping out all those vines yesterday by the back door."

"But I wasn't sleepwalking last night."

"You said a lot of nasty things, Chris. There's no point in repeating them. And you also said some pretty weird things. But you can understand why we're a little upset. We're not sure how to feel. I know that moving to Oregon has been really stressful for you." Nicole took a deep breath here and looked at the ceiling. "And you did something."

Wordlessly, Alphonse and Nicole walked to the farthest corner of the family room. On the floor, the children's tea set from the secret room in the attic had been carefully set up in a circle, only each little cup and every little plate was up-side-down. It was so amateurish in its creepiness that I had to laugh.

"That's ridiculous! I didn't do that!"

"I know that it's scary, thinking that you did stuff while you were asleep—"

"Then how do you know that one of you didn't do it while you were asleep?"

Alphonse had to concede to logic. "We don't. But you were acting so bizarrely—"

"What do you mean?"

"Just not like you."

I was much angrier than I should have been. I realized that even as I was experiencing it. There was still a little rationality left in me, though; everything that they'd accused me of could have happened. What really enraged me was the fact that they weren't listening to me, that they refused even to acknowledge that Nicole might have been sleepwalking.

These were my friends; this was my family, such as it was. I ached to ask them how the house could be responsible for all of this, to discuss what we all knew was happening to us. But I'd just appear to be in some state of denial if I did, and something told me that this would be the worst thing to do at that moment.

So instead: "What did I say?"

Nicole crossed her arms. "Let's just forget about it right now, okay? I don't think that talking about it is going to help anything."

I bent over to pick up the little plastic plates as if I'd left them there to begin with. Why did I feel as if I had to return them to that little room and set them up exactly as I'd found them? "Well, I'm sorry for whatever it was that I said." I could tell that they wanted me to say more, to say that none of it had been true, but without knowing what they claimed I said, how could I be sure it wasn't? I just wanted to be away from them, to gather my thoughts and figure out how all this was connected to everything else that was happening in Penobscot Road.

I stood up with the tea set piled in my hands and froze. The presence had returned and was clinging to every part of me that wasn't visible to Alphonse and Nicole, a dance partner shadowing my every move.

"What's wrong?" The undercurrent of annoyance in Alphonse's voice was one thing too many for me. The entity was slithering around on my skin, feeding off of the situation, and not only did my friends think that I was growing increasingly abnormal, but their sympathy for me was becoming remarkably limited.

"What do you care?!" I couldn't stay there, in front of them, with that thing on me, so I retreated to my room, where the presence immediately dissolved into the space, a tarantula returning to its box. The thing had surprised me, but it hadn't scared me at all this time, and realizing this was so awful that I found myself crying into my pillow. It was the first time that I'd cried since arriving—possibly the first time in years—and I remember reveling in the self-pity, finding strength in it to contemplate foul things:

How did I know that Alphonse and Nicole hadn't made up the story about my sleepwalking? Could they have set up the tea set on purpose? Maybe Nicole's pretend sleepwalking had been a part of it, some kind of plan that they were perpetrating on me. The house could have been making them do nasty, convoluted things, too. After all, I knew that they would've never been so dismissive of me before. They would've never played such a cruel, elaborate trick on me when we'd lived in Sacramento. So why bother now? I looked around that room—my room—and realized that part of embracing my dark side would have to include questioning everything I'd believed in.

Is all of this entertaining for you, witnessing the betrayal of the only friends I'd ever had? Because privately questioning Nicole and Alphonse was just as treacherous as accusing them of my suspicions outright. Our relationships may have always been codependent, but we'd also struggled together to master the essentials of true friendship, including trust. After that morning, this was no longer true, and my tears made me feel as if I were mourning a grandparent who'd ceased to remember who I was.

Anyway, I hope this is entertaining for you because then I'd at least be rendering something of value out of all of it. Even this intensely personal pain is provided for your intensely personal pleasure. So return the favor.

Play a little game with me. It would bring me an infinitesimal amount of satisfaction, which is, as you know, the only amount I can hope to ever experience again. And you are the only person who can provide it.

What I'd really like to know is what you want me to do next. Imagine: you're crying like a child into your pillow, the vapors of Penobscot Road's second floor seeping into your mind, the entity observing you coolly, determining its next feint or stab with some unknowable logic. The only people in the world who matter to you are downstairs, probably whispering to each other about their concern for you, their growing revulsion toward you. Your only chance of redemption is Evan and Suzy's occult—and very possibly misguided and dangerous—insight into the house and what it's doing to you.

So everything doesn't seem inevitable yet, does it? What should I do?

Instead of an answer, you might presently find yourself asking a question of your own: why on earth would I bother asking this? Well, as you know, I want so badly to share everything with you: my body, my mind, my soul. It's truly the only reason I continue, either in this endeavor of ours or any other. And now I find that I'd like to share something else with you, too: responsibility. If your choice for my next act matches mine, then morally at least, you are just as accountable as I am for everything that happens from this point on. Think of how much closer that would bring us. You would be doing more than simply causing all of this to re-exist by continuing on with me—which you should take credit for. You would also be my active colluder, a partner whose instincts are in perfect concert with mine. And although slight, this would bring me actual *gratification*, an emotion I've been given far too rarely in my short life.

Of course, time and distance continue to separate us; I'll never be able to forget that. So I may never know the actual path you decide on. And you could very well make a choice different from my own, which, for you at least, might constitute a weakness in our relationship, as it would prove that we share even less than I've dared suggest. But remember that as for me, I'll never know, so even your generous gesture of considering my next move is a kind of tacit sharing. Knowing you're actively engaging in my situation, granting my request, is enough for me. In fact, it's more than enough. It's the only belief that can help push me through the next series of events in my story.

So I ask you to take the next moment, just a short moment, to determine what you would do at this juncture if you were me. Here, I'll tail off my writing as gently as possible, allowing your mind to go from receiving to generating, a small shift that will bring such relief to me, your eyes quietly passing over the three asterisks below that I use to indicate the passage of time for my story, only this time, they'll represent the passage of time for you as you pause…

*　　*　　*

Here's what I did:

After I heard Alphonse and Nicole part downstairs, and the creaking water pipes from the back bathroom indicate that one of them was taking a shower, I dug through my last box of belongings that hadn't yet been put away. At the bottom, I found an old bicycle lock.

I was glad to see that Nicole's door was open down the back hallway, which meant that she was the one in the shower. Quietly returning to the kitchen to grab a baggy, I deliberately stomped around, pausing at Alphonse's closed door.

"Alphonse, Nicole has the masking tape, right?" I knew that Nicole had mentioned looking for it when she'd lied about being in the dining room a few nights earlier.

"I guess," came the muffled reply.

"Maybe it's in her room."

So I walked back down the hallway and entered Nicole's room and tipped toward the wall next to me, resting my head there, nearly passing out. It was difficult not to make a noise, but I knew I couldn't afford to. The room still contained the presence of the old woman, but this was beginning to melt into Nicole's presence, somehow. Her traces weren't overpowering the old woman's, nor did they exist in tandem. Instead, their auras were combining into an entirely new element that filled the space like heavy sand. Taken on its own, what had been left of the old woman seemed just as innocuous as Nicole's presence, yet this new hybrid wasn't meant to exist. It was unnatural, and being there, in the midst of it, took my breath away.

But I had a job to do, and so I forced my way over to Nicole's dresser and emptied a third of her talcum powder into the baggy. She'd picked up the old-fashioned habit from her grandmother, who'd always smelled of the stuff, and this helped me understand that this was a point of intersection: the old woman had used powder, too, which had always been kept in the exact same spot in the room. I can only explain this as general knowledge, made clear by the walls, the ceiling and the floor. Information reverberated here; it was trapped and couldn't pass easily away.

If the powder had just been Nicole's, I wouldn't have been afraid of the consequences. But in that room, it belonged to the both of them, and as I rushed into the hall, I sensed some sort of new, muffled risk due to my theft.

"Did she have it?" The fact that Alphonse yelled this through his door meant that he was attempting to normalize things after our sleepwalking discussion.

I was only too glad to join him. "I couldn't find any, but it's no big deal. Hey, have you guys checked out the third floor, yet?"

The pause was so slight that no one else on the planet would've recognized it but me. "No. What's it like?"

"Kind of the same as the rest of the place. Big."

There had been a time, only a couple of weeks before, when I would've never asked Nicole or Alphonse if they'd gone somewhere without me. We'd always done things as a group, and the few times we hadn't, the two of them would tell me what they'd been up to as soon as they could. It had to do with trust, somehow, and I only realized this now, as I asked such a nonchalant question and received such a nonchalant reply.

"Oh. Is that right." Alphonse always could sound quickly and easily bored.

I remembered putting some string in one of the kitchen drawers and so began to quietly search there, the plumbing system reporting that Nicole was done with her shower. Before I'd made it through half the cabinets, she was standing behind me.

"What are you looking for?"

I couldn't afford to pause; I didn't even look up. "Remember that string that we had? I know I put it in here, somewhere, but I can't remember where now."

She reached for something in the cabinet over my head. "I put it in that back storage room. Where those stairs are."

"How come?" I carefully rose with my back toward her.

"When was the last time you needed string for cooking? We used to keep it in the kitchen because we had nowhere else to put it, but we've got space now. We might as well use it, right?" Nicole sounded a little conciliatory, too. Maybe the two of them had discussed how poorly they'd treated me earlier. Maybe they'd realized that they hadn't been all that fair.

"Sure."

"Why do you need string?"

I turned to her and shook my head as if it weren't even worth discussing. "Oh, I want to use it to tie up a box."

"Okay. So it's what, the 1800s? Did I not get the memo?"

"Hey. Don't knock the 1800s. When they wanted a box shut, it stayed shut."

"What were you doing in my room?"

I maintained the casual glance, but my brain squirmed behind my eyes. I would've heard if Alphonse had tattled on me; the door to his room was right there. I'd been very careful not to disturb anything; even the powder had been returned to its exact location, its precise angle.

Were the traces I'd left in her room bouncing around it, too, as blatant as hers and the old woman's?

"I was looking for the masking tape."

"For the box."

"But then I thought: string. Much better."

"The masking tape was right on top of my dresser."

I was going to make it: "Exactly." I walked past her, lightly. "But string is going to work much better."

"We've got all this space, Chris."

Maybe I wasn't going to make it. I turned. "Yeah?"

"So we don't need to, you know, be in each other's business so much. We've got the room to spread out a little."

"True."

I know that living in close quarters with others is supposed to make private space all the more precious, but it hadn't been that way with Nicole, Alphonse and me in Sacramento. Our entire apartment had been communal; each of us treated anything and everything as our own. So this was the first time Nicole had ever asked me to keep out of her things, and although she was right—the house afforded us with an amazing level of privacy—her warning was about more than entering her room. Something else was going on.

As I mounted the stairs, it dawned on me that the strange sensation I'd had of risky behavior in Nicole's room, that whispered threat, had come to pass: I'd been told to stay away. By the both of them. And I couldn't help but notice, once I closed my door against the others, that contrary to my experience of her room, mine was devoid of any trace of me. The space was a black pit into which my presence was dropped and lost, forcefully negated. I was inside it right now, but I was unremarkable, somehow, no longer worth noting. An ant in the corner of a prison cell held the same value. It would be easy to say that the entity was occupying all the space instead, pushing me to its edges, but it wasn't even there. I was completely alone in my bedroom and yet hardly there at all.

I'd always been the one who just wasn't noticed, the one who didn't really matter all that much. But I'd been changing since my time in Penobscot Road. My rage came out now. And so I banged on the walls to hear my fists pounding, to feel my power over at least the physical realm. I turned on the light in my bathroom and saw myself in the mirror, that wallpaper repeating and repeating behind me. Appearing to myself was an act of defiance. No matter what the room told me, *I was there.*

But I had to do more than just passively exist within it, and so I grabbed the bubbling corner of one of the sheets of wallpaper and ripped it down. The crumbling, yellowed crust behind it arced across the air for a moment, and I felt it on my face, my arms. *I'd* done that; the room was wrong about my impotence. Now I knew more about the room, about the house, and knowledge was power. I discovered that my room had once been painted Wedgewood blue, and as I crushed the wallpaper in my hands, feeling it yield to my strength, I noticed an odd crescent of black at the edge of the naked wall.

Pulling down the next two strips of wallpaper revealed a very careful, almost meticulous drawing, done in thick, black ink, of a row of trees. Each tree was exactly human-sized, and as I stared at what was facing me, I couldn't help but get the feeling that the scene was familiar. Slowly, I turned to my right and beheld the exact same arrangement outside my window, each tree the same shape, the same distance from the next as the cipher on my wall. The row of pines that faced the house had always struck me as especially melancholy, but this foul likeness was more than just depressing; the image was a cryptograph, a symbol for something much worse, although I couldn't have said what at the time.

So what other arcane meanings were scratched on the walls of my room, kept from me by only the thinnest sheet of vinyl? I looked around, devastated by yet another layer of filth that Penobscot Road surrounded me with, packing me even more tightly into whatever was left of the personal space I held around myself and used as a buffer. And there was something else, too, something about the tree hieroglyph that bothered me; I just couldn't put my finger on it.

So even my act of defiance, as pathetic and random as it was, had been cancelled out by the house. I couldn't even vandalize the place without the remains of my confidence being vandalized in return. It seemed as if Penobscot Road knew all the punches I was going to throw and already had its each and every counterpunch lined up and ready. It was just waiting for me to stumble onto my next, mistaken move. Or perhaps the building was just so saturated in wrongdoing that no matter what I did, where I turned, there would be something vile waiting for me there.

I'd seen an old paint can somewhere, and realizing that it had been under the back porch, dented and rusting, I raced downstairs and out the back door. The wet weeds growing around it wouldn't give it up easily, but I persisted, as there was still something sloshing around inside. We didn't have a paintbrush, so I decided to use an old rag.

Alphonse was in the kitchen, and as I passed by the doorway, he looked down at the filthy old can in my hand.

"What are you doing with that?"

I didn't even slow down, only yelled over my shoulder: "Just a little touch-up work."

Back in my room, I was dismayed to find that the drawing of the trees was now dominating everything else. In fact, I could sense that the presence would no longer be returning there. Just as the room had decided to deny my existence, the uncovering of the symbol seemed to indicate that there was now no longer any space for the entity, either. With me, this refusal had been slight, but with the presence, I could tell it was dangerous, and so the promise of a place where the malignant force couldn't interrogate me, antagonize me, wasn't the relief I would've hoped for. It still had the rest of the world to harass me, and the trees and what they stood for were infinitely worse, anyway.

But I wasn't so easily defeated. After hacking at the lid for a while, I finally managed to open the can and found that it contained pale yellow paint, a color I hadn't seen anywhere in the house. Of course, I still hadn't seen the attic or the basement, and this realization was just as draining as stirring the paint and watching the viscous fluid on top refuse to reincorporate with the pigment below. But I grabbed an old pair of underwear and did what I could to smear the trees over. When they were out of sight, the room immediately calmed, although it would never be what a bedroom should be. I'd never have that kind of rest.

I'd gathered the powder and the lock. Now I returned to the back storeroom, where I also retrieved a screwdriver and a heavy stone paperweight. But I didn't even look for the string there.

Returning to my room, I discovered that the corridor outside my room wasn't as intense as usual. As I walked toward the back of the house, I felt only the sensation that the family could be returning at any minute, rather than the threat that they were just around the corner, right behind a door. Which was just as well, as I was about to make a lot of noise.

I'd decided to break open the locked door at the end of the hall that led to the back stairs. Having to take the long way to get to the rear of the first floor had begun to feel like a manipulation, somehow, and I no longer thought it wise to allow Penobscot Road to control my movements so proficiently.

The door was so cheap that I could've put my fist right through it if I'd wanted to, but instead, I worked at busting off the hollow, thin door handle. Refusing to acknowledge what the door was screaming at me, I jammed the screw driver behind the escutcheon and banged it in with the paperweight. Of course, I could've gone down to the storage room and up the back stairs to see if I could unlock the door from the other side, but even doing that felt as if I were bending to the will of the house. And I wanted to do it this way: I wanted to enter the storage room from upstairs. Smashing at the door handle felt marvelous.

It wasn't as easy as I thought it would be, however, and by the end, I was simply banging the paperweight directly against the handle. Eventually, I managed to break it off, and I paused, no longer able to ignore the fact that the straight, flat, everyday lines of the door clearly stated the name of brutality. Still, the momentum I'd developed proved to be stronger than my fear, and I threw the door open to reveal nothing more than a shallow closet lined with shelves. On one of them was a newspaper, The Pacific Bay Echo, still pristinely folded, dated January 16, 1965. It was placed right in the middle of the middle shelf, an offering of some kind, and its headline read: "Nigerian Coup Threatens Stability in Sub-Saharan Africa."

Where did the back stairs lead if they didn't lead to a room here? And why would they lock a closet with only a newspaper in it, which had apparently been shut for 50 years? It was another score for the house, another score against me.

You see, to understand Penobscot Street's layout, the facts of its walls and corners and windows, was to understand its secret, and to prevent this, it frustrated my expectations at every turn. All those previous builders must have colluded in erecting a structure that defied common sense, and now these dead-ends and strange, tortured corridors seemed to trap bad things, to hold onto them when they might have otherwise dissipated into the sodden Oregon air. And for the first time, as I stared at the empty, mocking shelves, I could see that I was one of those trapped things, struggling to correct what wasn't right about the house, yet completely tangled in it. I pictured the wings of a fly terminally stuck to flypaper, ruined.

"What did you do?" I hadn't heard Alphonse and Nicole come up behind me; the sounds of all the breakage was still ringing in my ears.

"I thought I could go downstairs through here."

"But you didn't have to fucking break the handle! We're going to have to pay for a new one, now!"

"I'll pay for it."

Alphonse had come up beside me and was staring into the closet. "Weird." And he picked up the newspaper. Immediately, I knew that disturbing it was bad, but I wasn't about to tell him that.

Instead, I said only: "So you could hear me?"

"Barely. What is that?" Nicole peered around Alphonse at what he had in his hands. The two of them didn't belong on the second floor, but I couldn't tell them that, either.

He gingerly unfolded the paper. "Some newspaper from 1965. Why would they lock it in there?"

"This place is so weird." But Nicole said it as if it were a good thing.

Now had to be the time. I wasn't prepared, but I knew I never would be, and so I cleared my throat and began. "Yeah, it's pretty weird. I think we need to kind of talk about that."

They were looking through the pages, their yellow edges chipping off and drifting to the floor. Nicole didn't even look up. "Oh my god! Look at that dress! It's so ugly. What do you mean? Talk about what?"

"The house. And what we're going to do about it."

The two of them exchanged a quick glance. "What do you mean?"

"There's stuff going on here. You know that." My voice echoed down the hall, prosecuting me, but I wasn't going to let anything intimidate me now. "The way the house makes you feel differently in different rooms, and sometimes do things. All the nasty residue of the people who were here before us. We can't act like we don't all know about it, anymore. We just can't. You guys have discussed it, haven't you?"

"What do you mean, 'it makes you feel differently and do things?' What have you done?" Nicole's voice had grown smaller; she was afraid.

"Well, I just pulled down my wallpaper and found a drawing of those trees that face the house. Of course, I painted over it. And I've contacted a couple of psychics to see if they can help us maybe get rid of it. They think it's a demon, but there's just too much going on for it to be one single thing."

"A demon?" Alphonse sounded very sad when he said this, the newspaper still open in his hands, forgotten. I could just make out an ad for cigarettes in the dim light.

"But *I* don't think it's that."

"God, Chris. How long have you been feeling like this?" Nicole actually managed to look perplexed, and my stomach clenched. Why was she acting as if she didn't know what I was talking about?

"As long as *you've* been feeling like this. Nicole. It's happening, whether you want to admit it or not."

"I didn't know that you were going through all of this, Chris. God! I mean, you've been acting a little weird since we got here, but you know, you *are* a little weird. I just figured the move and everything. That you were just adjusting or something. So you've been worried that the place is haunted? I mean, it's a shithole, but that's not any poltergeist's fault." She laughed a lot longer and a lot harder at this than she should have. Nicole's rare humor had always been blunt, her laughter earnest and unapologetic, but now it sounded almost cruel. I momentarily flashed on the warning she'd just given me in the kitchen.

My voice sounded hollow. "But you're different, too, because of this place!"

"Of course, I am! That was the whole point of moving here! I want to be different. But that doesn't mean I'm possessed." Again, she laughed at me. "Sorry! This is just all a little... you know I don't deal well with shit like this."

"Shit like what?"

"Chris. You're having some kind of a crisis or something. And I'm starting a new job, and we've just moved to a whole new town, and this place needs so much work. It's just a really bad time for you to be having one of your—"

"One of my what?"

"One of your dramas. I just can't, like, be a part of it right now. I'm sorry." She chuckled as she took one last look at the closet, and then she walked away from Alphonse and me. "But I do admit that this place is weird."

When Alphonse finally realized that he still had the newspaper open, he folded it into its original shape and placed it back into position. I'd just noticed that there was no dust on the shelves when he spoke:

"I know what you're talking about." And I received one of his longer, more heartfelt shrugs.

So how do you feel right now? I know you've continued to suspect that I was insane, that this was all going to end with me in a mental institution. But surely by now you know that I wouldn't waste your time on a revelation like that! It would be too pat an explanation for everything that happened, and you know I would never dream of disappointing you with such a predictable device.

Still, you've done something worse to me, haven't you. I've laid myself completely bare, shared everything that happened exactly the way in which it happened because I trusted that you believed in me and what I was doing for you. I've sugar-coated nothing, even when I've cast myself in a negative light. But all the while, you fully expected that Alphonse would accuse me of a "crisis," too, so that you could roll your eyes and pass judgment on crazy me, nothing more than a predictable waste of your time. That's a really comfortable position to be in, isn't it?

That's exactly what it is, and I'd end all of this right now, keep the rest from you out of spite and maybe out of love, but I can't. I can't. Pulling you off of your perch above me seems punishment enough, and anyway, I knew what you'd suspected all along. I could've done more than just promise you that I wasn't deranged; I could've told you right from the start that Alphonse knew about the house, too. But I wanted to make all of this more interesting; I didn't want to spoil things for you. I suppose this only confirms that I'm your torturer, your jailor, your lover.

But then you're my general, my confessor, my lover. I suppose we're even.

"I've kind of noticed some stuff," said Alphonse as he stared over my shoulder into the faceless dark. "Like up here."

He was whispering, but I was so overjoyed by the confirmation that I immediately forgot about it. "Exactly! So you feel that family, too, how they're always just on the other side of a door or a corner or about to come back upstairs and find you."

Alphonse's eyes returned to me; he was baffled. "Family?"

"Or whatever they are. Isn't that what you feel up here? That they're just about to find you in their house, like you're trespassing or something? And then each of the rooms up here—each one of them has kind of a different force."

His eyes slipped off of me, and he grimaced at his feet. "God. That sounds a little... strange."

"What do you mean? You're not noticing the same things? What about the bump on the kitchen floor? Where Nicole and I said all of that weird stuff?" His frown only deepened, and I began to worry that he was figuring out a way to tell me that I was just being "dramatic," too. But he was even less tactful than Nicole; if that had been his concern, he'd have said it long before thinking about how to say it. Something else was making him reticent. He shifted his legs in a very awkward manner, almost defensively.

Now I was worried that he was going to leave. "Alphonse, what have you felt up here?"

"You know, maybe we should stop all this talk because, I don't know, I think we're just working ourselves up. Mass hysteria on a small scale."

I took a deep breath. The subject was difficult enough, but Alphonse was spooked. Every word had to be the right one now. "Okay. But I'm really worried about us. I think we should tell each other what we're going through. It may help us to understand what's happening. So that maybe we can fix it."

"No! No, that's a bad idea. Don't tell me anything else."

"Okay, I won't. But why is that not a good thing?"

Again, he stared over my shoulder and into the shadowed hallway, his eyes almost seeming to follow something, although he could've just been inspecting the baseboard. I received a very apologetic shrug. "Because listening to you makes me feel crazier. Or more ridiculous."

This was the blunt Alphonse I knew and loved. It was an immediate relief. "Well, why don't you just tell me what's you're feeling now?"

And then I realized why he was moving his legs the way he was.

"No, Chris, I'm just going to forget about all of this. We don't need Nicole pissed at both of us."

He was attempting to hide the fact that he was sexually excited. And before I was able even to begin to process this, a cold wave of sexual desire poured down through me.

This must have made me look as if I'd come to the same conclusion about Nicole he had, because he turned away, loping toward the stairs.

I couldn't shake the image of his body's urgency, so I spoke more loudly to beat down the feelings, the breathlessness in my voice: "So you think that what we're feeling gives Nicole the right to be pissed at us?"

"Shut up! And, yeah, kind of. We'd be wrecking her dream, Chris. This isn't the way things were supposed to go."

"Are you're whispering because you're worried that Nicole is going to find out something's happening to you, too?"

"How did that work out for you?"

"So you're just going to ignore what we both feel?"

He paused at the third-floor staircase, his hand caressing the bannister. "Pretty much. You should, too."

As he disappeared around the corner, I found my eyes resting on the curve of his buttocks. But this sexual response to Alphonse's was so divorced from my thoughts and emotions that I found it quite easy to discount it and then forget it as I stood at the far end of the hallway, my stimulation radiating into and then entirely consumed by the dank air all around me.

Instead, I considered both Nicole and Alphonse's recent behavior. If all this had happened in Sacramento, they would have been fascinated, titillated and intrigued, in their own ways. Nicole would've made a huge deal of it and then delighted in the prospect of being part of a psychic investigation. It wouldn't have mattered whether she believed any of it; it just would have been fun, a story. And Alphonse would've been interested, if for nothing else than to see just how stupid people could be.

As long as I'd known him, he'd never been even so much as mildly interested in keeping anything from anybody. And I'd never known Nicole to make fun of someone and then walk away from them. But now, standing there, in the bowels of the second floor, the closet door slowly, slowly creaking open to show me the newspaper again, to taunt me with it, I felt more alone than I ever had in my life. Nothing much had ever happened to me before. But now that I was finally faced with something momentous, something I couldn't handle on my own, I'd just been abandoned by the only two people in the world I'd ever trusted.

Returning to my room, I found that the drawing of the trees had completely bled through the paint I'd just covered it with. And no matter what I did, I'd always know it was there, a few feet away from where I slept.

I had to do something.

"Hello?" Unfortunately, I got Evan.

"Hey, Evan. It's Chris from yesterday."

"Yeah, I know which Chris it is." But at least he didn't hang up.

"Listen, things are kind of escalating here."

"Well, I'm sorry about that. I really am."

"And I just can't do this on my own. I just talked about it with my roommates."

I paused and could feel his interest in the silence.

"One of them acted as if she didn't know what I was talking about, and the other one won't tell me what's happened to him since we've been here. But something's happened. They're both really scared."

Still more silence. Then there was some rustling on his end, some muffled voices.

"—back to your pickling! For pity's sake! Suzy—!"

And I heard her voice. *"Chris? What's happening?"*

"Things are getting bad."

"We're coming down right now."

I still wasn't at all sure if it was a good idea to have Suzy and Evan ghost bust, but I knew that the one thing I could no longer afford to do was hesitate. We'd already lost so much ground to Penobscot Road, and I had a feeling that there wasn't much left to lose.

"Thank you."

As soon as I hung up, my gratefulness felt only like a kind of condemnation, and the markings on the wall somehow perfectly confirmed this. I could see then that this was one of the image's functions, to reinforce misfortune, to amplify it, and I quickly looked away, my eyes settling on the stand of trees facing my window.

Their meaning was that there was no longer any meaning in anything other than Penobscot Road, and I felt my world shrink around me, tighter and tighter.

*   *   *

"It's not right!" Even before they rang the doorbell, I could hear Evan screaming, whether at Suzy, me, or the house, I couldn't be sure.

I was even more surprised when I opened the door and the two of them pushed past me and into the front hallway. Suzy was holding a balled up towel against her face.

"Where's a bathroom or kitchen or something." Evan had his hands on Suzy's shoulders, one of which barely made it across her back.

"Evan, calm down! Hi, Chris."

"She's got a really bad nosebleed."

I guided them into the kitchen, and Evan helped Suzy bend over the sink. There was a lot of blood, and I quickly backed up, already wondering if I should call an ambulance.

"Evan. Just let me—" And her fat fingers grappled with his.

"Let you what? Bleed to death through your nose?"

Suzy managed to snort out a laugh at this. "Oh, god! Imagine my obituary!"

"Where are your paper towels?" But he saw them as soon as he asked and grabbed the roll. "We're leaving after we get this cleaned up."

"Evan! Chris?"

I'd positioned myself directly behind Suzy so that I couldn't see what was happening in the sink. "Yeah?"

"What do you know about the driveway? Near the road? That bunch of pine trees?"

"What do I know about it?"

"Has anything happened to you there?"

"Not exactly there."

"Because that was where my nose started bleeding."

I opened my mouth to tell her that those were the very same trees that cursed my bedroom, but she was already onto her next question.

"Where are your roommates?"

"When I told them you guys were coming, they both left."

She was silent for a while as she rolled up some of the paper towel. I guessed that the worst was over. "That's too bad. Evan, it's starting. I haven't even—" At this point, she lowered her voice to a harsh, unfamiliar whisper. "Bill Brinkman and the horse with wings. Pegasus—"

"No, no, no. We're leaving right now." But then he paused, his small face mashing up for a fraction of a second. I definitely saw it.

Suzy rose up with the paper towel against her nose. It was already beginning to turn red. She spoke normally again. "It's too late! It's too strong. Chris, what's that room behind you? Quick."

"The family room, we call it."

"Okay, we have to go in there first. I normally like to go over…"

But she faltered here as Evan pulled her toward the front hall. "Come on."

"Tell Chris, Evan." As her big frame pivoted toward the family room, there wasn't much Evan could do to stop her, his tiny hands grappling with and slipping off of her soft roundness.

"For Pete's sake, man! Chris, please! We can't let her do this. It's going to kill her!"

But she'd already wandered past me and through the doorway, where she stood in the middle of the room.

Evan came up next to me, cursing under his breath. I could hear him nervously scraping his fingers against his palms as we watched her. They both seemed overly theatric, as if merely behaving like this somehow made what they were doing real. But I knew I had a real problem, and as far as I could tell, Suzy's blood was real. And even though I could imagine Suzy getting herself so worked up that her nose just spontaneously erupted, I didn't have many other options at this point.

Evan sighed dramatically. "Do you have a pad and pen?"

I could hear Suzy mumbling something, over and over, the cadence hypnotic.

"Hey, is there something to write on around here?! Don't bother listening to her because it's not going to make any sense to you."

We only had a Chinese take-away menu lying around, so I handed it to him along with a pink marker.

He frowned at what I handed him. "I left all my stuff in the car."

When we came up to Suzy, she was vibrating slightly, as if her knees were going to give out. But what was slight for her was considerable for us, because her large body amplified the shaking dramatically. I stared at the side of her behind, spellbound. Once again, even though I knew that there were bad things inside the house, I couldn't help but feel as if Suzy were just working herself into a self-induced trance, her ardent desire to be psychic generating all the paranormal energy she needed. Still, it didn't seem to be for my benefit: if she were fooling anyone, it was mostly herself.

And Evan. I could see that, too. He was earnestly writing down what she was whispering: "San Onofre voodoo doll." He was right; I had no idea what she was meant.

Abruptly, she turned around and walked swiftly through to the dining room, where she once again stopped in the dead center. Her eyes were half-closed, and I knew then what a person who sleeps with their eyes open looks like.

"Ashes. Typewriter. Ashes and typewriter. Curve in the road ashes typewriter."

"Shoot." Evan shook his head about something, but I had to back away. The process was a runaway train.

At this point, she careened out of the dining room and into the parlor, listing slightly. "Catacombs in Rome brown recluse." And she kept going, right out to the front hallway, where she stopped and mechanically pivoted toward the small window by the door. Evan was bent over the Chinese menu, so I was the first to notice that she'd stopped breathing and was just trembling.

"Evan?"

He looked up at her and again, his face contorted. Suzy was aghast, her eyes seeing something beyond the window, beyond the yard, and this came as a surprise to Evan. "She's not saying anything."

"She's not breathing!"

As soon as Evan made a move toward her, she broke from the episode and turned toward the stairs, going up halfway, then turning around and returning to the hallway. I imagined the sight of Evan and me racing behind her, up and then right back down, and I could only think of the Marx Brothers. If she had a heart attack, it wouldn't be the house; it would be her erratic, frantic behavior.

"Candy cane!" But she was already heading toward the back hallway.

Evan nodded emphatically. "That's what I thought."

She threw open Alphonse's door and barged in, whimpering once she'd gotten inside. "Oh, oh. Lilacs." This room seemed to make her sad, and we paused here, a trio of mourners. I jumped when she rushed past me and through the kitchen to the back hallway, passing the next door in the hall and then pausing at Nicole's. Here, she quaked, facing the closed door, and a wail slowly built in her lungs until she was screeching.

Strangely, Evan didn't seem at all perturbed by this, and only scribbled on the menu, apparently timing her on his digital watch.

It was only when she whispered, "Ram van," that he looked up, frowned at her and then frowned at the door.

Suzy's nose had started to bleed again, and it was dripping down her neck. Evan made a motion to wipe it with the wad of paper towels she was still holding to her face, but she mechanically turned and hurried back toward the front door. I assumed she was going to go upstairs, but she began to pull on the door to the basement. It seemed locked, which relieved me enormously, as I still hadn't mustered the courage to go down there. But her most violent jerk freed it, and she disappeared down the dark stairway. A blast of fetid, underground air hit us, but there was something else, too, a sweet, burned smell that I couldn't identify. Evan hurried after her, but I stood at the top of the stairs, knowing that whatever was down there would make everything worse. I just knew it.

"Chris!" Evan was hissing up at me, now. "Come on!"

"I'm not really comfortable going down there. You guys go ahead and let me know what's up."

"Jiminy Christmas! Are you kidding me? Get down here!"

"That's okay."

"Okay?! We're here because you..." But then he stopped, and a moment later, I could hear him gagging. Then he threw up. The entire time, Suzy was repeating a phrase over and over again, which sounded like "Oreo nice."

The heavy squeaking on the stairs told me that Suzy was coming back up. When she emerged in the gray light of the hallway, she was covered in cobwebs and grit, and a red bloom was spreading on her pink blouse.

"You're really bleeding—" But she pushed past me before I could finish the sentence, still deep in her trance, if that was really what was happening. I realized a second later that the dirt was sticking to her face because she was sweating so profusely.

This time, she didn't hesitate on the staircase. She was on the second floor before Evan even made it to out of the basement.

He looked exhausted. "What is wrong with you people?"

"What do you mean?"

But his head pivoted one way, then the other. "Where is she?"

"She went upstairs."

"She can't take all of this running around!" And he pushed past me, too, racing up the stairs.

I brought up the rear, wondering what they'd seen in the basement and knowing that I'd be unable to ever ask them. I could hear Evan's light footfall farther down the hallway and knew that he was trying to find Suzy, but her weird chanting had evaporated. She'd disappeared.

"Suzy?" I opened the door to my room and was immediately confronted by the warning on the wall, and its black outline seemed to have grown even heavier, more definite. The size and shape of the trees were a testament that all of this was futile, a message sent from the past to this very second. It was an indicator of frustration and loss.

The symbols also made clear where Suzy was, where I guess I knew she'd been all along, and I called out to Evan.

He appeared a second later, panting. "Where is she? Is she all right?"

Wordlessly, I left my room and strode out into the hall. I could almost feel her gravity through the door to the little room near the front staircase where I'd found Nicole the night before.

"She's going to be face down on the floor, scratching at the baseboard."

"What?!" And Evan pushed me out of the way and opened the door. Of course, I was right.

"Suze? Suze!" Once again, his little hands grabbed onto the gradual curves of her body, unable to gain any useful purchase. "Honey, let's just get out of here, okay?"

I found myself wishing they would do just that, knowing now that this was all just a doomed exercise. But she would still have to complete the sequence of actions. I knew that much.

And sure enough, Suzy rose, sightless, and walked down the hall to the second bedroom on the right, the one with the stickers. Evan was directly behind her, but I didn't want to see what she was doing in there, so I paused just shy of the door.

"Suzy!" Evan sounded incensed and scared all at once.

"Evan? Is she taking off her clothes?"

For a moment, I could only hear the quiet grunts of a struggle, then no sound.

Finally, I heard Evan gasp for air, and Suzy emerged from the door. She had removed her top, and her huge breasts swung over the mound of her stomach, covered in blood.

"Suzy, man, come on!" Evan staggered out behind her, his face and hair smeared with her blood, too. He looked gruesome. But instead of following her, he grabbed my arms.

"We've got to stop her! She isn't even talking or anything, it's like she's—how did you know what she was going to do up here?"

"One of my roommates was sleepwalking and did the same thing. It's some kind of ritual, maybe—"

He looked nervously over my shoulder down the black hall into which Suzy had just disappeared. "So is that all there is to it?!"

"I woke Nicole up in there."

"So?"

"So I don't know if that's the end of it."

"Suzy!" And again, I chased after Evan, who was chasing after his wife.

She was in the bathroom, turned toward the door and calmly waiting for us. She was actually smiling, and her bright teeth contrasted sharply with the blood on her lips and chin. I could see this, and the fact that her eyes were closed, because she'd turned on the light.

Evan grabbed her arms, his fingers disappearing into the fat there. "Suzy, let's just go now. We've done enough. Suzy?"

Although her eyes were closed, her head seemed to follow me as I entered the room, as if she were staring at me through her eyelids. She was ignoring Evan, so I approached to help. "Hey, Suzy, maybe Evan's right. This is all a little crazy—"

She slapped me across the face, hard, and then frowned. "You tricked us and destroyed us but it's going to be so much worse for you." Her voice sounded so light and calm, nothing like the scratchy whispering she'd been doing, that if her eyes weren't closed, I would've believed that she was conscious of what she'd just done.

"Uhh—" But before I could get anything else out, she pushed past me and back down the hallway.

Evan snatched my arm and shook it. "We've got to stop this. If we both grab her and pull her outside, she'll probably snap out of it."

"Okay." But then I heard steps creaking. I hoped for a moment she was headed downstairs, but she wasn't. "She can't go up there. It's even crazier."

"What do you mean, crazier?"

"Intense. It's too much. I don't know. We've got to get her out of there."

But she'd already reached the third-floor hallway before we'd started up the stairs, and I could hear her racing around the two blind rooms up there, the floor banging with each step.

"What is she doing?!" Evan's voice was cracking now; he'd been pushed to his limit.

"Let's just get her out of there." I could hear her moaning as she ran from room to room and knew just what she was experiencing. The house was winning.

But it all stopped when we reached the top of the stairs. I turned on the light, and there she was, standing in the center of the hallway, her head limp, her frizzy perm hanging down, as the blood dripped from her nose onto the flesh between her breasts.

There was something about her that froze Evan and me to the spot. Approaching her was dangerous, for some reason. Slowly, her head rose and then continued until it was facing the ceiling, her mouth gaping open. She was standing directly underneath the panel to the attic.

Suzy began to cry then, and her face, which was normally so pleasant, now shattered with pain. This seemed to rouse Evan from his inertia, and he grabbed my arm, pulling me toward her. "Come on!"

Just as we were about to reach her, though, she turned and ran down the hall, the walls banging with her footfall. Considering her size, her speed was almost supernatural, and I was so astonished that I was a few seconds slower than I could have been. It was a good thing, though, because without even slowing down, she ran face-first into a wall and was flung violently onto her back. The floor screamed at this, and I could hear some plaster cracking downstairs.

"No." Evan came up to Suzy and was whimpering her name over and over as he attempted to revive her. I was about to join him when I looked up and realized that she hadn't run into a wall or a door or anything else in the middle of the corridor. She'd been thrown back by nothing more than the nonmaterial divide between the original part of the house and the hall that had been tacked on later. The third-floor addition had physically rejected her.

"We've got to get her downstairs. Grab her legs." Suzy still appeared to be unconscious, or possibly worse, so I didn't want to argue with Evan. As I attempted to stretch my hands around her ankles, though, I knew that the two of us wouldn't be able to lift her, let alone get her down two flights of stairs. Plus, I hadn't been back on the third floor since my first visit, and I felt it straining to excrete me, too. It was as if I were inside of a threat, as if it occupied all the space around me and therefore possessed every opportunity to harm me.

But I tried to help Evan move Suzy. He strained and grunted, but we could only manage to slide her to the top of the stairs.

"Maybe if I got a piece of cardboard or a rug or something, we could put it under her and then slide her down that way?" I'd moved a few, large pieces of furniture in my time. "But we should really call 911—"

"We need to get her out of here! She'll be all right once we get her out of here! Come on!"

"We can't *carry* her down! Let me see if I can find something to slide her on."

"We've got to get her out now! She's dying!"

She was turning gray, and I couldn't help but wonder if she weren't already dead.

Evan was backing down the stairs now, trying his best to keep her level. My choices were to pull on her legs, walk away, or help.

We'd gotten her about halfway down the stairs when the weight became too much for Evan, and his knees buckled. He lost his footing and collapsed underneath Suzy's back, the two of them crashing to the bottom of the stairs. It was terrible, standing there, grasping the rail and watching this take place. I knew it was the house's doing, but it was mine, too. It was mine.

Amazingly, Suzy suddenly jumped up and ran off, leaving Evan in a broken pile. He was screaming in pain when I reached him.

"Evan, what hurts?"

"Is she gone? Is she all right?"

"Yeah. I think she's okay, but I'm worried about you right now."

Their presence was so substantial that I could almost see the family coming up the stairs. And they weren't the kind of family that would appreciate finding an injured stranger thrashing around outside of their bedrooms. They were the kind of family that slaughtered young animals frequently and had no time for pain or emotions or charity. I could tell that even the children had had all the whimsy beaten out of them, their lives just rows of muddy furrows and muddy stalls. In fact, the young ones were the most dangerous of all because while they'd learned not to experience joy, they hadn't yet learned to conserve their energy by moderating their cruelty. That's how close they were getting to me. And while they'd never materialized before, I could tell that they were very near the gauzy muslin that separated our times.

Still, I didn't tell Evan to stop groaning.

"My chest, I guess my ribs. And my arm. The right one."

Sure enough, when he tried to raise it, I could clearly see that his arm was broken between his wrist and elbow.

Injured people aren't supposed to be moved, so I felt for my phone. "Okay, I'm going to call 911—"

"No, no, no!"

"Why not?"

"Because I don't want you to!"

"But your arm looks like it might be… hurt."

"I can fix that up myself."

"And your ribs?"

"Just get me down to the car, and we'll be out of your hair."

"But you're hurt, and Suzy might be, too!"

"Look. Suzy and I are kind of off the grid."

"I don't know what that means—"

"I don't care if you do or you don't! Just help me downstairs!"

It was almost as if there were still a great weight on Evan, and he could only thrash around on a horizontal plane while trying to get up. Once more, I had little choice, so I grabbed his good arm, and together, we gradually got him to sit up and then stand. I could see through to my bathroom mirror for a moment, which again held up to me the trees on my wall, now a kind of map of the afternoon, all false starts and dead ends. I could see, somewhere in all that black that had bled through to me, the future mapped out, too. And it was my future, although I couldn't quite make out exactly what that would be. But I knew that the longer I remained in the house, the more it seeped into me, its language and motives and will. Soon enough, I'd be able to read that map perfectly. And even a person exposed to the image for the first time would see that mine was not a promising future at all.

"Suze!" Evan couldn't raise his voice, and his breathing was shallow and strained.

"I'll find her. Don't worry. Let's just get you out to the car."

"Where is she? She can't be here, anymore."

"I know. I'll get her, I promise."

It was very difficult for Evan to move, and any bouncing had to be smoothed out, so going down the last flight of stairs was slow going.

"What's going on here? I've never seen her react like that to anything."

"I don't know. It's the house."

"She looked really bad up there! God, where is she? Suzy?"

But he couldn't take deep breaths, so I yelled for her until we made it to the front door, which was slightly ajar. She was standing next to the car, an oil-stained towel wrapped around her shoulders. She was just looking down at the mud pensively, the saturated paper towels once again at her nose.

"She's never going to be the same."

I knew that Evan was right, and again, I sensed my responsibility in what had just happened, a cold, heavy weight in my stomach. None of us would ever be the same. Standing there once more, in that spot near the front door, I came to understand the little window a bit better. Its prism of dread consisted of the accumulation of the residue of all the views it had framed in the past. Most of them had been just as dispiriting as this one, and they'd continue to be, to the point that now even the looking turned what was seen outside into something worse than it was, a kind of light beam that no longer just illuminated, but altered trajectories and reconstituted matter into something more painful and less viable, somehow. Furthermore, the things I could see through that window were made worse by my looking, so I quickly turned my eyes away, aware now of how the house had been changing since it was built, how it had used up all of its inhabitants to mutate into something active, deliberate.

"Suze!" Evan tenderly walked out to her, his broken arm stiff at his side.

Astonishingly, she just looked up, any trace of the trauma she'd endured gone. "What happened to you?!"

"Don't touch me! I hurt my ribs and arm."

"We've got to get you to a doctor! What happened?" Now she was looking at me. "What happened to my shirt?"

"It was the house." I didn't know what else to say.

"Did I go in? I don't even remember going in there. And my nose." But Evan had reached the car and was gingerly lowering himself into the passenger seat, so she couldn't stare at me any longer. As she hurried around to the driver's door, I imagined her being gone, of them both heading up the coast, and it was too much for me.

"Can I come with you? Please! I can't live here, anymore. More people are going to be hurt, and if I stay, it'll be my fault, too. I have to leave now. I think you might be my only chance."

Suzy started to say something, but her eyes fell on Evan, who was nearest me. He glared out the windshield and up the driveway toward freedom.

"Evan, I think—"

"No. We can't. Sorry, Chris, but we can't."

"Evan! Come on—"

He turned to Suzy. "Will you listen to me, please? Please. I know what happened in there. What you said."

Her eyes roamed over his face, oblivious to the source of the tension she saw there. "Chris, grab a few things and come on back out. Whatever I said, it can't be that bad."

"Thank you, Suzy."

It was actually easier to go back in there, to be inside of it and feel the forces pulling on me, making me feel things, suspect things. Even when the presence from my room suddenly flung itself at my chest, now only a few molecules from making contact with my skin, I only momentarily paused on the stairs before pushing on, through the vestiges of the family as they went about their business upstairs: normal, everyday farm things and sinister things, too. But my decision to leave had drained from the entity much of what was menacing about it, and I could feel it feebly dissipate as I approached my room, the house already closing up the wound—the scratch—that had been me.

Still, the scribbled-out trees on my wall were too much to look at. I kept my eyes from them as I gathered a few things, knowing that their cryptic power was increasing, just like the other forces in the house that over the years had stolen power. They would continue on, undeterred, until reaching a point at which they could no longer fester unseen. I did not want to be there when they ruptured.

My tremendous sense of relief was moderated, though, by my concern for Nicole and Alphonse. I was beginning to recognize that their denial, their attempts to ignore what was happening to us, was a kind of offering to the house, and this only provided more of the kind of energy it needed to do them further harm. I had no idea what I would do once I was past the stand of trees that stood outside my window, that borderline with the regular world, but I knew that once out there, I'd have more power to help my roommates untangle themselves from the morass that was Penobscot Road. I wasn't a coward; I was a friend. I wasn't running away; I was getting away. I'd squarely faced the forces of the house, and although something of myself had been taken from me in there, in those rooms and corners and shadows, I'd also gained something: I was finally running my own life. So I would be the one responsible for the rescue of our family, and once I'd gotten Alphonse and Nicole out of the house, they would finally appreciate this. Appreciate me.

I hadn't experienced anything like joy in years, so it shocked me then, blooming inside me as I foresaw my new role within my group, despite the terrible pictogram behind me, despite the faceless people wandering closer and closer to me on the other side of my door, despite the house and its plans for us. Over my life, I'd learned to forget why people *wanted* to be alive, rather than just submitting to everything, and this realization put my experience in Oregon into a completely different context. I'd needed to battle with something like this, to outsmart it, in order to develop as a human being. Living in the house had been terrible, but it was over now and I hadn't been completely ruined. Someday soon, I'd see that it had all been worth it.

At that moment, I was absently studying the stand of trees facing the house, and they indicated to me that the happiness I felt was much more powerful than I could have imagined. Because it was precisely the ingredient—some kind of fuel or payment—needed to decipher a particular truth, something I'd managed so far to suspect only vaguely. And as my pleasure was used up, sucked out of me by the house, I finally understood what had been bothering me about the trees on my wall: although they'd been drawn years before I'd moved in, they mirrored what the trees outside my window looked like now. Those pines must have grown and changed over the decades since my wallpaper had gone up, so the sketch had always been meant for me.

As the last vestiges of pride and hope drained from me, I heard Suzy and Evan's car quickly drive out through those sad woods and away from me and my house. Everything that was about to happen in Penobscot Road had been and always would be inevitable.

The bag in my hand dropped to the ground, and I fell onto my bed, suddenly too fatigued to think or feel or want anything more.

*   *   *

I awoke to the sound of Alphonse and Nicole at the front door. Everything had changed. With the defeat of my will and acceptance of the house's came a steadiness that I would've called peace if it weren't so malevolent. I finally understood then that I had to abandon myself just as Evan and Suzy just had, and if they had been able to do it, to leave me here, writhing in the middle of this maelstrom, so could I.

I also realized that Alphonse and Nicole had forsaken me much earlier than I'd realized.

"Chris!" I was already at the top of the stairs when Nicole called for me. "Where did all of this blood come from? Are you okay?"

"Suzy had a nose bleed."

"Oh, for Christ's sake." Nicole had been careful to give the impression that she didn't believe I'd really invited a psychic over to the house. She came upstairs and began to pull my sweater back from my wrists while running her eyes briefly over whatever parts of my skin were exposed. "Did you cut yourself?"

Part of abandoning myself was abandoning Nicole. "The bleeding's stopped."

"Good. Then you can clean it up." She turned around and headed back toward the front door, speaking over her shoulder. "But help us out here first. We bought some chairs to go with the dining room table for whenever we get a dining room table. From an estate sale."

A dead person's furniture seemed especially appropriate, and so I threw on some boots and headed outside. It was worse out here because I could actually see, could feel freedom so close by, a convict standing outside the prison walls waiting to be shot. I grabbed one of the old chairs they'd managed to stuff into the back seat.

"There's blood in there?" Alphonse did believe that Suzy and Evan had come over, but I could only reply: "I'll clean it up." Nicole was right behind me.

"Oh." They shared one of their knowing looks—which I should have been sharing with Alphonse—and we hauled the chairs inside. I could tell that they'd had some sort of conversation in the car about me because the atmosphere among us was even tenser than before they'd left, although I had no idea what conclusions they'd reached. I intended to find out from Alphonse.

Drizzle had followed the path of my backbone and soaked into the cloth gathered at my belt. I welcomed the wetness because it made me just as uncomfortably damp as the dining room, and I wanted to feel at home, part of the force there. "They're nice chairs. How much did they cost?"

"Only ten bucks apiece." Apparently, Nicole wanted to position them around the table that we didn't as yet have, so we set the chairs up in a circle. It was strange to see them like that, disconcerting. But it was right, too, because I knew we'd never eat in the room. It was for different things.

We each sat down, looking at each other over the phantom table top.

"Have you guys been down to the basement yet?"

Nicole and Alphonse looked at each other. Nicole spoke for them both. "Why do you ask?"

"Because Evan and Suzy went down there. Whatever it was that they saw freaked them out pretty badly. Evan threw up. He was pretty upset."

Nicole crossed her arms. "Did you really have people in here?"

"They left before I could find out what was down there."

"So you've never been down there?"

"Are you guys doing things that I don't know about?"

Nicole rose, shaking her head. "Fuck, Chris. We're working, we're cleaning, we're fixing up the place. We're fucking busy! The question is: what are *you* doing that we don't know about? Because you're going from weird to creepy really fast, lurking around this place all the time. And..."

She seemed to think better of something. The old Chris would have joined her in the denial, but the new Chris couldn't do that. The new Chris had to sink completely into whatever was required and remain there until it was over.

"And what?"

"And we're finding some stuff that's a little fucking creepy, too."

"Such as?"

"Such as that tea set. And that weird picture on your wall."

They'd gone into my bedroom? "And of course, you think all of that was me."

"And the old syringe on my pillow."

Now I got up. I had to get Alphonse alone. Nicole was still too closed off to what was happening.

"Whatever."

"And, god, Chris, we know about you pissing on the floor in the downstairs bathroom. We both use it! It's fucking disgusting, but we're more worried than anything else. Because something isn't right."

"I know!" I looked over at Alphonse, who continued to look at his hands.

"With you!"

"With all of us, Nicole." But she wasn't ready, so I didn't also say that turning on each other was the worst thing we could do because Penobscot Road wanted that. I didn't say that the most we could do would be to tie ourselves to the mast and occasionally throw a prayer in one another's direction. I didn't say that our old relationship was over, that we'd been broken apart by the house, but that giving in to selfish motives was exactly what we had to fight.

Her face softened. "I just don't want you to get any more upset, Chris. I mean, there's, like, eccentric, and then there's fucking state institution. How about I see if I can find you someone to talk to in town?"

Her motive wasn't completely selfish. "Actually, that would be good."

"Awesome! Thank god! I think you're just having some issues with adjusting—" But I was already leaving the room. I would never be able to get Alphonse alone, so I needed to take a different tack.

I had to find out what Suzy had meant while she was in her trance, what they'd experienced in the basement. And tracking down a psychologist would keep my roommates busy for a while.

As I headed up the stairs, Nicole shouted out, "You owe us twenty for the chairs."

After everything was over, maybe Alphonse and Nicole would understand how much they owed me. But even that didn't matter, anymore, because soon, we'd be parted forever. Our relationship was already dead and, in fact, was now something very like a cadaver, viable only in appearance, which was also rapidly declining. If I had been the old Chris, I would've been in mourning, but now, I just wanted us to salvage whatever little was left of the individuals Nicole and Alphonse had once been. I'd lost faith in our relationship just as I'd lost faith I could do anything to save myself, as I had allowed too much of the house inside me. But I still hoped I could save my friends.

Instinctively, I also knew that uncovering exactly what was generating all of our misfortune would make it finish more quickly because complete knowledge led to termination. What I couldn't say was whether accelerating the process meant escape or annihilation for Nicole and Alphonse. Either way, I just wanted it over.

So I had to make another trip to Seville.

The Ninth Day

October in Oregon was like having summer ripped away from me forever. I knew that fall in Penobscot Road would continue to grow colder, darker, that the dawns would break over the mountains like increasingly feeble afterthoughts. But June had been pushed so far away that it joined the ranks of all the other things that were impossible for me now. And summertime hadn't just been eradicated from Pacific Bay. The essence of that season, a kind of relaxation into the environment, had been taken from me no matter where I'd find myself when the days lengthened and temperatures increased. The foundations of my old reality were being steadily, meticulously removed.

But maybe you know exactly what I mean. Maybe you've experienced this yourself. I have only your continued participation in all of this as an indication of who you are. Of course, the fact that you soldier on with me in reconstructing all of this tells me all I want and need to know about you because it tells me that you have something to lose, now, too. So thank you for that.

Since we are in such perfect concert, you must have correctly predicted what I was about to do when I asked you what my next move should be. Remember? You paused then, carefully considering the issue because your increasing respect and affection for me could allow no less. I know that you would've never simply passed over the request, more interested in what happened next than in truly joining me in my struggle. What would I do if I thought you were capable of something like that?

No, you understand me so well now that we are almost of one mind. So you already know why I gathered up my old bicycle lock, Nicole's talcum powder and the string: it's what *you* wanted to do at that exact moment, to actively look for evidence that would convince Alphonse and Nicole to leave with me, just as Evan had suggested. And he'd been right. The internet was packed with all sorts of ghost tests.

So the night before, I'd sprinkled the talcum powder on the hallway floor to reveal any footprints in the morning. I was sure that the family was now passing back and forth between dimensions, and proof of their existence would go a long way with Alphonse, if not Nicole.

I used the lock to secure the room where sleepwalkers would scratch the baseboard, the first location of the strange, night ritual. This way, when Nicole, or the next victim, found him or herself in a trance at the door, the rite could progress no further—hopefully leading to consciousness and understanding, instead.

And I tied one end of the string to my toe and the other to my bedpost. If they told me that I was the one sleepwalking, I wanted to know if it was true.

See? Everything was exactly as you predicted. We've achieved a profound state of mutual understanding, uncanny proof of the true depth of our relationship.

Yet you don't know what happened next:

When I awoke on the morning of the ninth day, I discovered that the string had vanished. And in the corridor outside my bedroom door, the talcum powder had been carefully swept away, the bicycle lock removed. It was devastating to find that Alphonse and Nicole had been so altered that they were beginning to work against me—or really you *and* me, because it had been just as much your plan as mine. How would they explain their actions? I was so aghast that I didn't even want to hear what they had to say.

So it was a relief to be back on the road to Seville. It proved that against all odds, my last, real act as a hero would be to save my roommates. But I was glad, too, to be away from Nicole and Alphonse because I no longer was certain what they were capable of.

This is my best chance yet to prove to you how worthy I am of your devotion:

Earlier, I'd stolen the car keys from Nicole's dresser, no longer concerned about smoothing things over. But I was painfully nervous. After I knew she'd left her room, I pushed into it, fighting against the mixture of familiarity and spiteful malevolence there, nauseated by the cloying old scent hanging in the air that was a mutation of Nicole's set of odors. I replayed the previous evening in my mind, how she'd suggested that I needed help, that our only problem was me. One of her eyebrows had been raised a little, almost out of spite, something I'd never seen her do before, and I realized that she was changing physically, too, the way she moved and her expressions joining the ingrained habits of a more aggressive personality.

Oddly, the claustrophobic smells in her room were somehow helping me decode these foreign movements and inflections I'd been too upset to notice earlier. In fact, ever since she'd moved into that beige room at the end of the hall, more and more of our communal property had been ending up there, some nebulous form of control. There were piles of belongings in each corner, and smaller items scattered on the dresser and floor. Worse yet, the odd amalgam of her energy and that of the old lady had become an almost physical barrier against anyone brave enough to attempt retrieving anything inside it. The new Nicole was becoming dangerous.

I left the house vowing to investigate this phenomenon when I returned, too. I believed that the sooner I uncovered everything, the sooner the house would do its worst to me and be done with them. It was the only thing I had left to believe in, and it proved to be the last.

Evan and Suzy must have seen me approaching because I heard their television very slowly lose volume as I walked up through the mud, and I realized just how much damage I'd done to them both. Now, I had come to do more. It was terrible, really, but I'd recently learned that for some victims, the process of victimization itself becomes demystified, and the fear of inflicting pain on others is no longer the unacceptable boundary it once was. I was also desperate.

"Evan?! Suzy? Look, I'm not mad or anything about you leaving me there. I'm not. And I'm not looking for you to save me or anything. I have to stay there until all of this is over, one way or the other. You know that, and now, so do I."

I could feel their attentive listening as if it were radiating out of every crack in that house.

"And I'm really sorry about your ribs and arm, Evan. And for any injuries to you, too, Suzy. I honestly didn't know that was going to happen. Well, I knew something bad was going to happen. I did. So I have to take some responsibility. And I'm sorry."

Just as I could sense their listening, I could also tell that my little speech wasn't working. Whatever Evan had told Suzy in the car that had convinced her to abandon me to the house was still potent enough to suppress her goodwill. I had to try a different tack.

"Look at what happened to you both, and you were only there for half an hour! My roommates and I actually *live* inside it! And something worse is going to happen to us if I don't figure out what's going on. I just came to find out what those things you said mean, Suzy, because I think they can help me. That's all, I swear!"

Silence. Because it had grown almost completely numb, I could only watch my fist as I knocked again, knowing how knocking should feel, rather than actually feeling it. The worst thing about the constant rain was having wet hands because it made me a part of it, spreading around that ice-cold drizzle every time I touched anything, a participant in making the place just a little more miserable. And there was nowhere for me to wipe my hands dry, no way to prevent the occasional drop from running down my arm whenever I raised it.

"You guys knew the risks, too! I'll take responsibility, but I can't take all of it. And you kind of owe me this, don't you? Look, you did the work, already; now all you have left to do is help me. Because when something bad happens to us, you're going to feel responsible if you don't!"

The door opened, and a young, thin woman briefly inspected me. "Who are you?"

"Chris Szabo."

"What are you here for?"

"Are Suzy and Evan here?"

She considered me for another moment, her expression dark, slippery. Finally, she decided that she could talk to me, but only on the porch. "I'll be right back. Okay, Dan?" She shouted this over her shoulder, but somehow, I knew she was alone. "Why do you want to know?"

"They were at my house yesterday. And Evan got hurt. I wanted to make sure he was okay."

"I just heard what you said."

"And they have some information I need, too. About my house. It's really important. Do you know where they are?"

She frowned, and I could see that she was not only humorless, but also not particularly intelligent. The smell of warm pot smoke further blurred her vicinity.

"It sounds like you know more than I do."

But this was all she said. I was unsure how to respond, her greasy hair and heavy eyelids irritating me more than they should have.

I held out my hand. "It sounds like maybe we could help each other out."

She glanced flatly at it for a moment before pushing hers, dry and limp, into it, and I could tell that she hadn't had the opportunity to shake many hands in her short life. The old Chris would have been pleased to meet someone who initially seemed in many respects so inferior, as I usually came from such a manifold position of weakness. These had been a rare kind of encounter for me.

The new Chris, however, was just annoyed. "And your name is…?"

"Carrie."

"Nice to meet you, Carrie. Do you think we can help each other out?"

"I don't know."

"Why don't we try? I'll answer your questions, and then you can answer mine."

She remained unconvinced. "So you don't know where they went to?"

"Do we have a deal?"

Apparently, my last challenge broke down whatever cloudy defenses Carrie had erected. I also suspected that she'd remained too long away from the bong for her liking. She disappeared back into the dark house, and I followed. Everything looked more or less just as I had last seen it.

She sat in Evan's chair, the television still flashing light into the room. I sat down on the couch, positioning myself parallel with her and hoping this would keep things a little less adversarial.

"So what questions do you have for me, Carrie?"

"Do you know where they're at?"

"No, but maybe I can help you figure that out."

"How?"

"Well, what do you know? Why are you here?"

"Evan emailed me and told me to, like, empty the refrigerator and turn it off and shut off the propane and shit like that because they're not coming back."

"Are you their neighbor or something?"

"Evan's my uncle. Do you smoke?"

"Not really. Did he say why he wanted you to do all of that?"

"He also told me to take all of their weed." And as if to confirm this statement, she lit the bong up again.

"So you've been basically closing down the house."

"I'm going to."

I wasn't convinced this was going to happen anytime soon, but I continued. "So they're not coming back for a while."

"I don't think they're ever coming back. He said they're never coming back."

"Did he say why?"

"No. It must be because of you, I bet. What happened?"

"They came over to my place, and Evan got hurt."

"How?"

"Well, Suzy fell on him by accident."

"Because what you were saying outside. It sounded, like, more than that." There was a flicker of intelligence in her eyes. "It's not any of that psychic shit, is it?"

What did I have to lose if I told her the truth? I was beginning to suspect that she might know more than she seemed to, that there were other motives behind all the haze. The question was, were our motives at cross purposes, or could I be honest?

"Yeah, it was. I'm having some problems at my new house."

"Like what?"

"It's hard to explain. The house makes you feel things. It puts ideas into your head."

"Really?"

"And I'm getting worried about me and my roommates."

"Why don't you move?"

"My roommates don't want to, yet. They don't totally see what's happening, and I can't just leave them there."

"You sound like you really believe it."

"You would, too, if you were inside that place for a little while."

She took another drag, and I could feel her moving farther away from me.

"What did Suzy and Evan say it was?"

"They didn't. Evan got hurt, and they left. That's why I came."

"You're not from Seville."

"Pacific Bay. We just moved there from Sacramento a little over a week ago."

Her eyes focused on the air in front of her for a moment. "Suzy's from Pacific Bay."

"I know. She told me."

"Where's your house?" She took a lungful immediately after saying this, as if to draw attention away from her interest.

"Outside of town. On Penobscot Road."

She slowly blew out the pot smoke, again as if to camouflage a more pointed response. "You know they're fake, don't you?"

"Evan and Suzy?"

"They're full of shit. They convince people that there's something going on in their house, and then they go and Suzy makes up all this shit on the spot. Nonsense words, and then Evan supposedly translates it like it actually means something, and then they charge you to clean the air in the house or whatever. It's all like a total scam. I mean, Evan's my uncle, and I love him and everything, but he's a fucking con artist."

The acrid smoke was becoming oppressive, and the heat that radiated off of the wood stove to my immediate right pushed me back onto the sofa.

"How do you know?"

"Fucking everybody knows." She put the bong down beside her and fiddled with the lighter in her hand. "Around here, anyway."

The little cabin was so overcrowded that there were only narrow passageways through the furniture to get around, and I began to wonder how anyone could escape quickly enough if they were trapped there. As I re-gauged my distance to the front door, which seemed farther away now, I began to suspect that my awareness was becoming more altered than Carrie's, somehow. It had to be a contact high.

Then I realized that she'd been studying me shrewdly, the lighter circling around and around in her hand. "So what did Suzy say when she was in her 'trance' or whatever the hell she told you it was?"

I didn't know how to answer. "I don't really remember."

"You didn't write nothing down?"

"Evan did." My responses felt like little hemorrhages now.

"Oh, he did, huh? He must have had one of his stupid yellow pads with him."

"So I guess you're not going to be able to figure out where they went until they get in touch with you." Getting up was harder than it should have been, and I swayed a little after standing up. "They don't even have a cell phone?"

"Are you kidding? They hate technology. Look at this place. They use public phones." And her eyes scanned the surfaces of the room carefully. I could tell that she was looking for something.

"Yeah. Well, thanks for your time, Carrie."

"Sure, I guess. So what kinds of things are, like, happening in your house?" She remained in Evan's chair, the TV flickering in her pupils, seemingly too high or bored to bother accompanying me to the door.

The farther I got from her, the clearer my mind became. "Oh, you know, the usual. Bumps in the night. Weird creaking noises. I guess I shouldn't have called Evan and Suzy."

"It is what it is." Now she directed her eyes toward the mute television. "But didn't you say that the house makes you feel things or something like that?"

I was at the door now. "Yeah, scared is what it makes me feel. But now that I know that it was just a scam, I feel better."

"You should. Bye." She didn't even bother to turn her head in my direction.

"Yeah, thanks."

I'd anticipated that the freezing drizzle would feel clarifying after my time in the hot, dark cabin, but it didn't. It was just another extreme, waking me up, but only to its own kind of oppression. Nothing seemed to have a chance to dry off in Oregon; it was as if everything in it were being held down, a kind of choking water torture. I thought of the smoggy, gray dust that coated everything in Sacramento and heard a soft groan leave me.

It was hard to turn around in the driveway, but eventually, I made it back down the hill. There, I parked, and climbed back up to the house, hiding myself as best I could among the dripping foliage. The window in the living room was bare, and I couldn't cross to the house without being seen, so I waited about ten minutes while I watched Carrie keenly search drawers and surfaces there. Finally, she passed into the kitchen, and I sprinted to the front wall of the house, the mud splashing across the cuffs of my jeans. From this angle, I could see Carrie rifling through a mound of paperwork on the kitchen table. Her eyes were wild, her fingers trembling but still nimble, such a profound contrast to her earlier behavior. She looked like a different person, and although it was hard to believe, I preferred the pothead. This woman was disturbingly panicked.

When she seemed convinced that she wouldn't find what she was looking for in the kitchen, she hurried down the corridor and out of sight. I crept around the back of the cabin, where the ground was less trodden and so was soft, deep mud. It clung to my shoes and immediately froze my feet, which hadn't been warm in a while, anyway. By the time I reached the bedroom window, I could hear Carrie shutting the front door.

My car was plainly visible at the bottom of the driveway. If I raced down the hill at that moment, I might've had a chance to move it, but assuming that Carrie was getting into her car, I would've had to have crossed her path. The sound of an ignition turning confirmed my concerns, but I remained rooted to the spot, my shoes three inches sub-merged. I didn't know what to do.

To make matters worse, the presence had been sliding over my skin since I'd left the house that morning. I could tell that it was feeding off of my fear, absorbing the sweat from my skin before it even had the chance to reach my clothing. There had always been a purpose lurking behind the thing's actions, and I sensed that its latest behavior was the first sign of its final plan for me. It was an awful realization to make at that moment, knowing that yet another danger was now standing in my way of saving Nicole and Alphonse. But there was nothing I could about it at the time, so I cast it from my thoughts.

Carrie's tires crunched and splashed down the driveway, and as soon as I was sure that she couldn't see me, I raced back into the woods, knowing that I would never reach my car in time. Sure enough, when I was halfway down, I could hear her car pause for a moment, then suddenly speed off. She only had one road to take for a while, though, so I continued to my car, hoping I could manage to follow her.

When I got in, I was unsure if I could even operate the pedals because of the heavy mud on my shoes, so I threw them into the passenger foot well and drove after Carrie in my socks. Unfortunately, they were soaking wet and slipped off of the clutch and brake so often that I thought I was going to run into the woods on the way down the mountain. In fact, my socks were too slick, and I realized the presence was altering their surface tension, acting as an additional lubricant.

Then I came to a series of switchbacks. At the corners were guardrails, but the straightaways provided nothing to keep a vehicle from slipping a few inches off the pavement and plunging two hundred feet straight down. As I approached the first unsafe portion of the road, the land falling violently away at my right, the entity forced my foot to slide off of the brake, and at the same time, my hands to lose their grip on the steering wheel. The right tires swerved to the edge of the pavement, and then off of it and onto the soft mud of the verge. I frantically pawed at the wheel, scraping it with my nails until I righted the car again. On the next straightaway, which provided an even deeper drop on my left side, the presence again caused my feet and hands to be so slick that the car became a careening box of metal around me, veering gradually across the road and toward the fall. My furious jabbing at the brake pedal and scratching at the wheel barely kept me from plunging off the cliff, although I couldn't help scraping against the edge of the next guardrail. Control of the car was then instantly given back to me until the next open drop. I could've stopped the car and gotten out, but I knew that the presence would've only performed other malignant acts upon me.

By the third straightaway, though, I realized that the entity was allowing me to barely avoid falling off the side of the mountain, and my grip on the wheel suddenly became normal again. The presence didn't want me dead, yet; something more obscure was at work.

At the bottom of the hill, I could go left or right. I knew that if I turned right, I'd be headed back to town, so I elected to do that. Seville was small, but I didn't know my way around it and Carrie did, so the chances of finding her seemed slight. And that was assuming that she wasn't driving out of town. Moreover, even if I did manage to catch up with her, how could I keep her from seeing me? The presence could start up with its antics at any time. And how far would I have to go? My low-fuel light had illuminated twenty miles before I'd even reached the area.

A quick glimpse through the pines below me revealed a flash of Carrie's car. It was a relief to know that I'd chosen the right direction, but she was driving much faster than I was and would reach town much sooner. I briefly considered speeding up, but at that exact same moment, my foot slipped off of the clutch, and the car lurched so violently that I hit my head on the top of the steering wheel. The entity wasn't through with me, yet.

After a drive that seemed so haltingly slow that I just assumed I'd lost her, I finally came into town. Our car was so old and beaten up that I could feel the attention it must have been attracting, ghostly stares hitting the exposed areas of my face and hands. I felt utterly exposed to Seville's citizens, all of whom apparently knew Evan and Suzy, and undoubtedly, Carrie. If she were hiding, waiting to follow me, there wasn't much I could do about it. And all the while, the thing continued to feast on my fear, slithering all over my body, enraptured. I was having an awful time trying to determine what to do next.

Driving up and down the streets in the hope that Carrie hadn't left town seemed like the best alternative, and yet I was sure that she'd see me before I saw her. She'd be looking for our car.

Then I considered the contents of the trunk and immediately parked. Before the move to Oregon, Nicole had packed the car with what she understood to be emergency supplies for cold climates, including an old, black coat. It was far too long for me, but it had a hood and looked nothing like my beige windbreaker. I figured that the hood would not only shield my face but might also keep some of the rain from pouring down into my clothing.

Seville was a smaller version of Pacific Bay, but not by much, and winding residential streets snaked off in every direction away from me. I had nothing to go on except for the fact that Suzy and Evan lived up in the hills, so I headed up into the higher elevations and hoped for the best. I was only too aware that a hooded stranger lurking on the side of the road—and presented in full figure by each house's picture window—had to be attracting some attention. It wasn't the kind of place and it wasn't the kind of day to be taking a stroll.

I was hungry and tired; this seemed to disappoint the presence. So, possibly to increase my stress, it began to move in ways that caused me to itch in sudden, random places all over my body. Every few hundred feet, I would stop and manically scratch myself, which had to further concern those residents who caught a glimpse of me. I must have looked insane, and after only a half an hour of this, a police car pulled up beside me.

"Hey, there." He was a kind-looking, older man with a gray moustache. "Can I ask what you're doing?"

The itching suddenly bloomed all over my body as my sweat glands fired up. "Hi. I'm just taking a walk."

"I guess you've been kind of walking up and down all the streets. Are you casing the area?" He said this with a smile.

"I'm actually from Pacific Bay and am thinking about moving here."

"Would you happen to have any identification on you?"

I could feel my jaw tightening from the intense urge to scratch myself, and the strained smile I flashed at the policeman must have been too much as I reached for my pocket. "Actually, why don't you stop what you're doing and put your hands on the roof of the car, okay? Now, I'm not arresting you, but I just want to grab that identification myself, all right?" Without ever taking his eyes from mine, he smoothly emerged from the car and frisked me, pulling my license from my windbreaker.

"I need to get a new one."

"Sacramento. So now, when did you move to Pacific Bay?"

"About a week ago, but it just isn't right for us. I'm sorry, but I'm having an allergic reaction or something, and I really need to scratch myself." The discomfort pushed my voice up an octave.

"Why don't you just hold on a second." He was looking through my wallet. "Are you on meth?"

"No. I'm sorry, I just—" And I scratched my legs and chest and arms and neck in quick succession.

My back was facing the cop, so I didn't see at first that he'd drawn his gun.

"Put your hands back on the cruiser. We're just going to have to take a trip down to the station."

I did as I was told, the itching so intense now that I was actually rubbing against the car.

If I didn't want to be spotted in Seville, this wasn't the way to go about it.

He handcuffed me, put me in the back seat and drove back down toward the beach. I felt as if I were in a movie.

"I think I have hives or something! It's just suddenly gotten so bad." I was at least able to reach some parts of my body with the handcuffs on, but it was so intense now that I was squirming around. "Maybe I should go to the hospital."

He said something into his radio, but I was too overcome to notice what. Then, almost as suddenly as it started, the itching stopped.

And looking up, I saw Carrie's car parked in front of a small, yellow house with dark green shutters that quickly passed from view.

It took about an hour for me to convince the people at the police station that I wasn't an addict or crazy person, and the only reason I was wearing the black coat and hood was because I didn't have an umbrella. The cop who'd arrested me insisted on driving me back to my car (on the surface a conciliatory gesture but in actuality, a way to be sure I really did have a car), so we drove around a while before I spotted it.

"—although other people think his mother was Spanish." He'd been explaining how the town had been named, but I was barely paying attention to him. I still hadn't spotted the yellow house.

"That would explain a lot. You know, I noticed a house with a for-rent sign that looked really nice. It was yellow with green shutters. You don't know anything about that, do you?"

"I don't think so." We'd been parked next to my car for a while, but the officer seemed in no hurry to get rid of me. I must have been the most excitement he'd had in weeks.

"No? Well, I'll see if I can find it." I opened the door.

"Wait, did you say yellow with *green* shutters?"

"Yeah."

"There is a place a couple of blocks over and a little closer to the harbor that's yellow with green shutters. On Monte Cristo, I think. I don't know anything about it, though. But are you sure you want to move here? After all of this?"

He was joking, so I smiled and assured him that it only made me feel safer, even though I couldn't imagine living anyplace where people were arrested simply for behaving a little oddly. No one was ever arrested for that in Sacramento.

He waited until I started my car and drove off before pulling away himself, and he followed me until I turned onto Monte Cristo.

Then I spotted the house. Carrie's car was gone, but there were two trucks in the driveway. There was no for-rent sign, however, so it was a good thing that the policeman hadn't followed me all of the way. I'd been very close to being arrested again.

Without even considering what to do next, I got out of the car and approached the front door. I wasn't even sure what I was looking for, but I had to do something. Of course, that something would probably land me back at the police station.

"Hello, I'm Chris Szabo."

A woman in her fifties had answered the door, and she frowned at me. I wasn't sure what—if anything—Carrie had told her, so I tried my best to instantly assess the situation. She was a little overweight with short brown hair and was very conservatively dressed in beige slacks and a dark green sweater. It looked as if she smoked because of all the small creases that pointed to her lips. She had similar little lines that seemed to indicate that she did a lot of eye-narrowing, too. Overall, my impression was that she wasn't a very joyful person, and I had no idea how to exploit this.

"What do you want?"

"I'm a friend of Carrie's?"

"I don't know any Carrie." And she made a move as if to close the door.

"Oh, oh, wait! That's just what we call her at work. I thought she said she was going to come to see you today. I thought I saw her car..."

"Christine?"

"Yeah, but we don't call her that."

"She ain't working."

"No, I know, but when she did. We called her Carrie."

"At the gas station?"

"Yeah."

"I never seen you there. Why would you call her Carrie?"

"Because we used to always have to carry everything for her."

At this, the woman let loose a loud gaffaw. "Yeah, that's Christine all right." But her scowl soon returned. "So why are you here? You ain't looking for meth, are you? Because if that's the case—"

"No, no, no! I'm just trying to find her."

"She owe you money?"

"Well…"

"She should be home by now."

"That's just it. I don't know where she moved to."

"But you said you talked to her."

"She called me today, but she didn't tell me where she moved to. So I figured I'd try and track her down."

The woman studied me carefully for a minute, my muddy shoes, the soaking black coat over the wind breaker. "Well, you are just completely full of shit, aren't you. But I've got to admit that you tried real hard here. I will admit that. You've got something to do with Evan and Suzy, don't you."

"Yeah."

"They screw you out of some money?"

"No. They just have some information I need."

"Oh! Oh." The woman's eyes glazed over, and I could tell that she was replaying Carrie's recent visit, picking through it for valuable material.

"Why did Christine stop by today? Did it have something to do with Evan and Suzy?"

"Did you follow her?!"

"I just happened to drive by and saw her car here." I would have apologized about deceiving her earlier, but I could tell that refusing to apologize for my bald-faced lies was precisely why she was taking me seriously now.

"God, it's cold out here." She stepped onto her little porch and closed the door behind her. "My husband's going to call the police on you if he hasn't already. If you know Christine, he don't like you."

"I don't, to be honest. I just met her when I went to Evan and Suzy's place."

"That's what I thought." But this was all she said. I was expected to continue.

"I must have said something important to her, because after I left, she started looking for something in their house."

"How do you know that if you left?" And again, she cackled. "No, don't answer that. I feel like I'm dealing with a spy or something. So you probably want to know why she came here."

"Yeah, I do."

"You know that Evan and Suzy believe their own bullshit, don't you? Well, they're the only two. They've been in town for years, sensing this, sensing that. Ghosts and the devil and whatever else they feel like. They just get themselves all worked up, looking like fools. In fact, Suzy got herself so worked up a little while back that she had a heart attack. They're just doing it to themselves. And I'm just as bad because they've been friends of mine for years. Only bit of excitement I'm ever going to get around here. Bob, my husband, he hates them. Absolutely hates them." Strangely, this seemed to please her.

"Is Christine Evan's niece?"

"God, it *is* like a spy movie! Is that what she told you? Because no. She ain't nobody's niece."

"Then what does she have to do with them?"

"She wants to be one of them. She's the only one who believes they're real! She's a trainee, or was before they tried to get out of the whole business. She thinks she has the gift or whatever. About the only thing she's got is the gift of bullshit, though. Just like them. I still think she's a meth addict."

"Why did she come?"

"Well, in case you don't know, the way they work is that Suzy says weird stuff, and Evan translates it. It's usually stuff from their past. They think they hide that from people, but we all got ears. And so Christine came here because she wanted to know what some stuff that Suzy said really means."

She must have found the Chinese menu.

"Did you tell her?"

"Suzy and Evan are friends of mine, but I don't know their weird, little language."

"Christine said that Evan and Suzy left town. Is that true?"

"I couldn't tell you. I mean, we all get together sometimes, but we're not *real* close or anything."

"I need to get in touch with them. It's really important."

She looked me up and down again, her frown deepening. "I'll let them know you came by or whatever, but I don't want to give you their number. Evan's weird about that stuff. He'll kill me."

"Yeah. Sure." I didn't know what to do next. "What did Christine tell you that Suzy said?"

She just looked at me flatly. Finally: "You know, this is fun and all, but I think I need to shut my trap. I think that's just what I need to do."

"Look, I know you don't know me, but I'm really worried about my safety. And my roommates', too. Figuring out whatever Suzy said is the only thing that can help, at this point."

"So you believe their bullshit, too?"

"Suzy knew things that she couldn't have known about my house. I swear. It was real."

I laid myself bare at the woman's feet; my honesty was simple, complete.

She merely pursed her lips. "Yeah, well I've got to go. I'll call them and let them know. Do they have your number?"

I sensed an opportunity. "Not my cell."

"I'll get a pad."

She stepped back into her house and disappeared down a hall to the right, the storm door slamming behind her. On the coffee table six feet in front of me was a cell phone.

Christine had told me that Evan hated technology, but he'd had a website built. And if the woman was going to call Evan and Suzy, and she knew that they weren't at home, they must have had a cell phone.

I quickly opened the door, and stepped inside. I had no idea if the husband was in the room, but as soon as I was sure he wasn't, I grabbed the phone and returned outside. The pneumatic door took a lifetime for me to push closed behind me.

At first, I was going to run away, but I realized that stealing a phone might not be my best move. The Seville police department had all of my information. Instead, I fiddled wildly with the phone to find its list of phone numbers. Eventually, I found an entry for Evan that I knew wasn't his home number.

It wasn't terribly hard to memorize, but at that moment, a cop car pulled up on the street, and the woman returned to the door.

She joined me on the porch, her arms on her hips as she scowled down her front yard. I was reasonably sure she hadn't seen me hide her phone behind my back. We both watched the cop as he approached us.

It was the same one who'd brought me in.

"You are really stirring things up around here." Again, he was smiling at me, but I didn't think he was very happy.

"Did my husband call you?"

"You know, I would've just driven by, but I couldn't help notice that there's no for-rent sign around here."

I threw the most significant look at the woman I could in the circumstances and watched her briefly weigh her options. It was at that precise moment that I simply knew she wouldn't turn me in, and I remember finally exhaling.

I was wrong: "There's never been any for-rent sign here."

"Is that right?"

I squinted up the street, searching for the elusive sign. "Oh, I thought—"

She interrupted. "Look, no laws have been broken. My husband's just a jerk. Chris came here looking for somebody, that's all."

"Lying to an officer of the law isn't exactly legal."

"Well, the real reason was too crazy to say." And she looked at me.

I had no choice: "I think my house is haunted."

Now it was the policeman's turn to weigh his options, and he divided his stare equally between me and the woman. I knew that I was becoming less amusing by the minute, but the woman was clearly telling the truth. If she wasn't worried, maybe the whole thing was a pardonable offense.

"Yeah, well, in the future, you might want to think about just telling the truth right out of the gate. So, Evan and Suzy?"

"Yes." The woman and I replied in unison, and it was the cop's turn to frown.

"Okay. I'm out of here." And he turned on his heels and headed for his cruiser. Over his shoulder: "I don't want any more calls about you, now, Chris. You might want to just get on home."

"I will."

Just as his door shut, the woman turned to me and held out her hand. "You just be sure to tell Evan that I didn't give you his number, all right?"

I returned the cell phone, merely nodding, and she returned inside without another look in my direction.

* * *

I'd planned to call Evan as soon as I was back on the road to Pacific Bay, but my coverage was so bad that I couldn't get a signal a mile outside of Seville. It's easy to say now how stupid I'd been not staying in Seville while I made the call, but I decided to wait until I returned home. Not only was I eager to get past the town limits, but I also told myself that at home, I could collect my wits, which had been frayed by the day's events so far.

In fact, it had been quite an adventure, and in spite of the entity's menacing acts, I'd never felt more effective, more in control of my situation. I'd more or less accomplished what I'd set out to do, and I'd done it by thinking on my feet. While I wasn't exactly elated, I felt much more powerful driving up to Penobscot Road than I had leaving it that morning.

But then there was the forlorn stand of trees that served as the gateway to my house's dominion, and there was the ugliness of the house, radiating out into the wet atmosphere of the front yard. The only reason I'd been so quick-witted in Seville was because of everything I'd been put through by the house.

So as I pulled up near the front door, any sense of accomplishment I'd managed to gain was drained from me, replaced with a sentence of present and future failure. Even though I'd just gone through hell, I still didn't know what Suzy's comments really meant, and the chances of Evan telling me seemed slim. Simply behaving heroically didn't necessarily lead to victory. History had long borne that out.

Still, I knew that the only chance for any kind of success was to pass through the worst that the house would put me through and come out the other side. I was right about that, at least.

But I'm troubled by your thoughts right now. On one hand, you think that I was a fool for even considering going back inside that house, for not trying anything that would involve attacking it from a distance. And you feel as if I was a coward for giving up any hope for my own salvation. You don't believe me when I say that I had no choice and no chance.

At the same time, you want me to go back inside that place, to relive all the awful things that were about to happen to us. After everything we've shared, I'm still just a thrill to you, an idiot who provides you with a moment's diversion. Can all my honest emotion compensate for your tenuous interest? Is there more of an imbalance in this thing we've created than I'll admit to? Am I being ultimately self-destructive?

I think my dread at reliving what happened next is hardening me to everything we share in the present, casting it all in a scarlet light. Or maybe it's helping me to see things more clearly.

I suppose I should continue.

Alphonse and Nicole were waiting for me in the front hall. Nicole's face was continuing to change. She'd always had a very lively set of facial expressions, and she would switch from one to the next as quickly as her emotions slid into each other. But now, her face was a barrier, a tool to misdirect. Her eyes moved on me, and her mouth followed the general rules of what constitutes the physical appearance of a smile, but she was a stranger.

Alphonse stood behind her, shrinking himself into the shadows as far as a tall man could, and I sensed that his increasing spinelessness would prove just as much a danger to me as Nicole's growing malice.

"Hey, Chris? Listen, we need to talk, like, now. Okay?" Nicole's voice was growing less and less familiar, too, yet Alphonse continued to stare at me as if *I* were the threat, the stranger.

In fact, there was something so awkward about the way the two of them were positioned in the hall that I froze. All I wanted to do was get out of my filthy clothes and call Evan, but I froze.

Neither one of them even asked why my shoes and jeans were caked in mud or why I'd stolen the car.

"We got a call from the police in Seville."

"Oh."

"He just wanted to check that you were telling the truth about living here. He said that you were wandering around, ringing people's door-bells."

"I was trying to find out some information about Evan and Suzy."

"I figured that was why you were there, so I asked about them."

"Did he know where they went?"

"He said he'd never heard of any Evan and Suzy living in Seville."

"Who'd you talk to?"

"Officer McConnell. He said that he was the one who picked you up."

The presence materialized, practically springing onto my groin. I tried not to react, but it was impossible.

"What's wrong?"

"I'm just surprised that he would say that." The entity was creating friction in an attempt to stimulate me sexually. "Because he mentioned them to me." I had to get to my room, the only place left where I could slough off the presence now. I must have looked and sounded insane because Nicole actually dropped the subject.

"Anyway, we got really worried about you, so…" She looked into the parlor, and I realized that there was someone else in there.

"What have you done?"

Wordlessly, she and Alphonse walked into the next room. I took the opportunity to try and rid myself of the entity, but grabbing at my crotch only seemed to make things worse. I couldn't remain in the hall for very long.

A thin, older man was standing by the mantel in a sincere effort to appear as if he hadn't been listening to our conversation. He was wearing a beige sweater, and his smile overpowered me for a moment.

"Hello, Chris."

The presence was now doing things to my body that I can't even repeat, but I did my level best to keep myself steady. I already knew how important my interaction with this man would be.

"Hello."

"Dr. Modelle. I'm a psychologist."

I couldn't appear resentful, so I extended my hand. "Nice to meet you."

His handshake was dry, with the perfect amount of pressure. He had blue eyes that hid nothing, that asked, rather than demanded. His grin was clearly something that often graced his face.

I couldn't help liking Dr. Modelle.

But I also had the entity taunting me, debasing me, and I had the house and now my roommates to contend with, so I couldn't relax. Liking anything or anyone at this point was simply a meaningless exertion.

"How are you doing?"

"I walked in some mud…"

But I couldn't be honest about the house with Dr. Modelle, at least not until I'd gained his trust. And I did think I could, because even though he was a psychologist, I sensed he would eventually listen to me with an open mind. Once he saw that I wasn't crazy.

Dr. Modelle looked briefly down at my jeans. Did he see the thing moving over my skin, insinuating itself into my private places? I couldn't tell him about the entity now, but I hoped that he'd remember whatever he'd just noticed when I finally could.

"May I sit down?" The doctor actually waited for a sign from me before he sat. "Can we talk for a little while?"

I joined him on the sofa, nonchalantly rubbing my legs together in an attempt to interfere with the presence. I'd hoped he wouldn't notice this, but he did.

"So, the house." And that was all he said. He wasn't going to beat around the bush; he was moving straight to the evaluation.

"I guess I've let my imagination run away with me a little bit."

"Is that what you think is happening?"

"You've seen the house. It isn't exactly a scary place."

"We all experience places differently. Has it been scary for you?"

"I guess that with the move and everything, I've been a little upset. I think subconsciously, I'm trying to blame my fear on something external."

Dr. Modelle smiled at this. "Sounds as if you know a bit about psychology."

"Do you think that I'm wrong?"

"Well, tell me: have you shared your psychological theory with anyone else?"

"I guess seeing you here has really made me conscious of the situation. I guess it's suddenly just become obvious to me, what I'm doing."

He nodded for a while, the rhythm and distance never wavering. Then he stopped. "So what *did* you believe was happening?"

Now the entity was trying to wriggle inside of me, and I suddenly rose. "It would be easier to show you." I had to get to my bedroom, or the presence was going to make me go insane right before the doctor's eyes.

Yet he remained seated, searching my face, a subdued version of his smile unnerving me. "All right." And only then did he rise.

"For instance, you were leaning against the mantel. I thought that there was something that attracted people to it, almost like a siren song. And I thought that attraction would end up being dangerous, somehow. But everyone is attracted to mantels if you think about it, aren't they? The hearth is the center of a home." I hoped that my strained, rushed speech wasn't too noticeable.

"It's a nice mantle."

I continued into the front hall. "I convinced myself certain things in the house, certain rooms and objects, had special powers or special effects on people. It sounds crazy to say it out loud now. But I thought that looking through this little window here, out into the front yard, made everything you saw actually sadder. It sort of made everything get worse. See? I told you it sounds crazy."

He looked out the window, and it seemed as if he flinched momentarily, although when he turned back to me, he was grinning again. "Oregon in October can be a pretty sad place."

"Exactly. I was just transferring my emotions onto the house. I'd convinced myself that other places downstairs were affecting me, too, but I sleep upstairs, so I had a lot of what I thought were experiences up there."

I could feel Alphonse and Nicole eavesdropping somewhere down the hall and realized this was the first time I'd ever vocalized many of the details of what had been happening in their presence. Alphonse had to listen to me now, and maybe Nicole would recognize one of the phenomena, herself. Maybe her terrible denial would begin to break down and her transformation reverse.

I strained to ascend the staircase steadily. "I also convinced myself that I could sense the presence of former residents on the second floor. A family who lived here when it was a farm. They had something wrong with them, and I thought they were somehow getting closer and closer to the present time, as if they wanted to break into it and do something bad to the people who are invading their privacy now. Don't worry. I can see how ridiculous that sounds."

And sure enough, when I reached the top of the stairs, I could almost feel the family members brushing past me, so close to recognizing what was happening to them. Realizing what they had to do to me. The danger was palpable, but I couldn't waver in the doctor's presence, so I continued in the direction of my bedroom.

The presence was getting more frantic, more audacious. Even though I was almost to the bedroom and it was about to be repelled, its efforts to stimulate me were beginning to pay off, so I moved as quickly as possible.

"Here's my bedroom. I was convinced there was an entity in here." How did it know what to do to me? It must have been watching me when

I was alone. I'd never felt more violated, but I only smiled wearily at Dr. Modelle as I opened the door. "I convinced myself that it liked to torment me."

He was squinting down the shadowed hall, as if he'd seen something. Or maybe he was simply interested in his patient's environment. Then he studied my face. "It seems as if it's tough for you to come up here." He paused at the door, waiting for a response, but I was practically at a sexual climax, so I merely suppressed my grimace and slipped inside the room.

The sudden relief of the entity's absence only made the contrast to my room's increasingly terrible atmosphere more difficult to bear. If anything, the trees on the wall had become stronger, more intense, and now, they spoke of an immediate threat, a near future of confusion and misery.

Dr. Modelle was staring at them, too, and I could tell that he was disturbed by what he saw. The house had managed to rob him of his smile. If he had an open mind, as I hoped and sensed he did, then very likely it was being turned. "Did you draw that?"

"I'm not that far gone. This was under the wallpaper. It's that stand of trees out front." I pointed out my window, and he slowly turned, the forlorn woods silencing him for a moment.

I was understandably surprised, then, when he said this: "Why do you think someone drew the trees outside onto the wall in here? Almost this exact view?"

He still believed that I'd drawn the trees. I could tell by the way he'd asked me, but I tried to keep any disappointment from my voice. "Maybe they were practicing their life-drawing skills?"

"But it's not an exact reproduction, is it. There seems to be more significance to the drawing. As if it's trying to say something more."

At least he sensed this! "It seemed that way to me."

"So what do you think it's trying to say?"

"Nothing. I see it's just a drawing now." He wasn't going to trick me with the present tense that easily.

"But before. What did you think it was saying when you thought that there was something odd about the house?"

I got the feeling that he was looking for some sort of affirmation of his own suspicions about the image of the trees—another good sign—so I decided to be straight with him. "Well, I know this sounds even worse than anything I've admitted so far, but it seemed as if the picture was communicating bad things that were about to happen. And what it suggested kept changing. Like an early warning system of some kind. Of course, when something bad did happen, I could just tell myself that it had been right all along. So in reality, it was just an effort to use an external fact to confirm my internal story. Like I said, I was a little delusional. I see that, now."

"Anything else go on in here?"

"Just that it seemed like ground zero for some kind of malevolence. I thought I'd seen another presence in here, a ghost or some replay of the past. All I can remember is that it was all in black. With shiny, black shoes." I'd never had this recollection before it came out of my mouth! At first, I thought I was saying things that the house was forcing me to say, that this phenomenon was similar to the one near the kitchen sink. But I quickly realized that this had really happened to me: there had been something else in my room. Why was I only remembering it now?

"Hmm." He nodded. "It must have been terrible, sleeping in here. How did you cope?"

I had to remain focused on the task at hand and so filed this latest occurrence away. I would investigate the figure in black when I didn't have a trained psychotherapist watching my every move. I forced myself to chuckle. "Well, obviously, I didn't cope. But I understand now that it's just a room. How could walls and a floor and a ceiling be evil? It's just wood and plaster. You need a brain to be evil, at the very least. You need a soul."

I got a searching stare from him at this comment. "I think you're right."

Suddenly, he turned and left the room. I expected him to head down the hallway to the darker parts of the floor, but he began to climb the stairs. "What's up here?"

"Don't—" Alphonse and Nicole must have told him about my dread of the third floor, but they didn't know what had happened to Suzy up there. They didn't know how much stronger it had grown.

"It's just the attic." I didn't want to leave my room for fear of what the entity would do to me, so I shouted this up to him from my doorway. "There's nothing really worth checking out up there. With me."

"Do you want to join me?" I couldn't see him, but I could tell that he'd paused on the stairs.

So Dr. Modelle was trying to force my hand. He was attempting to get me to admit that I still believed the house was powerful. If I went up, I might flinch. And if I didn't go up, then I was clearly still scared of something. He was a fast worker.

But what he didn't understand was that I wasn't scared for myself, although I couldn't have said that at the time. In fact, I couldn't say anything; I could only follow him up, and so I stepped out into the corridor.

And then, just outside my door, I actually saw a flash of one of the family members at the top of the front stairs. A small child was walking away from me, dragging something behind it on the floor. It was gone in an instant.

Oddly, I didn't yell out or jump back or even freeze. The appearance was too sudden, too anomalous to give me a chance to generate fear. More than anything, it mesmerized me, seeing something that was never supposed to happen in real life. Three-dimensional matter doesn't just disappear before your eyes. I wish I could say that it had been like watching a movie, but while you're watching them, you know that movies aren't real. It's something you can only really appreciate when something like this happens to you. Movie ghosts aren't reality at all.

Still, Dr. Modelle seemed to notice that something had happened. "Everything okay?" He was watching me from the middle of the stairs.

"Yeah." And I turned toward him, knowing that I'd have to process what was happening on the second floor later. The shift that I'd feared was beginning to take place, but I had to deal with one thing at a time. Dr. Modelle posed a greater danger because he'd prevent me from saving Nicole and Alphonse if he took me away.

He was already at the top of the stairs, handling the deadbolt. "Somebody had this floor locked up pretty tightly."

"Before our time."

"Did you experience some sexual things, too?"

Now my mouth did drop open. He must have recognized what the entity had been doing to me. But before I could even respond, he continued with his line of questioning.

"What did you feel was happening up here?" He swung the door open, and almost immediately, I could smell the foul, strangely sweet smell drifting down the staircase. Instinctively, I paused, but he continued into the area beyond.

It seemed to me that having Dr. Modelle see the third floor for himself might actually be a good thing. After all, anyone who experienced the secret room up there would have to admit that something wasn't entirely right with the people who'd built it. And even *he* would have to admit that stepping into a bedroom with no windows would disturb the sanest person on the planet. At least a little. And maybe being up there wouldn't affect him as seriously as it had Suzy.

When I reached the top step, the presence instantaneously materialized right in front of me, in effect pushing me backwards and almost causing me to fall down the stairs. And as fast as it had come, it was gone, and I felt the situation hurtling downward, the threat accelerating minute by minute.

It almost seemed like further proof when I looked down the hall and found that the doctor was nowhere to be seen.

"Hello?" Suzy had immediately gone berserk when she'd reached this floor, but she was also prone to hysteria. Dr. Modelle was nothing like that.

Still, he didn't respond.

"Dr. Modelle?"

Dusk was quickly robbing the last of whatever meager light the third floor allowed inside, but I hesitated to flip the switch next to me. I was growing concerned by what it might reveal, so I just called out his name again. The silence seemed to indicate that he planned to remain hidden in the cold darkness of one of the rooms. Possibly, it was some kind of test. I prayed it was some kind of test.

I was frozen to the spot. Getting Alphonse and Nicole up to witness whatever was going to happen next seemed like my best move, but something caused me to pause. On one hand, I wanted to spare them any real trauma, and on the other, I wondered if the third floor could really change people as much and as quickly as it had changed Suzy. It seemed to have affected the doctor already; what would it turn my roommates into? I might not stand a chance if I were the only rational person left in the house.

Or I could just return downstairs. Eventually, Nicole and Alphonse would realize that something was wrong with Dr. Modelle, and therefore, that nothing was wrong with me.

What I knew I wasn't going to do was to walk farther into the third floor.

"Chris?" The voice was muffled, and it sounded as if it were coming from every room and none of the rooms at the same time, but it was Dr. Modelle's. And he sounded sane.

"Dr. Modelle?"

"Can you come here?"

"I don't know where you are. Are you okay?"

No response.

"Dr. Modelle? I'm just by the stairs."

He certainly sounded calm, and so I began to wonder if it really were some kind of test. But why try to pass it? At this point, I wanted to prove to him that the house had something wrong with it, not that I was no longer scared of it. If he hadn't figured out by this time that things weren't right in Penobscot Road, demonstrating my bravery by walking into that blackness wouldn't do any good.

He still hadn't responded, so I turned to go back downstairs.

"I need you to see this."

It sounded as if his voice were coming from somewhere new, but I would've heard him if he'd moved. The whole thing was becoming so ridiculous that I surprised myself by laughing at the cliché of a situation. It was like every horror movie ever shot.

This made me feel a little bolder, so I turned on the light, but the bulb was so ineffectual that it only made things worse. Any humor I'd found was immediately extinguished. "Dr. Modelle, anyone would be scared right now. You're hiding from me."

Nothing.

In the past five minutes, I'd actually seen a child from the bad family, and the entity had tried to rape and then hurt me. The forces in the house were escalating rapidly, possibly to the point that the doctor had become a threat to me now, too.

"Dr. Modelle. I'll just see you downstairs—"

"I need your help." Again, it sounded as if his voice were coming from somewhere new.

"What's wrong?"

"Please."

"Where are you?"

Again, nothing.

I wasn't budging. "If the house isn't doing anything to you, why don't you come out from wherever you are? You don't have to test me this way."

"Have you ever thought about hurting yourself, Chris?"

This sounded so conversational, so casual, that I almost replied as naturally. But why on earth would he ask this, and in such a way?

I didn't respond. Instead, I called for Nicole and Alphonse, although I knew that unless they'd followed us up to the second floor, they'd never hear me. And my cell phone was in my room. I wanted to get my room-mates, but I didn't want to leave the doctor all alone. I was afraid of what might happen.

"Have you ever thought about hurting someone else?" Now, his voice sounded farther away, as though he'd turned his head away from me.

"Why are you asking me these questions?"

Again, he failed to respond, so I thought I'd press my advantage. "There are things going on in this house. You know that now, don't you?"

"The weakest area of the skull is the temple. The bone is thinnest there."

This was no test—at least not one being conducted by Dr. Modelle. I turned to get away, but the entity enfolded me, impeding my movements to the point that I seemed trapped in a terrible pantomime of slow motion. It was as if I were suddenly in a vat of syrup, and the harder I pushed against it, the harder it pushed back. So in a matter of seconds, I was winded and covered in sweat, yet had hardly moved at all.

I could hear the doctor behind me now, walking toward me, although I could no longer turn my head. My back was completely exposed to him, as was my skull. I couldn't even move my mouth to form words, and it dawned on me that I was actually living out a nightmare.

"The brain continues to function for five seconds after being separat-ed from the body."

He was right behind me, and all of my muscles strained against the thick miasma that prevented my escape. Pressure was building on my chest now, too, and I found that it was becoming harder to breathe, which only caused me to panic more.

"The facial muscles continue to contract and relax, possibly indicating intense pain from the severing of the spinal column."

My inability to breathe made me pull back from the entity, and I found that this was much easier to do than push against it. Although the last thing in the world I wanted to do was move any closer to Dr. Modelle, I put all of my strength into pulling backward and toward him. Immediately, the presence released me, and I was flung violently back, my elbow smashing into the doctor's torso. When I turned to face him, he was on the floor next to me, clutching at his chest and smiling up at me, almost apologetically. I could only stare back at him in horror. Had he only been trying to scare me? It made no sense whatsoever, yet sense was the last thing I expected at this point. He still hadn't taken a breath, and the veins in his neck were bulging and twisting, yet he continued to grin up at me as his face turned purple. I could only think to race downstairs to retrieve Nicole, who had some basic training in medical emergencies.

I yelled for her on the way down, and met her and Alphonse at the bottom of the front hallway steps.

"What is it?"

"He looks as if he's having a heart attack or something."

"What?!" And the two of them followed me back. When we reached the third floor, he was gone. I was a few steps ahead of my friends, so I kept them from coming all the way up.

"He moved. He was here."

"We'd better find him, then—"

"I don't think it's a good idea for you guys to come up here."

"Why? What did you do?"

"He went kind of crazy when he got up here. I don't want it to happen to you."

"What do you mean 'crazy?' He might be having a heart attack!"

"Maybe he went downstairs—"

"Move, Chris."

She tried to push me aside, but I held myself in front of her. "He might be dangerous. I think he was going to attack me."

At this she stopped pulling at me and just studied my face, as if she were searching for some kind of evidence. She was looking for a sign of sanity. "He tried to attack you?" And her tone told me that she hadn't found one.

Just as she studied my face, I studied hers. "You don't have to believe me, but I need my old friends now. If you go up there, I'm going to lose you."

A kind of mild snarl crossed her lips that was completely foreign to her palette of expressions, and she cocked her head at an angle that she would never have cocked it before. Nicole was gone.

She looked over my shoulder. "Dr. Modelle? Are you okay?"

When it was clear that he wouldn't be responding, she returned her attention to me. How strange it was to find that by contracting just a few miniscule muscles in her face, I could see exactly how the new Nicole would study a stranger. She seemed no longer even to know me.

"You stay with him." And turning away from me, she motioned to Alphonse. He came up behind her and suddenly grabbed my arm, an act that would have mortified me if he hadn't been shaking so badly. But Alphonse, at least, was still Alphonse, and so realizing that my friend was assaulting me—actually becoming the threat I'd feared—wasn't quite as heart-wrenching as it could have been.

And then there was the fact that it had been so long since anyone had touched me, been next to me like this. The last time had been when I'd put my arms around my friends in the room with the Scooby-Doo sticker, and that may have just been a dream. I became intensely aware of the heat that we were trapping together where our clothing separated our bodies. I thought that his erection was pressing into the back of my leg.

Alphonse and I watched Nicole carefully walk down that grim corridor, looking in each room as she passed it, being gradually taken in by the increasing darkness of the hall until disappearing into one of the rooms at the end.

"Alphonse, being in there is going to change her! It changed Suzy, and it changed Dr. Modelle. You know this isn't happening because of me."

"I'm going to let you go."

"It's too late, now, anyway."

I only realized the shock of being restrained after it was gone—I hadn't been grabbed like that since I was a child. And now, Alphonse's closeness was gone, too. An instant later, my desire for this contact repulsed me.

Too much was happening at once, and I felt myself losing the flapping strands of it all. So I focused on the scratched bannister in my hand, which was just an old piece of wood, which felt just like an old piece of wood and looked just like an old piece of wood, and I pushed everything back but the immediate danger. The black hallway was digesting Nicole and the doctor.

"We've got to do something! And the only way to completely get away from this is to figure out what's happening. Why the house is like this."

"What are you talking about?" Alphonse was still attempting to sound as if he had no idea.

"It's trying to tell us something. Everything that's going on seems like some kind of communication. Maybe making us see and hear and feel all of this is a way of making us understand something. But I don't know what."

Nicole hadn't yet emerged from the room, and Alphonse called out to her. She didn't answer.

"Alphonse, you know something's going on here."

"Yeah. But…"

"But what?"

"Nicole?!"

"But what?"

"I'm going to see what's going on in there—"

Now I found myself pressed against him, holding his arm. "But what, Alphonse?"

"But maybe it *is* you! You know, like a poltergeist. You're making all of this happen. Your energy or whatever. Don't tell me that you haven't wondered about that."

"*I'm* making Nicole change like that? How?"

"I don't know. It all seems to involve you."

"Like what? What's happened to you since you've been here?"

"Look. Let go of me. I'm going to see what's going on. Nicole?!"

"She's not going to answer!"

But then: "Alphonse, come here."

And with that, he pulled free of me, and I knew I'd never get the answer from him that I needed.

He hurried into a room at the end of the hallway, and I could hear the both of them talking, although I couldn't make out what they were saying. After a moment, the door to the room slowly shut, and the sound of its lock turning seemed amplified by the space.

They hadn't locked the door against the house; they'd locked it against me. Was there anything left of my friends? If there were, then this proved that they thought I was insane. But if there was nothing left, if they were now as altered as Suzy and Dr. Modelle had become, then locking the door wasn't to keep me from harming them, it was to keep me from knowing what was happening in that room.

By now, the weak dusk was gone, and the dim passageway contracted, some obscene throat waiting to constrict around me. I felt more alone in that house than I had when Alphonse and Nicole had left me behind to go into town. And even though I'm beginning to realize that the only reason you've come this far with me is for a few momentary, salacious sensations, I still have to cling to your presence in order to move forward. Anyone is better than no one at this point, and at least this way, I know someone's with me there. So I have to repeat it to myself: I'm not alone, even at the mouth of Penobscot Road's third floor.

Eventually, I tried to gather my wits. I could call an ambulance for Dr. Modelle, but if there was any way of helping him, Nicole would've already called. I could walk down the fifty feet stretching out before me and knock on the door that had been closed against me, but I knew that I couldn't step foot on that floor—the danger was too palpable, and I could see no way of reversing what would change in me if I did. I could return downstairs and wait for the situation to resolve itself, but that somehow seemed the worst course of action of all.

But then I remembered that I hadn't yet called Evan. This left me with the short distance of the steep staircase and the brief walk down the second-floor hallway to my room, a prospect that wouldn't have been particularly daunting if it weren't for the presence's increasingly dangerous behavior on the stairs and the family now emerging out of the past directly beneath me.

I could only grip the bannister with both hands as I slowly descended. The dark air around me buzzed with negative potential, but as I got closer and closer to the bottom of the staircase, I felt that potential diminish. The entity wouldn't be throwing me down the stairs. And I was even more surprised to find that the family was nowhere to be seen once I reached the second floor. In fact, the darkness was calmer here than it had ever been before, which would have been a great relief if it hadn't represented the next, significant phrase of Penobscot Road's communication.

The membrane that had separated me from the family, as disconcerting as cobwebs entangling me in the dark, was gone. And it had been replaced with nothing, with empty space that simply opened into itself. They were with me, now.

As quietly as I could, I stepped into my room, closed the door behind myself, and slowly locked it. It was a relief to know that the family never seemed to pass into my room, but if I thought about that too much, it was worrying, too. I just had to focus on getting a hold of Evan, and so I turned my brain off, kept my eyes on the floor, and reached for my phone.

I got voicemail. "Evan, it's Chris. Please call me back. I just need to know what Suzy meant yesterday, and then I'll leave you alone forever. Please. My roommates have locked themselves in a room on the third floor with someone who might be hurt, and you're my last chance to help them! Please call me back as soon as possible."

Now I would have to wait. Careful to keep my back to the drawing on the wall, I furiously grappled with how I could best understand what the house was doing and why. Almost instantly, I understood what I had to do, but what occurred to me was so unexpected, so repellent that I attempted to continue on, to run through all of my other options instead. But it was no use. The thought had been injected into my brain, and in fact there was something so alien about it that I knew I hadn't even generated it myself. I would have never suspected how unnerving a truly foreign idea could be, but it was a violation that left me feeling more defenseless than ever. Now the house was inside my mind, too.

I understood that there was no use trying to fight anything that was about to happen, so I merely walked to my door, unlocked it and stepped into the hallway. They were in the shadows there, waiting for me. Watching me. I could make out the soft outlines of their hair and the random flashings of their eyes in the dark. The same thought that had been implanted in me had been implanted in them, too, and so we were each playing our part, although I could tell that the family's potential for danger was still very real. We shared this unnatural knowledge, but they possessed other, deeper understandings to which I had no access.

Entering the small room on the other side of the third-floor stairs, I knelt down next to the wall and began to scratch at the wood next to my fingers, my hand naturally falling to the same spot that had been clawed at by so many others. I could feel the physical damage they'd done to the wood and wondered what had been going on in their minds when they'd been in the same position I now found myself.

And then I did know what the others had gone through because occupying the same space now equaled occupying the same time, in some way.

Penobscot Road was robbing me of this dimension, too, and so I knew that everyone else who'd lived through what I was now experiencing had been conscious only of what they had to do. They hadn't been worried about why they were doing it or what was forcing them to do it. A flash of envy passed through me, but I had to continue. This was indicated to me.

I rose, feeling the stagnant air rush to fill the vacuum I'd created in that special place on the floor just as it had countless times before. The darkness seemed to amplify the damp, hanging mold spores and filthy dust motes feeding off the space, swelling as they clung to me.

The family now hid in the rooms on either side of me, quietly and attentively listening to my progress down the hall. I was surprised to find that my consciousness hadn't altered during the ritual so far; I still possessed my faculties. This was different from the other people who'd been forced into it, and this gave me courage, for some reason. It was comforting to know that I was the exception, although I knew that being aware of the whole process as it took place was going to be worse.

Sure enough, there was someone else in the room I next had to visit, someone who was waiting for me. I couldn't see an inch in front of my face when I entered, but I felt the other's intentions directed toward me in the blackness.

I had to remove my clothing, but the ritual revealed itself no further than this, so I merely did as I was required. Only when my bare skin was exposed to the clammy air did I become aware of how much sweat covered my body—and now that body was completely exposed to whatever was before it, there in the darkness. Instinctively, my arms drew up across my chest, the rest of me forsaken, marginally more expendable.

"A controlled bleeding-out allows victims to be aware of their impending death."

I squealed in terror as soon as I heard his voice but understood enough to be quiet and still as soon as I could. Dr. Modelle was in the room with me.

"Those afraid of heights are actually afraid of the certainty that they're about to die. The period of knowing."

The proximity of his voice told me he'd just come closer. I slowly took a step back toward the door. "Why are you saying that?"

Instinctively, I fell backwards, and my neck hit the edge of the door frame behind me. He was now only a few inches from my face.

"Don't hurt me."

My hand had been making its way up the door frame and now hit the light switch. The blinding glare allowed me to see only a movement of color next to me as Dr. Modelle left the room. But being able to see wasn't part of the ritual, and I immediately knew that I'd made a terrible error. It felt as if I'd stopped in the middle of a surgery, and the weight of regretful consequence pushed me to the floor. I could see all the closed doors down the hallway, the anger I'd engendered seeping under them, a kind of electrical buzzing that was almost visible in the harsh light I'd just unleashed. The others had retreated from the light, too.

I was no longer sure if I was expected to continue the process or not. It was a strange moment as I rose in the middle of the hall, naked and cold, the offending light casting my shadow where no shadow was meant to be. I knew that Suzy had next proceeded to the bathroom, but the directions were no longer blooming in my mind as needed; that method of control had been banished by the light, too. And a moment later, I'd recognized that *everything was gone*. The family, who just a few minutes earlier had entered my plane of existence, had passed back to their own, and even the potentiality of the presence had evaporated from the heavy atmosphere, my body somehow more my own than it had been in a week.

I could hear Alphonse and Nicole walking down the squeaky hallway upstairs, and the prosaic reflex of rushing to get dressed was somehow incredibly comforting because it was normal; it was pointed in the direction of rational living. There simply was nothing stopping me from putting my clothes back on, or even from wanting to put my clothes on.

I had entered a new phase.

"Chris?"

I rushed toward the front of the second floor. "Nicole?"

"We can't find Dr. Modelle. Is he down here?"

"Oh, he left." I didn't even think through my response; it was simply the only one I had to offer.

"Really? Oh. Well, how did it go?"

The three of us were standing on the second-floor landing, speaking perfectly naturally, as if nothing strange had happened. I remembered everything that we'd just lived through, but it seemed as if Alphonse and Nicole did not.

I wasn't about to remind them.

"Good."

"That's fucking awesome." I could tell that she really meant this; the old woman's influence had completely released her face, her movements, the way she spoke. She was Nicole again.

"Yeah, because you were going off the deep end there for a while. We were going to call the men in the white uniforms to come and get you." And Alphonse was still Alphonse; the ability to keep things to himself had disappeared, too. "You're just lucky that we couldn't do without your rent money."

I could feel the door to my room behind me. Had everything that had gone wrong really dissipated? "Well, anyway. I'll be down in a minute." And without even waiting to see them descend the stairs, I turned back to my room and passed inside, keeping my eyes cast down until I came up to the drawing. Denying so much as a moment's hesitation, I threw my head up and stared openly at it, keeping myself even from blinking.

It was a series of dark lines. That was all. Any cryptic significance had been eradicated, leaving merely a childlike scribble that made me question why I'd ever been worried about it in the first place. I knew there were other pictures still under the wallpaper—things hadn't changed that much. But now, I also knew that they were more of the same: just trails of charcoal embedded in the rough undulations of latex. Their power was gone, and I was shocked to find myself wondering if it had ever been there to begin with. In fact, this was the first time I realized that whatever constitutes reality for the human mind is like a magnet; we're compelled to return to it at every opportunity, even when its very evidence urges us to do otherwise.

Yet I couldn't so quickly and completely let go of what had taken place for me since moving to Penobscot Road. The place now felt like a damp, run-down old farmhouse and nothing more. Interrupting the strange ritual just couldn't have been enough to do it—and of course, I realize that you're thinking the exact same thing. It was all too easy. You want me to live through much worse before this is over and you're satisfied. You'd feel cheated if you didn't see me really suffer.

Well, I'm sorry to report that on inspection, each room on the second floor was just a room. Their odd urgings and atmospheres were no more, leaving only the dull markings of previous inhabitants and the filth of time. The same was true of the first floor: the parlor's mantle no longer held its sick, overly sweet attraction, and the dining room no longer repulsed.

This was also the first time I acknowledged to myself that a room existed between Alphonse's and Nicole's. I and, as far as I knew, everyone else had completely ignored its reality, passing the door almost as if it were false, as if it were only a decoration whose original intent had been lost to the past. But it led to a room, and I was about to enter it when I heard Alphonse and Nicole arguing across the hall in the kitchen.

The bump on the kitchen floor. It had been one of the places that held an especially strong kind of power over me. I was overtaken by a sudden, consuming desire to see if the bump could still affect me, a kind of final proof that Penobscot Road's supernatural influence was truly gone.

"We just met him! How could you forget that fast?"

"I can't believe this! Chris, did Dr. Modelle have a moustache?" Nicole was only a foot away from the bump; it would be awkward to stand that close to her.

"What? Are you guys having a fight about that?"

"Just answer the question. Did he or did he not have a moustache?"

"He had a beard." I walked toward the sink, my hands held out as if I needed to wash them, and Nicole moved aside.

As usual, Alphonse had folded himself up at the far end of the kitchen table. "We know that. But did he have a moustache, too?"

"You mean, did he have one of those, like, Amish beards or whatever?"

"Yes! Did he have a moustache or not?"

I was on the bump! I stood there a moment, pushing gently down on it, waiting for something to take me over, for the strange comments to rise up out of my mouth and push sinister thoughts into the room.

"Uhh, Chris? Are you having a stroke?"

"He had a moustache."

Nothing. Even that was gone. The house was calm, empty now of everything except for us. I was so relieved that I never bothered to wonder why my roommates remembered Dr. Modelle so well yet had completely lost their concern over my strange behavior.

It was as if we were back in Sacramento.

"I told you!" Apparently, Alphonse was the victor in this one.

"Whatever. I still want proof. Let's see if we can get a picture of him online or something. If he did have a moustache, it was pretty fucking light."

"Bummer! I should have put some money on it."

*   *   *

That night, in my room as I got ready to sleep, I could look at my bed and see only a place of comfort, of soft, relaxing surfaces and warmth. There were no amorphous threats, no nightmares cracking the surface and spilling over into my waking life. My room was enormous, and for the first time, I was able to appreciate what a luxury space was, how it took nearly four seconds to walk from one corner to the other! Before, the scale of the house had only made me feel small and ineffective, but now I was in charge. Space existed to accommodate me.

Of course, I also understood that this period was only a temporary lull, but it was the first time in days that I felt as if I could catch my breath. So I suspended any thought of what was to come and instead madly focused on my warm bed and the still, cool air around me. It must have been like the Hawaiian R & R Vietnam soldiers hungrily consumed, never knowing if it would be the last time they'd hold a Heinz ketchup bottle or look out onto the ocean without the need to listen for peculiar noises behind them. But the worst of it was that just as those soldiers must have realized, as they sat on those endless, blinding beaches, that their ears could never stop wading through sounds for Viet Cong, I knew that I could never again completely relax into my old certainties. I had only this weak, cardboard present; any faith in the future had been ripped from me, a kind of childhood I was no longer allowed.

You should stop here.

The Tenth Day

The buzzing vibration started at 2:41. I can still see those numbers, burning red in the darkness of my bedroom, signaling that the present too soon was robbing me of any peace, any numbness. I'd already forgotten how deep the sleep of the ignorant could be, and my struggling to consciousness had been quite an effort. I didn't want to wake up. But when I finally squinted at the clock, the first thing I did was the math: not even eight hours—more evidence that I'd never totally abandoned myself to the blank pause. For some reason, I'd expected a longer break. Still, the hours and the minutes were the same; they were just as unfeeling in their exactness as ever. That, at least, was a kind of comfort.

The room still felt harmless, and my eyes came to rest on the black space that held the black drawing and its black meanings. I sensed nothing from it but knew I had to be sure, so I stepped out into the freezing, damp draughts swirling in the room and turned on the light, immediately swiveling to face the wall.

The drawing was still nothing, and this would have been a tremendous relief but for the insistent humming coming from beyond my door. Just as I knew that my room was empty of any forces but me, I knew that the buzzing was wrong, that it was the start of something much worse. And it wasn't something I could avoid or ignore; the bad time had started again.

As if smoke were seeping under it, I pressed my hands against the door in an attempt to sense what was on the other side. Again, the experience was nothing more than touching a thin layer of paint over some ancient wood, so I opened it and stood in the hall. The light from my room was more than enough to illuminate anyone in the shadows, watching me, waiting for me nearby. But the hallway was clear, and the rooms were empty. The only proof I'd entered a new phase of my ordeal in Penobscot Road was that muffled, dull buzzing.

It was coming from the other end of the passage, and so I walked past the doors, past the invisible line to the newer sections of the house, past the sites of so many painful, inexplicable episodes. By the time I'd reached the bathroom, I knew that the sound was coming from the door at the end of the hall.

The closet door knob now hung at a strange angle, useless, yet I was still able to pull the door open, and the moment I did, the buzzing stopped. There before me were the inexplicable shelves and the same, old newspaper. The vibration had been coming from behind the closet, from the cut-off room at the top of the back staircase that I'd always known was the beginning of something much worse.

I didn't think I could face walking all the way back to the front stairs and then all the way to the rear of the first floor to find out what was happening. Because Penobscot Road still felt precarious, its potential crackling in the air and ready to return at any moment—at which point I'd be caught racing around in the blackness of the middle of the night, made even more exposed and vulnerable by the threat of surprise. It would be so much easier just to go back to sleep and allow the house to do whatever it wanted to me. Nothing I could do would stop this, anyway.

But even though I'd been changed beyond redemption, my old roommates had just been their old selves for a short while, at least. If they'd done it once, they could do it again. But in order to make that happen, I had to go through everything in order to come out the other side, and so I strode back toward the front of the house, every creak and every echo a new torture.

I walked through the parlor, dining room and family room to avoid awakening Alphonse and Nicole because I knew this would be dangerous for some reason. I had to face whatever was causing the noise alone. Still, my path led past Nicole's room, and I could hear her mumbling in her sleep, repeating what sounded like "dough" over and over.

Then I passed her door and somehow knew she wasn't sleeping at all—she was sitting up in her bed, staring at the door, almost *through* it at me, and what she was repeating wasn't "dough," it was "don't." Things were getting worse, and I ran even more quickly away from her, the leaden miasma behind me seemingly getting closer and closer.

The storeroom was now before me, and as I hurried to close its door against whatever was building up in the rear hall, I realized that I was still on the wrong side of it. It couldn't have been more than 40 degrees in there, and the presence of some horrific event permeated every surface, every molecule in the room, so much so that my body physically recoiled as if a furnace door were flung open before me. But this was different from anything that had happened in the house before: it wasn't the traces of some ancient occurrence that had seeped into the fundament of Penobscot Road and was now being released, nor was it some nebulous, hateful force rising up in the night. Whatever it was, it was of my time and of my reality, there with me in the dark.

At least I still had control over that, and so I reached out, my face to the wall, and turned on the light. A harsh hum accompanied the merciless, blue fluorescent light that flooded the room, and I winced for a moment, dismissing this noise as too weak to be what I'd heard earlier. By this point, I'd learned that in situations like this, I had to act without thinking, and so I turned around to face the room, my back pressed against the wall. Even though everything looked as if it were normal, the few belongings of ours piled up in the corners were now complicit with the rest of the space, tainted by something awful. There was an old printer in its original box to my right, and I couldn't help but marvel at how its label, "Brother HL-2040," now screamed bloody murder, its tame, original meaning as lost as mine.

But the event hadn't taken place in the room. I felt that, too. Rather, it was above me, the foulness radiating overhead. I knew that the poorly built stairs were behind the door in front of me, but I did not know what lay at their end. As far as I was aware, none of us had ever explored the area before, and I found myself sorry this was the case, as it meant that I had nothing to compare the upcoming circumstances with.

Of course, there was no light switch in the enclosed staircase, so I had to proceed with only the gray reflections of the first floor fixture. This wasn't an issue for the first seven stairs, but the structure doubled back on itself, and as I came to its crooked landing, I looked up into a murky hole, a closed door just visible above me. I could feel the stairs, the whole building waiting patiently for me to continue up, almost as if its breath were being held, and so I did, praying that the worst wasn't as bad as I expected. The room I was about to enter announced itself with a sour, abandoned stench, years of neglect translated into some kind of airborne retaliation.

Then the dented door handle was there, right next to my hand, and I found I couldn't reach out for it. On the other side a few inches away from me lay something real, something that could never be worked through or reversed or denied because it was too immense. The house's brutality had bled through too far there. And so for the first time, everything was completely real—there would be no more alternate explanations or dangers enigmatically cloaked.

My resolve to run the house's gauntlet had suddenly and completely drained away, and I could think of nothing else but the cracked dashboard of our car and its stained carpeting under my feet as I pressed down on the accelerator, escape a physical action that still made the old kind of sense.

This was an experience that must have been like dying: a leaving of the body and all that its past was mired in—the relationships and responsibilities and everything else petty and worldly. If I hadn't known better, I would've sworn that my soul was hovering high above me at that moment, out of the house and away from the series of regrettable decisions I'd made since moving to Oregon. But it wasn't my soul; it was the last vestige of my former self and its final impulse of self-preservation to get away before I opened that door and allowed Penobscot Road to completely devour me and my reality. I had to run away.

But you want me to open that door. This is as clear to me as that night still is. You're hoping for the worst, and that desire is so strong that it radiates out, reaching even as far away as I am from you. In fact, I think I even felt you that night, as I stared at the door knob, your hunger so deep, so absolute that whatever mortal corner left of me that still clung to my body simply continued to rise up and away, and I was left with only the twisted logic of the house. So you get your wish: I didn't save myself. I opened the door. But know that I continue with this only to satisfy my own needs now.

The light from downstairs barely managed to illuminate the floor and wall immediately in front of me, so I could make out only a scattering of debris across the floorboards, chunks of plaster and splinters of wood coated with gritty dust. It was even colder in here, so much so that it seemed as if a window were open, although clearly none existed. The space around me was so profoundly dark that it felt as if it were pulling at me, a vacuum eager to draw away what was left of my existence.

Yet the room exuded the presence of something horrendous; it was so overpowering that I actually felt nauseous as I stepped inside. Every molecule in the room reflected an atrocity, something so awful that it wasn't supposed to be seen or felt, and any contact with it made it an even worse kind of abomination. So my participation somehow completed the act. (Still, I wonder if it really isn't your participation that does this, a kind of final ingredient in the progression, in the knowing. Your desire for me to enter that terrible room might be what was always meant to happen.)

In fact, I understand now that you were there with me that night, a hungry witness in the darkness. Your eager anticipation swirled around the room, and you observed me fumbling for a light switch on the wall directly before me, shuffling into the shadows, feeling blindly. Then the door to the stairs squealed closed, leaving me with no ability to see, my hand frantically reaching out, every crack and bump producing a jolt of unwelcome adrenalin.

You watched me follow two walls and delighted in my dismay: instead of coming to a corner that would lead me back toward where I started, I faced an area that extended farther toward the back of the house. Almost immediately, my scalp was ripped open by an exposed nail, and based on this and the way sound was immediately thrown back in my face, I realized that this section was under some cobweb-covered eaves angling down toward my left. And then the ceiling began to lower before me, too, and I stopped. There would be no light switch back there. This is where you hid.

Something hollow dropped at the end of the space then. I pressed myself against the wall, the terror forcing a wave of sweat out of me. I knew that there was something farther back there, something aware of me, but I also sensed that you weren't part of the event I had to see. Your only act of violence at this point had been to hunger for the worst, and so I quickly backed away from you, stumbling back into the darkness until I came upon the outer wall of the room again. Settling back into the foulness of your crevice, you were perversely satisfied to be the torturer and not the tortured, to know that deep in those shadows, nothing worse could ever exist than you.

Then you squirmed, stimulated by my panic at finding another corner that I wasn't expecting. The structure built around the staircase shouldn't have met my hand for another five feet or so, but there it was. Following it to its next corner ended my confusion: before me were an open doorway and a step leading up. A staircase to the third floor. I threw up then, the leaden air from above carrying with it a scent that I didn't consciously recognize yet identified on an instinctive level, the word not accessible, but its danger palpable. You may even smell it now.

Whatever I was compelled to join was still above me, and for the first time, I felt how distant I was from Nicole and Alphonse, how much detritus I would have to stumble over to reach the comparative safety of their company. Even worse: I hadn't seen a back staircase when I'd searched the third floor and so was about to enter another secret section of the house, profanity solidified into plaster and linoleum. But what most distressed me was that this staircase was inexplicably narrow, and I knew that the space was about to constrict around me, crushing out my thin buffer of safety and robbing me of any easy escape from whatever waited in the darkness above.

You writhed ecstatically in my fear then as I passed out of the room, and as you know, a part of you is in that forgotten corner still, gathered up and left waiting for the next one that comes. Of course, this calving could have never happened if it hadn't been for our communion, so I don't know whether to feel remorse at this fragment I've torn from you or satisfaction in knowing that I am no longer the only one stripped of something vital.

It was so black inside the staircase that the smell became a physical assault, the creaking and scraping of my steps amplified into pitiless concussions. I had time enough at this point to consider how I would find what I was looking for—would I just feel around, sightless until my hands crashed into whatever was waiting for me up there? Would I wait for it to charge me? It was clear that none of these spaces were lit; they'd always had purposes other than to be lived in, to be seen.

The staircase turned back on itself, too, but the eaves above me were so close that I had to actually crawl up the last section. Here, I found quite a bit of what felt like trash under my hands, plastic bags and pieces of cardboard along with the dried feces of various animals and insects. At its top was a wooden door only about three feet high that refused to open, and so there I remained, my body extended over those filthy stairs, trying to force open a plywood flap and failing because something was behind it, something that felt soft and heavy and resistant.

I was glad then that I'd been made blind because otherwise, I would have seen how restrictive the space was, how the rafters prevented me even from sitting up, the walls on either side of me keeping my arms pinned down at my side. Then the resistance to my blows against the door evaporated, and it slammed open.

The strangely familiar, acrid smell was so strong here that it almost made the air solid, and I held my nose for a moment, too overcome to proceed. I could tell by the muffled echoes that whatever space before me was very small and full of objects that were absorbing most of my noise. It seemed as if it were a large closet. I just couldn't see what it was filled with.

When I reached out to climb in, my hands sank into a foot of trash on the floor covered in a coating of damp grime. I'd managed to drag myself halfway into the room when I grabbed onto something sharp, and I pulled back so violently that I slammed my elbow into the underside of the roof. There was a second of waiting, then a blooming of pain that forced everything from my mind but the sensation, and then not even that. Of all things, I actually heard myself laughing, the buildup of emotion too much for me to endure any longer. And besides, I was doing something so completely idiotic that even I was able to see the morbid humor of it. Now, it's hard to believe that I could have ever giggled up there in that hateful room, but at the time, I didn't know what was going to happen. Now, that knowledge is the filter through which I view that room: sharper, plunging, terminal.

The first thing I regained after my episode was the odor, and then the sense of claustrophobia. I pressed myself to the floor mostly because I didn't want to know how close the ceiling was, but the stillness that replaced my thin laughter was too insidious, and so I waded into the filth, pulling myself up into a ball, only one arm reaching out to feel for whatever awaited me.

The walls were unfinished, and so I pushed my hand into complex spider webs and lethal splinters of wood and what felt like some sort of crunchy, hollow nests built by a mass of unknown insects. There were other things on the walls that my hand would occasionally brush, and they felt like pieces of paper and the frames of pictures, but I ignored them, glad to be sightless at least of these artifacts. There were also stiff rags that could have once been clothing and desiccated, balding stuffed animals, and I refused to consider why they were there, the last place on earth I ought to have found evidence of habitation.

Then I had to shift my position to feel farther down the wall, and the sound of shuffling garbage was extended by another noise nearby, something almost like a sigh. After that, I kept the trash in a state of constant clamor, even though I knew I was stirring up the dangerous items mixed in with the benign—jagged and pointed and pinching things that had already sliced my skin open in several places. It helped that I was shivering, as this reverberated through some of the more flimsy pieces of trash that came into contact with my body, muffling the other, inexplicable noises.

Finally, I had to move my position to continue the search, and when I did, my face ran into something standing in the middle of the space, something solid and wooden. A moment's groping in the dark told me that it was a ladder affixed to the floor, and I actually spoke.

"Oh, no."

My devastation was absorbed by the house; I could actually feel it being extracted by the darkness. But any disgust at this paled in comparison to the truth I was faced with: the house was still waiting. Whatever I had to find wasn't in this foul, little space on the third floor, either. It was above me in the attic.

I had to force myself even deeper into Penobscot Road, the worst thing I could possibly imagine. It was worse than if I'd come face to face with whatever was pushing its way into my world because then I'd at least know what it was and could respond in some informed way. But I had to continue groping my way farther into the trap, still a witless victim.

I was curled up into a ball, and I drew my arm back to myself and stopped moving, face down in all that garbage. After all of my determination to see this hunt through—whatever it was—I didn't know where I would find the strength to climb the ladder. I was virtually trapped now, by the blackness, by the constriction of space that denied me any kind of easy escape. I was so far from the familiar areas of the house, which at least offered room to move and a light switch. How could it possibly get worse? My heart slammed out its beats against my forearms, and freezing sweat gathered at the tip of my nose, sensations that reminded me I was a biological organism whose life could be ended by any number of traumas.

Then the sweat mingled with tears, and I dragged myself to the base of the ladder, pressing against it as I grabbed for a rung. I hardly had room behind me to bend my legs and gain purchase, and short nails coming through the underside of the roof continually grabbed at me, but I only focused on the next step, driving everything else from my mind. It had to be done.

At the top was another piece of plywood, and feeling around the edges, it seemed as if it were built to slide to the right on a rough kind of track. Unfortunately, the area had swollen due to some kind of thick moisture, and so the door wouldn't slide open. My first reaction was relief, as it meant I wouldn't have to enter the attic, but I carefully excised that emotion and began pulling at the edges of the board. It was flimsy, and I believed I could break it in two—or at least bend it enough to pull it out of its tracks. But not being able to see what I was doing put too much of my awareness in my fingers, in feeling the flakes of wood dig into my flesh, because it took too long before I noticed the sounds coming from the area behind it. Once I stopped my assault, I could hear real breathing—a phenomenon from my old world and not the kind of fear the house could cruelly inflict on my range of senses. Someone was in the attic.

I had to break the spell: "Hello?"

The breathing stopped for a moment, then began again, shallower.

"Who's up here?"

No response. The house had driven me this far; I had to proceed, regardless of what I found, who I found in the attic.

I began tugging at the door again, and almost immediately, I sensed some play in the bottom track, so I pulled on it until I felt the board release itself. Immediately, I was blasted with even colder air and a smell that was so close now that I was able put a name to it: under the mildew and under the rotten garbage and under the myriad kinds of slick feces rotting everywhere around me was what I now recognized as the scent of blood. This, too, was not a spectral materialization perpetrated by Penobscot Road.

With the opening now uncovered, I listened for any signs of the other person. The breathing continued, but I could now tell it was farther down on my right, so I grabbed into the darkness to find a few loose planks in front of me and pulled myself in. My hands were instantly covered in something like cold motor oil, and I forcibly clung to that explanation as I dragged myself farther into the attic. I'd reached some sort of limit for processing things as they were happening.

The sides of the roof came together only three feet above my head, and my shoulders barely cleared the rafters on either side of me. I found that I could only move forward by grabbing onto the beams at my sides and pulling myself along, the wet filth on the floor pushing into my clothing and against my skin, my cellphone threatening to rip through my sweatpants. After a few moments of this awkwardness, I realized that the only way I could get out of the attic now was to push myself backwards into the darkness with no idea of what was behind me, my sensory organs at the wrong end of my body.

The attic must have run the entire length of the house because I could hear strange echoes reaching far out in front of me. What I couldn't tell was exactly where the other person was because the breathing merely ricocheted around the space whenever I stopped to listen. Now, I can't believe that I ever crawled along that narrow passage, dragging myself directly at someone waiting for me in the pitch black, but I'd managed to shut down as many emotions as I could. Unfortunately, most of them were the alarms that triggered my self-preservation instinct.

Then I stopped. Cell phone. I'd instinctively grabbed my phone before leaving my room, and it had a flashlight function! It was an idea with its own set of horrors, but there was someone up there with me. I needed to see them, regardless of whatever else was in the attic with us.

I retrieved my cell and fumbled with it until managing to get the screen to illuminate. Instantly, I felt the blue glow cover my face, the vulnerability so palpable it felt like a charge of electricity across my skin. Panicking, I began mashing the keys to find the flashlight function but only became more disoriented, and so I simply turned the screen toward the area in front of me and Dr. Modelle was an inch away from my hand, his face turned toward me in an unnatural angle, a dark bubble at the corner of his mouth, his eyes squeezed shut. Then they were open and looking at me, terrified, and he said, "No," and more blood spilled out of his mouth, and he was on top of the trap door over the third-floor hallway and although I could see that it was sagging precariously under his weight, I moved up closer to him, and the whole thing cracked away from the plaster, Dr. Modelle sliding head first into the space below then hitting the floor, a sharp, muffled crack reverberating below that I somehow knew had come from inside his body. He was silent for a moment, then made a weak choking noise and died.

There. Finally. You have your real, live death. In fact, you've been remarkably patient, sticking with me through all of this, putting up with my self-pity and endless pleas for a little support as I relived for you what were the most awful moments of my life. You deserve a medal for your endurance. And you've even managed to gloss over my belief that you return some level of affection, that you could never truly want anything horrendous to happen to me. Bravo. But I won't ask you if it's been worth it yet, because there is still so much more to live through.

That crack when Dr. Modelle hit the floor (looking down into the cellphone-lit hallway, it was clear that it was his neck) was the beginning of the next phase. I think I understood this, even then. Finally, I had taken a stand against the house by actively trying to save one of its victims, and this had pushed everything else into gear for some reason.

The short period that followed is still a confusion of mashed-up memories and glimpses of hell.

I do remember jumping on the doctor's body. I wasn't about to back up into the attic to escape, and the floor below me was at least ten feet away, so I used his body to cushion my fall. His ribs cracked under my feet as an exhalation of air wheezed past his lips. Because of the length of his throat and the shape of his mouth, the noise produced sounded like Dr. Modelle.

The next thing was to walk into one of the rooms at the back of the house. I didn't even think about this, I just did it, as if it were something I'd been meaning to do but just hadn't had time for yet. Looking out through the torn screen and filthy glass, I could just make out the forms of cars below me, all lined up in the backyard. Dozens of people had suddenly descended on Penobscot Road. So how had I known they'd come? And where were they now?

But no one had come because some of the cars had been rotting back there for years. Others were newer though, and even our car had been carefully lined up and integrated into the ranks.

It was true that I'd avoided the backyard—we all had—but how had we missed this? And why had someone parked our car back there? None of this was exactly right, and it made me realize that the change that had taken place after the snap of the doctor's spine also meant that I was seeing things differently. My overdue act of defiance against Penobscot Road was clearing its haze. I understood enough now to know that I had to get my roommates out before they were killed, and so I immediately raced down to their rooms, the power of the house gone out of the frail, teasing phenomena of the second-floor family and the presence in my room. Penobscot Road had now bled completely into my reality. The house was fully actuated, it had surfaced, and so I was no longer just frightened of what lurked in the shadows; I was directly threatened.

I rushed first into Alphonse's room. His bed was empty, and the calm in his room indicated it had been empty for a long time. It didn't make any sense, and then it did.

And so I ran down the hall to Nicole's room, and it was exactly the same. Empty, and empty for a while. Certainly empty of the residue of the old woman. It was the empty that fills up a room never be occupied again. I looked up then at her Marilyn Monroe picture, and it was as if I'd lately been looking at it cross-eyed, seeing two images indistinct and incomplete, and only now could I truly comprehend it. What I saw was that it had been hanging alone in there, its old value gone for some time and a new one taking its place: a memento mori.

And so I reentered the hallway, the freezing temperature there appropriate for my home now because it reflected the consistency of everything else there except for me. Emptiness, stillness. I was the only squirming, hot organic matter left, and soon enough I would be stilled, too. But I had to be sure I was alone inside of it, so I opened the door to the silent room between Alphonse's and Nicole's, the room that none of us had ever acknowledged despite knowing it had been there all along.

I was knocked back by the stench, and before I could even reach for the light switch, I felt my face and hands covered by crawling things, a swarm of flies, and then I did find the switch and piled up in the corner were purple masses of shiny, bloated flesh wearing Nicole and Alphonse's clothing, only now the clothing was stained with yellow and brown fluids and covered with quivering insects and the faces were so swollen that they looked like cartoon characters of fat people, even though I knew they were Nicole and Alphonse and that they had been gone for a while. My first response was disbelief: I couldn't have lost so much time since I'd last seen them. Replaying the most recent series of events, I looked for the crack in time, glad at least that it gave me something to think about at that moment beside the deaths of my only friends, but soon enough, I stopped looking for the crack and instead left the room, closing the door as gently as possible, as if I could still wake them.

I then crossed the corridor to the basement door. If I'd never been down there before, I wasn't at all sure how I knew that the light switch was next to the third step down or how I instinctively took myself on a tour of the area, a kind of blooming re-acquaintance. It was even damper down there, but warmer, the smell of various molds and mildew merging with a slightly different stink of decay than upstairs. I found Evan's vomit dried at the foot of the stairs, and that I was actually comforted by this disturbed me more than had anything else in this new stage of my life because comfort was an aberration and therefore somehow dangerous.

Rooms had been built into the basement, too, terrible dark rooms that were meant to house people, with dirty tiny windows that featured only a dim view of mud outside. No one had bothered to remove any of the furniture down there, so one room had a stingy, narrow bed with a moldering, black-stained coverlet offering a repulsive invitation to lie down. Another had a cheap chest of drawers that leaned to the left, millimeters away from collapsing under the rotten moisture that had risen up through the filthy carpeting beneath it. In the farthest corner of the cellar and at the end of the hall stood a tilted toilet on cracked, black-lined tile and a showerhead standing over a sewer drain that had been providing entrance and exit to a variety of insects and animals for years. Decomposing droppings were scattered everywhere, the last place on earth that anyone should have located a place for inhabitants to clean themselves. It would have been squalid even on the day it had been completed.

Then there was the final door on the left, and I opened it to find Evan tied up to a bed, small cuts covering his body that had scabbed up and were now oozing other kinds of liquids produced by the decaying of a corpse, and Suzy, her arms secured to a pipe running near the ceiling. She was also covered with long, straight cuts that seemed to deny the many curves and folds of her body, but hers was still breathing, the rasping sound the only one in this subterranean void that absorbed sound and other insistences of life. Her corpulence hung around her, shrunken and dry, and her skin, once rosy and glowing, now just wrinkled up at the heaviest ends of her extremities. A gummy pool of urine circled her on the curling linoleum and darker drippings nearer the wall evidenced her still functioning biology.

Suzy's body was shutting down, but she still managed to moan at my presence, her eyes slitting slightly to indicate the last vestiges of comprehension. I wondered a little what she saw when she looked at me, and the easiest way to stop wondering was to leave the room and close the door behind me. There, a shadow crossed mine, and I gasped until I realized it was just my own, generated by a cracked mirror further down the hall that reflected a naked bulb overhead. The substance, the actuality of the house was beginning to re-coalesce for me. I felt as if I were sinking into a fever.

I knew what was in the dining room, but I had to look at it for the first time again, and so I returned upstairs and turned on the ugly dining-room chandelier over our circle of chairs. At the center of them was Melissa's body, twisted and rotting, too, and then I remembered that this was what the chairs had been arranged around. They'd been placed this way because stepping over the legs and around the flayed arms had become increasingly unpleasant. This was unpleasant as it was the kind of repeated action that had the best chance of rising up through everything else and into my range of memory, so after her ending, the other bodies were placed in rooms that could be closed off and so avoided and then expunged.

These were the people closest to the surface, but there were others, and as I stared at the terrible vinyl wallpaper that bubbled in front of me, I was able now to access them, too. And so I returned to the front hallway and glanced out the small window by the door into the darkness and saw only myself in answer, my calmness framed by the edges of the glass, concentrated and contained. Upstairs, I passed by all the doors until I came to the large room that had smelled so bad when I'd first entered it a few days earlier. The room with the Christmas lights. The family that had been haunting me was there, unfamiliar and familiar at the same time, their remains all lined up and decomposing, too, only most of their moisture had escaped them by now, and so their solids were being broken down, minced apart both by invisible forces and the kind I could see: maggots, roaches. I noted that the children had come apart much more quickly than the adults, which brought to mind their smooth skin and narrow, precise little fingers, the absence of wear proclaimed in their every atom. The stench was so unbelievable that it had actually managed to break through when I'd last entered. At this point, I made a mental note to investigate all the phenomena that had managed to reach me despite the house's deceptions once I had a moment to think. Perhaps they all had something in common.

Am I losing you?

And standing there, the room whole again before me, I was allowed to go a bit further back, back to the old lady and the sick lady, the people who had occupied Nicole and Alphonse's rooms before, only it hadn't been years before, it had been days, and I was also allowed to regain the fact that what was left of their bodies was among the trees, the stand at the front of the yard that was scrawled across my bedroom wall. So I returned there to look at the drawing and could now plainly see that it had been a proclamation all along—at first a eulogy for the slaughtered old ladies dumped in the woods but now a warning, a message meant for me that could communicate only horror and therefore could not be interpreted for any kind of direct usefulness. It was at this moment I understood that the traces of these previous inhabitants had been so palpable because they'd been so recently in existence, their scents still trapped in corners, their fingerprints still pressed onto handles. I must have ingested their strands of hair, their skin flakes.

None of this was surprising to me, nor did it increase my dismay. I'd been upset since the day I'd come to Penobscot Road, and now I knew again why. Or at least I knew again that the house had prevented me from sensing the dead people lying around me since my arrival. I'd spent the last ten days surrounded by rotting corpses, robbed not only of the ability to see them but also of the chance to act on this knowledge. If the house had revealed them to me sooner, who knows how many lives I would have saved? My own, at least.

There were other secrets that the house had buried into me, and they had also been laid bare to me now, although I refused to acknowledge them.

And so, alone again in my bedroom, I felt Penobscot Road standing all around me, and it was both less and more than it had been. The deceitful fog that it had released into itself had been sucked back up into the walls, and in its place was the kind of waste that was part of the past, the waste of lives, of futures. I'd been stranded back in my old world, back into its laws and procedures, but I would have given anything to be swallowed up again by the house's hallucinations. It had been easier to be afraid and not know why.

It would be easier to leave you now with your fear, never completely knowing why, so I think I'm going to end this now.

But that would be merciful, and you don't deserve to feel any more satisfaction in my suffering than I've given you already. To stop now would be to show you the kind of respect I finally realize you've never shown me. After all, you must have noticed how your heart quickened at these recent revelations, how you became overwhelmed by the desire for the particulars of agony and death. There is no place for respect there. And I'd tell you again that your hunger is so profound that it has echoed back to those days, back to the time I first set eyes on Penobscot Road, and that it was the catalyst for everything I've just shared with you. I'd tell you again, but your thoughts would only glance over this, scrabbling for the next disclosure of horror. Nonetheless, in a very real sense, your black desires are the black desires of that house.

But you have your distance, your superiority and your knowledge. You feel certain that things would have turned out differently if you'd been in my place because you would have been much smarter and stronger than I was. But is it strength that allows you to dismiss the central question: Who else but for you did all of this happen? No amount of superiority can deny the truth that still squirms in your heart. Your bloodlust did this to me.

So, yes, I will continue. But I continue to honor what is left of me, not to satisfy your prurient urges. And I will use this desire you have to be cozily horrified as a tool to drag you closer, a weapon to use against you. See if you don't help me.

Underneath the killings were the events that had led to them. This was the next layer down, and the instant Dr. Modelle's neck broke was the instant this knowledge was again made available to me. Standing in my room, the terrible scribblings on the wall trying to keep me from remembering yet all the while screaming at me, I began to drop further into the obscured past. Being there, in the room in which I'd slept, first brought to mind the mystery that had been borne there: the entity that had persecuted me over the past few days. Its truth now rose to the surface, although in some sense, this truth had always been close by and so had prevented me from fearing the presence as much as I should have. You see, the presence had been me, or rather a part of me that had broken off, had survived and so represented my survival instinct. It had been a shard of the old me that remembered, and its compulsion hadn't been to torture me at all. At first, its goal had been to shock me into seeing what was really happening, then to kill me so that I would never have to face what had taken place. But it had been weak and failed miserably, more proof that it had only been me.

The thought that my soul had struggled in this way saddened me, and as I stood at the center of that room, my arms folded to protect myself from nothing, I mourned the passing of what I had once been. But then my pulse quickened: this mourning was an act that could only be generated and experienced by my former self! Somewhere in the shock of the release of all this information, I had been released, too. And if I was free, if I had my real senses back, it was possible that I might still have a chance to defeat Penobscot Road.

In fact, it was good to rid myself of that weak entity that had only beaten against me like a tiny insect, because a strange response rose in me: I became angry. I hadn't yet been ripped apart physically by the house, but it had violated what I had been, and this aroused a plume of rage that I calmly identified as a weapon—my first and possibly only one. Whatever was left of me was what had endured the house, and in so being, had power.

All of these thoughts were tangling in my mind as I stood at the center of that room, the dead all around me. I wasn't sure why the house had spared me this long, but I wanted to use my newfound hatred to ensure that it could never destroy anyone again. I also knew that I didn't have much time.

Realizing that I wasn't yet able to face how everyone had died, I turned away from them and instead revisited the areas in the house that had evoked strange responses in me, hoping that there would be some common link to help me make sense of what was happening. My first stop was the little bump in the kitchen floor. Standing on it now was an anti-experience; it was less than trivial. But only days before, it had been a place where I'd heard words erupting from my own mouth, disturbing comments I would have never uttered on my own. Something had pushed through to me here, but how? Why?

The mantel in the parlor was another spot, and so I inspected it, too. It had evoked an overly euphoric feeling in me, the sensation of being drunk just before transitioning into a hangover. I looked more closely at the mantel itself: some sort of stone that had been slathered in white latex paint years before. So was it something about its exact location in the house? The intersection of cruel ley lines? Was it the accumulation of past experiences there, one of the few areas in the house that hadn't yet been stained with pain or terror? Or was it some kind of bait that had been used to trap us? After all, Alphonse had been drawn here the first time we'd been inside, and he'd stroked the mantel carnally, murmuring that he didn't like the place. But there had been so much lust in his voice.

The clarity of anger was quickly pulling me out of the confusion of the past ten days, and I walked down the back hall toward the bathroom, the enormity of loss at last crushing me as I passed the door that hid Alphonse and Nicole's bodies. It was a physical assault, as if I'd walked into a wall, and a groan escaped me, a sound from my old life again. For some nebulous reason, the house had chosen this moment to be cruelest to me, forcing me to fully see what it was and what it had done to everyone in it. And so I began to weep even as I promised myself that I would put an end to the violence that was Penobscot Road. It was very possible that its cruelty could somehow be used against it.

The bathroom was as foul as ever, and I inspected the scuffed, soiled flooring for some kind of sign. I'd been convinced that Alphonse had been urinating there, but both he and Nicole believed that it had been me.

Was the house generating it? Or perhaps it was just another specter created to confuse us. As I stared at the floor, I realized that I had to relieve myself, and out of spite and curiosity, I did so right in the middle of the room. I wanted at least this memory to be real in some way, to take it back, rather than knowing that it was caused and owned by the house. Although it splashed back on my feet, the sensation of actually *doing* something to Penobscot Road, of communicating my hatred in return, was a momentary relief. As my piss gathered in an indentation and then ran off toward the farthest corner, I managed to turn one of my sobs into an awful cackle, and the sound was wholly mine. I needed to win because that was all I had become.

But before I'd even had a chance to allow the laughter to fade away, it caught in my throat. There was a noise upstairs, something real, and I found that I was quickly relearning how reality differed from the phantom phenomena perpetrated by the house—another tool in my arsenal. Suzy would soon be dead; I knew that in my heart. But perhaps there was another survivor still trapped with me who could be saved! Only then did I realize how desperately I wanted to share these experiences with someone, to stagger out of the house together and always know that I was understood, even as the rest of mankind doubtlessly would shun us. Another victim might even have the insight I needed to determine what was happening in the house and why. And so as I emerged from the twilight the house had forced upon me, my pain continuing to intensify, I prayed that sharing my ordeal would give me some kind of relief.

I had hoped that partner would be you.

Returning to the hallway, I heard more movement above me and only then reined in my optimism. Who could be left? Everyone who'd entered Penobscot Road had left behind a ruined body. As I approached the front staircase, I allowed myself to remember that there had been other people inside, official people who the house knew enough not to destroy but only to fool, so that they, too, walked past the scenes of brutality, blinded. I recalled my strange memory of a black pant leg standing next to me as I crouched next to my bed in a corner, a pair of shiny uniform shoes pointed at me that spoke distantly of the old kind of protection. At the time, the house had obscured the police officer's presence to such an extent that his legs had become an abstract thought, his thick, jangling belt merely a series of sudden movements and flashes of light. The house extracted meaning in that way. So all I'd been left with had been the ghostly tracings of the policeman, suspicions and sensations that I'd only been able to interpret as imaginary at the time, as hallucinations. And likewise, he must have dismissed me as merely a faint specter, an inconsequential feeling near his feet—meaning that the house had skinned me of my validity as a human being, too. In a very real sense, it had decided what existed and what did not.

And then more, that distant day: beyond the leg, across the room, another mass of sound and movement had barely registered on my senses. Melissa's boyfriend. He had been there, too, and the desperation radiating off of him had been his only detail that had managed to reach me, a kind of inchoate dread I'd only found puzzling, random. I was beginning to recognize this, too, as I stood at the foot of the stairs, again staring out that awful little window next to the front door. The spell Penobscot Road had inflicted on me was broken, but did that include the other people in the house? They might still be operating in the shadowy half-world that the house had left draped over them. I knew I would see them, but would they see me? Because even though I wasn't yet ready to admit it, on some level I knew that this spell did more than just blind us, confuse us. It made us do things to each other.

"Hello? Is anybody here?" If the house's shroud had been universally lifted, I needed to convert whoever was with me to allies as soon as possible because they would've seen the carnage at this point, too. But if the house was deceiving them, the strangers might only interpret me as a ghost or a feeling—if even that. Either way, how would they react when I found them?

"Are you okay?"

And if the strangers believed that I was coming to kill them, I'd just given away my location, my identity. It was a risk.

Complete silence. "I'm not a ghost. Or your imagination." What else could I say to convince the other people—or person—that I was just as innocent as they were? "Do you need help? I've called the police, so they should be here any minute."

Nothing. I could go up and present myself, but that seemed unduly reckless. Or I could wait there, at the bottom of the stairs. Eventually, whoever was with me in the house would have to come down, and I'd stand a much better chance of defending myself if need be. But that would mean standing there, in the middle of Penobscot Road, as the knowledge of the last ten days fully returned to me.

And then, almost as if in answer to my dread: "Help." A woman's voice, weakened by something. Even if she were being tricked to call out to me, she was still a human being, she still really did need help. So many things had happened within those walls, and I was somehow complicit; finally understanding this, I could not allow anything else to take place.

"I'm coming!" And so I mounted the stairs, cursing the creaky wood that robbed me of any ability to hear other movements in the vicinity. The light over the front door had seemed sufficient for the second-story hall, but as I rose into the dimness there, I realized that it wasn't. The shadows that had once hidden the memories of the slaughtered family were now pregnant with other kinds of danger. I paused at the top of the stairs, the surrounding silence enfolding me. "Hello?"

But the woman had now almost completely dropped out of my field of attention, because I flicked on a light to find that the veils were continuing to drop from Penobscot Road.

As my eyes adjusted to the glare, I was able to make out scribblings and drawings that had always been on the walls, floors and ceiling of the hallway, long passages written in a tight, neat hand and large sprawling phrases and diagrams of rooms and procedures, and what appeared to be lists like recipes of some kind. Much of it had been written on top of other words, as if the authors couldn't tell that someone else had already scrawled something there. I couldn't immediately make out the smaller script—and didn't want to at that point—but I could read the larger print: "You won't get out," and "It wasn't me," and "Don't forget us." There was a very careful drawing of the outside of the house, with arrows pointing to various windows along with explanations written nearby of their significance. A young person had drawn an animal of some kind with what appeared to be its guts hanging underneath it. Hundreds of crucifixes had been scratched into the paint on the door to the room in which the ritual began. There were brown splatterings that I suspected were blood.

Over the previous ten days, none of these warnings left by previous inhabitants had made it through the veil to me. Except for the trees in my room. I couldn't determine why those had been visible to me, how they had somehow pushed through the house's power and reached my eyes, imploring.

And then I understood: I'd drawn them in some somnambulant state, peeling back the wallpaper and then carefully replacing it with a kind of flour paste I must have concocted. That I *did* concoct. As with the entity,

I must have been semi-conscious of what was happening and desperate to warn myself before it was too late. That had been why I'd had the urge to rip the wallpaper off—on some level, I'd known that the message was waiting for me there. In fact, Alphonse and Nicole had warned me that I'd been sleepwalking, doing things I wasn't aware of—but then I froze.

Had they really warned me? By the state of their corpses, they'd been dead for a few days, yet I'd spoken with them only a few hours earlier. I grew nauseous: the house had not only obscured people's physical existence, it had conjured them when necessary. So had the three of us really baked cookies together, looking forward to meeting Nicole's new friend? Had they really hiked up the hill with me behind our house, eager to help me become a better Chris? Had we really wasted an afternoon trying to figure out where Nicole's poster should go?

Or had I been living inside of Penobscot Road, alone, begging thin air to listen to me, to help me, to leave with me before it was too late? I'd had full-blown, detailed conversations with memories. So at what point had they died? This knowledge I knew the house would never give up, and as tears wet my face, I wondered how many days I'd been completely alone in there, trying to save two people who were already dead.

Finding myself collapsed onto the floor, I could feel all those messages on the wall screaming for help against my back. In a strange way, I found that the scribbling the others had left behind was somehow comforting to me. I hadn't been totally alone; the horror of Penobscot Road had been perpetrated on countless inhabitants before me. We were all victims. Anything I'd done, they'd done, too, trapped into a pattern of degradation that had established itself years before and would doubtlessly continue on into the future, merciless, superior.

Unless I could determine a way to end it now.

I was finally allowed to see all of these signs and warnings; perhaps there was a solution buried in them, or one that could be added up, this accumulation of terror somehow rendering a buried weakness of Penobscot Road. It was only at this point that I realized I'd rejected the most obvious retaliation from the first moment I'd stepped foot in the house. To burn it down would've only made things worse, concentrating its energy in a way that would've led to an even more powerful structure being erected on the spot. There was some kind of refusal, a prohibition in every atom of the house to this course of action that did, in fact, reveal not only a weakness, but also an assured consequence. This was a seed that had been planted in every captive's mind the moment they set eyes on the place. It was inviolate.

So there was at least one vulnerability the house guarded against. Were there others that even it hadn't imagined yet? I turned toward the wall to my left, which had something scribbled out in pencil that began *"the Secret is to..."* when I heard a noise nearby. I turned to face the door that had been slashed over and over with crosses. The other person in the house was right behind it. And sure enough, I thought I could hear scratching, so the person must have been crouched down, her nails digging into the woodwork nearby. The ritual must have begun.

"Hello? Look, we can help each other—" But before I could finish my sentence, she threw open the door and bolted down the hallway, slamming a door to one of the rooms at the far end. It was Carrie—or Christine—the woman whom I'd discovered in Evan and Suzy's house. She was fast, but not fast enough to hide the wound-up way that she moved, or that she was profoundly terrified. Of me.

I was about to follow her when something caught my attention in the room she'd just left. In the farthest corner was a crumpled-up mass of dusty bones protruding out of a tattered, gray night gown. A human skull was at one end, which had rolled in a way that its face now turned to the floor, as if even dried-out remains could try to block out what surrounded them. There was no real way to tell, but somehow, I knew that this had once been an adolescent girl.

So the remnants of a much earlier victim were now being revealed to me. Just as everything covering the walls, I was oddly relieved to see this, as it put the more recent murders into perspective, merely a continuation of what the house was capable of. So just as I wasn't at all responsible for the death of the girl before me, I wasn't responsible for the deaths of everyone presently decomposing in and around Penobscot Road. Not really.

The walls of the room were barren, though—no drawings or words, just what Carrie had been scratching into the wood: *Help me god.* She hadn't struck me as a religious person at all.

"Carrie? Or Christine? Don't worry; I'm not going to hurt you!" She was able to see me, so she wasn't under the influence of the house after all. I had to convince her that I could help her. And if the house wasn't tricking her, she'd probably seen all the dead people, too, so I'd have to figure out a way to make her understand that I wasn't the real threat.

Quietly, I approached the closed door that, needless to say, led to the room in which everyone took off their clothing and went into some kind of cruel heat. She could no longer control her sounds and was gasping rapidly in between furious sobs.

"Look, I think I can get you out of here alive, but you have to do what I say. Carrie? You have to do exactly what I tell you to right now!"

She was at the far end of the room. I could tell because of the amount of echo in her weeping.

"Okay."

And so I slowly opened the door, the light from the hallway immediately illuminating one of her breasts and the left third of her face. She was pulling her shirt off, her face red and shiny with tears.

"What are you doing?"

"Just please don't hurt me." I could barely understand it.

"I'm not going to hurt you! But you have to do what I say—"

"I will, just please don't hurt me!" And she began to unbutton her pants.

"I don't mean that! I mean that I can help you get out of here, but you have to listen to me."

She stopped what she was doing, her eyes glittering at me through puffy, matted lids. There was an alertness there that I would only really recognize later, thinking back.

"The house has done all of this, not me. And if you don't get out, it's going to work you into its pattern. That's the way it traps people. And you're already—"

But she pushed past me and ran down the hall, sliding on the floor as she scrambled for a foothold. Maybe she was locked into the pattern, the ritual, because I didn't even have to follow her out to know where she'd gone. Yet she'd seemed entirely conscious of what she was saying and doing. So I just stood there, my back to the door, no longer concerned because I knew that the danger had shifted, and the hidden things in the house, the bad things, were no longer lurking in corners. They'd moved. But had they moved into Carrie, or were they simply latent, feeding off of the consequences of their design?

"Carrie? Christine? I don't want to scare you, but you're doing exactly what the house wants you to. I know where you are."

Sure enough, when I returned to the corridor, I saw her, standing in the bathroom at the end of it, her face thrown into a deep shadow. She wasn't sobbing now, although she was still taking in deep breaths as if to steady herself, and this abruptly composed state unnerved me.

"Carrie. Look, I knew you were going to be in there. It's part of the pattern!" She remained motionless. "Listen to me, please! You're going to want to run upstairs after this, but you need to get out. Do not go upstairs. Just go downstairs and out the front door. I think once you pass the trees at the end of the yard, you'll be okay."

She was shivering, too, but controlling it now, her left hand grabbing at the material of her pants and kneading it, rhythmically, almost methodically.

"You don't believe me, I know, but you have to listen to me. You have to break the pattern. *Do not go upstairs!*"

By now, I was ten feet away from her and could see that she wasn't looking me in the face; she was watching my arms, my hands for any sudden movements. She was waiting for me to attack her.

I stopped. "Okay. How about I go upstairs, and that way you can get out of the house. When you hear me up there, you'll know that I can't get to you. How does that sound?"

She was different now, a little more as I remembered her in Seville: crafty, evasive. Taking a deep breath, her eyes came up to mine. "Where's Evan and Suzy?"

She must have seen me wince because she immediately began to cry again, although she held her eyes up, her head steady.

"Look at the walls! This has been going on for years. It isn't me!" But her stare remained cold, dismissive. Was the house letting her see everything? If not, then this last comment would have sounded as if it had come from an insane person.

There was nothing more I could say or do. I just had to hope that she would leave after I'd removed myself as a perceived danger. "I'm going to go upstairs, now. Go out the front door and don't stop until you've gone past the trees at the front of the yard, okay? Otherwise, you're never going to get out."

I quickly turned and walked up to the third-floor steps. She could see me mounting them, disappearing into the blackness above. As I looked back, the flint in her eyes told me that much of her fear had dissipated for some reason.

The third floor was as dormant as the rest of Penobscot Road. When I turned on the light, there was only Dr. Modelle's body in the hallway, snapped into unnatural angles, to remind me of the house's potential. Even the walls in the passageway were clear of writing or drawing. This struck me as especially significant, although at the time, I couldn't have determined why.

"Okay, Carrie! I'm upstairs! So get out! Now!"

I could hear her moving below me, the floor creaking. I couldn't tell where she'd gone, but who would stay in a house with a mass murderer? Because I was sure she still believed that. I would have, if I'd been in her shoes.

I hadn't looked around the third floor since the house had allowed things to be seen, and I hoped that I might now find something there that could help me keep the cycle from starting up again. Of course, Carrie would immediately contact the police—and if she could see me, they might now be able to, as well. But it was strange: I wasn't worried about what would happen to me afterward because I knew that whatever it was, it couldn't possibly be as bad as what I'd just lived through. What I was still living through. The future would just be four walls that held nothing at all but me, nothing hidden, nothing determining new ways to take advantage of me. I wondered if Oregon had the death penalty. In fact, I was hoping Carrie was already on the phone, telling someone to come and get me.

But being locked up wouldn't stop what the house was doing, and so I ducked into one of the big, windowless rooms near the staircase. The light no longer worked in here, so I couldn't see much at first. But I could tell that there were things in here, in the corners, pushed into the shadows. The room revealed itself as holding more than the nasty bunk bed screwed to the wall. As my eyes adjusted, I could see the outlines of small boxes and cans and plastic bags. The room was filled with groceries, toilet paper, cleaning supplies—and they were all relatively new. Someone had very recently filled this room, and filled it while I'd been living in the house, as if they were planning on remaining for a long time. It must have been Carrie. But how long had she been hiding? Had she followed me from Seville? If so, she'd probably seen me conversing with no one, at which point she'd have to think I was insane. But what exactly was she planning on doing?

I heard another creak from downstairs and knew that she hadn't taken my advice to escape. So within the ritual, the bathroom must have represented a place to gather strength, or more accurately, to forget fear.

Suzy had actually slapped me across the face there, blaming me for everything. But thinking back, I wasn't sure if that had actually been her. She and Evan had gone down into the cellar beforehand, and I couldn't shake the feeling that they'd never come back up. So why had the house wanted me to think they'd been okay? And why had it done this with the memory of Alphonse and Nicole, too, hiding their bodies, their smell?

The questions I'd been repressing began to rise up and tear at me. What had been Alphonse and Nicole's last memory of me? What had they felt toward me at that moment—fear or sadness or just a kind of inevitable acquiescence? Had they finally understood that it had been the house all along? If nothing else, I hoped that they'd been given that because all of this was a crueler theft than their murders, and I knew it would hobble me forever.

Still, the secret to defeating the house might have been lurking within the tricks it played on me, a kind of defense mechanism hiding some obscure vulnerability. Why hadn't it just tricked me into believing that my friends had escaped, as it had with Melissa and Evan and Suzy? But then I knew the answer: if I'd realized that I'd been alone days earlier, I would've had no reason to stay.

The ice was too thin here, and so I resumed my investigation of the rest of the third floor. Stepping over the doctor's body, I passed into the back, into those filthy, cramped rooms gathered at the end of the hall. The stink of mildew and other things back there were pushed into me by the low ceilings and claustrophobic spaces, and I fought back an urge to retch. It was easy to recognize now that this part of the attic had never been meant to be inhabited when it had been built, but something about the house, the strange compulsion to add on, must have maddened the previous occupants to the point that they'd actually constructed rooms that felt like bad mistakes. And then they'd put their own children in them. It's true: there is no better way to describe the rear of the third floor of Penobscot Road. It was something to regret, an error of judgment that surrounded me, its walls pressing in to crush whatever came inside it.

I opened the flimsy door to my left, and the dim light caught the contour of something in there that I hadn't seen before. Then Carrie was behind me and I turned and she was grasping a knife that was slashing through the space between us. I fell back into the room and she tripped on my feet and hit the floor to my left and I could see that it wasn't a knife but a sharp nail file. I grabbed at the corner of the door to get out of the room but she raised the file again and so I kicked at her stomach to throw off her aim and got up and ran into the next room and slammed the door behind myself. The light switch was right there, pushing into my elbow, and so I flipped it on and found that the room now revealed a large cage. A little, soiled mattress was inside, along with old, dirty toys face down in ancient newspaper that had been covered many times by human excrement, and so children had been imprisoned up here, left to play in their own filth. And then I saw the folded-up bones in the corner of the cage, the newspaper eaten away around them and I knew that this child had been forgotten and had curled up and slowly lost consciousness alone, wondering why the people no longer visited her to throw food at her or to watch her, feeding off of her misery. This was one of the rooms in which the screens had been clawed at, and I hoped that at least someone had escaped, jumping out of the window to fall on her head and quickly die.

But everything had grown quiet. Carrie was waiting for me.

My first impulse was to plead with her, but this only seemed to make things worse. My weak begging had acted as an accelerant, causing everything to happen faster than it would have, otherwise. I'd have been happy to wait for her to leave, but the doors were so thin. Soon enough, she would realize how easy it was simply to stab her way into the room.

Then there was a loud click, and the room went black. She'd found an electrical box, although I couldn't see how the darkness would help her kill me. But then, very loudly, she walked down the hallway and into one of the windowless rooms in the old part of the house—probably the one that she'd filled with supplies that would last for months. Maybe waiting her out was a bad idea.

So where would I leave the tangle of my bones? In the corner behind the cage, my fetal position perfectly preserved? Right under the door, where I'd spend the last days of my life listening for a change on the other side? I could curl up around what was left of the little child, the thought of dying in the same spot somehow edifying to me. But I had the window and then the fall! I could erase everything I now knew with a simple, quick snap. Of course, I could also sneak out when Carrie was sleeping, but that would only feed the house, that particular surrender making me the worst kind of victim yet. The one who continues on, knowing.

The thought of rotting alone in that room was too satisfying, though, too appropriate for me not to wonder why my first impulse had been to remain trapped in there, rather than to continue seeking a way to save Carrie and conquer the house. I was untangling the house's web a bit more with this question, exposing it, and this in turn, seemed to open up more of my immediate past. The first thing I understood again was the spot in the kitchen, the almost organic bump that seemed to inspire strange comments from me. In actuality, it had been the place where Nicole had first spoken aloud of her fear of Penobscot Road—the first time any of us had. It was a memory that had been taken away from me, but now it was suddenly back in my brain, and only then, crouched down and frozen in that horrible room, did I understand just how dangerous it was to be robbed of a part of my past like that. Because it was only through my memories that I was able to learn, and without them, I was prevented from making good decisions. The right decisions. And so I'd been making the wrong ones since the first moment I'd stepped foot in Penobscot Road.

My eyes were open, muffled by the darkness, and yet I could feel them straining to see what I was now recalling. Nicole had stopped on that spot, a frying pan full of scrambled eggs in one hand and a spatula in the other, and she'd turned to Alphonse and me, a false smile on her face. She'd made a joke of it, something about the house needing an exorcism, but it had been the wrong thing to say, and so Penobscot Road had sucked it up, pulled it away from me. It had been early in our stay, probably the first morning we'd been there, and instead, I'd been given the information that at that time, Nicole and Alphonse had been comfortable in the house and distrusted my uneasiness. So this memory meant that she'd really been alive then, that first or second morning, and I couldn't help wondering if my response to her fear hadn't been altered too, at the time, so that I made her feel silly and mistaken. I couldn't help wondering if she would have gotten out in time if it hadn't have been for what I'd said, convincing her that it was only her imagination.

Then I remembered more. We'd all been up to the second floor on the first day, too—we hadn't really avoided it for days. And the upstairs room in which I remembered us lingering, losing time in some kind of euphoric trance—the carnal room—had really been the place where we'd first discussed going back to Sacramento. Alphonse had broached the subject only hours after we'd arrived, the house too big and awful for him to seriously contemplate living in. And so he'd suggested that we'd just had a little adventure, a momentary lapse in judgment, and all we really had to do was to get into our U-haul van and return home. It was still packed up and right outside, a few hundred feet away, and so was our path, just one road after another joining up, an uninterrupted asphalt surface right back to California. It was so comforting to think of all of that continuous blacktop leading home, how it was unbroken, an actual, physical link stretching back to real life.

So it hadn't taken us days before we'd admitted the danger to each other—we'd known right from the start that there was something wrong with Penobscot Road! The house had effaced the memories that were closest to reality and transformed them into bizarre falsities, as if eliminating the eyes of someone in a photograph with black boxes. By transforming these events into areas within itself, it subsumed the truth and spit it back up as some kind of emotional artifact that it now owned. Yet this was a thought that soothed some wounds too obscure for me to name, and it encouraged me. I felt my strength returning.

In reality, Alphonse and Nicole had harbored more doubts than I had about the house. They'd realized more quickly that it was a bad place. So I was chosen to be tortured like this because I was the slow one. Then, I remembered that they'd tried to get out, and that was why they'd died. On some level, I'd always known that escaping meant death, which was why I kept coming back, why I persisted in trying to fight back in other ways.

Now I could see that the house had manipulated me there, too, allowing me to believe that it could be conquered if I just continued to search its halls for the answer. But I'd been made to remove the string I'd tied to my toe the night before, so there was no way to recognize my nocturnal activity. And I'd been made to sweep up the powder I'd sprinkled on the floor outside my door, so there could be no way of ever seeing only my own footprints crossing back and forth, back and forth in a jumble of strange, lost movement.

I was nothing more than a kind of pack animal doing the house's bidding, and it couldn't be stopped, at least by someone like me. Someone as profoundly weak.

Then the other memories crashed down on me, a tangle of pain so intense that I writhed on the floor, the poison released into my body, catastrophic, permanent. And my lack of surprise at everything I remembered told me it was all true

"What happened here?" Carrie was right outside the door. The shock forced me to surface, although I'd lost the need to communicate. Instead,

I was strangely fascinated by the fact that she'd asked the very question at the very moment that I could fully answer it. I wondered if the house had done that, too.

"Hey, you mother fucker! Why did you do this?!"

And then I wanted to squeeze out the poison, to relieve the pressure inside me, if only slightly. Carrie would have to be the unfortunate receptacle.

"Everybody died."

"Did you kill them?" She was putting her entire soul into sounding as if she weren't terrified.

"The house did. Yes."

"What the fuck does that mean?"

"Why did you come here?"

"Because Evan and Suzy told me they were coming here. Where are they?"

"Why didn't you call the police?"

"I don't have to answer your fucking questions! I've got a knife."

"A nail file."

"Where are Suzy and Evan?"

"Why don't you call the cops now?"

"I already did. They're going to get here any second, so you better tell me what fucking happened!"

"You came all the way out here, and you didn't call the cops because the house has got you, too."

"Fuck you!" But her voice cracked.

"Everything that's going to happen has been in place for a long time. I'm sorry."

"What's that supposed to mean?"

"Fighting it only makes it worse. But it makes it better for the house. Squirming."

She paused, and I could hear her force her own breathing to slow.

"Is that what you did to them? Mess with their minds?"

"Me? No. I'm too pathetic. My god, can't you tell?"

"So how did all of these people die?"

There was no alternative. There never had been. "The family that lived here before was bad. The house wants to be the bad one; it doesn't want the rest of us to have that kind of power. So they had to go. We gassed them in the middle of the night with canisters of carbon monoxide I bought over the internet from China. Everyone looked sunburned when we were done. The old woman downstairs heard us, though—I think it was my oxygen mask—and so her screaming needed to be stopped right away. We hit her head with the oxygen tank until her face was moved to the right, and then we did the same thing to the sick lady in the room two doors down from her. She didn't fight much because she could tell that there was no point. Because they knew about us, they had to be taken outside and buried, and so we put them under the stand of trees at the front, near the road. Do you understand?"

Carrie was crying, but she didn't move away from the door.

"Why aren't you leaving? Do you still think you can do something?"

"You asshole!" Yet she remained.

"If I didn't know better now, I would've said that the property manager was a spur-of-the-moment thing. But there's nothing random about any of this. I found an old can of hair spray, and as soon as she led me into the back yard, we used it as a kind of flame thrower. I don't know how the body can keep living for so long like that, after it's been cooked. Her name was Flo, but I remember now wondering when a name no longer applies. At what exact point did she stop being Flo and start being just meat?"

She screamed; I apologized and continued.

"Then my roommates, Alphonse and Nicole." I paused, surprisingly. But only for a second. "Then Alphonse and Nicole. Nicole had been hiding in the small room at the front of the second floor, hiding there because she'd suspected something about me. When I found her, she pulled me into the room farther down the hall, acting as if she were interested in me. Sexually. Just like you did, Carrie. But when she realized that we couldn't allow her to leave, she ran to the bathroom. Sound familiar? You think that it's just me, but it isn't. Because just like you, she pushed past me and ran upstairs, came up here, only she had to stop in the middle of the hallway, and we had to cut her throat open. It doesn't allow anyone to leave. Not really. So what I said before—well, I was wrong about escaping. If I'd known how cruel it was, I never would have suggested it."

Now she was sobbing.

I had to ask: "Do you still think you're staying because you want to?"

"I'm staying because I'm going to fucking kill you!"

"You don't know how much I wish that were true."

Crying seemed to settle her mind a little. "Why are you doing this?"

I actually sighed at this question. I was wasting my breath on her, but it had to be discharged into the air. "When someone closes a door, does it matter if they use their right hand or their left hand? All that matters is that the door is closed. Nicole and Alphonse understood this too early. And too late."

"Is he still here?"

"Alphonse? No one's here but you and I, Carrie."

"So you killed him, too?"

"What the house made Alphonse and Nicole do always seemed to be closer to the surface for them. They suspected something earlier. They almost remembered. So after Nicole, Alphonse had to be gone, too. I still had blood on my wrist; I could feel it drying on my skin when Alphonse and I talked. He saw it, too. But we had a good conversation. I think we both knew that it was going to be the last time for us, a conversation like the old days. He talked mostly about the smart phone he wanted to buy. We were by the fireplace in the parlor. Then he went into the dining room, and we stabbed him right next to his spine and to the right, about eight inches below his neck. The knife rotated in my hand to fit between his ribs. He wasn't surprised at all. I think that helps people die faster. Maybe that's why I'm telling you all of this. Maybe that's why you're listening."

Carrie began to howl again, and I knew the sound was being absorbed by Penobscot Road, savored. I could at least stop that. "Carrie! I can tell you about Evan and Suzy now. Carrie. You have to be quiet."

"You fucking psycho." But she stopped screaming, and I felt that I could continue.

"Like I said, I'm a weak person. I haven't had the strength to remember anything but strange details until right now, and they didn't seem to amount to much. The house gave me just enough to want to get to the bottom of everything, to figure out what was going on. So I contacted a psychic in town, and she came over, and I think she was able to see the things that the house was hiding from me, like the bodies and the blood and the smell. And so we had to kill her right away, and we grabbed a heavy metal lamp and hit her in the head with it. She was still conscious after the first blow, so we had to slam it into her face several times before life left her. It wouldn't let go for the longest time. Her name was Melissa."

The sobbing began again.

"Too much was happening for me to forget it all, to have it completely taken away from me. The house gave me a different series of events to remember with Melissa, too, but still I was aware of her body a bit more than with the others. She's the one in the dining room. We surrounded her with chairs, so I wouldn't step on her."

"Where are Suzy and Evan?!"

"I got in touch with them after Melissa. Remember that at that time, I still thought there was something I could do, at least to save my friends. Of course, they were already dead. Evan didn't want to come, but Suzy... I just wish she'd been more clairvoyant. But she did seem to sense something when she got here. Just not enough. We tied them up in the basement and made small cuts in them. Evan died pretty quickly. Suzy's almost dead."

Immediately I could hear Carrie fumbling down the black hall toward the stairs, screaming when she tripped over Dr. Modele. She was doing exactly what she was supposed to do, but how could I make her understand that?

I was myself again. I had most of my real memories back, and so I knew that I couldn't be used to stop Carrie. That was all over now. So how was the house going to do it? I followed her down the corridor, feeling my way along the wall, toward the one place she should never have gone and the only place she could go. At this point, I just wanted to know how it would happen; it seemed the only thing left for me to do. And then, I would be alone in the house again, left to fester with the knowledge of my actions and my inability to see what had been happening until it was too late. The only reason the house let me continue to live was because it knew I'd never been any kind of threat.

And so I descended, passing down one hallway after another, seeing the house for what it truly was, all the bodies and gore and desperate scrawling that I would have to face for the rest of my life. Of course, by now I understood that all the supplies on the third floor hadn't been gathered by Carrie; I'd bought them. Honestly, it was a slight relief to see how finite my life was going to be now: I'd live only as long as my canned goods held out. I no longer had to battle against the house. The responsibility for all of that had evaporated, leaving only a dull ache and a kind of terrible peace.

Carrie must have followed the stench that Evan was producing, because when I finally made it to the room in which he and Suzy had been tied up—where we had tied them up—she was already there, desperately and ineffectually cutting at the rope with the nail file. There was a corner near the basement stairs in which a few old tools had been piled up, so I retrieved an old hack saw.

As soon as she heard me crashing around in the junk, Carrie screamed. "Stay the fuck away from us!" And when I returned to the room, she was hiding behind Suzy's swaying body, only her file peeking out.

"I'm just going to put this on the floor. You'll be able to get through those ropes better with it."

She only stared at me, her eyes glassy with terror. I backed up and into the shadows, unable to allow myself to hope that the two of them would make it out alive, but curious, nonetheless. I could tell that she'd lost sight of me because she was staring wildly around the space, and once I was perfectly still, she lunged for the saw. Although she was too scared to make a good job of it, it wasn't more than a minute before she'd gotten through the ropes, and Suzy fell, unconscious to the floor. Carrie continued to hold up the rusty hacksaw, a warning to me.

"You come anywhere near us, and I'm going to use this thing on you!" And then she started grappling with Suzy's now floppy, wrinkled skin. "Come on! We've got to get out of here! Suzy, it's Christine! Suzy!"

Suzy looked as if she were on the very verge of death, and if I could have, I would have prayed that she'd die so that Carrie might save herself. I knew I couldn't help her carry the woman out of the house; at this point and forever more, I would be merely a passive force, my observations the only actions I'd ever take. I suspect that this was because I'd brought in all the people the house could get me to bring. So I had to get used to peering through the shadows, still and silent.

Only at this point did Carrie think to pull out her cellphone, swearing when she found that there was no signal. It was only more proof that the house was influencing her.

Then Suzy was up and kneeling over Carrie, and when I shifted my position, I could see that what was left of Suzy was choking her. The preternatural strength that exploded in her body was fascinating to watch. It was almost external, as if Suzy were a marionette, and I finally understood why the house had grown dormant: it had been building up its strength for this single act. I'm still haunted by the fact that my first response to the murder taking place before my eyes was that I was glad Penobscot Road was using someone else.

So was this what I'd look like when we'd killed everyone? It was a relief to realize that I'd appeared to be no more than a tool because even if the victims observing me could've possessed memories for no more than a moment, they would've at least seen that I wasn't responsible for most of what we were doing to them. At least for the few moments before they died, all of those people had understood that it wasn't just me.

Yet even this wasn't true with everyone. I remembered now that I'd initially called Dr. Modelle during a particularly lucid period to prove to myself that I wasn't insane. Once he arrived, we attacked him, although he managed to escape. I hadn't consciously known that he was hiding from me in the attic; the house had led me up there. But I'd been all too aware that the trap door he was cowering on couldn't take any more weight, and just as Carrie's desire to save Suzy was now leading to her death, my conscious actions had been used to accomplish the house's will. The trap door had fallen in because I'd knowingly crawled onto it, and Dr. Modelle had died. So even completely aware, I'd colluded with the house to murder because in some sense, I'd known just what I was doing— whether for mercy, convenience, or both, I could only consider later. Something told me that this confession had been Penobscot Road's true goal all along.

From my vantage point, I could see Suzy's eyes close, and I wondered what she thought she was seeing. I hoped she were brain dead.

Carrie turned red and then purple, and was totally unable to gasp or choke. She hit Suzy with the saw, but it was turned sideways, so it couldn't do any damage. The veins in her eyes burst after a long time, and then she died, too. I think I'd been screaming "no" during the killing, but the metallic echoes of the basement had gone, and the noises escaping me were immediately absorbed, as if I were suspended in gelatin. As soon as Carrie was dead, the house dropped Suzy on top of her, every muscle as limp as before.

If you're wondering whether all of this was just a memory implanted in my brain by the house and that I had, in fact, killed Carrie, I can only say that it was different from the other times. Penobscot Road no longer had any reason to lie to me because it had won, and its reward was to make me witness all of this. To make me know again.

And to make you know, too.

After

You see? If I'd told you everything right from the start, you'd never have stayed with me. Never. I had to reveal things as they were revealed to me, so hate me if you'd like. If it makes you feel any better, I continue to remember things—worse and worse things that the house metes out to me to keep me cowed. This morning, I was given back the memory that I'd been sleeping with Alphonse and Nicole's decomposing corpses at night, a pathetic, unconscious expression of my grief at losing them. I've even gone in search of the Halloween decorations I recalled us buying to confirm that my roommates had really been alive at that point, to prove that something of our relationship had been real, at least then. I never found them, and it's terrible to realize that even this proves nothing.

I'm running out of space, anyway, so what's the point? Now you know that my frailty was not only responsible for causing more deaths than otherwise would have taken place in Penobscot Road, but also for spreading this knowledge to you like a disease. A stronger person would have let it die with them, because the sharing of it is an abomination.

Yet you earned it. You wanted to feed off of my pain, eat up my suffering just as the house did. By now, you must realize that it's your insatiability that fuels the house. It needs people like you to continue to exist. Even more than it needs people like me.

The police were here again today. Forensics. I have to say, it's fascinating to watch how the house stops them just before they step on any of the bodies, how they look past everything scrawled on the wall, oblivious. The stench has only worsened, yet they don't so much as wrinkle their noses. In fact, I can stand directly before one, screaming into his face that two feet behind him is a pile of rotting corpses, and my outburst is so violent that his hair will actually be blown backward. But he will merely stare through me, only the slightest whisper of concern at the corner of his eyes, as if he's wondering if he's heard the trace of a wail carried on the wind. I know that if I try to leave with them, there will only be more death, and so I linger in the corners of Penobscot Road, now a kind of phantom myself. As long as I'm here and living, nothing else can happen.

The police are utterly stymied, and it's frustrating the hell out of them. They simply can't determine what's happened to all of the people who've lived in the house, all the people who've visited. Penobscot Road seems to be the common link, but it's just an old, rambling, empty structure with no incriminating evidence whatsoever, no clues that might lead to the missing people or their potential killer. All the blood's dried, so they can't even slip on it.

Sooner or later the legend is going to spread—if it hasn't already—and they're going to pull down the house. It won't matter if they do because whatever it is that killed all these people and continues to entrap me is borne in the hearts of people like you and lives there, ready to swell and materialize at will. The only act left to me is to make you face your role in all of this, a hollow retribution but retribution, nonetheless.

Of course, you and I share another punishment: the impenetrability of so much of what has happened here. I feel in my soul that there is an urgent significance to, for instance, the second-floor ritual, the newspaper in the closet, the window next to the front door, yet their meaning is profoundly inaccessible. And just as I can make sense of so little of what has happened to me here, neither can you. While this disadvantage will be as short-lived for me as my remaining few moments on earth, this house's unfathomable logic may frustrate you for decades yet.

Of course, I'm hounded day and night by only one thought: had I known all along that the trap door would never hold my weight? Was this the real reason the house finally gave me free will—because it knew that it could trust me to kill Dr. Modelle on my own? Because even though the house has given me back my memories, I wonder if anything can clear completely the fog of the human soul.

I'm sure you'll be glad to know that I ate the last can of corn yesterday, and since I've been rationing the food so carefully, I'm already so thin that my death can't be too far off. That's been its plan all along: to ensure that I had just enough sustenance to scribble out this story on the walls of the third floor. Of course, I'm ending my story here, in the little hidden room at the front of the house, only the dreadful stand of trees to look at until finally I die. Up here, they are at the exact same angle as the drawing on my bedroom wall. I see that now.

Perhaps since you're reading this, you're inside the house and have been manipulated by it, too, a prisoner of different rooms and therefore a victim of further atrocities. I still wonder about all those unrevealed places meant for others, like the room next to mine with the brown stain in the carpet. Nothing is random in Penobscot Road; it's simply that my key didn't fit. And perhaps it's done with you, too, only now allowing you to see my writing on the wall.

But I've never believed that. I've always suspected that the house would find some way of releasing my story into the world, a way of spreading its strength and potential. So I've always imagined you safe and far from Penobscot Road. This distance of yours is how I convinced myself for so long that you could be innocent and voracious at once, and that only through teaming up with you could I take back my past in this way. I thought you would be the perfect partner for me. Instead, you've been a perfect partner for the house: you may feed on what it's done to me, but ultimately, it's feeding on you.

I only have this little space left on the walls of the third floor, and of course it's here, just above the children's tea set. In fact, I've left the set alone, set up exactly as it always has been because I'd like to think that whoever once placed it here was still a regular little kid doing regular kid's stuff, at least for a short while. Maybe preserving it—just like this—is the only thing I can do to stand up to the house: leaving evidence inside of it of the power of normality.

But maybe there's something more I can do. Even though I despise how your salaciousness has fueled my story, I've lost whatever strength I had to resent it. I certainly no longer have the strength to hate you and, in fact, often wonder if the erotic frisson I offered you so long ago will prove to be my final good deed on earth. So I'm going to share one last secret with you, something I've been thinking about for the past months.

You see, I'd believed that there was no way to fight the kind of evil that resides here. But perhaps I'd just been coerced into believing this. Because I spent countless hours poring over all of the communications left by former inhabitants on the walls, and I think I've found a common thread—something that no one has recognized before. I think I've discovered a way to end Penobscot Road. And maybe the real reason you're reading this is because you're the one destined to stop the horror forever.

It's really quite simple, a seemingly innocuous aberration in the house that I've already mentioned to you, as a matter of fact, and to put an end to it would prevent so much more misery. Please, for your own sake, if no one else's, come and undo some of the damage you and I have done here and prevent what I couldn't. All you have to do is

www.ingramcontent.com/pod-product-compliance
Lightning Source LLC
Chambersburg PA
CBHW050418260626

47156CB00003B/1068